THE MATRIARCH CHRONICLES
BOOK I

THE MAIDEN'S HUSBAND

MORGAN CHRISTENSEN

Book Cover by MiblArt

Paperback ISBN 979-8-9899750-0-6

Hardcover ISBN 979-8-9899750-1-3

E-Book ISBN 979-8-9899750-2-0

First edition published in 2024

To Dad for introducing me to *Vikings*, which inspired this book, its world, and its characters. That and everything you have done for me. Love you. Skål.

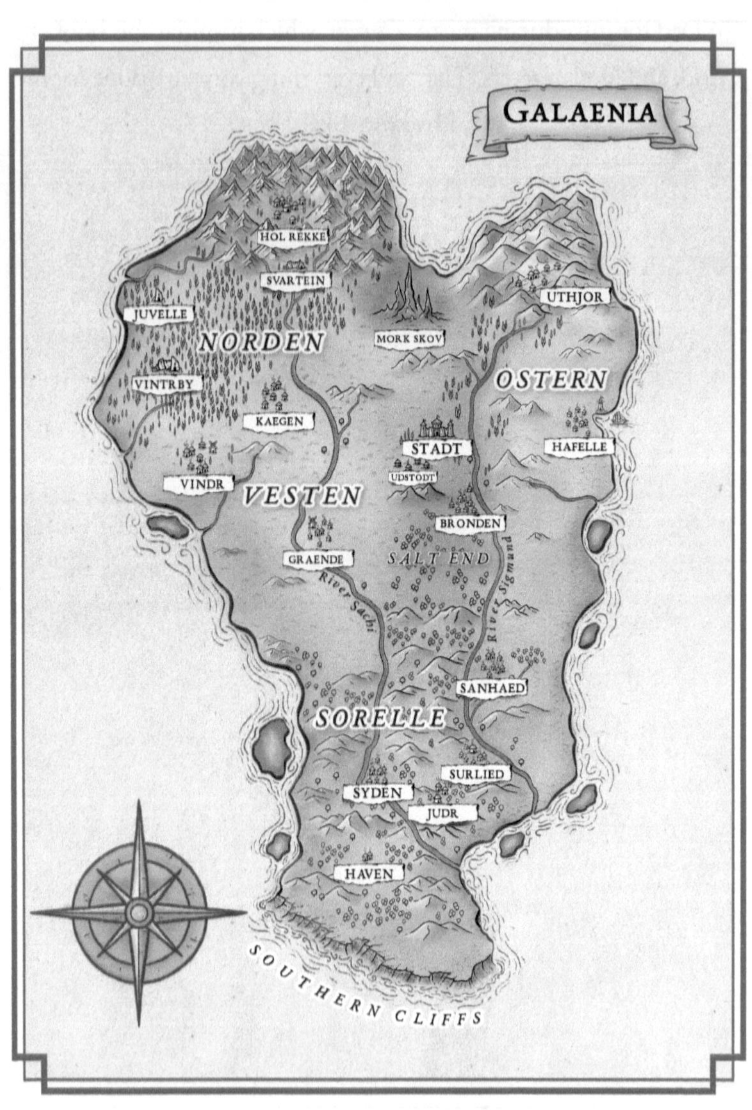
GALAENIA
HOL REKKE
SVARTEIN
JUVELLE
NORDEN
MORK SKOV
UTHJOR
VINTRBY
OSTERN
KAEGEN
STADT
HAFELLE
VINDR
UDSTODT
VESTEN
BRONDEN
GRAENDE
SALT END
River Sachi
River Sigmunds
SANHAED
SORELLE
SURLIED
SYDEN
JUDR
HAVEN
SOUTHERN CLIFFS

Content Warning

The Maiden's Husband is a dark epic fantasy with **adult language** and content. Harsh battles are fought with **blood and gore,** and despite the efforts of the matriarchy, **violence** is ever present. Galaenian law prohibits **sexual violence**, but such cruel acts are inflicted on page. The All-Mother wills **death** is a part of life, and so, a part of this story. Reader discretion is advised.

Prologue

Raegna

Pain ripped through Raegna, and a scream erupted from her throat. Sweat slicked her back, soaking her nightgown. Tears blurred her vision and spilled over her cheeks when she shut her eyes tight. The midwife aimed a beady gaze between her legs while her mother, Jaleesa, stood on the other side of her, clutching Raegna's arm. Through the agony, her mother's touch should have been comforting, yet it sent her skin crawling. She gathered the bedsheets in her fists.

Bai leaned against the opposite wall. The candlelight illuminated his warm, beige skin with an orange tint and cast sharp shadows under his protruding brow. He did not need to be here. Raegna glowered at him until a contraction took her again, and she growled.

Her throat burned, rubbed raw from her cries. Her belly wrenched and her back became an anvil for some unseen hammer, but she refused to give in. The babe moved, expanding her in ways she didn't think possible. Raegna let out a battle cry she was sure all of Syden could hear.

"Easy," the midwife said. "You're doing well."

"Come now, daughter," Jaleesa urged, without missing a beat. "You have the strength to do this."

Raegna gritted her teeth at them, her tall looming mother and the portly midwife, who both stared at her womanhood. Two peering old women were better than her own husband.

Bai looked on with those profound gold eyes. Raegna would show him just how powerful she was, despite what he had done to her. After all, this was a battle many women fought before. A lowly man would crumble under the immense pain.

A cool breeze brushed Raegna's skin. The midwife held the babe and grinned as she wrapped it in a cloth.

"Congratulations. Gaea has blessed you with a beautiful daughter."

Jaleesa's smile spread from ear to ear, and she gave Raegna's arm a firm squeeze. "You've done it, my girl. Thank Gaea above, a daughter!"

A daughter. Raegna stifled a sob of relief. Her body shook as she watched the midwife take her baby girl to the dresser, where Bai stiffened in place.

"Won't—Won't you bring her to me?" Raegna croaked.

"Patience," tittered the midwife, as if Raegna were a child waiting for a treat. "I'll get her clean for you. Then the father can give her to you."

No.

Raegna opened her mouth to protest, but her gaze found Bai's and they locked on each other for a fleeting moment. It could have been a trick of the candlelight, but he appeared unnerved, the whites of his eyes flashing as they darted and his face paling. He spun away before she could be sure of it.

The hairs on the back of Raegna's neck prickled when Bai inched toward the child she had kept in her womb all these moons. If she could, she would have rushed to the dresser and snatched the babe from the midwife's hands so Bai wouldn't touch her, but she could barely raise her head in her exhaustion.

Jaleesa sat on the edge of the bed beside her and brushed wet strands of hair away from her forehead. "It is tradition, Raegna."

Everything between Raegna and Bai deviated from tradition. Raegna would not have had him in the room at all, much less let him even look at the babe as he was now, craning to see over the dresser. It was unfair to have the father present the babe to its mother. Raegna gave her daughter birth, and all Bai had done was...

With her fists still clenched over the damp bed sheets, her jaw set as the midwife showed Bai how to hold a newborn. His forearm cradled her body with her head in his palm. He pivoted to face the bed, the shape of the baby girl swaddled in his arms. A cry escaped her tiny mouth and the angles in Bai's face softened, his eyes not as fierce. A crooked smile pulled at one corner of his mouth.

With a deep frown, Raegna cleared her throat. Bai glanced up at her as if he had just acknowledged her presence and drifted to her bedside. The tenderness in his features retreated, and he handed their daughter into her care. Raegna inched away and disregarded him, enfolding her babe the moment her tiny body curled against her mother's chest.

Still, Bai remained there, standing above her and watching like a raven in the treetops.

The babe arched her back, unleashing her voice. Something came over Raegna as she looked at her. Instinct, one could call it, but if that were so, instinct was so much more intense than she ever imagined. The immense feeling washed over her like a high tide and filled her with warmth. She let the babe lie bare in her arms.

Jaleesa sighed and ran her long fingers through Raegna's hair. "Praise Gaea. What a beautiful granddaughter for the family."

Raegna's daughter settled into her snug embrace, the rhythm of her mother's heartbeat in her ears once more. She blinked with large brown eyes and strands of blonde hair lined her head.

The babe traded her wailing for coos and whimpers. Her cheek pressed to her mother's chest. Dread had plagued Raegna for months with the anticipation of how she would react to her newborn and how her newborn would react to her. All the expected fear and reluctance melted away. Raegna stroked her flat back with gentle finger pads, her pink skin soft and new.

A fresh set of tears rolled down Raegna's face as she kissed the newborn's head. "Adabelle. My Adabelle..."

Chapter I

Raegna

Raegna scowled as she stood before the house where she had been born and raised, her heart caving in on itself. The morning light etched the cracks in the foreboding wood rafters and rickety porch rails under the sod roof coated in grass and birch. Adabelle cast her large brown eyes up at her mother, her little hand encased in Raegna's. Wisps of blonde hair floated about her round, rosy face.

"Mama?" she chirped, more than likely curious why they were stopped before her grandmother's house.

Raegna chewed the inside of her cheek and steeled herself. "Everything's all right," she said, more to assure herself than her daughter. "Let's go in."

Raegna marched forward. It was pointless avoiding the inevitable. She just had to speak with her mother and get what she truly came for. Adabelle waddled along as they conquered the porch steps and pushed through the front door.

Smoke swirled from wall to wall. Incense and sage burned from every corner of the main room and the kitchen, throwing a gray veil over the furniture. Adabelle wrinkled her nose and coughed. The thick air stung Raegna's nostrils, though her lungs had acclimated to the strong scents over several visits. She tilted her head to follow the rising clouds to the ceiling, where her prize waited in the rafters.

The healer appeared from the bedroom door at the sound of their entrance. The creases in her worried face told Raegna everything.

"Young Raegna." She wiped her hands on the apron around her dress. "I'm glad you've come. She'll be pleased too."

Raegna's mouth twisted. "Will you look after my daughter?"

"Of course," the healer said. "Please, whatever you need, just ask."

Giving a distracted nod of thanks, Raegna knelt before Adabelle and squeezed her hands. "Stay here, sweetling. I must talk with your grandmother. I'll only be a moment, all right?"

"Is it because Grandmother is sick?" Adabelle asked. "Is that why there's so much smoke?"

Raegna faltered and collected herself with a swift breath before she could break. "Yes. She's very unwell. This... this happens sometimes. Be good for the kind healer. I'll be right back, my love."

"All right, Mama."

Envying her innocence, Raegna planted a kiss on her cheek and rose to confront her mother. Under no circumstances was she going to let Adabelle pass through that door. Not when there was so much to say.

In a few strides, Raegna crossed the floor and steadied a trembling hand on the doorknob. She entered the dreadful room where the windows were shut. More smoke clouds rested along the walls. Raegna waited for her vision to adjust before taking another step.

Shadows spanned the bed, concealing the withered form of her once mighty and revered mother. Lady Jaleesa wheezed with every breath, her parchment-like skin sunken over the bony creases of her face. Her deep brown eyes found Raegna in the haze despite her apparent struggle to keep them open. "Daughter."

"Mother," Raegna said.

Long, knobby fingers gestured to the edge of the bed. "Sit with me, my sweet one."

Despite herself, Raegna sat. Jaleesa placed a hand over hers, unable to grip them and give them a squeeze, as Raegna knew she meant to do. Her voice droned over her thin lips, laboriously slow. "You know what to do for my lifting."

"Yes, Mother. The temple, the bed, and everything."

"And be sure to appear as if you're suffering my loss." Jaleesa coughed. Red spittle drizzled over her chin.

Raegna's shoulders slumped. "Of course, I'll suffer. You needn't worry."

"I've never cared for those quips and you know it. I say this so the village may see you and care for you. Take pity on you."

Not to mention portraying that the love between them was like that of any mother and daughter. That could not be further from the truth. Raegna bunched the bedsheets in her free hand and bit her tongue to hold back another quick remark.

"Everything I have done, I have done because I care for you and your future," Jaleesa lectured, as she had hundreds of times before. The words fell hollow on Raegna's ears as her contempt continued to build. "As my only child and daughter, it is crucial that you lead a successful life and further the family bloodline. We must preserve the legacy your grandmother Ragna wished for, becoming prestigious women without steel and bloodshed. Your daughter will do the same when her time comes."

Every muscle in Raegna's body grew taut. "Adabelle will not—"

"She will if you know what is good for her." Jaleesa cut her off, only to throw herself into another coughing fit. When it ceased, she took a staggering breath. "It is the way of things. The best a woman can do is use her ambition to aid her Matriarch if not her Queen, find a good man and then sow her success on the daughters he gives her. I'm not sure how else I will get that through to you."

"That will be Adabelle's choice and not mine or anyone else's," Raegna hissed. "I won't force her into anything as you have me."

"Force was necessary because you are so stubborn and idiotic, traits you've unfortunately inherited from your ungrateful father."

Raegna did not wish to delve into the subject of her father, so she kept her mouth shut. She knew little about him since he had died before she could create memories, but she imagined the statement wasn't true. Jaleesa herself packed the attitude of ten mules, and Raegna had dealt with every one of them.

What Jaleesa referred to was Raegna's undying dream that had taken her far from the path her mother had envisioned for her. A wish Raegna had possessed since childhood to give up a comfortable, homely life and swear an oath to Galaenia as an elite Maiden.

Jaleesa had eradicated any chance Raegna might have had among their ranks years ago, for the Maidens did not marry, nor did they bear children.

"Thank Gaea I caught you before you left and I'd lost you to the wilderness forever," Jaleesa went on, her voice croaking. "You could never be a Maiden, Raegna. Getting yourself killed on horseback with no man or children to your name. Barren spinsters and tomcats become part of the Maidens' ranks, and you are neither of those. Nor will your daughter be."

Only if she wanted that. Raegna straightened and pulled her hand from under her mother's. "Is there anything else?"

"Yes." Jaleesa wiped her mouth with what little strength she had left. "I will be with Gaea soon. Do not think you can throw away everything we've worked for. You will keep the family you have, and make me proud."

A wavering breath caught in Raegna's chest. "And if I were to divorce my husband, all you have done would be for nothing."

Another cough rasped from her mother's throat. "Such cruel words to say to your mother, and about your lovely and giving husband. Divorce him if you wish, but it makes no difference. You will protect my granddaughter and teach her everything I've taught you. Like a sensible girl, she shall prosper as any woman should."

Raegna's anger broiled as if it might spew and scour the dying woman. Yet she learned from every slap on the wrist and cheek to suppress that fury and instead sit poised and calm. Her right eyebrow arched as she hid a glare. Tears threatened behind her eyes, and she swallowed hard.

"Now stay with me, daughter. Let that be my final wish."

Raegna yearned to storm out of the room, leave her mother behind in this darkness, and never have to see her face or hear her voice again. Willpower alone kept her in place, because she could not return to Adabelle with this much wrath coursing through her veins. For all the poor girl would know, her loving grandmother would be dead and she would need comfort. Raegna remained at the bedside and Jaleesa's hand lay over hers once more, every tiny finger bone burrowing into her skin.

"Good girl. You have always been so precious to me, my beautiful Raegna."

Turning away, Raegna forced herself to breathe deep. *Just a little longer. Endure her for just a little longer.*

Jaleesa closed her wilting eyelids and drew a few more gasps. Raegna listened to each one, waiting. The dying woman must have held out until she spoke her last threats to her daughter. That was just her nature.

An eternity went by in the stagnant, smoke-filled room. A hard stone cut the inside of Raegna's throat and tears blurred her vision. What she wished for in her heart was wrong, but didn't her mother deserve it?

A long, unsettling groan crawled from Jaleesa's lips.

Raegna turned and examined her stillness. Jaleesa's flat, ribbed chest did not rise again. She lay a decaying shroud of what she once was, bound for a lifting bed in the temple.

Raegna stood for the door. In the main room, the healer and Adabelle looked up at her. The healer went to Raegna's side, brushing away tears Raegna had not noticed.

"Oh, there now," the healer soothed. "She'll be with Gaea soon. I'll make her ready."

"Mama?" Adabelle spoke up, cocking her head.

Raegna pulled from the healer and strode to the kitchen. There, she retrieved a wooden stool to reach the rafters. Adabelle and the healer gaped when she jumped and gripped a beam. Raegna grunted as she hauled herself up and swung a leg over the beam, ducking under the earthy ceiling.

"Raegna!" The healer's palms pressed to her chest. "What in Gaea's name are you *doing*? You'll get hurt!"

"Mama's very good at climbing," Adabelle remarked matter-of-factly.

Above them, Raegna coughed on the smoke and searched along the length of the beams for what her mother hid from her. In her old age,

Jaleesa had instructed the Matriarch's two sons to strap it to a rafter. She had invited the young men to her house before Adabelle was born and had sworn them to secrecy from her daughter, information which Raegna had extracted from one of them with a bit of blackmail.

"Your mother needn't know how you get the extra coin from your business in the tavern," she told him. At once, the boy obliged her.

For a moment, Raegna thought he had lied. She scanned the beams and came up with nothing. *Damnable man.*

A metallic glint caught her eye through the pluming smoke. The slanted rafter just above her mother's bedroom door had a thicker width. Raegna shimmied down the main beam, hissing at splinters and cursing when she nearly rolled off her perch.

Finally, it lay beside her. The petal pommel of her grandmother's abandoned sword rested closest to her. The rest of the weapon remained sheathed and buckled to the beam. Raegna leaned over the sword to unfasten the belt that kept it in place. One hand fiddled with the buckle while the other clawed into the wood. When it clinked loose, Raegna smirked and unwrapped the weapon from its binding.

The sword clattered to the floor, making Adabelle squeal. Raegna sighed and lowered herself from the ceiling. The healer stared at her with a furrowed brow, but Raegna ignored her, picked up her prize, and fitted the belt to her waist.

"Come, love," she said and took Adabelle's hand. "There's something I have to tell you."

***

The sunset lit the congregation in Gaea's temple on the northern rim of the village. Many of Jaleesa's old friends and colleagues attended her lifting, most of them aging crones with withered faces. At the head of the temple stood Matriarch Alv, her silver hair in tight curls, her copper skin soaked in the orange light from the temple's open dome ceiling. For Jaleesa's lifting, she had chosen a faded green dress with a brown sash stitched in gold runes over each shoulder.

Wearing a plain, dark blue dress, Raegna twisted a braid above her ear. The rest of her chestnut locks tumbled past her shoulders. Sweat adhered loose strands to her temple. She gripped the hilt of the sword hanging from her belt.

Adabelle hid beside her while they overlooked the pyre. She sniffled into Raegna's skirts, rubbing her cherub cheeks raw. With a tender touch, Raegna stroked her hair.

On the other side of Raegna, her childhood friend Pinar held her hand in support. Tears rested between the corners of her long nose and tinted her snowy complexion red. A ruddy olive dress hugged her slender body. Her single silvery braid stretched down her back.

Raegna attempted to produce tears as well and appear smothered in grief, but her eyes remained dry. Witnessing her mother draw her last breath had left her heart carved out like an empty gourd. That must have looked sorrowful enough.

Three priestesses circled Jaleesa's body where it rested under a linen sheet. They repeated an incantation she had chosen from the scriptures before she died. But Raegna tuned out every word.

The lighting of the pyre drew her from her daze and the small group watched the flames lap over the body before consuming it. Smoke, much thicker than that of the incense and sage that had filled her house, climbed through the open skylight in the dome ceiling, cloaking the congregation in shadows.

Pinar turned and wrapped Raegna in a hug. Returning the embrace, Raegna tipped her head toward her friend. Adabelle inserted herself between them and the two women pulled her close.

The lifting ceremony ended. As the gathering exited, the priestesses saw to the rest of the burning. Raegna stood outside the temple doors with Pinar and Adabelle, while those in attendance gave her their condolences. Raegna nodded to each of them and thanked them for coming, taking their hands in hers.

The last to approach her was Matriarch Alv, with tears fogging her brown eyes. Syden's Commander Berthe flanked her with one other warrior, both of them clad in leather armor. The Commander raised an eyebrow at Raegna's sword. Noting this, Raegna straightened.

"Young Raegna," Matriarch Alv said, opening her palm.

Raegna shoved her pride down and placed her hand there. "Matriarch. Thank you for attending. My mother would have appreciated it."

"Of course, my dear," Alv cooed and touched Raegna's arm. "I knew your mother well. We practically grew up together. Be strong as she was and keep her in your heart. I promise it will get easier."

Raegna forced a twitching smile. She fixed her sight on the Matriarch's grasp that tightened around her wrist before Alv left her to mourn, Commander Berthe and her warrior trailing behind her. The last guests filtered out of the temple and dispersed into the streets of Syden, illuminated by the waning sunlight.

Things could begin as planned.

Adabelle curled in Raegna's arms, spent from her crying. Pinar walked them home and wiped away one of Adabelle's old tears. "Poor thing. Hopefully, she'll sleep tonight."

"Hopefully," Raegna sighed.

"I pray you do too," Pinar told her. "You deserve nothing less."

Raegna gave her a smile of genuine thanks. "It has been a long day, seeing her and preparing... I think I will."

"I know you're tired of hearing this," Pinar started as they reached the village, "but if you need anything at all, I'm here. A few meals or someone to look after Adabelle. She's always welcome at our home. Estrid loves to have another girl in the house and it's sweet to see our daughters together."

"Yes. It is. I was going to stop by the butcher's before she closed her shop. Wanted to try a stew tonight. You can come." After today, some normalcy would do her good. Raegna yearned for a mindless task to organize her thoughts and plans.

"The butcher?" Pinar repeated. "You know, we have venison from Naleem and Hadwin's last hunt. You can bring some home."

Raegna frowned. "Pinar, you... I couldn't. That meat is for your family and your children would—"

"Oh, hush," Pinar said with a dismissive wave of her hand. "There's plenty. Besides, we have the next two seasons to send the men hunting again. Those two would take any excuse to be in the forest. Come along. Perhaps it would cheer Adabelle up to visit Estrid too."

Her daughter's weight grew heavier in Raegna's arms. Buying meat from the butcher would do, but her experience with Pinar's generosity told Raegna she couldn't refuse the offer.

"Very well," she agreed. "Thank you, my friend."

"It's no trouble, you know that." Pinar placed an arm around Raegna's shoulders. "Let's go see if my husband could manage the children on his own."

By evening, tucked in the center of Syden, the bustling market fell to a tranquil routine of merchants packing up for the night. One storekeeper swept the dust collected by patrons over her porch. Those who preferred to complete their errands late walked from tent to shop, perusing the wares.

A shepherd girl herded goats moseying at a steady pace, ready to turn into their pen after a long day. Gritty smoke wafted from the blacksmith's forge as she continued to pound her hammer against red-hot metal even when evening quieted the village. Her striking echoed across the road.

Pinar and Raegna stuck close together, their boots crunching over gravel. Along the way, familiar faces greeted with solemn glances at Raegna. Eventually, everyone would learn about her mother's death and offer condolences, but Raegna nodded back to them in greeting as if nothing had changed. Such was a habit she learned from Jaleesa.

"Always greet your fellow women, Raegna," she told her long ago. "It is polite, and some who do not receive acknowledgment may hold it against you."

Jaleesa smacked Raegna's hand if she did not follow her instruction. A good and friendly reputation was the key to making friends and allies and keeping them. Recalling the lesson left a sour taste in Raegna's mouth.

Adabelle stirred in her mother's arms and mumbled, "Papa?"

Raegna winced and patted her back. "No, sweetling. It's Mama and Aunt Pinar."

"Aren't we home yet?" Adabelle whimpered. "I want Papa."

Of course, you do. Fortunately, Raegna did not have to hide her disdain as Adabelle faced away from her with her chin on her shoulder. "He's not here, Ada."

"Is he working the fields today?" Pinar asked. "I thought you might at least have him attend the lifting."

"His place is with the rest of the men," Raegna said. "Pulling him for the day isn't necessary."

A line creased between Pinar's eyebrows.

Dissatisfied with these answers, Adabelle kicked her legs out and wriggled in Raegna's grasp. "Won't Papa be home soon?"

"Yes," Raegna said. "And so will we."

They approached the little house at the end of the market strip. The quaint and cozy place displayed Pinar's famous wildflower arrangements along the porch rails beneath the pointed sod roof.

On the steps, two young boys and a girl sat enraptured in a game of stones, several smooth pebbles splayed between them. The girl had the same silver locks as Pinar, the same chin that curved up in her profile. In front of her, the boys scratched their mops of brunette hair over their sister's next move. The only thing that pulled them from their play was their mother's voice.

"Has your father already kicked you out of the house, sweetlings?" Pinar teased them.

Dakarai, Estrid, and Cadoc perked to attention. They beamed at the sight of their mother before they bounded from the steps. "Mama! Mama! Mama's home!"

Pinar knelt to catch the three of them in a hug. "Yes, Mama is home. Now dinner can begin, eh?" She stood and gestured to Raegna. "Will you all say hello to Lady Raegna and little Adabelle?"

Each of them bowed as Raegna knew their mother had taught them. "Hello, Lady Raegna. Hello, Adabelle."

Dredging up a smile, Raegna nodded back to them. "Hello, children. It's good to see you."

Raegna set Adabelle on the ground and combed her fingers through her hair. Estrid came forward to greet her much younger friend but frowned at the dried tear tracks on Adabelle's face.

"Adabelle? What's wrong?"

"She's had a very hard day," Raegna explained tentatively. "Her grandmother was lifted today."

Ever the nurturing eldest sister, Estrid brushed a strand from Adabelle's face. "Aw. Everything will be all right, Ada. You'll see."

"Estrid, why don't you pick our flowers for Adabelle?" Pinar suggested. "I think that might light up the day."

Estrid jumped in place. "And I can braid them in your hair! Mama showed me. Would you like that, Adabelle?"

With a shrug of her shoulders, Adabelle sniffled.

Raegna gave her a slight nudge. "You may if you would like, Ada. You love Pinar's flowers."

Estrid took Adabelle's hand and guided her to the porch. "Come on. Mama and I got these purple ones yesterday. Let me show you!"

Dakarai let out a huff and followed his sister. "Estrid, what about the stones? Aren't you going to finish the game?"

"This is more important, *Dakarai*," Estrid insisted, helping Adabelle up the porch steps.

As they ascended, Pinar's husband, Naleem, emerged from the house. In his arms, he balanced the swaddled bundle of baby Nalani. His dark brown eyes tracked Estrid and Adabelle inside. Dakarai and Cadoc tramped after them.

"Be kind, all of you," Naleem called after them.

Their voices echoed out the front door. "Yes, Papa!"

Raegna braced herself for cordial acts of affection, which would surely take place as Naleem approached his wife. A sweet smile stretched above his squared chin and jawline where black stubble dotted cool ash skin. They didn't disappoint; the couple nuzzled their noses and kissed, Pinar on the tips of her toes and Naleem leaning down just enough to reach her. Thankfully, they kept it short and Naleem handed their babe to Pinar.

"Hello, Raegna," he said, turning to her. "I'm very sorry to hear about your mother. We'll pray to the goddesses to bring your family comfort."

Raegna cast her eyes to the side, unwilling to let the condolences go on any longer. "Thank you. I appreciate that."

"I thought Bai might be with you," Naleem went on, and Pinar stiffened beside him. "Did you send him home after the lifting?"

Raegna clutched the hilt of her sword. "He's working the field today."

"Oh." Naleem shifted his weight. "I see…"

"Darling, why don't you cut up some of that venison for Raegna and her family?" Pinar interjected. "It is the least we could do to help."

After looking between them, Naleem nodded and kissed Pinar's cheek. "Of course, love. Whatever you or Bai need, Raegna."

If her mother were here, she would remark that a *Lady* would suffice before a woman's name. Especially from a man. Raegna ignored her churning stomach at the thought. "Thank you."

Trotting up the porch, Naleem disappeared inside the house as the children had. Their babe gurgled in Pinar's arms.

"You could take some vegetables and bread for a stew too," she suggested.

"You've done enough for me today, Pinar," Raegna told her with her palms up. "I'm grateful, but at this rate, I'll make a dent in your winter stores. Besides, we have food at home."

"O-of course," Pinar stammered. "Well, let us know... Raegna. May I ask... what will you do about Bai?"

Raegna blinked and then pursed her lips when a few ideas came to mind. The sword grew heavy over her hip. "I'm not sure yet."

"Well... He seems to be a decent husband and father," Pinar said, bouncing her babe. "And a fine worker, according to Naleem and Hadwin. They've all become good friends in the fields, by the sound of it. It would be a shame to put him out on his own."

Raegna held her tongue. A part of her couldn't blame Pinar for dissuading her from taking rightful actions. As far as Pinar knew, the arranged marriage was awkward and uncomfortable. She didn't know what more Raegna suffered. And Raegna could never tell her, no matter how she yearned to confide in her friend.

"Let's check on the girls," she said instead, walking past Pinar. "When that meat is cut, we need to head home."

Behind her, Pinar sighed, but followed. "All right."

Chapter 2

Bai

Sweat drenched Bai's shirt as he toiled over the weeds that sprouted from the crop. It dripped off his brow and stung his eyes, seeping through the sash he layered around his head to soak up the moisture. Bai straightened and dried his face with his sleeve.

The other men tended to the field, plowing, pruning, or digging. Bai watched them, taking in the sea of crops that would not only feed Syden, but would contribute to neighboring villages and realms across Galaenia. The aisles of vegetation flushed green despite the wet heat that boiled the men while they worked.

Beyond the fields rolled the southern hills of forest and more green, where the sun dipped behind pine tops, marking the end of midday and the start of the evening. Bai admired the vibrant orange color melting beneath pale pink, purple, and blue.

"Sunset, boys," the overseer called out as she walked the aisle. She wiped her forehead, splotched with grime. "Rip up what you can and start heading home."

The others stretched and rose to finish their work. Bai managed a few more handfuls of weeds and tossed them into his basket. He followed the overseer alongside the rest of the men, who carried their baskets over their shoulders.

"Another productive day, I'd say," a voice spoke beside him.

Bai glanced sideways at Hadwin, who offered a friendly grin. He paid no mind to the sun that made his skin match his tawny hair, which was slicked with sweat and plastered to his forehead.

"Yes. Tomorrow there will be more to do."

"It'll be worth it when Leaf Fall Gift comes," Hadwin assured him, ever one to see the positive side of things. He wrestled with the basket he carried. "And it's always worth the return home to a cool bath and a good meal."

"Hmph," Bai grunted. "A good meal."

A meal Raegna might poison. To his wife's credit, Bai always received food when he returned home and woke up in perfect health the next morning.

"Tomorrow is a fishing day," Hadwin said, breaking Bai from his thoughts. "Naleem and I are taking the boys. Teach them how to cast the reel. Think you'll show Adabelle?"

Bai snorted. "You honestly believe my wife would let Ada out of the house and near the river with me? Besides, Ada is still too little. I'd be afraid of her falling in."

Hadwin shrugged. "I suppose so."

"Where is Naleem?" Bai asked to change the subject.

"Oh, I'm sure he's around," Hadwin answered with a wave of his hand. "Mayhap he took off early to steal some time with his lady love. *Alone.*"

"Disgusting."

"I'll say." Hadwin stumbled when he nearly dropped his basket. "At least they bed-play while I'm away."

They tossed their weeds and continued on their way home. Every man dispersed through the streets, relieved to be free of work until sunrise. A breeze cooled Bai's skin while he and Hadwin walked back to Syden. The roads lay quiet as shops closed for the night. Merchants and business-women prepared to be with their families over dinner. Bai's least favorite part of the day.

Orange sunset disappeared and left the land gray and dull when they reached the village. Hadwin picked up his pace.

"I should make it to the house before supper," he said as he started jogging ahead. "Goodnight, Bai!"

"Goodnight," Bai called back. "I may meet you all to fish tomorrow."

"We'll save you a reel, then!" Hadwin shouted over his shoulder and fled down the road.

As he treaded home, Bai wondered if Raegna would notice if he went fishing instead of working the field. He doubted she would care if he fled for the woods and never returned. His mother-in-law would send a hunting party after him. Even in her current feeble state.

Their house stood in the middle of the northern side of Syden. The other little houses all sat side by side in no particular pattern, as if Syden's founders homesteaded upon whatever plot of land lay unclaimed. Each had the same pointed arch for a roof, blanketed by moss and grass, above the same rectangle porch with rickety wooden stairs and splintery railing. The wood boards groaned under Bai's feet as he ascended and approached the door.

The knob turned and gave in, though Bai awaited the day Raegna locked him out. In the beginning, he might not have minded, willing to venture the streets, maybe leave the village altogether. Evade any dogs and huntresses Jaleesa sent on his trail.

With Adabelle on the other side, what lengths would he take to get past that door?

The hinges shuddered, and Bai entered. The main room conjoined with the dining area, a kitchen to the right, and their bedroom beyond that. The front door faced the fireplace on the opposite wall. Raegna knelt before a pot over the fire. Embers sparked and danced about her. The flames highlighted the warm bronze undertones of her soft cheekbones down to her rounded chin. She flipped her chestnut hair and glanced over her shoulder at him with eyes dark as wet soil. Fixing dinner must have taken half the day.

A sheathed sword leaned beside the fireplace. Worn leather wrapped around the grip under the petaled pommel and matched the scabbard, which had a tattered brown belt looped down its length. The sight of it wrenched Bai's gut.

Adabelle bolted toward him, her skirt floating beneath her. "Papa!"

Bai gulped down his worry, and his heart floated as he scooped her into his arms. "Ah! My beautiful girl! How are you today?"

Raegna's piercing stare hovered over him as she stood from the hearth, ever vigilant. She looked perturbed, with her small nose wrinkled, though it could have been her usual greeting to him. At least whatever she had cooked smelled good this time, the tangy aroma of stew hanging in the air.

Excitement at the prospect of supper vanished when Adabelle buried her face in his shoulder, the wildflowers in her hair grazing his jaw. "Papa. Grandmother had to go to Gaea today."

"What?" He balanced her on his hip to better see her. When tears shimmered in her eyes, he pressed his forehead to hers.

"She was sick," Adabelle whimpered. "Mama said she had to be lifted. We did at the temple."

Bai's chest squeezed as he took a breath. *Jaleesa is gone.*

Adabelle became heavy in his arms, and Bai caught himself in a stagger. He fought the urge to survey Raegna once more. Upon first glance, she had appeared to be her normal, detestable self. Not as if she lost her mother forever. That might mean nothing after what Jaleesa had done. Even Bai thought he should rejoice that the old witch could never torment them again. But her death changed everything.

He gripped Adabelle tighter. "It's all right... These things happen."

"Adabelle," Raegna said in hushed tones as she hefted the sword from its place and paced into the kitchen. "Come help me set the table for supper."

"Yes, Mama," Adabelle replied with a disheartened sigh. Bai let her down so she could rush to the table, as she always did. Instead, her feet shuffled over the floorboards. Raegna did not spare Bai another glance.

While they prepared the table, Bai retreated to the bedroom, his heart drumming against his chest. Shoving his work bag into their tiny closet below Raegna's dresses and skirts, he attempted to calm himself and collect his thoughts.

His clothes sat folded on the closet floor. No matter her ignorance of him, Raegna tolerated him in the littlest ways: allowing his belongings in the same closet, letting him at least sleep indoors, but not in the same bed.

Bai looked upon the bed Raegna had moved from its original place beside the far window after Adabelle was born. The little girl's own bed filled the space beneath the windowsill. Every time Bai entered the room, he did not have to be reminded of that horrible night Jaleesa had orchestrated. Perhaps that was Raegna's reason for moving it.

A painful wave of guilt burst in his chest, coupled with the unhinged fear of what might come from Jaleesa's passing. Raegna's new sword had to be a part of it. Bai rolled his shoulders. He shut the closet door to join his family for dinner.

When the stew boiled over the cauldron, Raegna poured it into bowls retrieved from the cupboard. She served one to Adabelle, one to herself, and one to Bai. This was a behavior she adopted after Jaleesa had found out she did not give her husband food, forcing him to fend for himself.

"That boy gave you a child," she had scolded with her finger pointed and wagging. "He works hard for your contribution to Syden and this is how you repay him?"

Bai didn't expect any result from the chiding, but the next day, Raegna threw jerky from the butcher at him and fled from sight. From then on, she attempted to become the home-cooking wife her mother could be proud of.

Raegna placed the hot stew in front of Bai. He remained motionless so as not to throw her off. Once she took her seat at the head of the table, he noted the sword rested against her chair. Bai cast his gaze into his bowl. The stew was supposed to be creamy, but it sat in the bowl like pond water. Standing, thin, and most likely tasteless. He did his best to hide the twist of his mouth, but Raegna noticed, closing her eyes in dismissal.

"Let us thank Gaea," she said, "for this meal she has given us."

"Thank Gaea," Bai agreed.

They slurped up spoonfuls of the stew. Just as Bai thought, it barely had flavor and no substance to fill a belly. He tried not to gag. In his peripheral view, Raegna twitched after her first taste, and quickly composed herself. Adabelle screwed up her button nose at her bowl and pushed it away.

"I don't want it, Mama," she said.

"You must eat it," Raegna told her as she scooped another spoonful. "You need it to grow."

"She can't grow on this," Bai mumbled.

He silently scolded himself. If only his tongue were not so quick.

Raegna tensed at the sound of his voice. Her spoon clanged against her bowl. Glaring at her stew, she spoke in a low growl. "What did you say, husband?"

Nothing is what he should have said. Bai pursed his lips instead, gripping his seat tight. Just because her mother was gone didn't mean Raegna's own wrath lifted with her. But he had dug a hole this deep. What would she do if he kept digging?

"She cannot grow on this," Bai repeated, meeting her glare. "This is nothing but soggy meat and water."

Every muscle in her face hardened in an unyielding calculation, unsure of what to do about him and his outburst. Bai had to admit, it was fascinating to see her pushed to her limit.

"It is a recipe to nourish," she said.

"If made correctly," he countered.

Their eyes locked on each other as they had only twice in their life together — when Adabelle was born and before her conception. It sent another pang of guilt through Bai's chest, but he held Raegna's gaze. An indentation popped above her jaw and her soil irises turned black.

"Well then, perhaps next time, you would like to take up woman's work," she snapped.

Something any petty wife might say, though Bai had a different perspective. He broke the stare and stood from the table. Adabelle and Raegna watched him go to a cupboard and find the burned loaf of bread Raegna had baked two days ago. He brought it back to them, took a knife, and sliced it.

"It may be a terrible stew," Bai said, "but it could pass for some kind of broth."

After handing a slice to Adabelle, he offered two slices to Raegna, who flinched at his outstretched hand. She scowled at the bread and then at him. Bai fixed his sight on the bread, waiting and watching for her hand to take it. Her sword sat between them and he prayed she wouldn't reach for it instead. Eventually, she swallowed her pride and seized the bread from his fingers.

"Dip it and eat it," Bai explained, nodding to Adabelle. "This loaf cannot go to waste. The stew will soften the burned crust."

Raegna's eyes narrowed on him, but Adabelle gobbled up the stew-soaked bread and asked for seconds. The three of them finished the loaf, and the stew disappeared with it.

After supper, Raegna washed the cauldron while Adabelle wiped the bowls and utensils. Bai went to bathe in the tub on the back porch.

Bai had the entire starry sky above him and the crickets chirping from the brush. Cleaning the day's grime away relaxed him on any other night. Tonight, his stomach churned as he listened to their chattering, and he envied them. Even the crickets could use their voices, but not him. Bai may have found his voice over dinner, but his outbursts did him no favors.

The old witch no longer loomed over this household and no longer dug her claws into Raegna's sides. But just because Jaleesa's reign ended did not mean Bai was free of a woman's name... not at once. Without her mother's control, what would Raegna do about him?

This fall marked seven years since their wedding in the temple. Surely Raegna dreaded every passing season as much as Bai did. The only reason she kept him was because of Jaleesa's obsessive control over her family's success.

If Raegna had it her way, she may never have married Bai or otherwise would have divorced him as soon as she breathed her vows. Should she have her way now, divorce may not have been an option. She might just reveal the true savage history her family carried and Syden would find another young husband dead in the village barn, like Raegna's own father. The sword remained with her tonight for a reason.

Bai sank deeper into the tub, soaking and contemplating with his nose over the water. In another life, he would have happily separated from her. Let her divorce him, let her kill him. He deserved as much. These days, only one thing kept him at her side, even without her mother's coercion. One thing would urge him to fight for his life should his wife choose to spill blood.

Adabelle cut a deep crevice into his heart the moment the midwife placed her in his arms, the moment she opened those precious eyes. He would do anything for her, and that included remaining married to her dangerous mother.

Watching the ripples in the water, Bai replayed Raegna's reactions over the table in his head. Certainly, her nasty looks showed the intention to kill if her sword didn't do that on its own, and Bai gave her every reason to, but she kept the peace. Maybe blood wasn't on her agenda, and maybe he had the chance to convince her to keep him. Then he could keep Adabelle within reach.

Things might be better with Jaleesa gone. At least she couldn't take charge of every aspect of their marriage and she couldn't force them to have another child.

Claws raked within his chest. Bai growled and pushed himself out of the tub. The water splashed over the rim and he pulled a towel around himself. Once he dried off and dressed, Bai snuck back inside.

What could he say to persuade her? Perhaps persuasion wasn't the answer. Perhaps he should apologize.

Apologize for everything.

Moonlight shone through the windows, serving Bai on his way to the bedroom. Raegna blew out the candles in the main room and kitchen before he could finish bathing. One candle burned in the bedroom and coated Raegna's form in a flickering light as she stood over Adabelle's bed.

Raegna plucked the last wildflower out of her hair and set it with the rest on the windowsill. The sword leaned on the wall next to Adabelle's bed. Adabelle glanced up at her father's entrance with mournful eyes. With her mother nearby, there was nothing Bai could do for her. He gave her an encouraging smile and went to make up the main bed. It was his turn to sleep there tonight.

"All right," Raegna whispered as she tucked the girl in. "That ought to keep you warm. You'll sleep tight tonight, won't you?"

Adabelle shook her head. "Not without Grandmother."

That makes all of us. Bai held his tongue this time.

"Ada, you must get some rest," Raegna told her. "You need your sleep. How about a story to take your mind off things?"

Adabelle pouted, folding her arms, but both her parents knew how she couldn't resist a story. Especially one her mother told. The corner of

Raegna's lip curled and she raised a smug eyebrow at the girl, knowing she won. "Remember the first story of Sachi and Sigmund?"

Adabelle shook her head, earning a click from Raegna's tongue before she continued. "See, Gaea became lonely after She created our world of Jorde, watching the land and making it go 'round. So with Her own power, She conceived a child and gave birth to a beautiful daughter She named Sachi. Gaea and Sachi lived on Jorde together and Gaea adored Her daughter. Sometimes, She had to leave Sachi alone to fulfill other duties as a Goddess, but She would always return to her."

Adabelle's eyes glittered with wonder while she listened to the story. Bai couldn't help but grin at her.

"One day, when Gaea was away, Sachi walked through the forests and happened upon the god Fan, the evil one. Fan was driven by Sachi's beauty to trick her and take her for his own. He did what he desired before Gaea returned and found Sachi lying on a forest path, weeping, pregnant, and slowly becoming human. Enraged, Gaea hunted the evil one down and punished him for what he did. She sent him to the underworld, the land called Helved."

"What about Sachi?" Adabelle asked, eyes wide.

"She had a child," Raegna answered. "A boy who was deformed and too weak to survive. This left Sachi scarred, childless and human. She couldn't see her mother in physical form anymore and wept every day for her."

"That's not fair," Adabelle protested.

Raegna brushed her daughter's blonde hair from her face. "Because She could not be with Sachi, could not comfort her and directly shield her from danger, Gaea made her a companion from the earth. The first man. His name was Sigmund. Gaea created him to protect Sachi, and provide for her and she fell in love. She wanted Sigmund to be her husband, and under Gaea, they were married."

"That's very nice," Adabelle cooed. "Did they have children?"

"Many, many, many children," Raegna told her. "You and I are descendants of Sachi. All of us are."

"Even Papa?"

Bai froze over the pillows he fluffed, listening to Raegna's answer.

"Erm. Well..." she stammered. "Yes. He, like all men, is a son of Sigmund. Like the first man, it is his job to protect us and provide for us. They must respect us."

"Uh-huh. Papa loves me," Adabelle chirped. "Papa's just like Sigmund."

Bai repressed a chuckle. Neither he nor his daughter helped his cause to be in Raegna's good graces. Or rather, tolerant graces.

Raegna breathed a hopeless sigh. "Perhaps. Now get some rest, sweet babe."

She leaned in and kissed her forehead, then got to her feet, snatching up her sword. She switched places with Bai as they had every night since Adabelle was old enough to beg for him to wish her goodnight. Bai knelt before her bed to lean in and give her a kiss. He smoothed the sheets around her.

"Papa, you always protect us, don't you?" asked Adabelle.

"I will," Bai assured. "No matter what. I love you. As much as the sky is wide, I love you."

"I love you too."

All fear of Raegna washed away as he nuzzled Adabelle and kissed her once more. "Sweet dreams, precious girl."

CHAPTER 3

RAEGNA

RAEGNA WAITED FOR BAI'S soft snoring. Every night, she ensured he fell asleep before her. After their marriage, Jaleesa made sure they shared the same bed, expecting it to lead to more. They ceased that tradition as soon as Adabelle grew into a bed big enough for two. Raegna slept beside Adabelle until she could speak and ask for her father to do the same. When Raegna refused, she wept for him. Thus, they took turns.

Tonight, Bai settled on his side, his back facing them. Tucked under the blankets, he never twitched as he would when he drifted off. His snores did not break the quiet air.

Adabelle had fallen asleep, her chest rising and falling under Raegna's arm. Raegna wrestled to control a fidget. Finding sleep proved difficult with the suspicion that Bai lay awake. Raegna heaved a hard breath and closed her eyes to get some rest, at least. More pressing things could keep her up, like waking early to fulfill their divorce.

Then Bai rolled, shifting the sheets. Raegna went rigid. Her nails dug into the pillow beneath her head, but she remained still so as not to disturb Adabelle. She glanced at the nightstand drawer less than a foot away from him. Her original choice of weapon — should Bai decide to do anything — lay within it. A knife he couldn't know was there.

Raegna eyed her sword resting against Adabelle's bedframe. It would be easy to rise and unsheathe it, dare him to come close. Raegna could bring it to his throat faster than he could touch her.

While all this swirled in her mind, Bai didn't move.

"I'm sorry," he whispered into the darkness.

Where was this sudden need for conversation coming from? First over dinner and now this? He had never spoken to her before. Was it her mother's absence that emboldened him? Did he want her to let her guard down?

With taut muscles, Raegna held her breath. In contrast, Adabelle dozed beside her. The girl's head lolled to the far side of the pillow. Her arm hung over the edge of the bed.

Bai shuffled beneath the blankets. "I am truly sorry for what... for what happened. I should have said so a long time ago. And I'm sorry about your mother. But you must know this... this changes everything. We can make our own choices now."

Teeth gritted, Raegna growled. "Nothing you say will change anything. Tomorrow, you're on your own. I'll give my case to the Matriarch and priestesses, and we will no longer be bound to each other. This is over."

He turned to face her, the sharp corner of his brow and hollow cheekbones highlighted by dim moonlight. "What about Adabelle?"

Raegna fought the urge to pull Adabelle toward her. She shouldn't disturb her sleep. "She isn't your concern. She never was."

"Please. She'll be heartbroken. If she's this upset about Jaleesa, imagine how she'd feel if I left. Please don't do this."

Tears brimmed her eyelids and Raegna blinked them away. "I don't want to hear another word out of you. She's young and she'll get over it. My mind is made up."

Bai inhaled a shuddering breath. "I won't leave her."

"You will when you are not mine," Raegna hissed. "And if you do not, I will have warriors escort you out. If you fight back, they will surely lock you up, if not kill you. You're a man and there is nothing you can do about this. If you know what's best, you'll leave Syden entirely and spare her more pain."

Silence fell over them. Bai finally rolled onto his side and pulled at the sheets as he curved in on himself. Raegna's drumming heart slowed and the last of her tears streamed over the bridge of her nose and down her temple. She controlled her quivering lip and oncoming gasps as she curled around Adabelle.

Of course, he would beg for a spot in Adabelle's life. Everything he said would come to pass. Adabelle would likely wail for her father for days once she realized he was gone. She may turn on her mother, but Raegna prepared herself for that. Nothing could deter her from her plan. Not even Adabelle and any desire to prevent her heartbreak. The little girl could not understand what had happened between her parents. What they were forced through... what Raegna had been forced through.

Swallowing a sob at the memory, Raegna dried her tears by nestling her face into the pillow. Tomorrow, she would set everything right. For now, she accepted she would not sleep, and braced to manage the following day in complete exhaustion.

Raegna must have dozed off, because she woke again to a blood-curdling shriek.

A woman's scream made its way into her home and echoed from wall to wall. The shrill sound of it chilled Raegna to her bones. She propped herself on one arm as the hairs on the nape of her neck stood on end.

Bai shot up in bed, his blond hair a tussled mess and his eyes darting around the room. He marked Adabelle, stirring in her sleep, and Raegna hovering above her, staring back in bewilderment.

"What was that?" he whispered, his voice edged with fear.

Before Raegna could answer, more terrified voices filled the night, and she sat up. Low shouts and ravaged screams carried through the village, ripping the quiet stillness to shreds. The faint, stinging smell of smoke wafted into their home. Had someone's house caught fire?

Worried for her neighbors and friends, Raegna crept over her daughter and slipped out of bed. Her sword clinked as she lifted it from the bedframe and padded across the floor. Adabelle awoke to the commotion drawing closer, rubbing her eyes.

"Mama?"

"Go to your father, Adabelle," Raegna instructed without hesitation, surprised at herself.

"Come here," Bai urged her, patting the sheets.

Adabelle climbed onto the bed and scrambled to him. Bai held her close and watched Raegna tiptoe out the door.

Her vision adjusted to the darkness to maneuver through the kitchen. Everything stood in place just as the family had left it before bed. The only disturbances were the fearful cries and the scent of smoke from outside. In the window, an orange glow of flickering fire lit up the main room instead of the usual fading moonlight.

Raegna almost knocked over a chair. She peered through the window and gasped at the scene.

Fires burned several houses along the road, lighting up the streets in a blaze. A shadow of black smoke emerged from the flames, cloaking the stars. A priestess might describe it as the end of days when Fan's prison in Helved would stretch and consume all Jorde.

Women and their children bolted past the enormous flames destroying their homes in their nightwear, screaming in terror. Raegna caught her breath as she discerned those who pursued them.

Silhouettes of tall, broad-shouldered figures bearing swords or axes chased after the villagers. They tore children from their mothers and struck deadly blows upon their victims. The intruders barked orders at each other in low voices. Raegna's heart seized as she realized they were men. Men wielding swords and shields as if they were warriors. Or even Fan's minions.

One mother twisted to retrieve her child, but a blade slashed across her belly. Blood poured onto the ground and soaked her dress, gushing from her mouth as she fell. Her daughter screamed for her in the invader's grasp and her young son cried over her fallen body. Raegna watched wide-eyed as the invader lifted the girl by her hair and slit her throat. He threw her into the dirt beside her mother. Their blood splashed across the boy's clothes and face, and he sobbed harder.

With a shout, a warrior sprang from behind the invader, wielding her sword. The invader whirled and countered her attack. They battled just before Raegna's house, frightening chickens in a nearby coop. A few birds escaped before the warrior crashed backward into the coop. Squawking hens flapped around her in a flurry of feathers. Concealed by the ruined coop, the warrior struggled to recover as the invader stood over her. He plunged his sword down with a *shunk* and the warrior gave a strangled grunt.

Countless attacks occurred all over the street beyond, too many for Raegna to witness at once. Warriors defended Syden while common folk ran or attempted to fight. Women and men alike clutched scythes, pitchforks, and even kitchen knives. The invaders cut them down alongside their trusted warriors.

The invader outside Raegna's home wiped his blade on his pants and raised his head. When their eyes met through the simmering night, Raegna snapped out of her trance, fist clenched around her sword. She spun back through the main room. They could not reach Adabelle.

Raegna unwound the belt from the sword's scabbard and wrapped it around her waist in her haste. Then she latched the buckle over her nightgown. She raced back to the bedroom, where Bai and Adabelle waited, and found a satchel underneath the bed.

"What's happening?" Bai asked.

"There are men out there," she said without thinking. "They're killing everyone. We need to go."

His sinewy arms held Adabelle tighter. "What?"

"Grab what you can carry," Raegna ordered, before turning for the kitchen. "Quickly. We're going to the stable before they reach it. Move!"

Bai scooped Adabelle up and fetched his work bag from the closet. He stuffed clothes into it on top of the supplies inside. Raegna filled her satchel with food from the cupboards, crumbs and herb leaves falling about the floor.

In the bedroom, she opened the nightstand drawer and handed Bai her knife. He hesitated at the sight of it, his brow raised. Raegna barely believed herself, trusting him with the blade she had always meant for him. But if he was carrying Adabelle, she wanted him armed with something. Raegna shoved the hilt of the knife into his hand and pushed him forward.

"Go now!" she snapped. "Out the window!"

Heavy footsteps came from the front of the house. Crunching blows sounded at the door. The wood splintered and the hinges popped.

Bai climbed through the bedroom window with Adabelle in one arm, and his bag slung over his shoulder. As he clambered down, he made sure the knife's edge would not touch Adabelle while she sobbed.

"Hush, Ada," he soothed her. "Everything's all right."

Raegna climbed after them. On the way out, she lost her footing and dropped to the ground. When she landed in an awkward crouch, a sharp pain spiked through her ankle. Raegna cried out and stumbled to her knees, smudging her nightgown skirt in the mud.

Bai turned to her, Adabelle on his hip. He must have been considering helping her and whether that was a good idea. Raegna gritted her teeth and ignored the pang as she stood.

"Move!" she growled. "Go!"

They sprinted across a barren road to the stables, avoiding any light that might spot them. Bai kept a short distance ahead, with Adabelle bouncing in his arms. Raegna hobbled on the dull ache in her ankle. The screams that followed them rang in her ears, but she propelled herself forward. They had to get Adabelle to safety.

Someone else trailed close behind them. The thudding vibrations of dense footfalls raced in time with theirs and Raegna's stomach clenched tight as she limped faster. At least Bai could hasten his pace, so Adabelle would be out of reach.

The pursuer caught up to them. Raegna gasped as he swiped her feet out from under her. She yelped when she fell on her side. Pain struck her shoulder and thigh. With a groan, Raegna pushed herself up to face her opponent: a large, muscular man with murder in his shrouded eyes under a thick brow and a crooked grin beneath a scraggly beard.

"Where are you goin', wench?" he gargled almost happily.

He drove his sword to slice her skull, but Raegna rolled away and stood. With her ankle screaming beneath her weight, she unsheathed her sword and faced the man who was twice her size. It was strange to see him with a sword like a warrior, or even like a Maiden. He certainly had no wife to take it from him, let alone scold him for using such vile language.

"Oh, a fighter, eh?" the man said. "I might just keep you alive to have fun at home."

Raegna shouted and lunged at him. Her sword slashed to make a cut to the neck. Instead, the blade clashed against his.

Playing swords as a girl never earned Raegna any true combat skills. She did the best she could, parrying and attempting fatal blows. But a moving target with a weapon of his own differed from the tree trunks she had hit with fallen branches. Raegna's old cries of strength and valor transformed into grunts of frustration as he continued to slam his blade against hers, pushing her backward.

After a few swift moves, he took her down. Her sword clattered on a stone two feet from her. Raegna landed flat on her back and gasped for air. Her racing heart sank as the invader pinned her arms above her head and straddled her.

"You know," he said, "I've got time. Let's have some fun right now."

NO.

He threw her skirt up, and though she fought, he widened the gap between her legs. Raegna let out a scream of defiance and her body strained to escape, her rigid muscles trembling so much she barely controlled them to attempt throwing him off. Her mind swirled and almost succumbed to darkness, avoiding the experience entirely, but Raegna willed herself to fight. He moved to unbuckle his belt when a thud came from behind his back.

A strange groan rolled over his lips as he arched backward, releasing Raegna from his grip. Relief tingled through her as she shimmied away over the dewy grass before he fell onto his belly. The hilt of her nightstand knife stuck out between his shoulder blades.

Bai stood behind him with Adabelle in one arm. The little girl's eyes grew wide as tea saucers while her father ripped the knife from the man's back.

A muscle curled above Bai's sharp jawline as he glared down at the invader. "Bastard."

Raegna stared and blinked hard to grasp what had just happened. She shook her swirling head and rose, wincing at the bolt of pain in her ankle.

"What are you doing?" she gasped out. With a quivering hand, she snatched Bai's sleeve and tugged him ahead of her. "Move! To the stables!"

They took off again, feet striking against the dirt path. The chaos of the burning village drowned out their labored breath. Tears fogged Raegna's vision, and each step elicited an agony that sprang up her leg, begging her to stop. Every other instinct within her urged her to live.

Raegna kept her sight on Adabelle, who buried her face in Bai's neck. Her tiny hands clutched his shirt, and her hair swept around her with Bai's stride. Raegna would have to survive for her. The determination fueled her to keep her moving.

They pushed through the stable doors and used them for cover. Inside, the aisle of stalls had no light, and various large equine heads raised to witness the family's entrance. Reflective eyes glittered and hooves shuffled straw.

In a mad rush, they found two horses, led them from their stalls, and fitted bridles over their ears. Raegna shoved Bai towards his horse, a brown gelding that hopped from hoof to hoof. "Get on, now!"

He placed Adabelle on the horse's bare back and mounted behind her.

The doors crashed open, and the horses whinnied, rearing. Adabelle screamed with them. Three men stood at the doorway, swords in hand. The glow of the fires outside veiled their silhouettes, and their shadows stretched across the hay-strewn floor.

Bai moved his horse to stand in front of Raegna and hide her, sandwiched between the beasts. Raegna held her breath, but the men didn't spot her in the dark of the murky stable.

"He's got a girl," one man stated with a gesture of his sword up at Bai and Adabelle.

"Brother, we're not here to harm you," another said, opening a palm. "It's all right. We only want to free you from this place. Free you from the tyranny of the Queen and her women."

Raegna stayed low, attempting with stealth to use her good ankle to swing onto her mount. Bai stared at them. His lips parted as if he meant to say something to deter them. Adabelle sobbed against his chest. Their gelding shifted and tossed his head.

"The girl will be safe," the same man assured. He gave Bai his warmest smile through the grime and blood on his face. "I promise. Everything is all right."

Once she settled on her horse, Raegna rode past Bai, unleashing a battle cry. She slashed her sword at the men as she fled the stable. The blade cut one down with a slice to his chest. Bai and Adabelle rode behind her.

The horses took a sharp turn from the village. They drifted through the inky crop fields with only the firelight to guide them. The wind whipped through Raegna's hair as she led them away from the carnage, a stark contrast to the heat of the fires.

They slowed when they reached the woods on the hill crest above Syden. Raegna halted them to look back at their home, and her heart plummeted between her heaving lungs.

Rooftops and houses burned. Black smoke devoured the starry night sky. Their people cried out louder than the crackling of flames or crumbling of debris. Raegna beheld this nightmarish sight with a lump in her throat painful enough for her to forget her throbbing ankle, unable to make sense of it. She didn't want to believe it. What terror had destroyed her childhood home...

Raegna scanned her surroundings on the hilltop. Nothing accompanied them there except the tree line, the trunks beckoning them to safety. No other families stood alongside hers and none made their way towards them. None had escaped.

Which meant Pinar was there with her children.

Raegna swallowed her tears and directed her horse forward. "Go to the woods. You'll be safe there."

"What?" Bai snapped at her. His gelding's hooves approached behind her. "Raegna, you're coming too!"

It was the first time she had heard her name on his tongue. Her veins lit like the fire below them, and she wheeled her mare around and faced him with a scowl.

"Do not tell me what to do, man," she snapped. "You do as I say. Ride into the woods and keep my daughter safe."

"Raegna, there is no one left down there," Bai protested. He rode his horse up to hers. "They're dead and if you go, you're dead too. I won't let you!"

Raegna's lip curled in a snarl, and she kicked her heels into her horse to start back down the hill. Bai followed at once and whirled the gelding around to cut the mare off. The lines on his angled face stretched with his glower. Raegna bared her teeth, knuckles white around the reins.

"You stubborn cock!" she cursed. "Get out of my—"

Bai smashed the hilt of the knife and his fist against her head. Raegna fell limp across her horse, astounded by the glint of his gold eyes in the firelight, just before everything went pitch black.

Chapter 4

Hadwin

HADWIN STUMBLED ALONG WITH his brother and nephews. The invaders had organized the surviving Syden men into a line that snaked down the market road. Flames engulfed their village and swelled around them, scorching the air and searing Hadwin's bruised skin. Young boys stood alongside their fathers, hiding their faces and weeping.

Hadwin's nephews remained by his brother's side. Dakarai clutched his hip, his thin face half-hidden as he peeked about with large, brown eyes that glistened with tears. Cadoc wailed in his father's grasp. His forehead pressed to Naleem's cheek, and the little boy nuzzled for comfort. Naleem kept a hand on Dakarai's head, his fingers combing through Dak's dark brunette hair that matched his own. A stream of blood trickled over his thick, furrowed brow.

With quaking fists, Hadwin watched the ruthless invaders walk up and down the line of Syden men to keep order.

Nobody knew where these men came from. Nor did they know why they attacked this small, insignificant village. They had targeted the women and girls, sparing the men and boys. Or at least, the ones who could not defend their wives, daughters, mothers, and sisters. Their bodies lay where they fell during the raid, blood flowing from their wounds and mouths to create red creeks along their humble main road. The invaders kicked at the corpses when they stepped over them. Hadwin's veins festered with rage at the sight.

The captured Syden men, placed shoulder to shoulder, ducked their heads as the invaders passed. While the flames consumed homes in black ash, they found more village men and added them beside Hadwin. They joined the line either stone-faced or weeping as the children did, their hands cupped over their faces. The invaders rounded them up and directed them with the points of their swords or axes.

Searching up and down the line, Hadwin hoped to find another familiar face. They had gathered the last living men in Syden. None of them were Bai.

If Bai wasn't among the other captives, perhaps he had met the same fate as all the others who lay before them. Would he have fought to protect his wife? He would have died for his daughter. Hadwin took a shuddering breath as a pang of grief reverberated through his chest.

Another friend, Seagr, sobbed over his young wife's body on the road. Hadwin remembered attending their wedding two springs ago. Now Seagr cradled her in his arms, pressing his bloodied forehead to hers. His cries tore at Hadwin's heart, urging him to console his friend, though his nerves told him otherwise. Too many blades glinted around them.

One raider stood over Seagr and kicked him in the ribs. "Get in line."

With a pained yell, Seagr lunged at him and wrapped his hands over the man's throat. "You killed her! Get away from her!"

"Seagr." Hadwin tried to intervene, taking a step forward. He stopped when Naleem snagged the back of his shirt.

The man rammed a punch into Seagr's gut and brought him to his knees. He swung his ax, and the blade ripped across Seagr's face. Blood sprayed the gravel and his dead wife's skirts. Seagr fell sideways to land on top of her legs with a gaping red gouge stretching from his temple to the opposite jawline. Hadwin snapped his eyes shut and turned away, his mind spinning at the sight of the swift violence.

By Gaea, there was so much death. The fires devoured whatever remained of Hadwin's home and childhood, and these monsters marched over blackened timbers and stiff bodies as if they were nothing. The world collapsed around him like an ancient, weakened fortress. Hadwin gritted his teeth when a hard lump formed in his throat. The tears that blurred his vision evaporated in the hot night air.

Once the invaders had scoured the village for survivors, they reported to each other that their captives were collected. Someone shouted a name down the road. A horse strode to the line, carrying a cloaked figure in the saddle.

The horse's coat gleamed a deep, dim garnet in the firelight and a shaggy, unkempt mane brushed over its neck and withers. A black-furred cloak covered the rider's shoulders and draped over the horse's hindquarters. The heavy fur distorted the rider's silhouette to make them appear bigger than even the horse, though they had to be human.

One gloved hand gripped the reins, the other held aloft a pike pole topped with a head. Silver curls waved around the rider's fist and blood dripped down the pole.

The Syden men stepped back as the rider approached, shaking in their places. Hadwin braced himself. The rider halted their horse and thrust the pike into the ground. The men murmured in anguish when they recognized Matriarch Alv's face, her mouth open and eyes rolled back. Hadwin and Naleem shrank back, shielding Dakarai, and Hadwin gulped the sharp pain in his throat.

The rider drew back the hood of their fur coat, and every Syden man holding his breath flinched.

A square-jawed man with sharp eyes and a straight nose looked at them from his horse. His lips curled into a gentleman-like smirk through his short, black beard as his gaze lingered over each villager.

Another beast of a man rode up beside him on an even larger steed. This man kept his furred hood over his head, but his broad shoulders were prominent under his cloak, as was the thick, red beard that protruded from under the hood and covered what was visible of his face.

The first rider ran his hand through his short-cropped black hair. His skin was flushed red from exertion and glistened with sweat in the heat of the fire. But he kept his composure as if it were the coolest night of the summer.

"Gentlemen," he greeted the line of villagers, "I apologize for waking you all like this. My name is Thenalious. My men and I are raiders, rebels against the Queen of Galaenia. Because of us, you may now consider yourselves free men. No woman has control over you or your sons now. Nor will they ever again. We have freed you from their clutches and that of your Matriarch here. But don't thank us. Let us instead thank our god Fan and his brother Sigmund for blessing us to ride forth and dominate the wenches of your village."

"Fan is a devil!" someone shouted from the line. "He works against Gaea and all Her people!"

Thenalious peered at the man who spoke. At the very end stood Obrecht, an elder of Syden with a spotted bald head and hanging wrinkled jowls like wet parchment. He had always been a firm believer in

Gaea and in all her ways. Though a hint of pride sparked in him that their elder would speak up against this evil, Hadwin's gut somersaulted as Thenalious walked his horse toward Obrecht.

The horse came to a halt before the elder. Thenalious leaned over the saddle horn. "My dear brother, Fan stands with us. He is on Sigmund's side, guiding him, so he too becomes strong and too good to serve woman and her Goddess."

"Fan deceives Sigmund and tempts him," Obrecht argued. He turned to those in line beside him with his tired eyes squinting against the flames. "Sigmund is our father and, like him, it is our duty to protect and provide for our wives, as he did for Sachi. Fan persuades him to disrespect her, harm her, and take advantage of her." He glared back at Thenalious. "That is not our way."

Thenalious' fingers flexed within his riding gloves. His steed snorted just above Obrecht's head. "Come, old-timer. In the words of Fan, women exist to have our children, raise them, remain home, and prepare supper after we've finished the true work." He looked down the line. "Don't you think you have done more than any woman? What do you get for it? Mistreatment? Indifference? Abuse? As your brothers, we did you a favor."

"They were our wives and daughters," a different villager snarled, stepping out of the line, "and you murdered them!"

Time slowed. The flickering of flames became steady walls of red as Thenalious' eyes rested over the villager. He unsheathed his sword, spun the horse around, and galloped to the man, who shouted in surprise. He bolted, but the raiders on foot blocked his path. Atop his horse, Thenalious picked the man from the crowd and swiped the blade across his collar.

The man's body dropped to the ground with a thud. A small fountain of blood squirted from his half-severed neck. He twitched for two terrifying seconds with a permanent look of shock on his face. Hadwin shielded his nephews from the sight and Naleem pulled them closer. But Dakarai had already seen and screamed into his father's hip. Cadoc wailed in fear along with the other children.

Thenalious gave a heavy sigh and rode back down the line. "Here's a new concept: Anyone who defends the Queen, the Goddess, or their worshipers will be executed. Does that give you any ideas?" He waited. "No? Good."

He turned to his men and nodded, giving them a silent order to move forward.

"Gentlemen," he addressed the villagers, "please do not be alarmed as my men cover your handsome heads. This is just a precaution."

The invaders approached them with vegetable sacks and forced them over their heads. Hadwin could barely see through the sack stitching. It scratched his skin and reeked of ammonia, like cat urine. He tried to breathe through his mouth instead, to lessen the stench.

"We can't have you escaping our base and sending word out of our location," Thenalious explained, his voice muffled by the sack. "So please, don't fuss. We will remove them once we get home. We welcome you as brothers and will do our best to treat you as such. Surely some of you are happy to be free of a wife's claws... Turn and we'll press on to our destination."

All of them obeyed. The shuffle of dirt sounded before Hadwin as Dakarai stumbled at his father's feet. Hadwin found the boy's hand to keep him stable. "Here, Dak. Stay with Uncle Hadwin, all right?"

"I want Papa," Dakarai whimpered. "I want to walk with Papa. I'm scared."

"I know, little one," Hadwin soothed, squinting through the fabric. He could pick out the shape of Dakarai before him and Cadoc tucked underneath Naleem's arm. Naleem stood with his shoulders back.

"Your father's right in front of us. If you reach, you can touch him." Hadwin touched his brother's shoulder. "See? Right in front of us."

Dakarai reached and found his father's hip again. Naleem slid his hand over Dakarai's and wrapped his fingers around it.

"He's there, Dak," Hadwin assured. "He just can't walk blindfolded with both of you holding onto him."

Dakarai leaned against his uncle. Hadwin drew him close. "It's all right, Dak. Uncle Hadwin's right here."

The line of Syden men moved forward, toward the hills and away from their burning village. Hadwin took his hand away from his brother and guided Dakarai the best he could. They hobbled with the others. Before him, Naleem's figure became a blur, with Cadoc peeking over one shoulder. Hadwin found it impossible to read him, especially with the sack over his head. After everything that happened, how could Naleem hold up?

He loved his wife and daughters and had never spoken of them as Thenalious described women. Neither had Hadwin thought of them in such a way. Pinar had always been a gracious and kind woman, even when she pursued Naleem. Back then, Hadwin had teased Naleem for being courted.

"What will she do for you today, brother?" he asked a lifetime ago in their childhood home, hopping in circles around Naleem. "Bring you flowers? Sing you a song? Kiss your fingertips as a lady does for a gentleman?"

"We're going for a walk in the forest," Naleem answered, fixing a vest over his shirt. "There are flowers involved. She wanted to show me where she finds the wildflowers she likes to arrange."

"Better not get lost in those flowers, Naleem. I'll tell Mother if you haven't returned by sunset!"

"Nothing is getting lost, Hadwin. I'll tell Mother you're being an imp if you don't stop this teasing when Pinar gets here."

When she arrived, they opened the door to her, and her bright smile flustered Naleem. Hadwin could tell by the way his shoulders bobbed and how his cheeks developed a tinge of pink. He couldn't blame him for it. Pinar had the prettiest smile in Syden that made her soft cheekbones rounder. Strands of her frost-like hair drifted behind her, tied in a half-braid. She seemed bashful about Naleem, too, her long eyelashes batting.

"Good day, Naleem," she chirped. "Before we go, I have something for you." From a skirt pocket, she produced an amulet in the shape of a raven and placed it in his hand. "It's the symbol of Sigmund, for when he transformed into one to find Sachi when they were separated. You said it was your favorite story, so I thought..."

"Oh, it's beautiful." Naleem slipped the necklace on to thumb the amulet carving at the base of his neck. "Thank you."

Hadwin snorted at their lovesick faces and their dumb, whispering voices. Then Pinar turned her attention to him. "You must be Hadwin. Naleem has told me all about you. I brought you something, too."

This time, she offered a parchment covering a circular object and unwrapped it. Hadwin gasped as she revealed a cinnamon pastry covered in a brown crumble. "A sugar roll! Thank you, thank you, thank you!"

From then on, he didn't poke fun at them. He looked forward to Pinar's visits with her various courtship gifts and sweet disposition. Eventually, he took her aside and asked, "When are you going to marry my brother?"

She laughed and showed him the ring she meant for Naleem, silver with forest vines and wildflower petals etched around it. "I'm trusting you, Hadwin. You can't tell him. All right?"

It was the hardest task of his young life. Hadwin bit his lip every time the news surfaced in his mind. Finally, she proposed in the forest among the flowers and they wed just a few weeks later. Though it was a happy occasion, it meant Naleem had to leave and begin a new family with Pinar. And Hadwin became utterly alone.

Hadwin counted on his mother to search for his match, but Lady Tessa did not seem so urgent about finding her youngest son a wife. All their childhood, she had kept an eye out for a suitable woman for Naleem, and Pinar's affection met her approval. The sweetest girl in the village was just right for her firstborn son. What would become of the second?

Hadwin waited, hearing the proposals and wedding ceremonies of everyone else his age in Syden. His mother hardly brought the idea of courtship up, nor did she appear to care. Then he came to his twentieth year.

"Now, Hadwin, you are a man grown," his mother said one day. "I cannot tend to you forever. If you can't find a wife, you must find other means of living."

"But, Mother, I thought—" Thought she might have put an effort into finding him one as she did for Naleem.

"You're not a child anymore," she went on, ignoring him. "The Matriarch has cut my income. I can't take care of you like a babe."

With that, she sent him out. Tears welling up in his eyes, Hadwin dragged his feet to the other end of Syden where he knew Naleem and Pinar lived and knocked on the door. The freshly built house didn't have a crack or rot in the wood and flowers grew on the windowsills. A buttery smell of bread baking over a fire wafted through an open window.

Pinar answered him with a hand under her round, pregnant belly. Younger Dakarai and Estrid peered at him from behind her skirt. "Hadwin?"

"Pinar. Hello. Is Naleem here?"

"Er, no. He's working in the field. I thought you might be there, too." Her voice came slow and steady, as if she was focused on figuring out a riddle, fingers absently twirling her children's hair. "He'll be home by sunset. Is there something I can help you with?"

"Well... I'm not sure. See, our mother... said she couldn't have me live with her anymore, since I am yet unmarried. I just had nowhere else to go."

Pinar raised an eyebrow, a deep frown breaking the serenity of her face. "What?"

"I'm sorry, I'll come back later when Naleem returns—"

"No!" She rushed forward and gripped his arm, startling the children. "Come inside this instant. We'll wait for him here. In fact, you can stay as long as you like. Are you hungry?"

When she told him as long as he liked, he did not think she meant it.

That evening when Naleem came home, Hadwin explained everything to him and kept a brave face. He despised speaking ill of their mother in front of Naleem, who loved her so. Naleem's gentle expression turned to stone as he listened to him, all three of them sitting at the kitchen table with Pinar's meadow pie cut up in slices before them, the children excused from the conversation to play on the floor in the main room.

"No, Hadwin," Naleem said, his knuckles white as he held his fork. "She shouldn't have sent you away like that. A mother doesn't do that to her son. I can't believe she's done this. Not even once looking for a girl for you."

"Well, she isn't getting any younger," Hadwin admitted with his chin in his palm. "And all the girls my age have been married. It's not a simple task."

"Would you want a wife, Hadwin?" Pinar asked.

Hadwin shrank in his seat. "Um. Aren't I supposed to?"

"You don't have to," she began and set her fork down. "Because I have an idea. I can't let you go after this. Why don't you stay here with us?"

Both brothers stared at her.

"For how long?" Naleem pressed when Hadwin couldn't find his voice.

"For however long he wants," she answered with a shrug. "You can be another man of the house and work for our compensation in the fields. Or you could be a house-husband without the law of marriage. We'll need the help with this little one on the way and more to come, Gaea willing."

Hadwin pushed pieces of his pie around his plate. "I... I wouldn't want to be a bother..."

"Nonsense! You've never been since I've been with Naleem, Hadwin. And to be honest, I missed your high spirits. So, what do you say?"

Hadwin looked at Naleem, but his brother leaped out of his chair and kissed Pinar. "You would truly do that for us?"

"Of course, my darling," Pinar said, cradling his cheek in her hand. "Anything for you and your brother. We are family, after all."

Hadwin beamed. "Then I suppose I'll have to stay!"

The years passed happily, surrounded by a family that grew. Hadwin spent Cadoc's birth watching over Dakarai and Estrid, reassuring them their mother would be all right. It ended with the newborn in his arms as Naleem and Pinar showed him how to hold the babe.

Three winters later, little Nalani followed, and each child brightened their lives, adding warmth to their hearth. Seeing Naleem and Pinar together, and raising their children alongside them, caused Hadwin to yearn for his own from time to time. Though he would trade nothing for the one he had.

And it had all been taken from him in a single night.

The screams had broken out in the house closest to theirs. Hadwin, Naleem, and Pinar rose to make sense of what was wrong. Pinar lit a candle and went to investigate with Naleem behind her. Hadwin stayed with the children in the bedroom. Dakarai and Estrid whined for their parents and Hadwin hushed them.

Was there a burglar in the village? Or had a wolf or mountain cat trespassed?

A great bang splintered the front door, causing Hadwin and the children to jump. Cadoc cried in his little bed across the room. Hadwin went to him to draw him in his arms, placing a hand over his mouth. Pinar shoved Naleem into the bedroom and whirled, a pitiful kitchen knife in her fist. She stood guard with such ferocity in her eyes Hadwin had never seen in her before.

Then the men entered, readying their swords as they studied the family close.

"Take the women," one ordered.

They lurched forward and snagged Pinar, twisting her wrist to seize her blade. Naleem lunged at them, throwing punches. Outnumbered half a dozen to one, they grappled him to the floor. Two of them grabbed him and threw him onto the bed.

Pinar fought to be free, lifting her head to see if her family was safe. When her babe Nalani wailed in her crib, Pinar let out a sob of her own. "Leave them be!"

"Call him off," the first man said. "We'll spare the men's lives. You'll give us your own."

Pinar ceased her struggle, hunched over with her hands wrenched behind her back. "Naleem, stop."

Hadwin curled around the children, who sobbed in his grasp. Naleem writhed under the raiders' grips, but obeyed his wife with a growl.

With a shudder, Pinar held the man's gaze. "You won't harm them?"

"Not the men and boys."

Hadwin's stomach dropped as she considered trading her life and the lives of her daughters for Naleem, Hadwin, and the boys.

Anything for you and your brother.

"Pinar," Naleem started, his voice cracking. Hadwin was unsure if it was a warning or a desperate plea.

Pinar shut her eyes tight, and a tendon protruded along her neck as she turned from them. Strands of her silvery hair fell in front of her face as she looked the invader straight in the eye. Her lips quivered and tears collected on the brims of her eyelids despite her sharp gaze.

"Leave them then. You'll have me."

Just as soon as she spoke, the man unsheathed his sword and ran it through her, beneath her sternum. He sliced down, gutting her.

Naleem screamed and attacked again. Two men held him back and knocked his head with a sword hilt. Four of them wrestled Estrid from Hadwin's arms before they drove a dagger upward under her jaw.

Hadwin cringed behind the sack over his head. He tried to drown out the memories of Nalani being strangled above her cradle, crying for rescue and comfort. The invaders had left the girls and Pinar inside the house and forced the men and boys out onto the street with the others.

Where would these men take them? After all the carnage, they could not be on their way to safety as they promised Pinar.

It wasn't easy hiking half-blind at night with a child who also couldn't see sticking close to him. Hadwin walked with caution, testing the ground with the tips of his toes. All the while, he kept Dakarai on his feet, though they both stumbled on stones, tree roots, or fallen branches. Once, Hadwin tripped and took his nephew with him. Dakarai had scraped his knees and cried, earning his father's attention. Naleem twisted and followed the sound of Dakarai's sob, with Cadoc by his side.

"Dak," he said. "What's wrong—"

"Move it!" a captor shouted and prodded Naleem with an ax haft. "Get going!"

"Don't worry, brother," Hadwin reassured him. "It was my fault." He searched for Dakarai with his hands and found the boy's arm shaking with his cries. "Come on, Dak. Let Uncle Hadwin carry you so you won't get hurt. Can't have you limping while you can't see."

Carrying the boy wasn't Hadwin's greatest idea. He walked slower, choosing his steps more carefully. The men urged them on until morning. Pale sunlight revealed silhouettes of those around him and redwoods towering hundreds of feet skyward. Hadwin had known those trees since childhood. He recognized a hunting trail and birds that sang through those intertwining branches. Surely every other Syden man could pinpoint how far they had gone by the familiar route.

But the flat forest turned into an uphill trek. The invaders ventured off the rather comforting path and up the hills that surrounded Sorelle. Switchbacks tilted beneath them and the enormous forests faded into weaker shrubs that grew off the side of the slopes. Hadwin put Dakarai down and bent over to climb. The group heaved for air. Some men stumbled and were kicked to their feet again.

Dakarai panted beside his uncle, his legs shaking when he stopped to catch his breath, which he did often.

"Keep going, Dak," Hadwin encouraged breathlessly. "You're strong. You can do it."

Naleem glanced over his shoulder. "Come along, son."

His father's voice sent Dakarai walking again, pushing through fatigue.

As the sunset melted from the sky, inviting the moon to take over for the night, the group settled to camp in a rugged, rocky clearing. The darkness carried a cold wind to shake the trees and raise goosebumps. The invaders started fires for themselves. Their prisoners absorbed the heat from a distance, but they were glad to rest.

One by one, each villager plotted a spot and dropped in exhaustion, their bodies spent. Little ones curled up with their fathers and brothers, whining after their long journey.

Hadwin and Naleem chose a piece of the ground farther away from the invaders' fires and made themselves comfortable. But Dakarai and Cadoc held onto either side of their father, so Naleem could not lie as easily as the others.

The invaders gave those who were conscious a ration of bread, stale but flaky and crunchy with oats. Such a portion hardly filled his stomach, but Hadwin chewed gratefully. His nephews munched on the crusts under the sacks that covered their heads, making a crumbly mess of themselves. They dozed off in Naleem's lap with his arms around each of them, soaking in their warmth.

Hadwin cleared his throat and leaned toward his brother, who was only a dim, obscure figure through the sack as evening turned into night. "Are you asleep, Naleem?"

"No," Naleem's worn voice grunted. Hadwin needed to get his spirits up.

"Dakarai is very brave, taking those scrapes," he joked half-heartedly. "I've got a few scrapes myself. It's amazing what rocks can do to us by just sitting there."

"Hm."

Hadwin counted that as a chuckle. "How are you, brother?"

Naleem wasn't as quick to respond. He sighed before replying, "I'm tired."

"Why don't you sleep? Feel the ground and find a soft spot. The boys can lie down with you."

Naleem did not search for optimal comfort. He lay back, taking the boys with him to sprawl on his chest. Neither of them stirred. Instead, they slumbered in a heap on top of him.

Hadwin took a deep breath. So much clouded his own mind, he couldn't imagine what Naleem could be going through. "I'm sorry, brother."

Naleem rubbed the raven amulet around his neck between his thumb and forefinger. "Me too."

CHAPTER 5
RAEGNA

FIRE RAVAGED SYDEN, CHARRING everything in sight. Embers rose around Raegna as the heat toasted the surface of her skin and singed the ends of her hair. Her childhood home became nothing but the fiery Helved. The old wooden houses cast blackened shadows, ash coated the streets, and the hot air reeked of burning wood and flesh.

An ominous presence surrounded her, whose rumbling laugh circled her above and below. The voice resonated like thunder, resounding in her bones and rattling her skull. Her nerves begged her to cower, to run as this deep, ancient baritone carried an unholy power that tore into her primal fears.

"Pinar!" Raegna yelled. Yes, that was her mission. She had to find her friend and escape with her and her family. No frightening voices could deter her from that. No matter how much her body trembled. "Pinar, where are you?"

The ground baked beneath her boots. The embers seared holes into her skirt. The torrid air was so stifling, Raegna struggled to breathe or think.

"Pinar!" she called out, though she feared her words became lost in the gusts. "Where are you?"

"Raegna!"

She spun, ash kicking up from her heels, and found her friend standing several feet before her, down the main road. Pinar's skin glowed white as a ghost, as if the flames could not touch it, yet her dress was plastered to her with sweat. Like blinding streaks of blizzard snow, her hair whipped and tangled about her in the scorching wind. Her eyes, once bright and loving, sank into their sockets. Spindly arms draped over her children, who were small, wispy shapes like the smoke.

Pinar visibly shivered despite the heat, desperate lines creasing in the gray circles under her eyes and the hollow crevices etched over her mouth. "Raegna, please!"

Raegna moved to take a step forward. The black cinders caked around her feet, locking her in place. She tried to kick and free herself, but it was no use. Ash turned into the stone that encased her boots.

"Pinar!" Raegna shouted, offering her hand. "Come, we'll get out of here! We can leave now!"

Pinar's lip quivered over her clenched teeth. Tears that streamed down her face evaporated into the air. "My family... My Naleem..."

Raegna threw her weight to combat the hardened ash. "What? Pinar!"

The malicious presence grew stronger, and, in a blur of motion, Pinar and her children became embers that flew. Laughter boomed and echoed with the crackling of flames.

"No!" Raegna jolted. Her skull pounded, and she fell back, staring up at Adabelle, who kneeled over her. The daylight overhead deepened the flush in her cheeks. Her tiny, brown velvet eyebrows rose with concern.

Adabelle blinked and tilted her head. "Mama? What's wrong?"

Raegna's vision swam, so she forced a "Nothing," in response.

Surveying the surrounding wood, she sat on a patch of clovers in a clearing with Adabelle, still in her nightdress and with the sword strapped to her belt. A canopy of trees floated above them. The branches swayed while the trunks stood firm. Sunlight stretched through the leaves and pine needles to reach the forest floor and scatter shadows upon it.

Across the clearing, Bai tended to the horses, his back to Raegna and Adabelle. When he turned, his angular profile peeked over his corded shoulders. The gold irises caught the light and glinted like coins. Raegna's head pounded harder, and she winced.

He hefted his work bag from his horse and plopped it beside her in the grass. "Good morning, wife. Or good afternoon."

Good afternoon, indeed. Raegna glowered at him as her veins steamed with rage. "Where are we, *husband*?"

Bai didn't glance at her. He fished through his bag to find an old piece of bread crust, then knelt to give it to Adabelle with a smile. "A few miles from the river. We had to create as much distance from Syden as we could."

Raegna got to her feet. Dizziness buzzed through her mind. Her ankle reminded her of the jump out the bedroom window with a pain that ripped through the muscle. Raegna hid a stumble by patting clover leaves off her nightgown. She straightened with spots dancing in her vision. "What did you do?"

Bai rose and stared down at her. His keen gaze made her heartbeat uneven, but she stood firm.

"I did what I could to protect you," he explained. "I knocked you out so you wouldn't foolishly kill yourself by trying to be heroic."

Raegna couldn't stand the knowing look in those eyes, the steadiness of his features. It made his words even more condescending. The ache in her ankle subsided as the years of hatred swelled within her. Speaking out of turn at home was one thing. Laying a blow to her, rendering her unconscious, and then dragging them through the woods—who in Gaea's name did he think he was? The wrath Raegna had fought so long to keep at a simmer boiled over to sizzle and spit.

Her hand raised and swiped across Bai's face with a hard smack. The blow was enough to make him stagger. His head turned from the force. Adabelle gasped and shrank back as she watched her mother shove her father backward.

"I'll decide what's foolish and what's not," Raegna snarled. "Remember your place. Just because we are out of the village doesn't make you a free man."

Adabelle sobbed and snapped Raegna out of her focus on Bai. They spun to her as fresh tears rolled down her cheeks, her lower lip quivering. For a second, neither parent moved. From the corner of her eye, Raegna caught Bai giving her a sideways glance and inching closer to Adabelle.

Instead of allowing such a thing, Raegna rushed forward and took Adabelle into her arms. The swift movement revived the pain in her ankle that fired up her leg with a vengeance.

"Shh," she soothed through clenched molars, combing Adabelle's messy hair with her fingers. "It's fine. You're all right, sweetling."

"But Papa" was all Adabelle could manage as she wept into her mother's shoulder. She wriggled to be let down, but Raegna held her tight.

"Nothing is wrong," Raegna said as calmly as she could. Her eyes narrowed as she glared at Bai. "Your father has spoken against me and physically harmed me. That is not acceptable."

Bai stood motionless, staring at her.

"He didn't mean it," Adabelle argued through muffled sobs. "He is just keeping us safe. Like Sigmund, like the story. Right, Mama?"

Raegna grimaced, suddenly regretting the story she had told her daughter. All she had wanted was to distract her from the sorrow of her grandmother's death. Yet it had only fueled her adoration for her father. This new lesson about a man's place in the world revived Jaleesa's teachings. Raegna would rather let them die with her.

She set Adabelle on the ground and knelt before her. "One day you'll understand."

She kissed the top of Adabelle's head, trying to reassure herself more than the girl. Adabelle's innocence left her oblivious now, but yes, in time she would realize her position among men. More likely when she is older and more experienced with well-behaved boys like Pinar's sons.

Pinar. The thought of her tore through Raegna like a knife through fabric. The horrific events of the night before crashed through her with another headache.

Had Pinar and her family survived as Raegna's had? Or had they met a terrible demise? She could not bear to imagine such a tragedy and could not fathom the fact that nothing would ever be the same. Her precious childhood friend, a woman she looked up to all her life, could be nothing but ash...

Don't say that, Raegna thought to herself. *You can find them. You will find them.*

"We must go back," she said aloud.

"What?" Bai blurted.

Ignoring him, Raegna peered at the tree trunks. The rugged redwoods towered above her. Growing up playing Maiden, Raegna had taught herself to climb the trees. The sheer size of these could lift her to see over the forest and view Syden. But her ankle throbbed in protest. Vertigo added to the ache in her head as her gaze scaled the trunks.

Raegna examined the other side of the clearing. The rising slope of a hill continued deeper into the wood. Younger trees grew from the incline, sitting among jutting boulders engraved by time. Raegna steeled herself, adjusted the belt with her sword over her shoulder instead of her waist, and hobbled past Bai and Adabelle.

Careful of her bad leg, Raegna teetered on the stone to reach the lower branches. She grasped the strongest and grunted to haul herself up with both arms and one good leg. Leaves fell over her with the shake of the tree. Recalling the days of her youth, she lifted herself and repeated the balanced action. Her ankle twinged when she used it.

An odd, small sense of freedom bloomed in Raegna's chest. Perhaps it was the simple nostalgic act of childhood play, and the distance she had put between herself and Bai. If only the circumstances were not so heartbreaking.

As a child, she might have climbed higher, but Raegna found her limit several feet from the very top of the trunk. Still, she had covered a considerable height. The branches curtained Bai and Adabelle below, tiny as mice. Raegna straddled a sturdy branch, her complaining ankle dangling beneath her. She pushed the canopy out of her line of sight.

Through the needles and leaves, the forest stretched out before her, rolling with the hills and dark green as ever. Beyond the hilltops stood the outline of the northern mountains, washed out in blue. Clouds dotted the faded afternoon sky and cast shadows over the greenery. One shadow clung to the landscape, refusing to be spurred on by the wind. It blemished the land like a blot of ink on parchment.

Syden. A wisp of smoke plume. The River Sachi wound around the blackened village, flowing from the east to the west.

Raegna squinted to make out roofs and buildings, but the distance was too great. Bai had taken them far from the village. She studied the sorry flaw in nature's beauty. How could the world ignore the remains of her home?

Gaea would not ignore it, Raegna assured herself.

She climbed down the trunk, silently constructing a plan. Once she slid over the nearest boulder, sure to land on her good foot, she limped to her horse.

"We are going back," she said. "We have to know if there are any survivors."

"Raegna..." Bai had been kneeling beside Adabelle, one arm over her shoulders.

"Pack your things, husband," Raegna ordered, holding her head high. "I want to make it there before it gets dark. So, hurry."

Before packing, Raegna removed her nightgown behind the trees. New holes had appeared in the skirt from riding unconscious through the forest. With a low growl, she bunched the gown up and cast it aside on a branch. The nerve he had...

Bai never once gave her reason to punish him before, not like this. All these years he remained quiet, withdrawn, and perhaps even nervous of her. What possessed him to disobey her? Jaleesa's death? He told her outright it changed everything. Yes, it would have. By now, she would have freed herself of his burden, finally free of her mother's control.

Jaleesa would reel in Heimelle above to see armed men taking Syden. Though seeing Raegna uncover her grandmother's sword from its place in the rafters would send her reeling further, let alone Bai's actions.

Raegna grabbed the dress Bai had retrieved from the bedroom closet the night before. Looping the belt around her waist, she tied the sheathed sword beside her hip and tapped the hilt. She arranged the top layer of her hair in a single braid, picking pine needles and twigs out of the loose chestnut locks.

When she emerged from the trees, she stopped in front of Adabelle, who had been waiting for her with her hands folded over her chest in her nightgown.

"Mama," she said sternly.

Raegna masked a grimace. "Yes, love?"

"Why'd you hurt Papa?" Adabelle asked. "He didn't mean to hit you."

"I told you, Ada, men are not supposed to mistreat women," Raegna explained, using as much patience as she could muster. Adabelle was still young. Too young to comprehend the extent of their situation long before they had to flee their home.

"But Papa didn't mean to," the girl protested.

Raegna glanced at Bai, who was preparing the horses. Mud and grass stained his white shirt. A tear in his sleeve exposed his elbow.

Combing back Adabelle's yellow hair, Raegna took in every beautiful, smooth feature as she had since her daughter was born. "I understand, sweetheart. But the Queen's word is law and Gaea's word is the law of Jorde. A man will not harm any woman for any reason, for she deserves the utmost respect from him. In the village, your father would have deserved worse. I showed him mercy."

Adabelle pouted. "I don't like the law."

"If it didn't exist, men could do what they pleased with us," Raegna countered. "There would be no punishment for those who mistreat us. Would you rather live in a world of injustice?"

"I just don't want you to hurt Papa," Adabelle said.

Such stubbornness for a child. She must have inherited it from Bai.

Raegna sighed. "It's over now, Ada. I won't punish him if he stays in his place."

Adabelle glared at the ground and huffed. Raegna swallowed her irritation. The girl had never seen her parents argue, or even speak to each other. She was frightened, and Raegna could not blame her for that.

Stooping down, Raegna squeezed Adabelle's shoulder. "I'm sorry, sweetling. But please understand that a man has no right to harm a woman for whatever reason. I promise, I will not strike him again so long as he listens, just as you need to listen to your mother. Is that all right?"

"... I suppose."

Raegna grinned and kissed her forehead. "I love you, my sweet girl. Now, let's get ready to ride back."

The family managed little supplies. While packing, Raegna took inventory of what they had escaped with as they fled Syden. Bai already had a few tools from working in the fields. He had brought one of Adabelle's dresses with them. He still held the nightstand dagger she gave him, so Raegna confiscated it. Men should never keep weapons. They were physically strong enough as it was. Bai had made a fine example of that last night.

Finally, Raegna found smashed leftover cheese bread squished at the bottom of Bai's work bag. She inspected it before splitting the flattened pieces between the three of them for breakfast. One bite each. That was until Bai gave his bite to Adabelle and, though she was reluctant to follow his lead, Raegna did the same.

After packing, they mounted their horses. Adabelle rode with Raegna this time. She didn't enjoy it, leaning away from her mother. Bai followed.

The horses trekked faster downhill than they did uphill, gravity leading them with an invisible rope. Raegna knew the basics of riding, but she hadn't needed it when she only traveled around Syden by foot. The chestnut mare she sat atop had a smooth gait without a saddle and did not shy at much. If Raegna had chosen to travel, she wouldn't have picked any other steed. Meanwhile, Bai's brown gelding gave him a rough ride, stopping and going, throwing his head back, and stomping his hooves.

A few hours through the woods passed before Syden appeared nestled in the hills below them. Bai had taken them farther than Raegna thought. All the more reason to justify his punishment.

They followed the light gray plumes of smoke that climbed into the air. Bai's horse trotted faster, recognizing the terrain. He halted and snorted when the scent of charred flesh hit his nostrils.

When they drew closer, Raegna's muscles quaked. This village, once familiar and comforting, was now filled with decay. There were no voices or signs of people from their distance. The invaders had not claimed Syden for their own. They must have raided and left. But they might have a mind to send scouts to ensure the village remained dead. Raegna planned to get in and out as quickly as possible, preferably unscathed.

The family entered Syden from the back roads and wound the same way they had escaped, passing barns devoid of any animals. Without the braying, snorting, and hoofbeats of the livestock, the rustic building contained an eerie silence. Raegna's mare started towards the stable to be placed in her stall, but Raegna urged her on down the road.

Homes scattered the edge of Syden and were usually lit with chatter and laughter and the smell of breakfast or supper. They scorched half of those quaint houses to the ground. Nothing but ash marked plotted land. The remaining structures had charcoaled roofs and doors thrown open with furniture and clothing strewn about.

Then they came upon the first bodies. Raegna pulled Adabelle close and covered her eyes.

The mother and daughter Raegna had watched through the window last night lay in the middle of the path where they had fallen, lips tinted blue on their ghost-like faces. Darkened blood pooled around them. The warrior who had fought to avenge them rested just beyond Raegna's little house beside the destroyed chicken coop.

Others lay about the road or just outside their homes. Faded red stains snaked from their bodies, their eyes, and mouths open and staring, eternally frozen in their terror.

Raegna pulled at the reins when her house appeared. The blackened rafters stuck up into the air, slanted, giving the building a deformed silhouette. The door hung by the bottom hinge and creaked as it teetered back and forth.

Raegna dismounted with a wince and left Adabelle on the mare. To keep her daughter from the sight of death, she turned the mare around and handed the reins to Bai on his gelding.

"You'll not go anywhere," she instructed him with a tight frown. "I'll be but a minute to gather what they missed."

Bai nodded a confirmation, his expression mirroring hers.

Inside the wrecked house, furniture had crumbled beneath the fire. Her cauldron was nowhere to be found, nor was the food she stored in the cupboards. The blankets on her bed, and everything she kept in a chest at the footboard—her coin pouch, furs, boots, trinkets, and jewelry—the invaders had raided it all. She found a small piece of flint near the hearth and put it into her pocket.

They hadn't touched her clothing or Adabelle's, but Bai's had vanished, leaving a vacant portion in her closet. Raegna gathered warmer dresses and cloaks for herself and Adabelle to keep the cold out at night. At least she had her sword and whatever Bai had shoved into that work bag of his.

When she returned to the porch, Raegna came to a standstill. Bai brought the horses to stand side by side so he could reach Adabelle. The little girl's shoulders shook as she sniffled.

"It's all right, love," Bai said, wiping her tears away with his thumb. "There's nothing to fear now."

He spotted Raegna and straightened. Raegna averted his stare and mounted her horse with fresh supplies, jerking the reins to ride away from Bai.

Adabelle squeezed herself against her mother's torso. "Mama, I want to go home. I want to go inside."

"I'm sorry, sweetheart." Raegna wrapped an arm around her. "We cannot stay here. But don't you worry, we will find a new home."

It was difficult to lighten the situation as the horses walked past corpses of people Raegna once knew. She could not let Adabelle be frightened.

They approached the main road and beheld a scene far more horrific than they had expected. Again, Raegna covered Adabelle's eyes so quickly, the little girl yelped.

The familiar dirt path of the marketplace was a red track scattered with the dead. Their blood trailed through the gravel. Slain children lay beside their fallen mothers. Men and warriors who did battle rested with gashes in their sides, their skulls crushed, and a few with heads sliced from their bodies. Crows and ravens circled the village and landed about the remains, cawing at the prospect of food.

A single head sat on a pike in the road. Raegna's gut rolled as they neared. They passed Matriarch Alv's head, her brittle hair flicking in the wind and her withering skin stretched over her gaping mouth. Raegna nearly lost the contents of her stomach but fixed her focus ahead and kept riding.

"By Gaea. They killed all of them..." Bai muttered.

Holding her breath from the stench of rotting flesh that drove bile to her throat, Raegna rode forward with her hand over Adabelle's eyes. Her mare twitched as she picked her way across the carnage. The horse's ears rotated back and forth, and she snorted.

Raegna's knuckles went white over her grip on the reins. Syden had become a torn battleground, littered with the bodies of her townspeople, murdered in cold blood by monsters of Fan's Helved. Through her terror, she made sure her horse stepped around each body out of respect.

These people needed to be lifted. Their souls could not return to Gaea in Heimelle if their flesh was not burned to free them. Otherwise, they would suffer in Fan's purgatory as tormented spirits. But with so many, how could they send them off? And without a priestess' blessing and guidance?

Her mare came upon the end of the market road where a once dear home rested, but Raegna hardly recognized it.

Charred pieces of Pinar's sod roof pointed to the sky, but the rest remained intact. The door stood wide open, the inside curtained in darkness. There was no sign of Pinar or her family among the dead, so there must still be hope...

Raegna gulped. Dismounting with Adabelle in her arms, she guided the girl's head into her shoulder to protect her from the surrounding sights. Raegna hesitated but hefted Adabelle to Bai, where she would sit in front of him, her face buried in his chest. He held Adabelle close, wrapping her in his cloak.

"Stay here," Raegna ordered, her fingertips pressed against Adabelle's back. "Do not look about, Adabelle. Understand?"

"Yes, Mama." Adabelle obeyed, on the verge of tears.

"Raegna, what are you doing?" Bai demanded.

Without a glance at him, she turned and climbed the porch steps. "Just do as you're told, husband."

She steeled herself as she entered. The house within had a heavy atmosphere as if a great thick cloud hung from the ceiling and pulled everything down. The morning light filtered through the burned roof. Ice-cold sweat prickled Raegna's neck as she gingerly stepped toward the main room where the flipped furniture sprawled over the floor. The floorboards groaned under her feet.

"Pinar?" she rasped. Her dream flashed at the forefront of her mind, with the image of a pale and horrified Pinar. Raegna shook the thought aside.

No answer came. The silence drained her hope, but she kept moving to the back of the house where the bedroom would be.

"Pinar, please," she stammered, a sense of foreboding washing over her. "Don't be afraid. It's only me, there's no reason to—"

Raegna halted at the door. Inside, Pinar's body lay before the threshold with her torso ripped open. Her innards spilled out on her nightgown, soaking her and the fabric with black blood. Her skin had turned the same ghost-white as she was in Raegna's dream, and her purple-hued eyelids remained closed. Blood caked over her thin, cracked lips and clustered under her nose. Raegna's hand fled to her mouth as a scream erupted from her.

Estrid's small feet appeared behind the bed, though Raegna dared not go closer. The babe's cradle rested sideways at the edge, dreadfully quiet.

A mournful sob hollowed Raegna's chest. She caught herself against the doorframe before crumbling to her knees. Her childhood friend, a young woman like a sister, was gone, her corpse only a hollow husk of gore. Raegna sobbed again, her head pounding with every beat of her heart.

"Raegna?" Bai called out so close he might have been at the door. "Raegna, what's happened? What's wrong?"

Stupid man. Leave me be...

Man. The thought of looking again made her stomach twist. The vision stamped in her memory for good. No men perished in the room. Pinar's husband and brother-in-law, her sons, none of them were to be seen. Where had they gone?

Perhaps they fled? Or perhaps they were dead with the others in the streets...

Raegna could not think of them clearly. These people, her closest friend, and her children—their souls would rot with their bodies if she did nothing. She could try to find a priestess to perform an unimaginable lifting ceremony in the neighboring village, Judr. But that would take too long. They had to be lifted before they suffered any longer.

Burning the village would take time as well. The invaders could be nearby. They could attack again at the first sign of life, but Raegna couldn't abandon Pinar like this. She had come to save her.

Teeth clenched to fight another sob, Raegna wobbled to her feet and turned back out of the house.

At the porch steps, Bai waited atop his gelding for her. His eyes searched hers with dread.

"Raegna—"

She avoided his gaze as she mounted her mare. Though she tried to steady her voice for a command, her words came out shaken and hoarse. "I'm going to the temple. They need to be lifted."

"You can't lift all of them," Bai protested. He kept hold of his reins as his gelding kicked his legs out from under him. "Not unless you... But Raegna, you're not a priestess."

Old and new tears burned Raegna's eyes while she rode in the other direction, northward, to Syden's temple. "The scriptures say, in times of hardship, Gaea will accept anyone willing. I know it to be true, and we must do something. But we have to move quickly."

The surreality of conversing with him matched that of Syden's destruction. Of course, the days she would speak to Bai would be the same days Helved swept the land with darkness. Raegna urged her horse into a swift trot.

The place ought to be as she left it the morning before, after her mother's lifting. Gaea's temple stood on the northern rim of Syden, a great house with a domed sod roof. A skylight surrounded by grass and birch would let light in and smoke out.

Syden's settlers had built the walls to be sturdy and withstand any attempted damage, carved with ancient Galaenian runes and illustrations of stories in Gaea's scripture. The front double doors depicted Gaea Herself as She cradled the world, Her dress and hair flowing about Her.

The fire pit was all that had survived, the walls and pews vanished as if they had never existed. The bare plot mirrored the emptiness of Raegna's heart as she surveyed it. How could they have desecrated Gaea's sanctum?

Raegna swung off her horse to approach the pit, for it was all that she needed. Behind her, gravel shifted as Bai and Adabelle dismounted to follow.

Kneeling, Raegna brushed away the ash that blanketed its stone encasement, her hands trembling. Underneath were the carvings of Galaenian ancestors. The first who sailed to the shores from a homeland left in a cold, frigid famine. Four women draped in robes held outstretched palms as if to push a door open.

Strict ceremonies made young women into priestesses. The rite of priestesshood was a holy ritual, performed by others among their ranks. Raegna had only herself and Gaea.

Taking a breath, Raegna rolled her shoulders. Her throat closed in on itself as she spoke. "All-Mother Gaea, beasts of Fan have committed an injustice here. They've destroyed Your daughters and Sigmund's loyal sons. I pray for You to welcome them as I lift them to You. I am no priestess, but I will sacrifice my life to You, for You, and for the fallen."

Using the small piece of flint from her house, Raegna created a fire for the rite. As she worked, Bai's unease practically screamed from behind her, though she ignored it and retrieved her knife. The sooner she finished this, the sooner she could lift Syden, and the sooner they could flee before more trouble appeared. Raegna pressed her lips into a thin line and held the blade against her palm.

With a swipe and a whimper, Raegna cut deep enough to bring blood to rise over the surface of her skin. Then she raised her hand over the fire and squeezed it into a tight fist. She cringed as the blood dripped and fell into the flames. There they seared and became her signature of the oath to her Goddess.

"I am a daughter sworn to You, All-Mother." Raegna gripped the knife at her side. "Accept me as I am. Use me as You will."

The fire dimmed and lit again, growing taller over the pit.

"Take them with You," Raegna shouted and lifted her bloodied palm up to the sky, the air stinging the open wound. "Take their souls and let them see You and surround You. Let them glorify You as I will for the rest of my days."

Embers shot from the flames and flew skyward. White smoke clouded the air. The blood that gushed from Raegna's palm rolled down her arm and dripped from her elbow onto her skirts, dotting the fabric. She tilted her head back, and her body grew faint from the weight of her losses: her friend, her village, her home.

Just as quickly, Raegna's chest opened, her heart skipped a beat, and she gasped. She knew what she needed to do.

Wiping the knife with her skirt, she turned and walked past both Bai and Adabelle but spoke only to him. "I'll need your help."

They left Adabelle with the horses and scoured Syden for oil, the additional corpses she discovered in their homes spurring Raegna on in her grief.

After hours of searching, they found oils hidden in the rubble, tucked beneath the floorboards of a storage house. They wouldn't produce the greatest flame, but they would suffice for their next task.

Collecting the dead.

Raegna and Bai labored the rest of the day, carrying the fallen to the temple. Some required them to work together, Bai hauling up the shoulders and Raegna the legs. Others they held with great respect, dismembered in pieces or burned to charcoal. Most of the women Bai carried in his arms, and Raegna over her shoulder. Children were the easiest but the most heartbreaking. Raegna let her tears fall over them while Bai hefted their mothers ahead of her.

In the temple, they placed the bodies side by side, resting families alongside each other. The number of people filled the place wall to wall.

Then they revisited Pinar's house. Raegna halted at the porch. Bai climbed but glanced over his shoulder at her. Raegna refused to meet his gaze and conquered the steps. Her head buzzed as she led him to the bedroom and stopped before the door. The tears came without warning, and she froze at the threshold.

Bai snapped her out of a blinding trance. "Get to Estrid and Nalani. I'll help Pinar."

Raegna bristled. "How do you know..."

"Naleem and Hadwin are my friends," he said, meeting her glare head-on. He gestured to the room. "They are family. But they aren't here. Neither are the boys."

Raegna's throat closed. "Gaea knows what happened."

Bai slipped past, careful not to touch her, and went for the bed. He pulled a sheet off and draped it over Pinar. Raegna stared with blurred vision, watching him wrap her friend with light hands. Respectful of her torn body, Bai picked her up into his arms and nodded to the turned cradle.

"Would she want her babe?" he asked.

Of course, she would, but Raegna didn't have the heart to scold him. Not here. She trembled as she crossed the room and knelt before the cradle. A blanket covered Nalani's small form. Raegna's sob caught when she scooped the babe up, marking the bruises around her neck.

Raegna placed Nalani on Pinar's chest, tears dripping down her face, and tucked her between the wrapped sheets. She retrieved Estrid next, holding her close. Bai adjusted his grip and carried Pinar and Nalani out of the house, Raegna behind him.

They placed Pinar and her daughters among the rest of their neighbors. Bai retrieved wood from building remains and the forest, while Raegna prepared the oil and doused it over the fallen. With the fire pit, Raegna made two torches and handed one to Bai. They let the flames lap at the oils, wood, and bodies.

As she worked, Raegna whispered, "May Gaea keep you all."

It took time, but the fire engulfed them, raising smoke over the temple ruins. Once their work was finished, Raegna and Bai retreated to Adabelle and the horses on the hill.

Raegna's sore muscles quaked, and her eyelids drooped, swollen from weeping so much. Pinar, her kindness and bravery, and her warm smile floated through Raegna's memory. What beautiful children she bore and what a terrible thing they suffered at such a young age…

Adabelle's crying broke Raegna from her thoughts. Her precious daughter huddled against her father's leg beneath his cloak as she wept. Her little shoulders shook while Bai stroked her hair. Glistening tears brimmed his gold eyes as he watched Syden burn.

Though her voice wavered, Raegna spoke with her chin up. "We'll ensure the lifting is complete. We'll stay the night in the tree line."

Bai nodded in agreement. So, they camped under the stars and let the horses graze at the top of the hill.

Adabelle snuggled close to Raegna as they lay on the hill's grassy crest with the outskirt trees hovering over them. Raegna, her hand newly bandaged, curled around her daughter. She kissed Adabelle's head and gave a silent, thankful prayer that the lifting was done and that her only babe rested safely in her arms.

Despite her exhaustion, after the day's events, Raegna fought to sleep. Adabelle let her tears take her into slumber. Raegna needed the nightly routine of listening for Bai to fall asleep first. He collapsed into a pile in the grass close by, his wiry form invisible in the darkness. For a long time, he too struggled for sleep, judging by his utter silence. Eventually, he inhaled and exhaled gentle snores as he always did.

Raegna took comfort in the familiar sounds of home that had not died with Syden. Her heavy eyes closed and, immediately, sleep took her.

Chapter 6

Hadwin

Early in the morning, the raiders kicked their captives awake and continued their journey in the breaking light of dawn before the birds even sang. Trudging uphill and navigating switchbacks made Hadwin's calves spasm. His lungs heaved in time with the other men as their captors led them through the southern hills. The sack over his head disrupted his vision, causing him to trip over forest debris. Loose gravel slipped under his feet.

Alongside Syden men and boys, the raiders trekked on foot, on horse-back, or by wagon. Hooves thudded against the soft soil, and wheels creaked over the trail. Some raiders talked and joked with each other while others labored like the village men.

Dakarai struggled at Hadwin's heels, stumbling but catching himself before a fall. Naleem walked behind them with Cadoc slung over his back in a makeshift pouch that used to be a shawl, which was difficult to create with their heads covered.

Hadwin's body stooped forward for the climb, exhaustion clouding his mind. He thought he might just tumble forward, and their captors would let the rest of the party trample over him.

The rushing of swift water sounded ahead of them and Hadwin perked to attention. Through the sack, he saw the shapes of tree trunks and the figures of the surrounding men. Their heads lifted to the sound. Another clue to where they were taking them. The only river remotely close to Syden was the River Sachi, named after the goddess.

Hadwin pondered how they would cross. It was too wide and strong to swim across, especially for the little ones. The group drew closer to the water until the roar of the current blasted in his ears. White foam streaked through the low visibility. The river cut through the woods and raced beneath the trees, making a great, watery chasm on their path.

But the men kept at the same pace. A shrill horn sounded ahead. The snap of wood snaked over the river's roar with a growing *crr-rack*. The Syden men jumped as a wall of tree trunks fell like a drawbridge over the river before the frontline. The ground trembled under the impact. Then the party crossed.

Hadwin took Dakarai's hand and followed. Along the bridge, they walked over rough bark and rustling leaves. The water sprayed up from under them. Hadwin stubbed his toe on the knots and balanced on their curved surface. He gripped Dakarai's hand tightly, careful should he slip and fall again.

The raiders had nailed fallen logs and connected them to make a wider bridge for their horses and wagons, allowing it to blend into the trees. Clever enough, Hadwin supposed. He noted they did indeed cross the River Sachi just as he remembered traveling on the hunting trails from Syden before going directly uphill.

Finally, the ground leveled with the river behind them and Hadwin's lungs could inflate with air without his torso hunched to climb. Branches scraped at his arms and legs. The forest grew denser, forcing him to lift his hands to defend against low-hanging vegetation.

Hadwin tracked the footsteps of the man in front of him through the bottom of the sack. When he came to a sudden stop, Hadwin halted, and Dakarai collided with him.

"Uncle Hadwin!" the boy complained.

"Hush." Hadwin peered through the sack to find what had stopped the group.

Those at the lead faced a wall of shrubbery. A rider dismounted and stood before the wall, guiding his horse. He gave three distinct knocks, and the sound was that of a thick door, the leaves rattling as it shook. Hadwin blinked incredulously as the forest parted like double-door gates before the traveling party.

All Hadwin saw through the irritating fabric was the backs of heads and not what the gates revealed. The rider mounted his horse again, and the group proceeded forward.

Once past the doors, those on horseback paraded out of sight. Those on foot shoved and arranged their captives into a line side by side.

Hadwin straightened beside his brother and nephews. Dakarai leaned against his father. Feet crunched the gravel as the raiders surrounded them, front and back. Those behind them removed the sacks as soon as the forest gates closed with a thud and rattle of leaves.

It took a moment to get his bearings. Hadwin's eyes adjusted to the sunlight of midmorning. Initially, he had the pleasure of glaring at the men before him and Thenalious atop his steed, smirking at the men of Syden under his command. His fur cloak was nowhere to be found; his broad shoulders covered by a wool jacket. Beyond them sat a camp packed with dozens of large war tents erected in a maze of paths crawling with men going about their business.

Smoke rose from fires above the tent canvases and the clang of metal on metal rang from various small forges. Men worked, shouted at each other, and discussed plans or tasks.

To the west, the roof of a great red barn with a curved arch stood above the commotion. Sheep and goats called out to make themselves known, along with an unseen donkey braying with all his might.

On their left overlooking the camp loomed a two-story house that appeared like a jagged version of a Matriarch's great house. Above its porch hung the skull of a bull elk, one that must have been massive, for its antlers protruded and curled over the shutters. The image sent a blade of fear through Hadwin's stomach. Antlers like that were a demonic symbol. Fan himself donned them like a crown.

The barn and the house were the only buildings towering over the white tents. The camp stretched several yards, contained within the forest and its trees. The clear sky above them had no canopy to cover it. In the structured chaos, there wasn't a woman in sight.

The men in camp peeked at the captives. The Syden men stared back at them and their ratted clothing and leather armor. Half of them brandished weapons. Some had long hair, and shaggy beards, and shaved or braided them in their own way.

Thenalious, unlike the others, kept his black hair cropped short with a cleanly cut beard to match. The sun rays brought a faint gold hue to his skin. His hazel eyes roamed over the villagers and he rode his horse before the line.

"My friends." He made a grand gesture behind him. "Welcome to Haven. A sanctuary from woman and her tyranny. Your new home. Years ago, a group of mistreated house-husbands and bachelors banded together, fed up with the injustice done to them and unable to watch their sons grow beneath the claws of the matriarchy. They fled to the woods where they built their own village. They used the trees to build their great house and barn, and began their new lives here, their Haven."

His horse whickered and swished its tail. Thenalious patted its neck as he went on. "Rumor of Haven spread from man to man. Those who believed came searching for their refuge. Others, such as yourselves, were found and rescued. The great house grew too crowded, so they set up camp and everyone pitched in for their share of the land. You will do just the same."

You didn't rescue us, Hadwin thought. *You took us away! And what if we do not want to do our share for this place?*

Thenalious' horse tossed its mane as a new man approached. The villagers fidgeted at the sight of him. A gangly creature with skin like rough clay dotted with ruddy freckles, wide, dreary eyes, and a long, toothy grin. He wore only a vest and pants covered in dirt, with tattered boots. Faint wisps of brown hair sat on top of his head. His beard too grew thin, like cat whiskers. That was what he reminded Hadwin of: a mangy feral cat.

"This is Wyn," Thenalious said. "He is in charge of the labor done in Haven. He will send you across camp where he sees fit to place you."

Wyn studied the Syden men with his odd, yellowed eyes.

"All young 'ins, eh?" When he spotted Naleem with Cadoc looking about over his shoulder and Dakarai at his side, Wyn's face lit up.

"Lookie, two of them!" He cackled, revealing brown teeth. "Wonder how you got the tiny one to follow you. Ones that young don't leave their mums, even after death."

Naleem shifted his weight and pulled Dakarai close. Hadwin inched forward, ready to defend. He had lost Pinar and his nieces. He would not let these brutes harm his brother and nephews.

Wyn raised a hairy eyebrow at him but did nothing but gift them with a nasty sneer.

Thenalious gathered his reins and turned his horse around. "I leave them to you. Show them our ways and hospitality."

"Of course, my lord," Wyn said, and they watched Thenalious ride off. Some raiders surrounding the villagers trailed after him. A few remained behind and guarded those in line.

Wyn put his hands over his hips. "For starters, any little pups left unattended, or, in the way, will be tossed into the wilderness. However, should they be old enough, I will put them to work myself."

Hadwin grimaced and side stepped closer to Dakarai.

"Now, I will justify where to place you with my several tests." Wyn approached the first villager, a young man about Hadwin's age who he knew was Bjarni.

Bjarni was the first father in line with a toddler son in his arms. He eyed Wyn.

"Put yer boy down," Wyn instructed.

Reluctantly, Bjarni placed his son on the ground and held his hand. The boy squeaked and reached for his father. "Papa!"

Bjarni ignored him as Wyn drew close, so they were nose to nose. He took Bjarni's stubbled chin and twisted his head from side to side, then jerked his mouth open and inspected his teeth like a horse. When he was done, he examined Bjarni's arms, strong and lined with muscle beneath dark beige skin from plowing the fields back home. Wyn nodded to himself.

"You'll work in the barn," he told Bjarni. "The horses need a handler. Listen to our horseman, Fritjof, will you?"

Moving down the line, Wyn evaluated each man by his fitness to assign him a job. He gave some men jobs with animals. Others went to clean weapons, dishes, and things no one would ever desire to clean. Then he stopped at Obrecht. Despite the terror of losing his village and speaking out the night before, Obrecht planted his feet and stared Wyn down with his tired eyes.

Wyn beheld the old man. "You're almost nearing yer time, aren't ya? Not as old as our forefather, Gudmund. What have ye to offer?"

He moved to inspect Obrecht, but the elder stepped back. "I will not serve the evil one."

The other villagers gazed at him in nervous awe.

"Who's evil?" Wyn asked with a dismayed hand to his chest. "Not I."

Obrecht looked up and down the line. "Stay strong. Rest in the faith of Gaea. For even in Fan's domain, She will protect you and provide for you. You must believe that She will!"

Wyn snorted. "I'd shut my mouth if I were you."

"Our All-Mother will be with us," Obrecht went on. "Her scriptures say, 'In the darkness of the clutches of Fan, Gaea shall prevail and smite the evil one. She will embrace Her children and wrap them in divine protection.'"

Wyn rolled his eyes and spun on the balls of his feet to another freedom fighter who lingered to guard the line of villagers. With a glance, they understood each other, and the guard slipped his ax from his belt, handing it to Wyn. The ax blade glinted in the sunlight as Wyn turned to the Syden elder.

"Stay strong, for Gaea is with you," Obrecht said to the group, glaring at Wyn with his chin raised and knotted fists at his sides.

Hadwin silently begged Obrecht to silence himself but could not help but admire his courage. The old man stared death in the face. He stared Fan in the face.

"All-Mother Gaea is good and loving," Obrecht persisted as Wyn approached him. "She is with us."

With a quick raise of the ax and a swipe, Wyn slashed Obrecht across the chest. A rasping gag escaped the old man's lips. Blood sprayed through the air over the gravel. Obrecht toppled to his knees and then landed face-first onto the dirt. His blood pooled around him.

As he fell, every villager jumped back, taking hold of their children, or crying out in shock. Naleem hid his sons' faces from the red froth the old man spit up. For extra measure, Wyn brought the blade down on Obrecht's neck and hacked at it. A young man had turned to vomit what little food they received the night before.

Bile streamed up Hadwin's throat. His heart rammed against his ribs as if it might break through them. A village mentor, a spiritual teacher, a true man of Gaea, was gone from this world. His head rolled to the side, splattered with dark crimson. No one here would lift his body to let his soul escape to Heimelle. Hadwin couldn't ponder that for long.

"Shut up!" Wyn shouted at the horrified men and boys. "Let this be yer warning! Our god is Fan! Our father is Sigmund! You worship them and them alone!"

He returned the bloodied ax to its owner without a word and continued down the line, leaving Obrecht's body on the ground.

Wyn came upon Naleem, who had to tear his eyes from Obrecht to focus on the frightening, thin man. Like the others, Wyn ordered

Naleem to remove Cadoc from the sling behind his back. Naleem did so and passed Cadoc over to Hadwin. Though Cadoc squirmed and kicked, Hadwin held him in place between the folds of the shawl. The poor little ones could not understand what went on, but they could feel the unease of their guardians.

Wyn's frown twisted as he examined Naleem's sturdy build.

"Not much to you, is there?" he said. "Just a handsome face. Mayhap you were finer once, but producing sons has ruined that." He glanced at Hadwin. "You let him protect you and yer boys. Ye husbands?"

Hadwin nearly choked. He and Naleem looked nothing alike, but no one had ever made that assumption before.

"Brothers," Naleem grunted.

Wyn giggled. He glanced at Hadwin and said, "The husbands will do laundry."

Chapter 7

Bai

C ANDLELIGHT FLICKERED IN THE room with an orange glow. Fall brought nothing but frigid weather and bitter news of Bai's betrothal. No amount of colored leaves could brighten his spirits that season. If only his mother and the whole arrangement could vanish and blow away with the brittle leaves in the woods. Now they drifted on the wind more like ashes than leaves.

Bai wanted only one sanctuary to be preserved. The warm center within his mother's cold house with its rigid rafters and creaking walls. He wished he could have seen that house set ablaze and crumble in charred pieces. He would have fought to see that the cozy center remained untouched by the flames. Bai had left it long ago but imagined it waiting for him whenever he could be free from an unwanted marriage.

Knowing nothing could have saved that familiar place from the fire, Bai dreamed the warm center survived with his old bed encircled by candles. Tiny flames danced over melting wax. He could curl into his father's arms and listen to his heartbeat as if he were a boy again.

"Let me hold you one last time, my Bai. My Bai."

But everything was taken from him, even that sacred refuge, just as Raegna took it before.

"Papa."

Bai shuddered in his sleep.

"Papa, I don't want to go!"

"Papa." Adabelle's voice broke through his dreams, and Bai woke with a start. She shook his shoulder with both hands to wake him.

"What is it?" he groaned, rubbing his eyes.

"Mama says we have to go," she explained.

Yes, of course.

Bai sat up and blinked to adjust his vision to the sunlight. Their makeshift camp stood just beyond the trees overlooking Syden, though he couldn't bring himself to glance at the aftermath. In his periphery, a scorched plain stretched out below them. Faint smoke strung up towards the blue sky. Their home would become a memory in time. Bai shoved that mess of feelings and the rest of his dreams down into his gut. He would have to face it later.

The shadow of Syden did nothing to the hills that surrounded it. The forests extended over the horizon in deep green above the ash-ridden remains of the village. A reminder that the world went on despite the circumstances.

Raegna limped and rummaged through satchels, gathering their supplies—what little they had—and loading them onto the horses. The light revealed a red tinge in her hair and its waves bounced over her shoulder as she turned to be sure he was awake. Her thin upper lip curled before she whirled back to her work.

"We need to move on," Raegna said as she piled clothes into a bag. "We can go east to Judr and warn them of this attack. They will know how to defend themselves. Perhaps send word to her majesty in Stadt."

Where did all of this come from in one morning? Had she even slept during the night?

Bai frowned. "Judr is a two-day ride. Stadt could take half a season."

Raegna scowled as she tightened the horses' saddles. A dark brown eyebrow arched, and her curved hips tilted as she kept her weight off one foot. "What do you want me to make of that?"

Before a witty comment surfaced on his tongue, Bai clamped his mouth shut and seethed.

Raegna's eyes narrowed on him before she ushered Adabelle to her. "It is our duty to bring news of this massacre to them before the raiders attack them, too. Besides, where there is a village, there is a Matriarch. She can send word to the Queen, who can send her Maidens. Unless you have any bright ideas?"

Something about her had become so irritatingly self-absorbed and pretentious. What was it that had changed?

Bai caught a glance of her hand, wrapped in a bandage stained with old blood. Ah yes, she was now a priestess. That much was debatable. If he remembered correctly, it required an assembly of priestesses to perform and witness such a ceremony. Raegna had taken it upon herself to become one. Now she had more cachet to hold over his head: woman, wife, and priestess.

"No, wife," he muttered.

"Very well."

He liked it better when she refused to even look at him.

On the ride back, Adabelle sat with Bai, reclining against his torso. The gelding they rode spooked at things now and again, but Bai controlled him before he would buck or bolt. Raegna led the way on her mare, using the trail that cut through the forest leading to Judr. The air filled with fresh pine, a pleasant change from burning wood and flesh.

Twigs and needles crunched under the horses' hooves while birds called to each other from tree to tree.

How nature went on when so many were lifted a few miles away, Bai didn't have a clue. The sun still rose, and the birds still chirped, while good acquaintances and friends lay in ashes within Syden's ruins.

Yet not all of them. Raegna's friend Pinar was Naleem's wife, Hadwin's sister-in-law. Knowing them, they wouldn't abandon her or the girls without a fight. Their bodies were not with them. Neither were the two boys. What happened to them? Did they perish some other way? Bai's gut rolled at a few horrific guesses.

He watched the back of Raegna's head as she bobbed with the horse's gait. Despite the illegitimacy of her priestesshood, the bold decision to lift the entire village was worth admiring. He wouldn't have thought she had it in her. Somehow, her courage had grown since her mother's death.

Which led to a more pressing issue. Why did Raegna allow him to tag along if she was determined to divorce him?

Striking her was the only thing Bai could think to do at that moment on the hill, their home ablaze and filled with the screams of their neighbors. If he hadn't stopped her, Raegna would have ridden back with her sword high, and gotten herself killed. Her corpse would have burned among the others. Adabelle wouldn't have her mother, and then where would they be? Knocking her out seemed to be the only option, though Bai knew he would regret it.

Naturally, after he rendered her mother unconscious, Adabelle sobbed through the woods, but Bai couldn't focus on her for the time being. He struggled to keep Raegna on her horse. Once they were safe and Raegna was on the ground, he reassured Ada and wondered what his wife would do to him when she woke up. Best case, she might chase him off with that sword. Worst, she might run him through right in front of Ada.

But she slapped him. And she let him stay. Ordered him around like the begrudging wife her mother could be proud of. Whatever compelled her to keep him was beyond Bai's comprehension. Without a Matriarch or priestesses to nullify their marriage, Raegna could simply get rid of him with no witness but their six-year-old. It would be all too easy.

So why tolerate him?

As the day wore on, gray clouds billowed on top of each other. The sunlight waned as they consumed the sky. Thunder rolled, emitting a low tremble in the ground that crawled up the tree trunks. With it came a silver drizzle of rain.

Bai wrapped Adabelle closer in his cloak and flipped his hood up. Raegna tipped her head back and scowled at the rain as if she would chide it next. With a gravelly sigh, she threw on her own hood. "Is Adabelle covered?"

No, I thought she might enjoy a fever after this lovely downpour. "Yes, wife."

Raegna grunted and veered off the trail. Despite the cover of the trees, the rain still reached them. The density of the forest dwindled. When a small clearing opened before them, Raegna brought her horse to a halt, and she dismounted.

"We'll make a shelter here," she said, grabbing the reins of Bai's gelding and moving to take Adabelle. "She'll stay with me. Go find some suitable firewood."

Bai blinked at her. "We can't stop here. This is wolf country."

"Which is why we need a fire." Raegna caught Adabelle as she slid off the horse's back. "The flames and my sword will keep any wolves at bay. Now go find firewood."

Across the clearing, she led Adabelle beneath a tree and got to work gathering branches for what Bai assumed was a shelter. Adabelle looked at her mother and then at her father with wide brown eyes, and her lips parted.

Bai forced a smile through the drizzle and dismounted. He tied the horses to a nearby branch and turned to the forest.

Pine needles and moss squished under his boots. An ashen mist hung between the tree trunks as the rain came down harder. Bai pulled his cloak tighter and gritted his teeth through the cold. Every stick he picked was damp. Perhaps the priestess thought she could make a fire out of anything.

A twig snapped behind him and Bai jolted upright. Nothing but darkness beyond a sheet of rain and shadows of trees greeted him. Ominous thunder rolled overhead. His clammy skin crawled, and he squared his shoulders to shake off his unease.

There was a reason Syden rested below the hills and not so close to the river. Wolves stalked the woods and hunted the game that hid in the trees. Bai gave his surroundings one more sweep before continuing with his haul, balancing wet sticks in his arms.

He trusted his memory, but relief warmed his bones nonetheless at the sight of Raegna and Adabelle in the distance. The horses remained tied, swishing their tails. A sad-looking, triangular shelter that Raegna fervently tended to, stood between the mother and daughter. In his absence, it must have become the new object of her frustration.

Bai took a breath and started toward them, marching through puddles as his hood loosened and raindrops struck his face and eyes. As he drew closer, Adabelle looked up and tilted her head at him. Bai smiled, wanting nothing more than to call out and assure her it was only him.

Instead, her own voice carried across the clearing. "...Mama?"

Why bring her *into this?*

Raegna stood up from her work and followed Adabelle's gaze, stumbling to keep off her bad foot. She gaped at him and grasped the hilt of her sword at her belt. "Run!"

Another twig snapped. The shuffling of four feet crept behind him. Bai glanced over his shoulder and metal rang as Raegna unsheathed her blade. A lightning bolt flashed and illuminated the trees, along with the two wolves that skulked in the tree line.

Their wide eyes reflected the light in that instant. How their ragged fur slicked with water, and their fangs hung over their black snarling lips, was like something out of Helved that would be imprinted into Bai's nightmares.

The pitch black of night swallowed the creatures in the forest with an earth-shattering clap of thunder. Bai bolted, clinging to his firewood despite himself. His biggest concern was not leading the wolves to Adabelle, so he steered to the left.

The rain stung his eyes. Adabelle's shriek tore through the rain. The horses whinnied. The trampling of paws reverberated on both sides until it was too late. Bai wrapped a fist around one branch and threw the rest of his haul at a wolf. The sticks splashed over the wet ground and the wolf snarled.

The second rushed up to him. Bai swung his branch with all his strength. The wood smacked somewhere, and the creature growled. Bai tried again, swiping nothing. The beast slipped beneath the strike.

Pain snatched Bai's calf and yanked hard. He screamed as teeth wrenched deep into his flesh and tore muscle like fabric. The first wolf crouched as Bai tumbled.

Before it could leap on him, Raegna's sword pierced the animal's side. Blood burst and mixed with the rain. The creature yelped and dropped. Raegna pulled her sword free and circled Bai to the other wolf, whose jaws clamped on his leg. Raegna's sword flashed with another bolt of lightning above. The point sank into its hide. The wolf released Bai with a harsh yelp.

Bai scrambled behind her, and Raegna defended his retreat. She just missed the wolf's neck, slicing fur.

The beast snarled and bared bloodied fangs at her, its soaked fur prickling. A gash on its flank oozed dark blood, and the wolf picked up a hind foot.

Raegna stood her ground, attempting a blow that nearly took off its ear. "Get away!"

With one last growl, the wolf shrank back and slinked for the trees. Lightning lit its path through the forest.

Raegna whirled on Bai, glaring at him under the downpour. Her hair turned black and plastered her ivory face. As she heaved for breath over her purpling lips, her shoulders rose and fell. Bai sat in the mud with his leg mangled. His heart rammed against his chest, and he gulped raindrops while he panted.

An eternity passed as they stared at each other. Raegna peeled a few strands from her forehead and sheathed her blade. "Can you walk?"

Bai wasn't sure if he could speak. He winced when he tested his leg but twisted onto his good side to push himself up. When he staggered, all his weight caught on the bitten leg and Bai snarled. Then Raegna was under his arm, bracing him on her shoulders.

"Thank you," he grunted.

She might have had something to say, hesitating for a moment before she ignored him again. Raegna guided him to her little shelter, her muscles tensed beneath his. Stealing a downward glance, he meant to search her face, but her hood obscured her profile. No matter, she was like a stone under him. This closeness clearly terrified her, so he measured the weight he placed on her.

Within the flimsy branches, Raegna helped Bai painfully rest on the damp ground. Adabelle knelt by his side, tears in her eyes and her lip quivering.

"Papa..."

Bai forced a brave grin. "I'm all right, Ada."

Truly, he was not so concerned about the pain but the wound itself. In all this mud and the fabric of his pants, the bite could fester. Adabelle huddled beside him, and, despite his worries, he draped an arm around her and pulled her close.

Raegna remained on the move, gathering the thrown twigs and bark to build a pile before them. Her cloak floated behind her as she went, heavy with moisture.

Bai frowned at her effort. "Raegna. If you're fixing a fire, it won't work. The wood is too wet."

She did not look at him when she said, "That bite will need burning."

Did she mean to help him more? Bai figured she would rather let him die of a fever in the wilderness. How could she stand to heal him?

After several minutes and various curses a priestess shouldn't make, a flame sparked in the pile of wood. Raegna retrieved her knife, then rested the blade on the fire. She plucked the hilt up, and the metal glowed red.

Bai gulped but shifted and rolled his pants leg up over his knee to give her a clear target for the bite. As Raegna lowered the knife's face over it, Adabelle gave a sharp gasp. "Mama!"

"Hush, Adabelle," Raegna scolded and pressed the hot metal to the wound.

The heat seared his skin with a hiss. Bai restrained a yell with a loud growl as tears brimmed over his eyelids. He took pain on top of pain with as much grace and dignity as he could muster. His fists clutched the soaked soil until his nails dug into his palms.

Raegna pulled the knife away to set it on a nearby tree root to cool. When raindrops fell on its blade, they sizzled and evaporated quicker than they appeared. Bai's injury transformed from an oozing gash to a roiling, misshapen mark stretching down either side of his calf.

Raegna slipped out of the shelter and tended the horses. She returned with a dress and ripped the skirt into strips. "Your horse fled. Broke the rope."

Maybe he'll stall the wolves. Bai refrained from saying it aloud for Adabelle's sake. Instead, he kissed her head. He was willing to feed a thousand horses to those wolves if that kept her safe. He peeked down at her, huddled against him, her cheek squished into his chest.

Raegna fashioned the fabric into a bandage and tied it around Bai's new burn. As he watched her work, the pain became more tolerable with the awe-inspiring sight of her treating him so diligently.

Their eyes settled on each other before Raegna turned to finish her work. "We'll reach Judr tomorrow."

The first howl of a lone wolf sounded. Then another. Two more harmonized through the rain. A chill shot up Bai's spine and the cold rain did not help.

Adabelle whimpered and collapsed onto her father's lap, burying her face in his chest. Bai cradled her, but he strained his ears to listen for the number of them. Based on the tension in Raegna's face, she did the same. The echo doubled with rainfall and thunder, making estimation difficult. Bai shuddered and his leg ached.

Raegna unsheathed her sword, then plucked the knife from the tree root to give it to Bai. In their seven years of marriage, he had never seen its edge until she pulled it from her nightstand drawer. He would bet good coin on how she had meant to use it, but she had given it to him when their home was invaded, in a time of uncertain danger. Surely, she didn't know how many wolves lurked outside, but she handed the knife to him now the same way.

As a last resort, she wanted him armed.

Raegna sat at the mouth of the shelter, her sword in hand. Bai kept Adabelle warm, gripping the hilt. Before Raegna's feet, the fire flickered as the drizzle dissipated. The flames might keep the wolves at bay, but their hollow, droning voices carried through the trees. Sleep may not be an option tonight.

Chapter 8

Hadwin

STEAM ROSE FROM THE wooden tub and drenched Hadwin's face. Sorelle's thick and sticky summer heat didn't help.

Laundry duty included cleaning leather armor and washing clothes over a large wooden tub of hot water that lay beneath a small, open tent. The task itself wasn't grueling, but the vapor clung to Hadwin's skin and stung his eyes as he worked.

Across from him, Naleem knelt with Dakarai and Cadoc. All three of them had their dark brown hair sticking to their foreheads. Naleem wrung out the soaked shirts and pants after Hadwin finished lathering them, then scrubbed the leather with a brush while he waited for another damp batch. Clothes hung from a line above them where they dried and dripped over their heads.

The real job was keeping Dakarai close by. Cadoc slept in a sling on his father's back, his little eyelids flitting even with the jolting movement of Naleem's scrubbing beside him. But Dakarai heaved a great sigh while he drew in the dirt with his finger. When he got bored, he wandered to the mouth of the tent where the rest of Haven stretched outside and peered at the dirt path.

"Dakarai," Naleem scolded.

The boy peeked over his shoulder.

"Come here, now."

Dakarai shuffled over to him. "What, Papa?"

"You need to stay with me," Naleem said. "Do not wander off or play games. I can't let them take you from me. Do you understand?"

Dakarai nodded to him and plopped by his side again. "Yes, Papa."

He stayed until a mouse skittered from the pile of soiled fabric hoarded behind Hadwin. The creature's scurrying caught the boy's attention. Dakarai darted after it when the mouse made its way toward the tent's open flap.

Hadwin dropped a shirt into the tub with a gasp. "Dak!"

Naleem turned to see his son running to a tent across the path. Two bristled, large men stood under its shade, watching the boy intently as he approached. Their weight shifted, and they gripped the axes at their belts.

"Dakarai!" Naleem shouted.

Dakarai skidded to a stop, kicking up dirt. He cowered at his father's scowl and slunk back to the laundry tent. Naleem grabbed him by the arm and pulled him down next to him with a rough thud.

"Stay with me," he growled.

"But, Papa, I don't want to do laundry," Dakarai said.

"You must," Naleem told him. "There's no getting out of it."

Dakarai pouted. "The water's too hot."

"I don't care," Naleem grunted, rubbing his forehead.

Hadwin cleared his throat. "Here, Dak. Come over here and hand Uncle Hadwin the clothes."

Beside his uncle, Dakarai investigated the heap of shirts and pants. His little nose wrinkled, and he shut his eyes tight as if he could block out the very memory of the stench. "It's smelly."

"That's why we must clean it," Hadwin chuckled. "Go on, hand one to me."

The three did laundry until the sun hovered over the horizon with a faint orange glow darkened by small, rolling rain clouds. Hadwin's hands burned red and sore from the hot water, his skin warm to the touch.

A horn blared throughout Haven. The pitch caused dogs to howl across the campground. Men and boys left their tents and stations to meander towards the great house with the elk skull. They seemed in good spirits with the day's end, laughing at the jokes they told as they paraded by.

"Where are they going, Papa?" Dakarai asked.

Hadwin sniffed the air. In the distance, a tangy scent of smoke carried towards them. "Smells like supper time. You three hungry?"

***

Gray clouds trailed the setting sun, bringing with them the scent of rain. Hadwin and Naleem followed the others through the dirt paths to the great house, which had transformed in the light of evening.

The shadows sharpened the archways and the elk's antlers that elongated over the rooftop. Flames from the torchlight beside the double doors flickered and gave the skull a more menacing look in its pitch-black sockets. Hadwin gulped as the men poured inside, the spicy aroma of cooked meat and the sting of burning wood hanging in the air.

The first floor made up the dining hall with long tables filled with platters of food. Every man in Haven had a seat, and each squished and shoved to take his place. To the far left, in the middle of a table,

Thenalious sat in a wooden chair decorated with antlers. Several men had similar seats about him: men in leather over their shirts, finer dressed than those that stuffed the hall. But none of them had a chair so grand. Thenalious held a drinking horn as he spoke to them.

Friends greeted each other with laughter and claps on their shoulders and took their seats. Hadwin and Naleem stood apart from the crowd and waited for open spots. The walls flooded with voices as more people piled in and sat themselves down. Among them, young men dashed about with food and pitchers to serve.

Two tapestries dangled and waved on either side of the room, one of Sigmund and the other of Fan. However, unlike in Syden's temple, Fan was not adorned by dark colors, snake pupils, and stag antlers. Instead, he wielded a sword and shield like a warrior with human eyes and a crown of antler points.

Sigmund even had a distinct atmosphere to him, bearing a submissive humbleness with a doe-like stare. A dainty elegance rather than godly strength. And he did not stand with his wife, Sachi. Hadwin frowned at the two images before Naleem nudged him.

"Let's find a place to sit before they are all taken," he suggested.

It took some negotiating with the other men to claim seats, but the brothers managed with Dakarai in Hadwin's lap and Cadoc in Naleem's. Dakarai complained he would rather have his own seat, but Hadwin ignored him and endured the tight fit between a burly warrior and Naleem.

Fortunately, the food before them appeared worth the trouble. Cooked pheasant with crispy, golden-brown skin made Hadwin's mouth water as it was passed on a platter. He picked pieces for himself and Dakarai, juices dripping from the meat.

The bird's presentation on silver platters was peculiar, as if it were prepared for a holiday. Hadwin noted every serving on the table and the sweet wine young men served to the others. He realized this was the sort of feast their Matriarch would serve for her own village for a Solstice Festival, Leaf Fall Gift, or Winter Mull.

Brow furrowed, Hadwin peered at the cloth that decorated the long wooden tables. The velvet gave under his fingers as it did each Winter Mull since he was a boy. Matriarch Alv laid it out every year for its deep forest-green color and gold borders.

The roast pigs stretched across platters, the sliced honeyed beef layered in roots and gravy, the pheasant covered with caramel grease. Every morsel from each plate came from Syden. This was Haven's bounty the men indulged themselves in, congratulating themselves on a job well done.

Hadwin's appetite vanished, despite the hard travel this morning and the day's work. The heartache in his chest throbbed far worse than his growling stomach as he remembered Pinar and his nieces, lost to them forever. The fellow Syden men who joined that garnished table at Winter Mull were prisoners or dead, their bodies left to Fan.

His hands balled into fists over the tablecloth. How dare they reward themselves for destroying his home and his family? Right in front of the victims of their raid? He wished he could do something, but there were many of them and one of him.

Whilst coming to this conclusion, his rumbling stomach caught his attention. Despite himself, Hadwin nibbled at a pheasant's leg. Cadoc ate off Naleem's plate while Dakarai gobbled up a roll of bread. At least they would get the nourishment they needed.

Hadwin gave Dakarai a weak grin. "You are hungry, aren't you?"

Dakarai beamed with food in his teeth.

"Cadoc," Naleem said beside Hadwin, "you need to eat more than that."

Hadwin turned to see Cadoc shake his head. Naleem picked up a piece of meat and brought it to the boy's lips. "Please. Eat more, son. We've had nothing but scraps for two days."

"Don't you want to grow big and strong like your father?" Hadwin added.

"Mama," Cadoc whined. "I want Mama."

Naleem froze up before blinking. "Your mother isn't here. Eat, Cadoc."

Tears sprung to the toddler's eyes, and he buried his face into Naleem's chest. "Mama..."

"Hush." Naleem tried to muffle his cries by holding him closer.

Across the table, a few ugly brutes raised their heads to the crying child and snorted jests. Crumbs and gravy smeared their beards. One with the scraggliest beard over fat, pink cheeks wiped his mouth with his sleeve and jeered, "Dealing with children is a woman's job. Give it a week and you'll desert them to work. They're not worth the effort."

Naleem ignored their words. "Cadoc, your mother isn't here. Papa is. I'm here. Please don't cry, and eat your dinner."

Cadoc sobbed harder, his face flushed and pinched, while the other men mocked him and Naleem.

"Give it up, boy!" One hoisted his drinking horn with a huge hand into the air and brown ale splashed out of it. "Your mother's dead!"

Another man tossed a bone at Naleem's plate. "You can't do a woman's job, foolish bastard!"

"Maybe he is a woman!"

Hadwin prayed to Gaea that Naleem would keep himself together. The tendons in his neck grew and his nails clawed the tablecloth with every word they threw at him. Hadwin himself struggled to control his temper as his grip tightened around Dakarai. These foul men could not understand what they put their captives through. They were far too simple-minded and cruel.

"Ignore them," he urged Naleem instead.

Some sweating, bald giant of a man slammed his mug of ale down on the table. "He let a woman break him. Look, boys, he won't even defend himself. He's broken. They've turned him into a pathetic babe-kissing cunt."

That did it.

Naleem chucked the remains of a drumstick at the burly giant. The hunk of meat and bone flew and smacked his bulbous nose, splattering him with grease. The man stared across the table, his flat jaw slack. Naleem glowered at him with dark eyes piercing beneath his knitted brow, ready to set Cadoc down for a fight.

"You little shit," the giant growled and stood from the table, clattering every plate and goblet. "Do you know who you're dealing with, woman's bitch?"

"An insolent, arrogant follower of Fan," Naleem snarled back. "I am a bitch to no one."

"You've made yourself one when you fucked a woman just to baby her brats," the man snapped. "They are better left in the dirt."

"You carry Fan's word," Naleem said. "He's a terrible god who did nothing but tempt and dissuade Sigmund. I follow Sigmund and he follows Gaea. He is loyal to his wife and children, and so I will be."

Hearing his brother say such things ignited a spark of pride in Hadwin's heart. But they reminded him of what Obrecht had preached in front of Wyn, and his stomach knotted with dread. These men didn't seem so offended by it. Perhaps they were too drunk to care.

The giant snorted. "Pathetic."

"If you're so loyal to your children, why don't you take them from us?"

Cadoc yelped as a second man from behind grabbed him by the sleeve under Naleem's arm and ripped him away. Hadwin and Naleem whirled to face a wiry man holding Cadoc by the wrist.

The boy cried out and reached with his tiny, outstretched fingers. "Papa!"

Naleem rose over the man, his shoulders hunched. "Let him go."

"Come get him, son of Sigmund," the man taunted, and swung Cadoc in his calloused hands. "Come save your child."

Naleem lunged and threw his fist into the man's face. Stumbling, the man fell backward and crashed into a tray of mashed roots. Ale spilled over him and splattered the table. In the mess of it, Naleem snatched Cadoc. A blow smashed into his nose, knocking him into Hadwin and Dakarai. Naleem recovered with his lip curled. He shoved Cadoc next to Hadwin to brawl with whoever neared.

"Naleem!" Hadwin yelled, his arms full of his nephews. Every man around them rose and cheered on Naleem's defeat. Hadwin kicked at any who came too close, but he knew he couldn't protect them through this chaos. "All of you, stop it!"

A great bang and the splintering of wood echoed on the tapestry-adorned walls. All the men in the hall came to a standstill and even cowered to look up in utter silence. Only distant thunder dared to rumble outside.

Thenalious stood over his table covered in half-empty platters and goblets of ale. An ax blade wedged into the tabletop and its green cloth. A deep frown morphed his close-cut beard. His sharp eyes blazed as they roamed over the room.

"That's enough!" he shouted. "We're brothers here. Act like it!"

"We only joked about the boy's maternal ways, and then he throws punches," someone said.

Naleem looked ready to throw another one.

Hadwin faced Thenalious, surreal as it was to speak to his menacing captor. "Sir, our youngest was taken from us. My brother was just trying to defend his son."

A beat passed before Thenalious nodded. "I understand."

He scanned the hall of men before him. Most could not bring themselves to meet his gaze. "What you all need to get through your heads is that they are new here. They have been taught the ways of Gaea and women, and they are not used to our customs. It's a new belief for all Galaenia to hear. If they feel their duty is to protect their young, let them."

Then he took in Hadwin and Naleem. "To the newcomers, I apologize for my brothers' incompetence. However, we have embraced faith not only in Sigmund but in his brother Fan. Perhaps you will seek and ask the elders and my fellow councilmen about it if you're curious. I've already lost a man to this foolishness. I don't want another one of you to suffer."

Somehow, he knew about Obrecht's death. Stranger still, somehow, he regretted it.

Thenalious pulled the ax blade from the wood and cloth to sit back down. Slowly, conversation resumed, and the other men shrank away from Naleem and Hadwin with murderous looks. Cadoc curled into Hadwin's body and sobbed in fear. Dakarai did his best to comfort his brother, brushing his shoulder as Hadwin clutched him.

Naleem's face swelled and bruised. As much as he detested him, Hadwin had to give Thenalious credit for stopping the fight. Otherwise, Naleem might be in worse shape. But this leader's words contradicted everything these men stood for. He killed those who spoke against his twisted beliefs and so had his men. Now he would instruct them to excuse a newcomer's ignorance. That had to be his persuasive tactic, which he had tried on those lined before him while Syden burned. A gentle push and a grotesque punishment.

***

After dinner, the men filed out of the great house, heading for their tents. A drizzle of rain hastened everyone's steps. Unnerved from the fight, Naleem and Hadwin led the boys to where the Syden men were told to bed down for the night.

Rows of cots lined the quaint space on either side of its walls. Some men had already bundled themselves up, while others found it more difficult to do so, what with young boys who threw tantrums. Their fathers couldn't hide their impatience. Despite the cruel jests at supper, it was the women who typically cared for the children at home. Many of these men may not have spent as much time with their children as

Naleem and Hadwin did. Were the Haven men right about children eventually being left behind? Would their fathers abandon them?

Shoving the thoughts out of his head, Hadwin chose the cot beside Naleem's and helped tuck the boys in for bed.

Dakarai pushed the wool blankets away and whined, "Papa, the blanket is itchy."

"That's all we have, Dak." Naleem tugged the blanket loose. "Now sleep. Tomorrow will be a harder day."

Dakarai obeyed and fidgeted when Naleem placed his brother beside him. "Uncle Hadwin, will you tell a story?"

Hadwin blinked. "Well, perhaps—"

"Not tonight, son," Naleem said.

"But, Papa, I can't sleep without one."

"I've seen you do it before."

"It's all right, brother." Hadwin perched himself on the edge of his cot. "It might help us all rest better. I know just the one."

"The one where Sigmund shows his power!" Dakarai told him, his eyes alight.

"That's the one," Hadwin agreed with a grin. He glanced at Naleem. "If you don't mind."

Naleem sighed and waved a hand before lounging beside his sons.

"Very well." Hadwin cleared his throat. "Long ago, after Sachi and Sigmund's deaths, their children lifted them to Heimelle, as we all will be. All took comfort that Sachi reunited with her Mother again and that she and Sigmund could live in peace. They watch over us now, and guide us, and protect us alongside Gaea Herself."

"Yes, but then Fan comes," Dakarai urged.

"I'll get to that," Hadwin teased and poked him. "One day, Sachi and Gaea were catching up in the forest and Sigmund wandered a distance away to give them time together. He found berries and flowers to pick for his wife when two feet plodded up to him and he looked up. Standing before him was the ancient, evil god, Fan, who sought to bring the daughters and sons of Gaea down to his level in the eternal dark land, Helved."

In his periphery, Hadwin noticed others in the tent listening. A frightening flush of embarrassment bubbled through him, but he kept his focus on his nephews, who were leaning forward in anticipation.

"'Hello, brother,' Fan said to Sigmund. 'What are you doing with those plants? Making a concoction?' Sigmund gathered his find and stood to face the god." Hadwin had chosen different voices to portray the gods when the children were just babes. Sigmund's voice was smooth and deep, while Fan's was snarling and cackling.

"'The flowers are for my wife,' he said. 'The berries are for us to eat later.'

"'Your wife?' Fan asked. 'The daughter of Gaea?' And once Fan knew of Sigmund's relation to Sachi, he connived an idea. 'Brother,' he said. 'Do you still serve your wife, even after death?'

"'Yes,' Sigmund replied. 'That is because I still love her.'

"'You do know you are immortal now,' Fan said. 'You are no longer bound to the law of humans.'

"'I understand,' Sigmund told him. 'But I will still give her these flowers.'

"'That's all well and good,' Fan told him. He stepped closer to Sigmund and said, 'But tell me: Since you've come to Gaea, how often have you brought your wife to bed?'

"Hearing this, Sigmund scowled at Fan. 'It is none of your business. There is no reason to bring her to bed. We've had all our children on Jorde.'

"Fan gave a sly grin. 'But, brother, to bed a goddess as a god is something no being should pass up! It's better than anything you or your wife would have experienced before.'

"Sigmund frowned at the god and shook his head again. 'If I do, she will have to agree.'

"'Didn't you know? You have a say in things! You are not a human man anymore, brother. You don't have to give in to her will or do as she says. Make off with her! Drag her to the nearest green patch and do as you wish! You're free now!'

"'I will not!' Sigmund grew angry, and the visibility of his wrath made Fan cower. 'She is my wife, and I will not dishonor her. Leave before I call Gaea and tell Her what you have tried to do. She will show you what happens to those who try to destroy Her daughter.'"

The entire tent was silent, deep in Hadwin's storytelling.

"Fan fled from Sigmund's power but turned back to shout, 'You will break for me! You will help me destroy Gaea and Her daughter! I swear on the lives of your children on Jorde!'

"Sigmund was glowing with an incredible power that shone like the sun and made Fan shrink away. 'Leave me!' he shouted, and the evil one was gone."

"Did Sachi and Gaea see?" Dakarai wondered aloud.

"They did," Hadwin answered. "Gaea did not approve of Fan's final words and knew them to be a curse. She feared someday Fan may tempt Sigmund and the faithful husband would give in. When that day comes,

Fan will take Jorde into his own hands and use all men and their desires to do his bidding and dismantle the reign of women."

"That won't happen, will it, Uncle Hadwin?" Dakarai asked.

"Sigmund has always been strong and has never dishonored or mistreated Sachi." Hadwin propped himself on one elbow. "As long as we do the same, Fan can do nothing to harm us."

Naleem yawned and pulled the wool blanket over the boys. "All right, your uncle has told you a story. Now go to bed."

The boys snuggled under their blankets and shut their eyes to sleep beside their father. The rest of the men drifted off as well once the story ended.

Hadwin lay on his back and stared up at the tent ceiling. The fabric waved and clapped ever so slightly as a night breeze picked up. Raindrops splattered here and there. Snores harmonized with each other across the rows of cots and Hadwin sighed.

Fan's curse may have come to pass with Haven attacking villages and taking men hostage. The story from Gaea's scripture seemed like a fairy tale to frighten children and encourage young boys to stay true to women as they grew older. But it was so real now that it made Hadwin shudder and turn over on his side.

This fear could not reach his nephews. He would keep their spirits lifted with stories of Gaea, Sachi, and Sigmund. Stories that could be all Dakarai and Cadoc had left of their home. He would protect them at all costs.

Chapter 9

Raegna

"**M**AMA, MY BUM HURTS from all this riding," Adabelle complained.

Raegna looked over her shoulder as she led her mare by the reins on foot, limping on her bad ankle. Atop the horse, Adabelle sat in front of Bai, both slumped over in their weariness from a hard night listening to wolves in the mud and rain. Bai's eyelids drooped and his head bobbed. Sometimes he jolted at the swing of the mare's gait when he drifted off. His torn and burned leg dangled over the horse's side, wrapped in the shredded fabric of Raegna's skirt. It was a wonder he didn't black out and fall off.

Leaning back against his torso, Adabelle may not have been helping his cause to stay conscious and upright. But her warmth was a much-needed remedy to protect her father from the chilly night and brisk morning after the rain.

"Just a little longer," Raegna assured. "Judr is nearby." If only the mare could carry three and gallop under all the weight. However, they would arrive there before the day's end.

The damp forest floor squished under Raegna's boots and the mare's hooves. The murky air clung to her skin, dress, and hair. Old rainwater dripped from the pine needles and fell onto them. Strands of Bai's hair glittered from their droplets, but he kept Adabelle dry under his cloak. They would soon have a place to rest with no more of the pine-soaked smell of the trees.

"Do you see anything from up there?" Raegna asked to entertain Adabelle.

"Nothing but more trees," Adabelle answered. "Papa's taller though."

Bai's dreary gold eyes peered over the trail. "There's smoke rising in the distance. They must be getting ready for breakfast."

At the mention of food, Raegna's stomach growled. She had given the last of their rations to Adabelle. Raegna and Bai hadn't eaten since the evening before, and that was a small portion of cheese. It was no wonder Bai had food on his mind.

Hopefully, Judr would be generous and give them plenty to eat. Perhaps Raegna could find a place for her family to stay. Then she could work for a house, and everything would go back to the way it was...

One task at a time, Raegna thought. Get to Judr first. And find a healer for Bai.

Raegna sucked in a rigid breath and exhaled to bite her lip. She had been wrong to stop them in that clearing, practically offering the three of them to the wolves. Worse yet was the fact that Bai had been right. If she had listened to him, they would have been safe.

His new wound was her own fault. Yet, after what he did to her, should she not have minded his suffering so much? Why did she feel so stricken with guilt for his injury? She had saved him, after all.

Beneath their pitiful shelter, Raegna had even handed him the night-stand knife before their world flipped onto its head. As he received it, Bai stared at her, dumbfounded. He still wore the blade on his hip, and she allowed it. The blade she had imagined sinking into his neck was now a tool to protect him.

Why did Raegna allow it? Could it have been Adabelle's anguish that tore at her? Not that Bai got hurt, but that because he did, Adabelle grieved. Her beloved father could have been killed. Then again, Adabelle had been terrified during all these recent situations. Raegna worried about her, but she always did. That wasn't it.

Her heart ached for Bai...

The reality of it became more infuriating the more Raegna puzzled over it. Hitting her over the head when they escaped was an act of protection. Though she would argue there were better ways to do so. She had punished him for it, struck him across the face, and he continued to follow her.

Why did he keep trying?

"Mama!" Adabelle cried, stretching high from the saddle. "Houses! I see houses!"

Raegna tore herself from her thoughts and looked ahead.

Below the hillcrest, nestled within the forest trees, and surrounded by a wall of timber, was Judr. A village much larger than their own, dotted with houses, shops, and barns. But every roof was covered in timber and not sod. To the right of it lay the fields of crops that fed them, lush green from last night's storm. The sunlight sat on rooftops, warming their structures after a chilled night. Smoke rose from chimneys and the faint scent of fresh, warm bread baking made Raegna's mouth water.

"Almost there," she breathed.

Down the hill and through the trees, they walked until they approached Judr's gates, which towered twenty feet above them. The wooden doors were carved with a small doe, a raven, and other woodland animals surrounding the Goddess, Gaea. Two watchtowers stood on either side, with a couple of guards in each. Raegna admired them. If Syden had built such a fortification, it might still stand this morning.

One guard caught sight of the family and leaned over her tower post to peer at them. "My lady, who are you? State your business here!"

Raegna glanced at Bai, though she was not sure why. Perhaps to remind herself that she was not alone before the gates of Judr, and these intimidating women to whom she was strange. Bai raised his eyebrows at her.

"My name is Raegna," she called back, cupping a hand around her mouth. "My family and I come from Syden. We bring grave news that it was attacked."

"Attacked? Sorry, our Matriarch does not get involved in village-to-village quarrels."

"No, it wasn't another village!" Raegna protested. "A group of brutal men invaded our homes and destroyed us. Please, we must speak to your Matriarch so she can send word of these raiders to the Queen!"

Small snickers echoed from the tower. "My lady, you say men raided your entire village? Is that what I heard?"

Raegna's patience faded. "Yes! Please, let us in. It would interest your Matriarch to hear about this, and we have a child who needs a warm place to rest. My husband is injured. He needs a healer!"

To prove it, she turned the mare so they could easily see Bai's leg from the height. He pulled his cloak to show them. The guards studied him, leaning over the rail.

After a heavy pause, a new guard said, "I am Ase, commander of the warriors here. You will be searched before entering these gates."

When Ase disappeared, the gate's doors creaked open with a rotating chain. Three guards emerged behind the door, dressed in leather armor. In the lead, Ase settled her hands on her belt, examining the family. Her black hair clung to her head in tight braids that stretched past her shoulders. Two pale scars striped her rich brown skin at her long jawline, and one crinkled above her right eyebrow.

Each warrior carried a sword on their hip and glared with mistrust at Raegna as they spotted her own weapon.

"Search them," Ase ordered.

They approached, the smallest one with an owl-like face inspecting Raegna's skirts and sword. "How were you able to afford such a blade?"

"It belonged to my grandmother," Raegna said. "We've kept it in shape since."

The taller guard's hand closed around the hilt at her belt as she instructed Bai to remove his cloak. He obliged, bracing Adabelle against him. The guard snatched his bag from his shoulder and picked through it. Satisfied, she returned it to him. Then her eyes lit up. "What's this?"

She slipped the nightstand knife from his hip, the flat of the blade gliding over his thigh. The guard held it up for her comrades. "He's armed too."

Ase narrowed her gaze on Raegna. "You allow your husband a weapon? We do not tolerate that here."

"I'll keep it with me then." Raegna opened her bandaged palm for the knife.

"Very well."

Once the visitors met their requirements, the guards had the gate drawn wider and the main road lay open to them. With a hard snort, Raegna's mare carried her family forward.

Houses and shops lined Judr's road, much like Syden. Instead of green hills roving behind rooftops, the forest pine wrapped the village walls. The path remained quiet, save for the men on their way to the fields. They gave Raegna and her family curious glances as they passed single-file like ants.

A stout woman on a lanky horse herded them, shouting at them with a shrill voice. "Move along, boys! We're late enough as it is!"

The pleasant peacefulness of Judr stirred Raegna's heart in an unexpected way. After the damage done to Syden, how could Judr stand just a few days' ride away, going on with business as usual?

At the end of the road, the guards marched the family to the great house, a two-story home with an elk skull above the sturdy porch. It belonged to a bull, but someone had sawed the antlers off. Flat stubs protruded above its sockets.

Whoever the Matriarch was, she did not favor male power or encouragement thereof with a symbol like that. Though Raegna might have commended the image before, the sight of stumps that were once great antlers made her skin crawl.

Two young girls sat on the porch steps, tying twine and strings in different knots. They jumped as the escort approached them.

Ase waved to them. "My ladies. Is your mother awake this morning?"

The eldest, a girl with light brown hair and fair fawn skin over long, sharp features, nodded and stood to retrieve her mother. The youngest, a copy of her sister, stayed behind, staring curiously at Raegna and her family encircled by the guards. Raegna offered a small smile of reassurance, and the girl did the same.

As they waited, Raegna focused on Bai and Adabelle. The little girl braided pieces of the mare's mane. Bai scanned their surroundings, his golden gaze drifting over the village houses and rooftops, then the Matriarch's house, before falling on Raegna and meeting her eyes.

She turned away. His stare had been so knowing, his face steady despite his fatigue and pain. Raegna squeezed her eyes shut and opened them when the front door clicked.

The eldest sister returned with three women behind her, all of whom stopped before the steps. The woman in the middle wore a regal dark blue dress in a style typically worn by wealthy noblewomen. Raegna guessed she was the Matriarch.

Thick sandy braids clung to her head. The rest fell about her shoulders. She studied Raegna with small, sage-colored eyes and her thin lips turned down into a frown. Her features were like that of the eldest girl's, long and sharp, but her nose carried more freckles across her tanned fawn skin.

The thinner woman to her right had a similar but paler complexion, with higher cheekbones below deep-set eyes. She wore a green dress that emphasized her irises, with a leather belt about her waist. Her dark brown hair was smoothed in two braids that trailed down her back. Her stare peered into Raegna's very soul.

The third woman stood to the Matriarch's left in a loose dress over her pregnant belly. Her round, white face tinged with gold-brown held a short nose, brown oval eyes, and brunette hair to match. She regarded the family with the same curiosity as the girls. Her hands rested under her belly.

"Good morning," the woman in the middle greeted with a rather dry tone. "I am Viona, Matriarch of Judr. What is your name?"

So much authority radiated from her in her straight, broad posture and the way she raised her chin, it caused Raegna to stand in a faint daze. With a hard blink, she shook her head to return to herself.

"Raegna, Matriarch," she answered, then gestured behind her. "This is my husband and daughter. We come from Syden."

Viona's gaze shifted. "Why have you come?"

"Our village was attacked," Raegna explained, "by strange men who came out of nowhere. No one survived, and we barely escaped."

"Your Matriarch didn't survive?" Viona asked.

"We found her head on a pike. See, we returned the morning after the attack and I lifted the entire village—er, with my husband's help." Raegna unwrapped the bandage around her hand. A red slash began below her index finger and extended to her wrist. She showed it to the Matriarch. "I begged Gaea to accept my sacrifice and bring our fallen to Heimelle."

At the sight of the cut, Viona raised an eyebrow. A hint of interest spread across her face.

"Raegna. Come inside." She turned to the skinny woman. "Femke, have our warriors take Raegna's horse to our stables."

"My husband needs a healer," Raegna blurted, taking a step forward.

The two looked at her with their thin frowns and sharp eyes. Raegna shrank back. Perhaps it was not wise to speak when not spoken to. But Bai needed help now.

She gulped. "Wolves attacked us. He was bitten, and the wound is still bleeding. This horse keeps him off the bad leg."

A line on the bridge of Viona's long nose creased as Raegna guided the mare to give her a clear view of Bai's leg. After inspecting not only the injury but Bai himself, his very existence, Viona nodded. "Femke, take Raegna and her family to Banu."

Before she could, Viona gripped Femke's arm to whisper something into her ear. Raegna waited with an eyebrow raised.

Femke inclined and walked down the porch steps. She gave Raegna a sideways glance as she passed saying, "This way."

Raegna hesitated and turned back to the Matriarch. "Will I be able to discuss what has befallen Syden with you?"

A smile tugged at the corners of Viona's mouth. "Of course, priestess. At a later date."

How much later? Was the matter not urgent enough? Just a moment ago, Viona invited them in. Bai could easily see the healer on his own. Raegna could remain to explain their story. But a wife ought to stand beside her husband when a healer treated his wounds. Especially after everything they had seen together. These people had reason to suspect this strange family that appeared out of thin air. If she abandoned Bai now, what would they think of them?

Raegna gave Viona a nod before guiding the mare after Femke. There was nothing she could do about it. Making a scene wouldn't do them good in a new village. For now, Bai needed a healer.

***

Femke took them down the dirt road, her skirts rasping with every stride. Judr came alive as children leaped about outside their homes. Women began their morning routines, and they paused only to show Femke respect with slight bows. Then they watched the unfamiliar family walk past. Raegna forced herself to hold her head high, something her mother had taught her since she was a child.

"A woman should never slouch or cower, Raegna," Lady Jaleesa had instructed when they traversed Syden's streets. Now nothing but rubble and ash. "We have a reputation to keep."

Especially among these strangers. No, Raegna was the stranger trudging behind a woman of great esteem, her intentions uncertain. Raegna smiled at those who met her gaze, though some did not return the favor.

Femke stopped before a quaint house where animal furs hung on either side of the door. Large beads and bones strung from the porch roof rattled when a breeze slithered through the rafters.

An old woman sat in a rocking chair, reading out of a book titled *Inger's Journal of Ancient Remedies*, the letters tooled across its leather binding. Her white-streaked, gray hair fell in giant waves over her shoulders, shadowing her weathered, russet skin. Crow's feet creased around her eyes as she read her book, and her small lips settled into a concentrated pout.

When her visitors approached, the woman tore her big, hooked nose from the yellowed pages and examined Raegna even as Femke climbed steps.

"Banu," Femke greeted, rather dully, at the top of the stairs.

The old woman, Banu, closed her book with a soft clap of paper and laid it on her lap. "What have you brought me now? I've never seen this girl before."

"Syden was attacked," Femke said and nodded to their visitors. "This is Raegna. She and her family are the only survivors. Her husband needs attention."

Banu's mouth warped into a smile between her wrinkled jowls as she beheld Bai and Adabelle atop the mare. Book in hand, she went for the door. "Bring the boy inside."

Raegna obeyed, picking Adabelle off the mare and onto the ground so Bai could swing his good leg over and dismount. He leaned against her for support. When his arm settled around her shoulders, her muscles seized. He was warm against her, towering and heavy as he had been...

With a jolt, Raegna snapped to the present. Her ankle throbbed, but she had the mare tied to the porch rail and continued to aid Bai up the steps. Adabelle clambered after them. The little girl held her father's hand and guided him, glancing between him, the path ahead, and back again.

The door opened into the kitchen, a wide room decked with wood counters, cupboards, and pantries. On the other side stood a long wooden table accompanied by various chairs tucked in beneath it. The table was piled with vials, bottles, books, linen, and candles with blackened wicks and drooping wax.

Another room lay beyond the kitchen, organized with two rows of cots for patients. Raegna expected Banu to direct them there. Instead, she pulled a chair out from under the cluttered table. "Sit here, boy."

With Raegna's help, Bai hobbled to the chair and Adabelle kept hold of his hand. He ruffled her hair.

Banu took a second chair and sat in front of Bai. "Let us see what is wrong."

Dexterous round fingers worked to unwrap the old, bloodied fabric so Banu could examine his leg. "A burn. Did you get in trouble with your wife?"

"It was a bite," Bai informed her. "She took a hot blade to it so it wouldn't get worse."

Banu's brow furrowed at Raegna. "Usually, I would refrain from burning a wound without proper knowledge. Then you very well could make it worse. I'm sure you thought there was nothing else you could do."

Raegna's gut somersaulted. She was already ravaged with enough guilt without knowing she could have sabotaged the situation further.

"But this is fine." Banu reached across the table for a strip of linen and a round glass bottle of clear, lime-green liquid. She held the cloth to the bottle's spout, then tipped the glass over to soak it. She gently dabbed the cloth against the bloodied wound with precision. Bai flinched and winced.

"No matter, your wife did well to bring you here. You are a lucky one to have her."

Raegna's eyes flicked to Bai where they met in a mutual gaze that meant, *She does not know what she speaks of.*

The surreality of willingly sharing a thought with him made Raegna avert her stare. When Banu finished cleaning most of the wound, she took Bai's chin between her thumb and index finger and turned his head from side to side.

"Handsome boy," she said with a wry smile. "Your mother picked a good one for you, girl. His eyes are bright." She forced his mouth open. "Teeth are good. He's as healthy as they come."

The way she touched him and inspected him like a workhorse at an auction made Raegna's blood simmer. Long ago, her mother had studied Bai the same way, finding the same traits for the prospect of her grandchildren.

"Will he heal?" Raegna asked, shaking the memory off.

Banu chose another clean piece of linen and soaked it with a cleanser. "Course he will. If anything was wrong, it would make itself known by now. He's fit as a fiddle, despite your attempt to mutilate him."

Raegna scowled.

"Oh, don't give me looks, girl," Banu scolded. "Who studies medicine here? Now, you came from Syden? It was attacked?"

"Yes." Raegna told Banu and Femke, who stood at the threshold, about the family's unfortunate experience. Leaving out the part where Bai knocked her unconscious, she explained how they returned to Syden the next morning to lift their people.

"That's very brave of you," Banu complimented. "And a long life of responsibility ahead of you. We haven't heard of any men like that." She looked at Femke. "Viona will look into it?"

"Our Matriarch can only do so much," Femke said with a wave of her hand. "The Maidens typically take defensive action. This requires a message to the Queen and her Duchess."

Banu rolled her eyes. "That'll take ages."

"That is, if these men exist," Femke added.

Raegna rounded on her. "Excuse me?"

Femke's face was ice cold even as the sun filtered through the doorway. "I'm sure my Matriarch sister will send a group of our women to see if Syden was actually destroyed. You could have been banished and sought pity."

"Banished?" Raegna scoffed.

"Mayhap you broke a law as a priestess just after completing the rites," Femke said with a shrug. "Indulged in more worldly pleasures, another man besides your husband. Perhaps even a tramp at your village brothel."

"And sent away with her husband and daughter?" Bai challenged behind Raegna. "Any right-minded Matriarch would keep a daughter for the future of the village. Then use a lonely husband for work and remarry him."

"A husband is the property of his wife," Femke snapped. "Where she goes, he is to follow." Then she glowered at Raegna. "Tell yours to watch his tongue. Lest we have it cut from his throat."

Raegna's nostrils flared, letting a heated stare settle on Femke's cold one with her chin level, far too grateful for Bai's words to silence him.

Femke turned on her heel. "I've done what was asked of me and brought you to Banu. A good day to you, priestess."

With that, she slammed the door shut. A cloud of dust billowed from the wood floor once she was gone.

Banu coughed. "Jealous wench."

Raegna whirled and shot Banu a look of warning. Adabelle stood on the other side of her, susceptible to such language.

Banu understood but shook her head. "My apologies, girl. I'm not sure what has gotten into that one, though I know there's plenty of weight on her shoulders. The death of our last Matriarch, their mother, has been difficult for her. But she's become quite the stiff."

"Seems like it," Bai grumbled.

Banu cackled. "You do have a tongue on you. I like that. But just so your wife can keep you, I advise you to heed that woman's words. Especially around the Matriarch and her sisters."

Collecting herself, Raegna turned to the old healer. "Thank you, Banu, for caring for my husband."

"Don't thank me yet, girl," Banu said. She finished cleaning and placed the linen and bottle on the table. "I imagine you three have nowhere to go. You certainly have not made a great first impression with Femke nor, in turn, Matriarch Viona. If you would like, my barn is open to you for now. I can't have families crowding my work, so I cannot give you the healing room."

"Oh, that's very generous," Raegna replied with a faint smile. "Thank you."

"But first, I will need names." Banu rose and went to the cupboards, retrieving more bandages.

"Ah. I am Raegna. My daughter is Adabelle, and my husband is Bai." More bizarre than sharing a moment of mutual agreement: speaking his name aloud.

Banu nodded to Adabelle. "Beauty." Then to Bai. "Purity." And to Raegna. "Yours is strange, girl. A combination of sorts. Ragna means wisdom, and Rae means friend of the lamb. Hmm, lambs often symbolize purity."

Hot bile burned the back of Raegna's throat.

"Banu, what do you think your Matriarch will do about Syden?" she asked to change the subject. "That Femke didn't believe me."

"Oh, they will send some warriors there eventually," Banu assured her as she started wrapping Bai's leg again. "When they do, they'll find the truth and send word to her majesty and the Maidens will look into it. Unfortunately, there is nothing more we can do from here. You've done the right thing, bringing your family here and lifting your village."

Raegna shifted her weight, folding her arms. "I'm not so sure."

"Be sure," the healer said. "Do you see? Your family is safe, Syden has a chance of being avenged, and you can stay with me until you are prepared to be on your own. Your presence may make things more interesting here in Judr, especially with a husband like that."

She sat up with her hands on her knees after tying the bandage togeth-er. "There now. How's that?"

"Better," Bai answered, flexing his leg.

For once in her married life, Raegna was glad her husband would be all right. But a sense of dread loomed. This Matriarch and her sisters were not quite what she had hoped for upon arrival. She prayed they would not dismiss her distress and the gravity of her story, but they were different women than she had ever encountered.

No, that was wrong. Her own mother had the same regal and author-itative posture as Viona's. If it were up to Jaleesa, she would have sneered at the exaggerated tale and called it Raegna's excuse to wield a sword.

As Matriarch, Viona bore the duty of protecting Judr and all those in it, not just her bloodline and a daughter's future, though such things must undoubtedly be on her plate. Raegna could not blame her for her distrust. A stranger and her family appearing in the village, spewing an extraordinary telling of men taking up weapons against their own people, would make any Matriarch bristle. Nothing like this had been heard of for centuries, not since Galaenia's Dark Days of civil war.

Perhaps it would serve Raegna well to earn the Matriarch's trust first, rather than advocate for the use of time and resources to investigate such a travesty. The urgency could not be pushed aside, but it could not be Raegna's only tool, either. Besides, as a newcomer to Judr, she should attempt to befriend her new Matriarch, regardless. Recalling her mother's teachings, Raegna groaned inwardly.

"Sit down, girl," Banu told her, tearing Raegna from her thoughts. "Let's take a look at that ankle."

Chapter 10

Naleem

Pinar danced before him, a silk white dress draping her body with the curve of her waist and hips. Daisies blazed in her brilliant, pale blonde hair. The elegance of her movements made Naleem's heart ache. She looked just as she had when they were young and courting. Her soft eyes lit up as she offered him her hand.

But rough, calloused hands seized her from his reach.

Then Pinar lay upon her back in bed beside him, bare skin glowing in the moonlight. She turned to meet his face, her hair tumbling over her shoulders and arms that reached over her head, and her fingers prettily rested on the headboard. Naleem hesitated to touch her for fear of ruining her very image and form but could not resist her delicate breasts and belly.

A sword plunged through her. Keen and frigid steel, hungry to tear her apart. The body he thought he would sleep with for the rest of his days, the belly that carried their children, the lips he kissed countless times...

...all doused in bright red blood.

Naleem jerked and sent clothes splashing into the hot water as he startled himself. Cadoc whimpered over his shoulder, a warning of an oncoming wail wrapped in the sling on his back.

"Shh," Naleem soothed, his chin over his collarbone to see him. "Shh."

The repetitive task of drying the laundry had not been mind-numbing enough. He hated the simple work and that it could not ward off dreams and visions. Sweat prickled his neck, even under the shade of the tent canvas, what with the heat from the steaming water meant to scrub these heathens' clothing clean. His shirt was soaked with Cadoc pressed against him, but at least his littlest son could not run, no matter how much he squirmed sometimes.

It was Dakarai he needed to worry about, trampling around to explore despite the numerous times Naleem chided him to stay nearby. The Haven men didn't intimidate the boy, even after being caught in the middle of that fight in the dining hall.

Watching Dakarai would be easier with a second pair of eyes. But that morning, Wyn had taken Hadwin by the arm and shoved him in the barn's direction.

"You husbands caused too much trouble at supper," Wyn sneered. "Better keep you apart."

These raiders were so bent on the fact that women treated them harshly, and yet they used each other the same way, if not worse. Naleem couldn't comprehend it but worked to maintain a low profile. After last night, he reckoned it would be in his best interest to not draw attention to himself or his family. There were many Haven men and only one of him.

With Hadwin gone, Naleem kept Dakarai busy by instructing him to clean the laundry as well. For a time, Dakarai sulked but accepted his lot and sank the filth-ridden fabrics in. The boy dunked the fabric into the hot tub to soak, being careful not to touch the evaporating water.

Then his hand slipped and dipped into the tub. He yelped and yanked back before his eyes brimmed with tears.

Naleem tossed a soaked shirt over the wire strung above them and knelt, cupping Dakarai's hands in his. "Here, son." He took a breath and blew cool air onto the boy's hand as the skin turned bright red from the burn. Dakarai's lips quivered.

"It's all right," Naleem soothed.

Boots crunched in the drying mud as someone approached behind him. "You there."

Naleem dropped Dakarai's hand and whirled toward the voice survival instincts had assured he'd never forget.

Thenalious stood over them, his hands resting gentleman-like behind his back, though he only wore a black shirt with a dark brown belt wrapped around it and black pants folded over leather boots. Naleem sized him up now that he was not sitting on a horse or at the head of a table. He must have been a year or two older than Naleem, going into his thirtieth, and two inches taller with lean shoulders. Strands of his tousled black hair fell over his forehead. A smile quirked beneath his beard.

Naleem prepared himself to defend Dakarai from being snatched away as he rose. Instead, the leader of Haven peeked over the hot tub and the clothes hanging over the wire.

"You've been doing this all by yourself?" he asked, his head tilted.

"My son helped," Naleem blurted. "He was cleaning, but the water burned him."

Thenalious raised an open palm, his light demeanor ever-present. "Don't worry, I don't intend to take him from you. You are doing fine. More than fine. Have you eaten at all?"

Naleem hesitated. "No..."

"A shame. Wyn should have given out afternoon rations." Another smile and Thenalious outstretched his hand to him. "Come. You can eat with me. I have plenty to share."

Naleem peered around the man at the tent down the dirt path, just outside the great house. Yellow canvas rippled in the breeze, giving glimpses of a table full of platters of food within. What food? Naleem could not tell from this distance. Why was Thenalious offering his luxuries to him of all the men here?

"Papa." Dakarai tugged on his father's shirt. Naleem looked down into his hopeful eyes. "I am hungry."

"Poor thing," Thenalious said. "Come along, we mustn't let the little ones starve."

Naleem still did not take his hand but begrudgingly followed Thenalious to the tent, Dakarai at his side, and Cadoc still slung on his back.

The yellow canvas splashed golden light over the table. Fruits and meats filled elegant platters with designs of vines and leaves decorating their rims. Goblets of wine rested on either end.

Two young men stood stiff in adjacent corners. One held a feather-plumed staff and the second a pitcher. When Thenalious took his seat, the boy moved to fill his goblet. The other fanned him with the feathers of blue and green, originating from a bird Naleem had never seen before.

Thenalious waved to the chair across from him. "Make yourself comfortable."

Naleem sat with Cadoc in his lap. At once, Dakarai went for a full bunch of grapes and started ripping them from their stems.

"Dakarai," Naleem snapped.

"It's all right," Thenalious assuaged with a laugh. "He can have all he likes. All three of you can. What's mine is yours."

Is it poisoned then? Naleem thought.

Perhaps he was not working as hard as Thenalious would have appreciated. Or his forgiving nature towards last night's brawl was all a ruse. Now Thenalious was going to kill him and his children covertly with some deadly toxin in these delectable foods. However, after gulping a dozen grapes, Dakarai had not keeled over... yet.

Naleem decided he would steer clear of the wine, no matter how tempting it was to quench his thirst, and went for the meat instead. He ate some himself before giving any to Cadoc, who whined in protest at the wait. Chewing slowly, Naleem tasted the savory spices that coated the chunk of beef he chose. Some poisons were tasteless, but any hint of bitterness and he would spit it into Thenalious' face.

All the while, Thenalious watched, hazel eyes full of mischief as if planning a move in a tactical board game. The look sent Naleem's heart drumming, pulsing a rampant fire through his veins.

Thenalious snapped his fingers at the young man who fanned him and gestured across the table. "You must be overheated from all this work. Summer is dreadful this year."

The boy scuffled over to Naleem and waved the feathers over his head. Wafts of hot air did nothing to cool him down, but the bobbing motion quieted Cadoc. Naleem's lip curled despite his efforts to keep a plain expression.

"You're from the recent raid, aren't you?" Thenalious asked as he reached for a peach among others in an elaborate bowl.

Naleem's chest contracted as if a hand squeezed his lungs. He tried to shove the memories of that horrific night from his thoughts to be strong for his sons and brother. The screams of his daughters and the blood of his wife scraped through his mind. Naleem touched the pendant shaped like a raven with outstretched wings around his neck.

He cast his gaze up from beneath his brow as Thenalious continued to speak. "My apologies. All this change must be frightening. Especially after the misfortune at dinner. I promise you have nothing to fear in Haven."

Be it the heat of the day or his fury, Naleem's blood sizzled. Thenalious sent these monsters into Syden, his home, and all he had to give was a quaint apology.

"What is your name?" Thenalious asked.

"Why does it matter?"

Thenalious sighed. "You don't trust me."

You slaughtered my family. Naleem clamped his mouth shut.

"That explains it." Thenalious relaxed against the armrest of his chair and cut into his peach with a knife. "The food isn't poisoned. I can have Leif sample everything if you wish."

The boy with the pitcher braced himself in his corner. Naleem refused to budge.

"Will you tell me your name?" Thenalious tried again.

"Not before you tell me why you brought me here."

There it was, that mischief glittering in his eyes as he looked up. A hint of a smirk darted across his lips and an eyebrow pricked up. "You've done well with the work we have given you. And you've kept not one, but two sons alive in the meantime. You seem to have a paternal skill few can offer in a place like this. You fought for your son's life last night."

Naleem lowered his voice. "They had no right to take him from me."

"You are absolutely right." Thenalious pointed at him with the end of a peach slice. "And though the others outnumbered you, you got him back. We can put any dog to work in the streets, but I would much rather have you in my household."

"Doing what?"

"We keep the councilmen's sons in the great house," Thenalious explained. "The men have their own responsibilities, and no time to care for them, so we have caregivers to watch over them. However, our most recent caregivers are ill-suited for the job. Some boys have been left alone or escaped into the woods or the barn. A babe died just a month ago from starvation, though a caregiver claimed he grew sickly."

How on Jorde did they have sons with no women? Did they find orphans and take them in to twist them into monsters?

Naleem sat still, holding his head high. "You wish for me to replace them."

"I see a good heart in you," Thenalious said. "You follow Sigmund's example in protecting these two, providing and being a good father. It seems a waste to have you wash laundry." He took a bite of the peach. "You would sleep in the house from now on. Not that frigid cold tent. Your sons may join you. They'll grow and play with the other boys like real children."

Play like real children? Naleem thought. *In this place? Do you not know what you have done to them?*

He did not dare express his rage aloud—he had seen what happened to those who spoke out against these men. He would have to settle for a glare at Thenalious instead, his hands balling into fists as he curled over Cadoc in his lap.

Thenalious' features became somber as he paused for a while. "We brought you here to save you and your sons. To protect you. Out there, they treat us like nothing but breeding stallions, good only for work and the herd's fertility. You and I both know we are more than that."

When Naleem stewed in his silence, never giving him what he wanted, Thenalious leaned forward and nodded to Dakarai. "I'm sure your wife was disappointed with having a son."

Dakarai froze in mid-bite to look up at him and then at his father, utter confusion smeared across his face. Naleem wrapped his arm around the boy's shoulder. "She was very proud of him, actually. He is our firstborn, and she was overjoyed after his birth. She named him Dakarai for those very reasons. *Exultation* to Gaea after such a blessing."

Thenalious' stare trailed from Naleem to Dakarai, who straightened his back and squared his small shoulders to copy his father's braced posture. Then he gave an amused huff.

"A fair woman your mother selected for you," Thenalious admitted. "But that is just it. Your mother and hers chose you for her. You were fortunate to have had a decent wife, but not all are so lucky. Most of us ran here for a better life. A life with purpose. We are here to serve our gods and our brothers, to create a more natural world. A world where we rule."

"That is the way of Fan." The rumbling of Naleem's voice resonated deep in his chest.

Thenalious traced the designs on the tablecloth with his middle finger. "Wyn told me your brother was telling tales about Fan and Sigmund in the tent last night. Do you always tell your boys stories?"

"Yes. We tell them about Gaea, Sachi, and Sigmund. I want them to be aware of all sides of all stories."

"I understand..." Thenalious placed his forearm on the table. "I want to make you aware that we don't worship Gaea or Her daughter here. To do that would give power to women. We can't give Her more strength and encouragement to strengthen and encourage them."

It was as if Naleem were a child being scolded and taught a lesson. Quite a change from being slaughtered on the spot. He lowered his eyes, not in any mood to argue with a demon-worshiping heretic.

"Instead, we praise Sigmund and his brother Fan for giving us our freedom and independence," Thenalious went on. "With them to guide us, we no longer cower beneath woman and her tyranny."

You needn't cower. Naleem raised his chin and settled in his chair. The boy's fanning eventually proved to be helpful in the summer heat that baked the inside of the tent, but it could not cool his growing temper. He would have to fan that himself.

"Of course, Haven's future rests in our young," Thenalious said, cutting another peach, "and they must be told stories of Sigmund and Fan. I know it will be challenging for you, but we can teach you those tales as well."

He took a bite of the slice and swallowed, letting the information rest where Naleem might consider it. When he said nothing, Naleem watched Thenalious grow impatient with a side glance at him.

"My offer stands," Thenalious told him. "Be our caregiver at least and watch over the children. You would do a far better job than the caregivers we have as it is. The council will protect you and your sons as if you were one of us. I'll tell you that councilhood is a high status here. You will be given a better life than most men in Haven."

To stay in this muck with the other captives meant the danger of being separated or killed at any moment. To take this job meant safety. A false sense of it, but safety.

Naleem absorbed this, taking a deep breath in and out of his nose. His eyes darted across the plates of food, a taste of the life Haven and Thenalious had to give. Holding Cadoc in his arms, he glanced at Dakarai, both of them fed and happier than they had been.

"I have a brother who Wyn moved to do different work today," Naleem said plainly.

Thenalious blinked before recognition took his expression, and he leaned back. "Ah, the young man who was with you last night. Of course, he can live in the great house as well. We could use a few kitchen boys."

An improvement from livestock. "All right. As long as everything you promise is given to us, I will do this work for you."

A grin played about Thenalious' face as his shoulders lifted. "Everything and more for you, son of Sigmund. More stubborn than I thought you would be."

Chapter 11

Bai

Resting at the table with his bandaged leg propped on a stool, Bai watched Adabelle clear the healer's tabletop and place books, candles, and papers where Banu directed her to. Pride swelled within him as Adabelle organized with no complaint. Her brown eyes sparkled beneath faint, raised brows, delighted to be of help while her mother and the healer prepared dinner. Wiping the surface with a rag, she caught her father's eye and gave him a cheerful beam.

Bai smiled back. "What a good girl you are. Helping Banu clean."

She nodded and assured him, "Supper will be ready soon, Papa."

"We'll see." Bai turned to view the work being done in the kitchen. His wife stirred the cauldron over the fire. The flames pulled the red color from Raegna's hair as it tumbled behind her round shoulders. With her back to him, she stood with her feet apart, her newly wrapped ankle showing under her skirt.

Raegna had never been the best cook, so when she offered to assist Banu with dinner, Bai groaned inwardly. What would Banu say when she tasted whatever Raegna arranged?

However, Banu supervised Raegna's preparation of their meal with her large fists on her hips and her thin, leather mouth wrung into a frown. When the old healer swatted Raegna's hand as she chopped vegetables, Bai bit his lip to keep from laughing.

"You want your babe to choke?" Banu snapped when Raegna gaped at the first blow. "Cut them smaller."

And then, "Gaea be good, girl. We want to crunch on these greens, not swallow them whole. That's what porridge is for. Don't let the pot boil like that!"

As much as Banu's chastising amused him, Bai kept himself in check. But he had to admit, Raegna was learning as Banu walked her through each ingredient. Soon enough, the old healer instructed Adabelle how to set the table while Raegna cooked.

Banu slapped a pile of cloth in front of Bai. "You can work, too. Fold these properly for our dining. You know how to do that?"

Bai picked one up. "Yes. My father taught me."

"Your father must have been a house-husband, not a worker," Banu thought aloud as she went to see Raegna's progress.

Bai did not answer. He folded the cloth as he remembered to do, with no intention of retelling any childhood memories to his wife and the healer. Adabelle took them and placed them beside each plate.

Peering over Raegna's shoulder and into the cauldron, Banu nodded. "Very good. Keep that meat from the bottom."

Raegna sighed in relief.

The front door opened, and every head turned to a warrior who shouldered her way in. Armor groaned over her movement as she halted and took in the healer's company. Bai studied her, his back straight as his chest squeezed. Had the Matriarch sent a warrior to take him for his quick tongue earlier?

Tight, black braids wove on all sides of the warrior's head. In her old age, wrinkles lined her rich brown skin under her large black eyes and at the corners of her plump lips. Muscles may have coursed under her arms once, but their mass was dissipating. Long, knobby fingers rested on her sword hilt as she shifted her weight.

"What have we here, Healer?" the warrior asked, scanning the family's faces. "I don't remember you mentioning we'd have company."

"You wouldn't even if I did." Banu crossed the room to her and gave the old warrior a kiss. "Femke brought them. They are survivors from Syden that needed attention."

The warrior cocked her head. "Survivors? Is this what the word around the village is?"

Banu gestured to each of her guests. "Meet Raegna, her husband, Bai, and their daughter, Adabelle. Everyone, this is my wife, Jora. She's an elder warrior and trains the green girls who dream of swords."

Bai jumped when Raegna nearly dropped her spoon into the cauldron. It skittered along the rim until she caught it and held it firm.

"It's always an honor to meet an elder," she stammered.

"The honor is mine." Jora unbuckled her belt and slipped two knives in their sheaths from it. She set them on the counter and wrapped the belt around her sword's scabbard, laying her blade beside Raegna's against the wall. "It seems you are a bit of a warrior yourself. If the rumor in the streets is true, you escaped an attack with this sword," she said, running her fingertips over the petaled pommel. "May I see it?"

"Er, of course." Raegna's cheeks flushed pink. The cauldron bubbled and spat behind her, so Banu came to its rescue, yanking the spoon from Raegna's grasp.

Jora plucked the sword off the wall and unsheathed it. The metal rang out of its scabbard, eliciting a sharp pang along with a blooming pride in Bai's chest. During their journey, he had resented that sword, knowing Raegna would use it on him. Yet, she slayed wolves with it to protect him. Now the elder warrior inspected the weapon with a gleam in her eye, a faint smile cracking on her face.

"She has seen more years than me." Jora tested its weight, flipping it in her hand. "Did you find it or buy it from someone?"

Raegna approached, her shoulders back but her voice low. "I've been told it was my grandmother's. My mother... she didn't appreciate the ways of being a warrior. She preferred I find my way in life elsewhere. It has sat in her house for years."

All of that sounded like Jaleesa. Though how her ancestors wielded swords, Bai wouldn't know. The word in Syden marked Raegna's mother as an uptight, prestigious woman, one who regarded a woman's ruling over her household and serving her Matriarch as the highest privilege. Such was her vision for Raegna as far as Bai understood.

It wasn't Raegna's calling.

Adabelle clinked a plate beside him and tore Bai from his thoughts.

Jora looked down the blade with narrowed eyes. "The stories this sword could tell. I'm certain it was used long before your grandmother. Just needs a little sharpening." She returned it to its scabbard. "Take good care of it to pass to the next generation."

She nodded to Adabelle, who paused her work to blink between the warrior and her mother. Raegna gave her a smile. "If she chooses."

"First, come finish what you've started, girl," Banu called over her shoulder. "Jora, love, wash up."

Jora and Raegna joined the healer in the kitchen, completing their instructed tasks. Jora dunked her hands into a water basin while Raegna stirred the cauldron.

"Banu," Raegna started, "could you tell me about your Matriarch? She was stoic when we met. What is she like?"

"Harsh." Banu leaned against the countertop and the wood creaked beneath her weight. "Other women of Judr cower at the sight of her. Matriarch Viona has a particular severeness toward men. She's been through two husbands. The first she had killed for giving her a son, who she cast aside as a bastard. The poor thing... The man she has now is her second and though she does not favor him for his looks, he's silent and has given her two daughters."

Jora drenched her face and shook her hands over the basin. Retrieving a cloth, she dried off. "Many consider her reign a blessing because they believe in a woman's iron rule."

Banu looked to Bai. "That is why I warn you to keep your wits about you and your head down. She would not take kindly to outbursts from a strange man."

Bai snorted in response.

"Husband," Raegna warned. "You will do as she says."

Hearing her address him, correcting him like a child instead of snapping at him, was enough to make him pause. Bai grimaced when his gut wrenched and looked away from her with a subtle nod. "Yes, wife."

Raegna glanced at him from the cauldron, her irises more brown than black. Rich with light, like Adabelle's. The darkness of them carried a shred of concern, but she gave her attention back to her work. Bai's chest fluttered as he continued folding the cloth.

"What of the youngest sister?" Raegna asked. "We've met Femke, and she's much like Viona, it seems."

"That is true." Banu inspected the stew with a knotted brow as Raegna stirred. "Well, the youngest is Iida, and she is the only sister to inherit her mother's kindness. Do not tell anyone I have told you this. I believe it's because she was just a babe when the late Matriarch found out her husband had been… harming her eldest daughters."

A shudder ran down Bai's spine. Raegna's stirring ceased before she looked at Banu, face slack with astonishment.

"Yes." Banu heaved a sorrowful sigh. "It's a sad thing that such a sick being ruined the future of our village. Of our Matriarch. Though she can be cruel, I think her trials have caused it. Surely she only means to protect her sisters and daughters. She cares for them."

"That she does," Jora agreed as she joined Bai at the table. "The harm dealt to them is something we will not tolerate from a man."

Bai's muscles grew taut. He gulped and shook himself back into reality and not the dark memory of that dim candlelit bedroom.

"Iida is the most tender of the three," Banu went on. "It's no surprise to me she has gained a husband faster than Femke, despite their age difference. He's a quiet one too. They have a babe on the way I am excited to bring to the world."

"That's good news," Raegna breathed.

Adabelle placed the last cloth Bai folded and stood away to admire her work. "Table's set!"

"A very good job, little one." Banu rose from the counter. "It seems supper is nearly done as well."

Raegna and the healer poured the stew into bowls and served it with roots and elk jerky. The five of them gave thanks to Gaea for the meal and ate.

After not having decent food in a few days, Bai slurped his bowl even when it burned his mouth and moved on to devour the rest. A full belly eased the gnawing ache the conversation left in his chest. He didn't glance at Raegna, who sipped from her spoon and picked at the jerky.

When dinner was over, Adabelle helped Banu clear the table again and Bai watched as the women cleaned. Jora excused herself to bathe. On a normal day, Bai would do the same, washing grime from working the fields. But normal days seemed far behind him and his family for now. They would have to pick up their daily lives here.

Here, of course, the Matriarch would be just as hateful toward men as any woman Bai ever met. He would hold his tongue for as long as he could, but what if he broke? As of late, his words betrayed him over and over, and he could not control them as he had before. What if a woman pushed him to the limit and he refused her commands? And what if she punished him? What could the women here be capable of if their Matriarch killed her husband for giving her a son?

He looked on as Banu ruffled Adabelle's hair beneath a meaty hand in praise for bringing the dishes to be washed. Raegna smiled at her with as much pride as Bai had. If anything happened to him, what would Adabelle do?

What would Raegna do?

Just two days ago, she would have begged Syden's Matriarch to rid her of him. But now, after all these years, she willingly spoke to him. Now and then she looked at him with worry. Not out of fear, but concern for him.

But that was absurd. She hated him for everything he had done to her, for the ball and chain he must be to her. Would she truly feel remorse should anything happen to him?

Banu and Jora showed the family to the barn behind their home where a mule slept in its stall and Raegna's mare rested on the opposite side. Beyond them, farming and riding equipment spread across the room, and hay piles and a tall bookshelf repurposed to nest a few chickens stood against the walls. The birds eyed their guests from their roosts but did not move.

Banu laid blankets over the hay. "I would have you sleep inside, but those sickbeds are for patients, and you don't want to know their stories. And in case of an emergency, I can't have the place crowded."

Jora and Raegna helped Bai onto a pile of hay and propped his leg on a pillow.

"Comfortable?" Raegna asked under her breath as she flattened the fabric underneath him.

Bai kept his sight on his leg as he adjusted it. "Yes... Thank you."

Raegna rose to her feet and went to thank the healer and the warrior for their hospitality. Bai slumped, his body at ease, as Adabelle sat beside him and nudged his arm.

"Does your leg hurt, Papa?" she asked.

"Hm. Only a little."

Adabelle lay at his side and snuggled into him, her small, round face pinching as she yawned. "That's good. I'm so tired, Papa."

He brushed a strand of blonde hair from her face. "Then sleep, sweet one."

It didn't take long. Adabelle fell fast asleep, her pink lips parted as she slumbered against him. Bai held her closer with a peck on the head. Then Raegna returned to the two of them in the hay.

For a moment, Bai feared she might separate them. Instead, her shoulders relaxed, and she shuffled to the blanket Banu laid for her close to Bai's. Raegna moved it to the other side of Adabelle. She lay across it and faced the little girl, closing her eyes. At least she would not turn her back to them.

Bai took a breath and kept his gaze on the barn's rafters and the chicken roosts as he stroked Adabelle's shoulder with a thumb. "Raegna."

She hesitated. "...Yes."

"What do you think of this place after everything Banu told us?" he asked. "Will we stay?"

Raegna's nose and eyelids scrunched. Folding her arm, she rested her head on her elbow like a pillow. "Do we have anywhere else to go?"

"Are you not worried about the Matriarch and her sisters?"

Her eyes flitted open, trained on Adabelle, and she seemed to absorb the very shape of her daughter as she slept. "Nothing will happen so long as you do what Banu has said. No matter where we go, some women are not kind. You are already wounded because... because of my ignorance. I won't have you harmed by this Matriarch."

What did she say? This time, Bai could not control himself. He chuckled. "You admit you were ignorant? I thought I would never hear such words come from you."

Raegna scowled and stiffened. "Be quiet or you will not hear any words for an eternity."

He withdrew his laughter in a wry smirk. "I'm sorry. I understand, and I will do my best to be obedient. As much as it torments me."

A huff of air escaped Raegna's nose, her face serene. "Perhaps we have been too tolerant of you men in Syden. Not that this Matriarch's ways are justifiable. Our Matriarch was firm, but she still cared for her husband and children."

"As you do," Bai said. He didn't know what reaction to expect from that remark and watched her closely. Raegna curled in on herself like a snake coiling, ready for defense, her gaze shifting. Bai gulped. "What I mean is, you've been... firm as well, but it feels as if you truly, um, mean well."

When she spoke, Raegna's voice came in a whisper. "You think... you believe I mean well?"

"...If I were honest," Bai started, "I would say I have been waiting for you to poison the food you serve me, but you haven't. If I weren't honest, it's been a delight to be married to you."

This time, she scoffed, the corners of her mouth curling up. Even her shoulders relaxed, and she stretched over the hay, releasing the tension in her back.

"But I know after what happened," Bai continued, "I deserve much worse. Perhaps I deserve to be murdered by this Matriarch."

She did not move an inch. "No... You were right. Adabelle would be heartbroken."

Adabelle. Bai peered at their daughter, asleep with her head on his chest, with little care in the world. Her eyelids flitted as she dreamed. Adabelle, the only beautiful thing to come from their marriage...

"You keep me alive for her... That didn't matter before."

Raegna swallowed hard. "I have tried to prevent it—her finding you. *Knowing* you. But she did and... fell for you. Though I detest it, you are precious to her. So, I will do my best to protect both of you. As much as that torments *me.*"

"Hm." Bai's smirk remained, the fluttering in his belly nearly painful. She actually made a joke with him. "Well, though we were forced together, it seems we at least have one thing in common."

"And what is that?"

"We both love Ada."

This time, he permitted himself to look at her as she wriggled in the hay to make herself comfortable. Raegna's black lashes lowered and touched soft, ivory cheekbones, concealing the warm brown irises. She inhaled deep and breathed out. "That much is true, I suppose."

This had to be the most incredible moment of his life. Raegna speaking to him and not in a closed-off way. She meant every word she said, and none of them intended to insult or threaten him. Maybe this was the time to speak genuinely...

"Raegna?"

Her face twitched on the cusp of sleep. "Hm?"

Bai clutched the blanket beneath him into a fist. "Just know that... That I am sorry for the pain I caused you, I truly am. And I will never harm you again. You never have to be afraid."

He craned his ears to listen to what she would have to say, his stomach tying in knots. Would she ever forgive him or give a sign that she had? When she lay silent, he thought she had fallen asleep before he could get his message across.

"Go to sleep, husband," she murmured, causing him to jump.

Bai glanced up at the ceiling, his chest constricting and opening on the terrible and conflicting verge of solace. His eyelids grew heavy, though thoughts filled his head with what her reply meant and what he might say next.

His body forced a yawn, and he said, "Goodnight, Raegna."

Bai was certain now she would be asleep, but Raegna whispered a final, "Goodnight."

Chapter 12

Hadwin

Hadwin poured rotting vegetables, broth, and some of last night's scraps into the pigs' trough from a bucket. The spongy greens oozed into the wood and the pigs rushed in to consume every morsel. They grunted and squealed, so Hadwin gave them room.

Working with the animals was like his work in Syden when the livestock needed extra tending, though different men and boys completed tasks all around him, not the familiar faces and voices he had grown up with. The surviving men were scattered across the campground. Hadwin spotted a few here and there, like Bjarni, who was first in line to be examined by Wyn upon their arrival to Haven. His young son scampered behind him as he fed and watered the horses. If only Dakarai was so obedient.

The barn rafters creaked over the snorting and braying of animals and the barking orders of men. With splintery beams and rust-coated nails sticking out of stall doors and pens, how the structure supported itself, Hadwin did not know. The barn harbored many animals to feed and serve every man in Haven. Hadwin still could not tell how many men. At least two or three hundred, after all those he saw bustling through tent-strewn paths and congregating in the dining hall.

The rickety barn held livestock to be slaughtered or produce milk. It sheltered cows in stalls and pens to one side with a bull to give them calves. Hadwin had to muck out their stalls later that day. They kept goats in a herd of thirty, including the kids that frolicked about their mothers. Two rams glared at passing men, their horns curving over their heads like crescent moons.

And, of course, the pigs that Hadwin fed lived in a pen at the front of the barn. Another smaller pen enclosed a sow and her piglets, over whom he stood to offer the last of the scraps. The sow snorted and lapped her dinner straight out of the bucket before she rolled and let her piglets suckle. Some of them skittered about instead, chasing each other with their curled tails wagging. Their inability to sit still reminded him of Dakarai again, and he smiled, then frowned in worry.

As he went to clean the bucket, Hadwin wondered how Naleem was doing, toiling over laundry by himself. Surely, Dakarai would do his best to help or at least stay out of trouble, and Cadoc would nap in the sling. The thought of them tugged at Hadwin's heart, though they were just across the camp. He prayed Naleem could care for the boys on his own. The prospect of what these brutes would do to abandoned children was unbearable to consider.

"You!"

Hadwin jumped as the booming voice ripped him from his thoughts. He faced Fritjof, the overseer of the barn and the animals, a very tall and large man with deep umber skin, long black hair braided down his back, and a great gray-streaked beard. Marching up to him, Fritjof kept a stony glare on Hadwin until he stood over him, his shoulders squared.

"You will work in the great house from now on, starting tomorrow," Fritjof told him. "Council's orders."

"Oh," Hadwin squeaked, grimacing. He would rather stand in front of the bull in his pen than this man made of bulk muscle. "What does that mean?"

"Ack!" Fritjof threw his wide hands in the air. "It means come tomorrow; you are not my problem."

For the rest of the day, Hadwin wrestled with the suspicion over yet another switch in occupation. What had he done to place him in the great house? How often did work change around here? Would he be closer to Naleem and the boys in this position?

All these questions and more swirled in his mind, distracting him enough to not see the oncoming bite of a cow he bothered as he cleaned her pen. The supper horn blared, and the men ceased their work to eat.

Plodding alongside the mass that headed into the dining hall, Hadwin knew where to find Naleem as soon as he entered the doors. The thick scent of sweat and cooked meat hung over the hall's great tables with the clamor of chatter and laughter. Standing on tiptoes, Hadwin found the place he and Naleem had chosen the night before, surprised when his brother was not there.

Hadwin claimed the seats and waited, though Naleem should already be present, as the laundry tent was closer to the great house than the barn. He searched the throng. It was not Naleem who arrived, but Wyn, looking as giddy and wiry as ever.

Wyn's yellow teeth stuck out in his crooked grin. "You've been invited to the council's table up front. Yer husband waits for you."

Hadwin frowned. "We're not—"

Before he could finish, Wyn snickered and disappeared into the crowd. Hadwin sighed and followed him. How could Naleem be at the head of the hall? Was he in some kind of trouble? Perhaps the men had punished him for last night's brawl by making a show of him, presenting him on a platter like a roast pig.

Hadwin picked up his pace and pushed through bodies. When he came upon the table, Naleem sat among the councilmen with Cadoc in his arms and Dakarai to his left, digging into tonight's feast.

"Uncle Hadwin!" the boy cried out with his mouth full. Naleem turned and met his brother's eyes, his face blank while Cadoc laughed in recognition of his uncle.

At least they were safe. Hadwin heaved a sigh, his entire being able to relax in his family's presence, and made his way to take Dakarai into his lap. Then he noticed Thenalious sitting beside Naleem, talking with other councilmen and then laughing.

Hadwin took his seat and bundled Dakarai in his grasp. He searched Naleem's face for some kind of explanation for this change. Naleem gave him a sideways glance, his brown eyes sparking like embers with a look that meant, *I'll tell you later.*

The plan must have been to act naturally. Hadwin hugged Dakarai as he ate. "How was your day, nephew?"

"Fine," Dakarai answered, still gorging himself. "We got to have lunch with Thenalious and play with the other children upstairs."

Hadwin raised an eyebrow at Naleem. A flat mouth and crinkled eyes promised a future discussion and nothing more.

"Well, that sounds... fun," Hadwin managed with a stiff shrug.

Thenalious shifted his weight over to Naleem, whose posture tightened. "How is the food?"

"All right," Naleem grumbled.

"I almost don't have to ask," Thenalious teased with a sly grin morphing his beard. "Your sons might devour every ham served tonight."

Dakarai always had a mind to eat something, but even Cadoc ate better than he had recently, gobbling every bite Naleem cut up for him. Naleem did not look at Thenalious when he said, "I'll be sure they don't."

"It's no trouble," Thenalious replied. "They will need it to grow strong." His bright hazel eyes landed on Hadwin, who had been staring in shock. "This is your brother?"

Naleem nodded.

"I'm Hadwin," he greeted and did his best to be polite. Perhaps then Thenalious would not be inclined to behead him.

"A pleasure," Thenalious said. He seemed a completely different man than the one who had ordered the destruction of Syden.

Hadwin's heart grew heavy, and he closed himself off, focusing only on Dakarai's movement in his lap. Why on Jorde were they dining next to this monster? What had Naleem done to earn this place beside Thenalious? How much did it hurt him to be this close to him?

Hadwin studied his brother and picked up on every little detail he had learned since they were children. Naleem's broad face was stern, and his lips curved in a tight frown. He curled over Cadoc as if those around him may leap up and attack at any moment. Hadwin thought perhaps that might be true.

The brothers ate in silence and kept a vigilant watch on those at the council table. The councilmen talked and joked among themselves and feasted as the average men in Haven did, tearing into the meat and gulping wine.

"What is it about good wine that makes food and company even more delectable?" Thenalious pondered aloud. He took a drink, his sights settling on Naleem past the rim of his goblet. "How do you like your wine, son of Sigmund? Sweet? Or bitter?"

Hadwin's nails sank into his palms in front of Dakarai. The way the man's head tilted implied the beginnings of drunkenness and his words seemed to imply a far different subject than wine.

Naleem dragged out his words in an irritable sigh. "I don't drink."

"You ought to. Might allow you to loosen up this evening. Have some fun."

If Hadwin did not know any better, he might peg the councilman's behavior as flirtatious with his eyes brightening with mischief upon Naleem. And all these jokes and comments were like an adolescent trying to woo a potential partner, but that . . . Hadwin tried to convince himself it could not be.

Whatever it was, Naleem did not fall for it and stayed silent throughout the entire feast. When half the hall left in full-to-bursting drunken stupors, Naleem and Hadwin excused themselves from the table. Most of the councilmen laughed with mugs and drinking horns in hand.

"So soon, son of Sigmund?" Thenalious asked, reaching to grab Naleem's wrist.

Naleem jerked away. "Yes. The children will need to sleep."

Thenalious gave a warm smile. "Of course. Do as you must."

On quick, light feet, Naleem led Hadwin and the boys to the other end of the dining hall. They passed through a hallway lit by candles and torches of bull horns and stag antlers.

The hallway transitioned into a main room with rugged couches, chairs, and a fireplace. There were doors on either side of the walls, lined in rows. A staircase ascended to the second floor.

"Naleem," Hadwin started once he was sure they were alone.

"Hush!" Naleem hissed and gathered Cadoc in one arm.

A man exited a door, tall with hard muscle weaving its way beneath his freckled, pink skin. A thick, rust-colored beard hid his lips, touching the top of his chest. Ruddy red hair fell past his shoulders even with most of it tied up in braids. By a black shirt hemmed in silver and a wide belt and buckle with crossed axes etched into it, Hadwin thought the man to be a councilman.

The man spotted them and let a long, glowering look settle on Naleem as he passed. The thudding of his boots drummed across the hollow floor. Naleem kept his eyes down.

As soon as the beast moved on, disappearing through the entry, Naleem continued and hurried Hadwin and Dakarai along.

"Who was that?" Hadwin urged. "Do you know him?"

"Hardly," Naleem whispered back. "I know his name is Reynold. Thenalious introduced me to every councilman in Haven."

Hadwin faltered behind him as they conquered the stairs, the wood creaking beneath their weight. Dakarai wanted to take the steps slowly to prevent a fall, but Hadwin hauled him up as quickly as possible to keep up with Naleem's pace.

"Why? Why are you here? Why were you sitting with Thenalious? Why was he acting so strange?"

"I wish I knew," Naleem said at the top of the staircase.

On the second floor, a hallway split in two directions. Each had doors on either side of the hall, though these were grander than the lackluster ones downstairs. Small carvings of ancient Galaenian runes climbed up the decorative panels. Sconces made of horns were lit by a red, ghostly fire on the walls.

"Is this where they sleep?" Hadwin asked.

"These are the councilmen's quarters, yes." Naleem tapped the first door on the left. "That is our new room."

Hadwin glimpsed the door before Naleem stopped in front of the second.

"This is where they keep their children." He pushed the door with a soft creak for Hadwin to peer in.

It was dark as pitch, but faint breaths came from the outlines of tiny beds arranged in rows alongside the walls. In a corner, the curving wood cradles sat still. His insides constricted, Hadwin withdrew, and Naleem clicked the door closed.

"They have children?" Hadwin asked. "How are they able to do that?"

"Papa, I'm tired," Dakarai complained at his side. Hadwin scooped him up and hefted him in his arms as Naleem went to the first room.

Inside, the room was simple, with four walls and two beds on either side. A small nightstand sat between them. Hadwin entered with his family and shut the door behind them.

"This is where we live now," Naleem told him.

Hadwin turned to him. "How—"

Naleem settled an already sleeping Cadoc on the right bed. "Let's put them to sleep."

"Do we get to stay here all the time, Papa?" Dakarai asked as Hadwin laid him down.

"We have work to do in the morning." Naleem tucked them both in. "Get some rest, son."

"We get to sleep here all the time?" Dakarai persisted. "Every night?"

"For a while." Naleem kissed his forehead. "Rest now. Goodnight."

Dakarai yawned beside his little brother. "Goodnight, Papa."

It was not long before he slipped into sleep. With the two of them resting, Hadwin could finally learn the truth. He sat on the opposite bed and rubbed his temples. "I don't understand what's going on, Naleem. How did you get yourself into the great house?"

Naleem slumped over the edge of the bed, smoothing out the blankets covering his sons. "I honestly don't know... We were just minding our own business when Thenalious came to us and invited us to his tent. He offered me a job as a caregiver to the councilmen's sons. We made an agreement that I would if you worked here as well."

"Ah," Hadwin grunted, recalling his encounter with Fritjof. "I am to be a kitchen boy."

"I suppose it is better than our original work," Naleem admitted with a sigh. "But I feel Thenalious has a different intent for this. He says they have caregivers, but they are not much help to the children. He thinks I can straighten them out."

"Well, how on Jorde do they have children?" Hadwin wondered aloud. "I haven't seen a woman walk this camp."

"I don't think I want to know the answer to that." Naleem cast his eyes to the floor. "In any case, they need care. Thenalious said that since I've been able to keep Dak and Cadoc alive, I was the one for the job."

Hadwin kicked off his shoes and brought his knees to his chest, wrapping his arms around his legs. "What is Thenalious doing anyway? He was trying to be friendly to you all evening."

"It's been that way all day," Naleem complained. "He's shown me around and introduced me to the councilmen so that I know who fathered which boy and so they know who is in charge of their keep."

"And that brute who gave you dagger eyes just now is one of them?"

"Yes." Naleem rubbed the nape of his neck. "He does not seem to like me. Not that I truly care if he does or not. But of all the men here, I prefer to be on the neutral side of that beast. Thenalious said he has two in the bunch and another on the way. Whatever that means."

"Do they steal orphans?" Hadwin asked. "Or do they claim our sons when they're left behind, is that it?"

"I've no idea."

"Wyn's a councilman." Hadwin's brow furrowed. "Do you think any of those children belong to that weasel?"

Naleem shrugged. "These children are innocent in this, as our boys are. As much as I loathe Thenalious and all these animals, I suppose caring for the little ones is a better, nobler option than washing their laundry."

"Speak for yourself." Hadwin jabbed a thumb into his chest. "I have to serve them food and drink and clean up after them." Then he straightened and held a palm up, balancing an invisible platter. "'Here is your ale, my councilman. It may or may not actually be horse piss I made especially for you.'"

Hadwin blinked as Naleem chuckled. It felt like ages since he last witnessed his brother smile.

"If you are successful in that, let me know," Naleem said with a smirk. "But for now, keep a low profile. These men are dangerous, and I don't trust Thenalious for a second, but he insists on making friendly advances. And we must protect the boys..."

Hadwin followed his gaze to Dakarai and Cadoc slumbering on the bed. His heart softened, and he set his shoulders back. "Of course."

Naleem sighed again. "Hadwin, I can't tell you how glad I am that we're together again. That you're all right."

"I've been worried about you three, too." Hadwin offered an encouraging grin. "Rest assured, brother, I'm here. We're still a family."

"Even so…" Naleem's words drifted, and his sight fixed on the boys. His heavy eyelids filled with sorrow so deep that an ache burst in Hadwin's lungs when he finally looked up. "There's more to do tomorrow. Goodnight, Had."

Hadwin watched him lie beside his sons before preparing himself for bed as well. "Goodnight. Sleep well."

As he rested his head against his pillow, Hadwin looked across the room to watch over his brother and nephews in their slumber before closing his eyes. Frost coated his blood at the very thought of losing his family, but he drew a breath and shoved the cold of it away. Naleem had suffered so much pain. Hadwin wanted to take it from him and use it and his own wrath to fight for him and the boys.

To soothe himself, he imagined falling asleep in Pinar's home with his entire family breathing around him in sleep. In the morning, he would wake to the playful wrestling of his niece and nephews. They would eat breakfast before he and Naleem headed for the field.

Hadwin's throat closed as he remembered his kind sister-in-law and two precious young nieces, all three of them torn from their lives forever. Naleem without his beloved wife and daughters. The boys without their adoring mother and sisters. Tears swelled behind Hadwin's eyelids. He shut them tight, allowing them to spill over the bridge of his nose, biting his lip to prevent a sob.

All-Mother Gaea, protect us now in this darkness.

Chapter 13
Raegna

A POUNDING IN HER hip woke Raegna, and she groaned, cursing the hay and wooden floorboards. She sat up to behold Adabelle pulling on Bai's arm as he dozed on his side.

"Come on, Papa!" the little girl urged, her small feet scraping the floor as she pulled with all her might. The tattered skirts of her dress swayed with her effort. "Banu has breakfast ready!"

"Breakfast?" Bai grumbled and shifted his weight to sit up. He winced as he moved his bandaged leg.

"Adabelle," Raegna warned. Her daughter looked at her as she rose and stretched. "Let him get up at his own pace. His leg hurts, remember?"

"Oh." Adabelle dropped his arm. "I'm sorry, Papa."

"No trouble, sweetling." Bai hobbled to his feet and balanced upright with a little help. He crinkled his nose and towered over Adabelle, tickling her cheek. "Now let's go eat."

Together, the family emerged from the barn. Bai and Raegna limped on their bad legs while Adabelle bounded ahead of them. Raegna rubbed her eyes and rolled her shoulders, envious of her daughter's energy.

They entered the house through the back door. The walls filled with the warm, sharp scent of oil and bread. With a pan over the fire, Banu fried round pieces of dough until they were golden, then placed them on a plate with a jar of honey beside it. Raegna's stomach rumbled at the sight of the crisp morsels. She couldn't recall the last time she had such a good, sweet breakfast.

Jora sat at the table in a leather breastplate, sharpening a knife. Three braids lined each side of her head. Her attention rose to the family as they entered. Her brown skin glowed in the sunlight and a line creased at the corner of her quirked mouth. "Our guests made it through the night."

Banu turned, her gray hair loose from any braids and hanging down to the middle of her wide back. A forest-green dress hugged her stout body with a leather belt around her waist. Lines deepened in her copper-toned face as she smiled at the three. "Good morning, all. Sleep well?"

"As I ever have," Bai answered, twisting before sitting down.

"Well, you'll thank us once you hear the stories of each healing bed." Jora ran her knife along the stone once more.

Banu brought a full plate and frowned at her. "Must you do that at the table? The rest of you, come and eat while it's hot."

Bai scarfed at least ten pieces of bread, and Adabelle hiccupped after just one. Raegna ate in as ladylike a fashion as she could with the finger food smothered in thick honey. This breakfast was more like a child's meal, truly, meant for stubby hands to pluck and inhale as Bai did. His lips were coated with the sweet stuff, much like a little boy's would be.

He licked his fingers, catching her gaze on him. Honey trailed down his chin and glistened on his hollowed cheeks. "What?"

Raegna grimaced, flipping a lock of hair, and averted her stare. "Clean yourself up. You eat like a pig."

Banu tossed a wet rag to him with a reminiscent smile. "I forgot what it was like to feed a man. Bottomless pits, you are."

"Need it for strength," Bai said with his chest out and washed his face. "Can't plow fields on an empty stomach."

"Hm. My mother said that was all we needed to keep our men obedient and at our sides, good food in their bellies." Banu glanced at her wife, who gulped the last of her breakfast. "It works on other women too, though."

"Strength in the field is enough," Raegna added. She finished her breakfast and leaned forward with her elbows on the edge of the table. "Today, we'll see if we can't get you set up with the laborer."

"With my leg like this?" Bai gestured to his bandage where a blood stain spread along his calf.

"That will need new bandages." Banu rose from her chair. "As well as time to air out."

Raegna closed her eyes and stood to clear the table. "Men are meant to work. Your leg will heal and when it does, you must make your contribution to me and this village."

"I thought we wouldn't stay long," Bai said.

Banu dunked the dishes in a tub of water and Jora halted mid-rise from the table. "You aren't?"

"No," Raegna corrected, turning on him. "I said, no matter where we go, there would be cruel women and we can't help that. You are safe if you do as you're told. You claimed you understood."

Bai frowned. "I suppose I did..."

His voice drifted with nothing else to say, his head down, though Raegna expected a quick remark or disdainful mumbling. Such was his newfound behavior as of late. Instead, he allowed Banu to replace his bandages. Jora buckled the rest of her armor while Raegna and Adabelle cleaned the kitchen.

Their conversation from the night before in the barn replayed in her memory, and she could not push it away. That he truly believed she meant well for him. That she was doing him some sort of service despite what he put her through, and how sorry he made himself sound fueled a hot fire in her veins.

No, you fool, she thought. *None of it is for you, but for her.*

The original plan to get rid of him was ruined and Raegna couldn't face turning him away. After striking him in the forest, she should have sent him off like releasing a dog into the wilderness. But the strike had frightened Adabelle and left her more disappointed and furious with Raegna than she knew a child so young was capable of.

Bai had been right when they spoke in Syden. If Raegna released him and made him leave, Adabelle would never forgive her. In a village surrounded by friends, neighbors, warriors, and a little house of her own, controlling the situation would have been much easier. But Syden was gone and Judr was far from familiar.

Raegna stole a glimpse of Adabelle drying the wet dishes she handed her, sitting in a chair and kicking her legs out. So young and carefree...

With a sigh, Raegna gave her a small, helpless grin. "Did you sleep well last night, sweetling?"

Adabelle nodded. "Yes, Mama. I had such a good dream that we picked flowers and had ponies to ride, and we went to the river and fished with Papa."

"...That is your good dream." Raegna's heart wrenched, and she let out a staggered breath. That was all her daughter wanted, her parents as she knew them: protective, nurturing, and together. What darkness she could not understand. What terrible truths Raegna had to keep from her to safeguard her innocence.

She and Bai both.

"Papa can take us fishing here, can't he?" Adabelle asked.

"The River Sachi is just through the woods," Banu told her as she wiped Bai's wound and prepared new bandages. "Plenty of fish there. Not too many men go without supervision, but when permitted by wives, they may cast a reel."

"They need their wife's permission to fish?" Bai blurted.

Jora bent over in a chair, tying her boots. "It is the Matriarch's law. Mainly to keep husbands and sons from fleeing Judr."

"Can't imagine why they would do that," Bai muttered, leaning back with his arms folded.

"Could we go fishing, Papa?" Adabelle asked.

"You heard Banu. We need your mother's permission."

Raegna broke from her thoughts as she finished the dishes and she turned to face him at the table. "There are better occupations to gain, and farming is one of them. We will start there this morning."

"Of course, wife," Bai agreed with an obedient nod.

"You all best move on then," Jora told them as she rose from her chair. "The Lady of Labor should already have the men in the fields. You'll talk to her."

Banu grinned at Adabelle. "If you do not want to endure the adults talking about work, you may stay with me, little one. If your mother doesn't mind."

Adabelle hesitated to answer and looked at her mother. Raegna gave her a warm smile and brushed the backs of her fingers over her cheek. "You can stay, sweetheart."

Adabelle studied her father as Bai stretched his leg under new bandages, then winced when he pushed his muscles too far.

"I'll help Papa walk," Adabelle announced, with her head high. Raegna sighed in defeat but allowed the little girl to aid Bai to his feet and guide him to the front door.

The sunlight toasted the ground by the time the family left the healer's house and the heat warmed Raegna's skin. At least a quiet wind that rattled the beads and flapped the furs on Banu's porch could cool them off. As Raegna and Adabelle helped Bai down the rickety steps, a few young boys raced by, pursued by a group of laughing girls who kicked up the dirt. Adabelle watched with a hint of longing in her eyes, and Bai ruffled her hair.

Jora brushed past them, her sword clinking at her side. "Good luck, all. Banu serves supper before sundown."

They watched her go before Raegna urged them down the road. "Come along. I'm sure the fields are this way."

Walking was slow going, with Bai limping and Adabelle's help. The other women of Judr who were in the midst of their routine paused when the small family passed. Raegna kept her shoulders back. When her eyes met another's, she would give a curt nod and smile before looking away.

Judr was more spacious than Syden, with houses spread out and a dainty marketplace in front of the great house. There seemed to be only a few vegetable tents, a blacksmith, a butcher, and a fur house. But no bakery or ink house, no dress or incense shops. Few women appeared to run independent businesses from their homes, as Pinar did with her flowers and blanket weaving. What was it that made Judr so poor compared to Syden?

"Priestess!" a cheerful voice spoke up.

Raegna jumped as she realized the voice came from the great house that overlooked the market. Bai and Adabelle halted behind her while she turned to see if she had somehow angered the Matriarch for even *thinking* her village was poor.

Yet it was not Matriarch Viona who sat in a rocking chair on the porch, but her youngest sister, Iida. She stood, balancing with a hand on an armrest and the other under her belly. From the shadows, a man leaning against the wall stepped forward. He reached to aid her.

"Oh, Asmund, I'm all right," Iida told him and looked to Raegna. "You're the priestess from Syden."

Raegna stammered. "Y-yes, my lady."

Iida waved the three of them closer. "Come, I'd like to speak with you."

Hesitant, Raegna approached with Bai and Adabelle in tow and stopped at the steps. Iida wore a plain blue dress that complemented her pale ashwood complexion. Without a braid to bind it, her brunette hair rolled in curls. Her smile brightened her round features, and her dark brown irises sparkled.

The man, Asmund she called him, who stood against the porch wall, was lanky, with light fawn skin and little muscle on his arms and shoulders. At least, no muscle like Bai. He may not have done any hard labor in his life. His mouse-brown hair stopped under his ears. He might be handsome if Raegna could see his face, but Asmund kept his chin tilted down.

Iida had both hands around her protruding belly. The babe could likely come any day, reminding Raegna of faint memories of pregnancy. "Forgive us. I don't believe my sisters offered you a proper welcome."

"Oh," Raegna breathed. "Well... your healer and her wife are most generous. They were kind to give us a place to stay and meals to eat."

"Banu and Jora have kind souls," Iida agreed. "I've known them all my life. I'm glad you are taken care of. How is your husband? You said he had an injury."

Raegna exchanged a look with Bai. He batted his eyelashes, being the docile husband she told him to be. Almost as docile as Asmund standing behind Iida.

"Yes. He's doing well, thank you. Banu saw to his wounds, and he will heal. We are looking for work for him."

"So soon?" Iida cocked her head. "Wouldn't you want him to rest?"

A quiet *humph* came from Bai's nose. Raegna forced herself to keep a pleasant expression while repressing a growl. "My husband is strong. Plenty of crippled men still tend the field. He can do the same. It is the least we can do for our new village and Matriarch."

Iida's bright disposition fell like a small raincloud blocked the sun. "I know my sisters can be... intimidating, but please, feel no urge to work your wounded husband. He'll need rest."

"Rest spoils a man." Raegna repeated the phrase her mother used to say. "His purpose is in the field, the barn, fishing along the river, whatever my Matriarch will bid me."

"...If he must work, make him a house-husband for now," Iida suggested. "I wish our house required some help, but my sisters already have servants and they prefer them to be female."

"Don't worry," Raegna assured her. "He's strong and obedient, we'll find something."

Iida nodded while she looked at Bai and Adabelle. "Such a sweet face your daughter has. Gaea has surely blessed her with such beauty."

That brought a proud smile to Raegna's lips as she followed Iida's sight to her daughter. "Thank you, my lady." She opened her palm and revealed her scar. "Perhaps my next act as a priestess will be to pray your child is blessed as well."

Iida beamed. "I would like to have a woman of Gaea by my side while I have this child. Both of us would, right, Asmund?"

Asmund glanced up, revealing blue eyes like the clear sky, and looked between the two women. He dipped his head again, nodding swiftly. What sort of woman did it take to break a man like this, Raegna wondered. This young man was no different from a beaten hound. It could not have been Iida's doing, what with her genuine, charming friendliness.

"Um, of course." Raegna blinked and shifted her weight off her aching ankle. "...Exactly what for, my lady?"

This time, Iida paused and her brown eyes darted about, matching her husband's. "For... guidance is all. And good luck. It will be nice to have an experienced mother with me."

Raegna shrugged. "If you wish, my lady. I would be happy to."

"Oh, please," Iida said, beaming. "Call me Iida. We'll be friends soon, I know it!"

"Very well, Iida." Raegna turned to lead Bai and Adabelle on. "We should be off, but I can meet you again here tomorrow morning."

Iida waved. "Until then!"

The dirt crunched beneath their feet as they walked, though Bai's footsteps were out of rhythm with his limping.

"Banu was right, she seemed kind," he spoke up behind Raegna. "Not at all like her sisters."

"I agree." Raegna did not look over her shoulder to speak to him. "Her friendship will be good here."

***

The fields stretched beyond the great house and outskirt homes of less fortunate families, which were mere shacks with withering wood walls and thatch roofs. Even the fields were small and frail. Men walked the lines and pulled weeds and dead crops from the soil.

Raegna scanned the field. There was no drought in Sorelle. It had rained on the way here. So, what caused Judr to have so little produce with so much room to grow and men to tend to it?

On the far side, sitting atop a large, gray horse, was the Lady of Labor. It was her job to record occupations and productions in Judr for her Matriarch. It surprised Raegna that she placed herself as overseer without the assistance of women under her command. A true Lady of Labor would have more important duties.

She was the woman to speak to in order to get Bai working again. Raegna nodded in her direction and motioned Bai and Adabelle to follow.

As the family approached, the woman glanced their way. After a double take, her blotchy, red face scrunched up. "Good day."

"Good day, my lady," Raegna greeted as politely as she could. Up close, the heavy-set woman had broad shoulders and arms. Raegna could have been only half her size. "I am Raegna, and this is my husband, Bai."

"You are the priestess who was banished from her village, aren't you?" the Lady interrupted.

Raegna's jaw set. "Syden was attacked."

"Yes, by a horde of men with weapons and shields." The woman snorted on laughter. "Sounds to me like you didn't have your men reined in over in our sister village. Discipline and assertion are all you need. Discipline and assertion."

"Yes, well, I've come to see if you will have my husband work." Raegna switched the subject quickly. "I would like to make my contribution to Judr."

The Lady peered at her and then at Bai, who jolted at her sharp-eyed gaze.

"We'll see," she said and dismounted.

Raegna noted the whip at her belt as its nine tails swung from her hip. She also carried a sword, though Raegna was unsure why she needed to be so heavily equipped when the men were defenseless.

The Lady stepped up to Bai, nearly as tall as him. Bai pushed Adabelle behind him under his cloak and stood straight with daring eyes. Not the eyes to show a lethal Lady of Labor. Raegna chewed on the inside of her cheek.

The woman took his chin in her hand, prying his jaw open. The jarring movement caused Bai to jump and pull away.

"Hm," the woman grunted and grabbed his wrist, feeling his forearm and bicep. She shoved his chest. Bai stumbled back, landing on his bad leg.

He gritted his teeth and winced, hissing as he inhaled. The Lady lifted an eyebrow. "He's lame."

"He was injured on our way here," Raegna explained. "Your healer says he will heal in time."

"Time is not something I have." The woman returned to her horse. "He's no use to me. I won't have him."

Raegna gaped at her. "But he's strong as a mule. He worked in our village."

"We have different requirements here." The Lady of Labor mounted the horse and rested in the saddle. "This one is worth less than a sick lamb to me."

Raegna searched for what this woman saw in him. Glowering, Bai's eyes sharpened like daggers on the woman atop her horse and his jaw clenched tight.

"Very well." Raegna took Bai by the crook of his arm and hauled him and Adabelle away. "Thank you for your time."

As soon as they were a safe distance, Bai could open his mouth. "Worth less than a sick lamb! I'll show her a sick lamb, that uptight, wretched cow!"

"Papa, that's not nice," Adabelle scolded with her brow furrowed.

"Try to keep your voice down," Raegna snapped at him, cringing over the ache in her ankle as she rushed them. "I agree she was... abrasive, but we must find you work to keep you out of trouble and away from the Matriarch."

Bai lowered his head and kept pace with her, grumbling under his breath.

There was not much to choose from in this poor village. Women who required work from a man already had husbands, sons, or brothers. Raegna had asked the butcher, blacksmith, even warriors. No one would have Bai because they had men, he wasn't physically fit or...

"Why would you present me a man with Fan's eyes?" the blacksmith snarled. "Better yet, why would your mother present you such a husband?"

"Fan's eyes?" Raegna repeated.

"There's a scar on your hand," the blacksmith noted as she dunked a hot nail into a bucket of water. "Aren't you a priestess? Surely, you of all people would refuse a husband with such obvious signs of corruption. I remember my scripture well enough to know the evil one has 'eyes gold like coins, for the lust and desire that gleamed in his irises.' Your man is no different."

Again, Raegna pulled Bai away before he could erupt in the blacksmith's face.

The family trod down the main street while the sun set in the west. Raegna carried Adabelle in her arms. The girl's slumbering weight added to the pain in Raegna's ankle. Bai limped behind them.

"It's no use, Raegna," he grumbled. "Maybe Banu will have me do something."

"No, healers don't need men." Raegna hefted Adabelle higher. "Besides, she would have to teach you medicine and that isn't a man's job."

"You don't think I can learn medicine?" Bai challenged.

"Can you read?"

"...No." He lifted his head. "But I could learn that too."

Raegna shook her head. Reading gave men ideas and knowledge, which could lead to insubordination. Bai had enough of that without knowing how to read. There had never been a male healer and never would be. Banu should agree with that as well.

"I am tired of being degraded all day, though," Bai spoke up as they walked. "Could we call this off? Perhaps Iida can find me something tomorrow when we meet her again."

Raegna stopped in her tracks and spun to face him, bracing Adabelle against her. "No, no, no, you are not meeting her and her sisters tomorrow. I am. You will just have to stay with Banu and Ada until I return, and then we will look some more."

"But Iida should know of every woman in Judr," Bai protested. "She might tell us who requires help."

"Then I will ask her tomorrow." Raegna headed for Banu's house. "I cannot risk putting you in front of that Matriarch again. Not after I had to excuse ourselves from every woman you nearly barked at today."

"I wouldn't have to bark if they did not first," Bai complained.

"...I know," she whispered so he could not hear. Raegna wanted to be rid of him. To find him work so everything could slowly go back to normal. But each terrible word each woman had for him heated her core. Should she not despise him as the others did? He had done nothing wrong to *them*.

Raegna's heart grew heavy and Adabelle heavier. Then footsteps rushed from behind them.

"Wait!" a voice called out.

Raegna and Bai turned to a woman jogging toward them. Her cherry-wood hair floated behind her small teardrop face. A sheen of sweat coated her red flushed skin. She came to a halt and panted. "My lady... Good evening."

"Good evening," Raegna said, blinking.

"Forgive me," the woman gasped as she caught her breath. "My name is Turid. I am a friend of the Matriarch and her sisters. Well, an adviser of finances and things of the like. Iida told me you were looking for an occupation for your husband."

"Did she?" Raegna asked, her voice higher in pitch than she intended.

Turid gave an eager nod. "You see, I lost my husband to sickness in the winter. It has been difficult to raise my children without him and to attend to my Matriarch when she requires me. I wondered if yours is good at caring for children and doing housework."

Raegna glanced at Bai. "He does well with our daughter. I've never seen him do housework—"

"I can sweep, clean dishes, and do laundry," Bai blurted.

Both women looked at him, Turid with her eyebrows arched and Raegna with her eyes wide. She expected Turid to reprimand him, but she laughed instead.

"Excellent!" she cheered with a grin that displayed a gap between her front teeth. "You can feed two children if I prepare meals the night before?"

"I can," Bai replied.

"Oh, this is wonderful!" Turid clapped her hands together. "I have a daughter and son who are the light of my world. Your daughter may join you. She and mine could be friends."

"Perhaps," Raegna stuttered with her throat closed.

"Iida did say your leg was bandaged but that isn't a problem." Turid's words raced from her lips. "Banu is a fine healer. She will have you fixed in no time! And the children are darling, they won't be a bother while they play. Would you be able to start tomorrow morning at dawn?"

Bai held his head higher. "Of course, m' lady. Whatever you'll have me do."

"Oh, thank you so much!" Turid nodded and came forward to squeeze his arm. Raegna straightened as Turid let her hand linger around his bicep before pulling away. "I'll see you tomorrow then! That is, if your wife permits it."

Raegna's mind swirled from the speed of the conversation. "Er, yes, of course. He may work for you."

"Wonderful! Thank you both!" Finally, Turid left them with a grateful wave. "Have a goodnight, you two!"

"Goodnight," Raegna repeated.

"I like her," Bai announced. "She treats me like a human being and not a draft horse."

Raegna wrinkled her nose and pressed on to the healing house. "Perhaps a little too much so."

"What do you mean?"

For prejudiced women to frustrate Raegna because they had no true reason to turn Bai away was one thing. But for Turid to tie her stomach because of her quick kindness and unnerving closeness to him...

No, it wasn't closeness. She was just being friendly like Iida this morning. It was polite of her to address Bai and speak to him about his capabilities, and put her hand on his arm...

Raegna shook the thought. Some women are simply prone to touch and that was clearly Turid's way: excited, loud, and friendly.

"Nothing," Raegna told him. "Let's go back to the house."

Chapter 14

Hadwin

Awakened by a flick to the forehead, Hadwin squinted up at whoever had disturbed him. He expected Dakarai or Cadoc, but a frowning young man with small eyes and a crooked nose like a hawk's beak stood over his bed instead, glowering.

Forcing his vision to clear, Hadwin sat up. "What? Who are you?"

"That matters not," the young man hissed. "You should have been in the kitchen before sunrise. Our lords need breakfast."

He must have been a kitchen boy and Hadwin prayed he wasn't the one in charge of him. His lower lip pouted in the pompous way that wealthy, well-off husbands who didn't work a day in their life showed when they did not get their way or were offended by common men. Hadwin despised him already.

With a glance across the room, he found Naleem sleeping with Dakarai and Cadoc. Dakarai stirred, rolling over in a dream.

"Forgive me, there are no windows in this room," Hadwin whispered. "How am I supposed to know it is sunrise?"

"You should just know," the young man scolded. "There's no use in arguing. Let's go before time's wasted!"

With that, he hastened to the door and waited for Hadwin. Though he would have liked to say good morning to his family first, Hadwin was sure if he did not hurry, this hawknose would only berate him more. Thus, he followed the young man downstairs and to the kitchen fixed just behind the dining hall, a bustling, steaming place of chatter and clattering pots and platters.

Three great ovens spread along the wall accompanied by several spits above fires of varying sizes to accommodate the size of the animals. One such was where a boy spun a cooking slab of meat—from what animal Hadwin could not distinguish. Fireplaces also kept cauldrons and soup pots filled with the smell of porridge. Each fireplace, pot, and spit were watched over by a kitchen boy or two, all of them Hadwin's age or a little younger than his twenty-four years.

"Your job is easy today, luckily for you and the time we have," Hawknose grumbled. He pushed Hadwin forward and gestured to a barrel at the far side of the room. "You'll fill the pitchers with ale. Can you handle that?"

Hadwin wrinkled his nose. "Yes, I can."

"See to it then, boy."

Boy? You're no older than me! Hadwin went to the barrel and found the pitchers nearby. Across from him were four giant tubs of hot water, much like the one he and Naleem washed laundry in, where some boys scrubbed dishes.

As Hadwin collected the pitchers onto a platter, a few of the boys turned for a better view of him. Their curiosity set a heavy weight over his shoulders, but Hadwin tried to ignore them and continue his small task.

One boy with a slanted, wide mouth and gray-circled eyes tilted his head and had the courage to speak to him. "You're the new nanny's brother, aren't you?"

Startled by his words, Hadwin jolted and glanced back at them. How news traveled fast. "I am."

"What is his name?" another boy with buckteeth inquired.

"...Naleem."

"And yours?"

"Hadwin." He hesitated, unsure of where they would take this.

"What has he done to earn Thenalious' right-hand seat?" the bucktoothed boy asked. "That seat is usually Reynold's."

Reynold. He was the giant man who had stared Naleem down last night. Was that the reason he seemed to despise him? Naleem took his place? A councilman's place? How, when Naleem was only a caregiver?

"May I ask what you know about that man?" Hadwin asked them and set a still-empty pitcher aside. "Why would Thenalious give my brother his seat?"

"That's what I just asked you," the bucktoothed boy replied.

"Reynold is a councilman who has been in Haven since he was a boy," another explained, refusing to look away from his work in the hot tub. A smug expression drew back the muscles in his golden-brown face. "He is also Thenalious' lover."

Hadwin's gut tightened. "Lover?"

"Yes, they've been together since they were young," the boy continued. "Before they were councilmen. In time, you'll hear them in Thenalious' chamber. They're not very quiet about themselves."

Hadwin gripped the edge of a barrel and shook his head. "You're telling me Thenalious gave Naleem his lover's seat?"

"Scandalous, isn't it?" Bucktooth commented. "He certainly has eyes for him. Oh, but you're new here. You're not accustomed to how things work in Haven. Don't worry, this is a good thing for you and your brother. You have Thenalious' favor."

"I've never seen the man look at anyone like that nanny," another added. "Not even Reynold. Have any of you?"

"No, and Thenalious is picky about who he beds." The smug boy still did not look up. "That's why he has no sons. He refuses to sleep with the women." Finally, he looked to Hadwin across two tubs. "He must see something in your brother."

But his voice didn't reach Hadwin's ears as his mind swam and all thoughts bubbled like boiling water. He could not find his bearings even when Hawknose returned to shout at him for not filling the pitchers. Hadwin obeyed, turning the knob to let the liquid pour as he listened to the other boys' chatter.

What was it about the new caregiver that stole Thenalious' heart? Was it his dark eyes like ebony, the wave of his hair, or did Thenalious truly appreciate his paternal nature? They heard rumors of Thenalious and Reynold having disagreements about how many times Reynold visited the women's shack. Was Thenalious jealous and seeking revenge?

A women's shack? The ale pitchers Hadwin held shook.

The group carried their servings out to the dining hall. The tables were rearranged to make one grand table large enough to fit a map of Galaenia, along with the plates, bowls, goblets, and platters. Sunlight poured in from rectangular windows above and soaked the room with early morning light. The great fireplace bloomed against the far wall but would likely be put out soon when the sun would warm the room better.

A few councilmen stood around the table, catching up after the night. Hadwin recognized Wyn but the other two councilmen he did not know.

Thenalious, Reynold, and the rest had not arrived yet. Hadwin helped distribute goblets and was ordered to give a pitcher to a serving boy so they could both refill the cups for their lords. Hadwin joined his friend to stand at one end and wait.

Once the food was served, more councilmen appeared, Thenalious being the first, in a casual white shirt with brown breeches and riding boots at his feet. All nine of them greeted each other with claps on the shoulders or handshakes. The last to arrive was Reynold, a wolf among mere dogs in a black tunic with patched elbows. He took the seat next to Thenalious, but neither turned to look at one another as they all sat before their food and the map.

Hadwin let his eyes fall to his feet with a gulp, copying the other boy's expression. He chewed his cheek as the councilmen ate and chatted more. An eerie presence settled over him until he could no longer ignore it. Hadwin glanced at the tapestry hanging over this grand table and Thenalious at the head of it. The tapestry of Fan.

This time, Hadwin noted ash, smoke, and the rock of Mork Skov surrounded the evil one. His fangs overlapped his lower lip, but he did not snarl the way he would in the temple of Gaea. Small antlers encircled his crown. Locks of red-brown hair fell over his shoulders. Yellow eyes oversaw everything in the dining hall and made Hadwin shudder.

"Our nannies are rather aggravated that you mean to replace them, Thenalious." A councilman with dark brown skin beneath a short black beard caught Hadwin's attention. "A man from the recent raid?"

"The one with two boys." Wyn cackled, his grin as wide and malicious as ever. "I believe Thenalious has taken a liking to him."

Hadwin stole a swift glance at Reynold and saw the boy beside him doing the same. Expressionless, the beast continued slurping up his last spoonful of porridge.

Thenalious hardly glanced at him and shrugged so casually, Hadwin wondered if he knew Reynold was in the same room. "I've just been intrigued by his paternal ability. Not all of us can live up to Sigmund's expectations of fatherhood like he can, so I think he makes the perfect addition to the nursery."

"We'll see." Reynold's voice rumbled so deep that it rattled Hadwin's bones. The beast wiped his mouth and red beard with his sleeve. "For now, we should discuss this past raid and look to the future. The women will become suspicious of these village attacks and send the Maidens our way."

And not soon enough, Hadwin thought.

"And what if the Maidens come?" one man remarked, cocking his bald head. "They're just a bunch of girls on horseback. That doesn't make them warriors."

"If there is any group you should not underestimate, it is the Maidens." Reynold pushed his bowl aside and leaned forward with his arms crossed over the table. "Unlike the Queen's army, they have no family to tie them down and no interest but in the safety of Galaenia. They are strong and experienced, and that makes women dangerous."

"The Queen only keeps a handful of Maidens," Wyn spoke up, gnawing on meat. "There are hundreds of us. More if we continue raiding."

"And more if we wait for the boys to grow," the man with the black beard said.

"We cannot sit and wait on mere babes to become men," Reynold protested with his lip curled. "And we cannot make tramps of ourselves in that barn and try to sire more sons. More often than not, those cows give us daughters. I swear it is Gaea's move against us."

Hadwin's mind whirled. These cows must have been the women they kept, and he understood where their sons came from with horrifying queasiness.

Thenalious rolled his eyes and waved his hand. "You all waste your time with the women. They're more trouble than they're worth. Even the babes."

"Which is why you gave them the new nanny?" Reynold grumbled, a low sound like a bear's growl.

"We need better nannies because the ones we have do not care for the children," Thenalious argued. "We wouldn't need any if all of you could keep your cocks out of cunts, but that is not what I am going to discuss."

He rose, placing his palms against the wood table. "This is our mission: We raid, we build our army, we let the women come to us because they will underestimate us. They think we are inexperienced and weak. As far as they will know, we are a small rebellion of farmers tucked within the forest. But we are more than that."

The councilmen nodded and grunted in agreement. All except Reynold, who festered in his seat, a vein in his neck bulging.

"They will hear word of us and send warriors to investigate," Thenalious went on. "When they do, we use our defenses, our organization, and kill them all. So, we will raid and strengthen our numbers when they send more of their warriors."

"The men we capture are raised in the belief in Gaea," the black-bearded man said. "What army can we build if they will not fight for us?"

Thenalious shrugged. "They're frightened and sorrowful. When we give them something to believe in, they'll fight. And if not, they can forge our weapons, make our bread, or be concubines for us. I hardly care."

Is that what he wanted? To make a concubine out of Naleem? Hadwin's blood seared his veins, and the pitcher quaked in his grip.

"Well, we've gathered more than we need from the last raid." The black-bearded man studied the map. "Perhaps it would do us good to lie low until we need supplies again. That shouldn't be for another winter or two."

"We cannot lie low when we destroyed a major village in Sorelle, Oberon," Thenalious protested.

"I suggested we take the eastern village of Sorelle, Judr," Reynold grumbled. "They are the poorest and no one would miss them until Harvest Union. That would give us plenty of time to prepare for an attack from the Maidens."

"We still can." Thenalious pointed to the map held down by goblets and empty breakfast bowls. "We have enough men for a second raid, and I know Judr. There are many warriors, but not enough to defend the village. Their men will be too docile to protect their families or fight back. The sooner we take Judr, the less likely its residents will notice Syden was attacked. The less likely their Queen is made aware."

"And more loot for us," Wyn cheered.

Oberon frowned. "Well then, if their men are docile, what use are they to us?"

"Their women are cruel," Thenalious explained. "They are more likely to join us and fight than any of these Gaea-worshiping tramps. I've wanted to plan the strategy soon. Judr is surrounded by a wall, easy to conquer if we take them by surprise." His eyes roved over the map. "...Until then, we have other things to attend to."

Reynold's voice boomed, more commanding than before. "We should send scouts around the perimeter and learn the wall's weakest points and the village routine, the perfect opportunities for us to make our move."

Thenalious kept his attention on the map, frowning. "Very well. Gather the men for a scouting party. Make sure you are not caught."

With that, Thenalious nodded to the councilmen. Each returned the gesture before he left his bowl and goblet behind. Hadwin watched him stride out through the creaking double doors with his head high.

The rest of the councilmen finished their breakfasts and called Hadwin and the other servant boy over for more drinks. As Hadwin filled Oberon's goblet, Reynold stood and skulked to exit, passing Hadwin like the shadow of a thunderstorm over a meadow. Hadwin stiffened, and only relaxed once he was gone.

"Don't let him frighten you." Oberon's voice made Hadwin jolt. The man regarded him with gentle eyes and offered an encouraging smile before taking a sip of his drink. "He's not as tough as he looks. He lets Thenalious get the better of him all the time."

Unsure of how to respond, Hadwin blinked and left him to refill someone else's goblet.

When all the councilmen finished their breakfast, the kitchen boys returned to clean the table. Hadwin did his part in a thick daze. So much information buzzed through his mind. A new raid, the women these men kept—though where they were, Hadwin wasn't sure—and what Thenalious meant to do with Naleem, how Naleem was caught between the relations of that snake and the beast.

One thing was clear: Hadwin must do whatever it took to protect his brother and nephews. Whatever Thenalious had planned for all of them would not be achieved.

The rest of the day continued with scrubbing dishes in hot water until his hands turned red and blistered from the heat. Hadwin and a few other boys suffered above the tubs, while the others scrambled to provide lunch for the councilmen and then dinner for the entire hall.

As he tried to be rid of a growing pile of dishes, Hadwin could only look forward to eating alongside his brother again and prayed their seats would not be next to Thenalious. But dinner drew closer. Hadwin's work seemed to never end.

Just as the tower of pots dwindled, Bucktooth approached with an armful of more stacked over his head and plopped them down beside Hadwin with a clamor.

"What's this?" he snapped at the boy.

Bucktooth paused and peered at him quizzically. "Used cookware?"

"How are we supposed to make it to dinner if we have all this work?" Hadwin demanded.

The other boys laughed as if he told the most hilarious joke in Galaenian history. He frowned at them. "What? Do they not want us to eat?"

"We'll eat," another said from across the tub. "But usually after everyone else has had their fill and all their dishes are clean."

Thus, Hadwin scrubbed on and listened to the roar of chatter coming from the dining hall while he and the other kitchen boys worked tirelessly.

Eventually, the hall quieted and when supper was over, they brought more dishes into the kitchen. When he thought his hands would shrivel into nothing, Hadwin's work was done, and it permitted him and the others to finish off leftovers and retire to their beds.

Hadwin hiked up the stairs and down the hallway to his room. Once he entered, Dakarai lunged for him. "Uncle Hadwin!"

Despite the day, Hadwin managed a grin and pulled his nephew close. "How are you, little one?"

"Uncle Hadwin, we've been inside all day!" Dakarai complained, tilting his head back to look up at him. "We wanted to go outside and play, but Papa wouldn't let us!"

Hadwin exchanged a look with Naleem at the foot of his bed, rocking Cadoc to sleep. The very embodiment of exhaustion, Naleem's eyes held a dreadful warning, circles looping underneath them. Hadwin had seen his brother this way only once when Dakarai was born, and he and Pinar spent sleepless nights caring for their first babe.

Hadwin pursed his lips. "Perhaps you can try again tomorrow." Another glance at Naleem and then, "Come now. Let's get you to sleep."

After guiding his nephew to the bed, Hadwin lifted the covers and Dakarai burrowed beneath them. Tucked in, the boy wriggled to get comfortable. "Will you tell a story, Uncle Hadwin?"

"It's very late, Dak," Hadwin whispered. "Perhaps tomorrow night. You need your rest. We all do."

A yawn rolled from Dakarai's mouth and his eyes shut. "Hm. All right."

"Good boy." Hadwin kissed his forehead and retreated to his bed. His back ached and popped as he lay across the mattress. Being hunched over scrubbing dishes made it the most luxurious thing in all Jorde.

Within minutes, Dakarai fell fast asleep and Naleem set Cadoc beside him. Sighing, he rubbed his tired eyes and stretched.

"You are all up rather late," Hadwin commented. "What kept you?"

"There were no other nannies today," Naleem growled. "Only one. He walked into the nursery, saw me, and left."

"Typical."

Naleem slumped onto the bed. "There are two dozen boys or more. I couldn't keep track of all of them. They ran about, made a mess, or hurt themselves. It was a miracle I could even put them down."

"But you were successful?"

"I suppose... I also suppose the thing to do is tell Thenalious, as much as I don't want to. Gaea, I hate this place."

"It's not Gaea's fault," Hadwin corrected, turning onto his side to face his brother. "I've seen enough of Thenalious and the other councilmen today."

"Quite the bunch, aren't they?" Naleem grumbled, placing his chin in his hand.

"They were making plans to attack Judr," Hadwin said. "...And a few other things came to light. Especially about Thenalious and Reynold."

"What do you mean?"

Hadwin propped himself on his elbow. "They are lovers. But there's something between them. I'm sure Reynold is jealous of Thenalious favoring you, and Thenalious must be using you for that exact purpose."

"What?" Naleem leaned in on the edge of his seat but retracted, rubbing his temples. "I truly despise this place."

"You must be careful around them," Hadwin urged. "That Reynold could crush your skull in his fist!"

"I'd like to see him try," Naleem said. "And Thenalious, that devil... I'll keep up the act. Tell him about the nannies." His brow raised. "Perhaps

I can convince him to let you help me. That way, I can keep you close and away from danger."

"And I won't have to worry about you," Hadwin agreed. "Or serve the bastards."

Naleem lay beside his sons. "That's settled then. I'll gain some trust from him in time. We could find a way out of here."

Hadwin's heart lifted, and he pushed himself higher. "How then?"

"The two of us together," Naleem breathed, slipping off into sleep. "We'll find a way."

"Together," Hadwin repeated. "All right. Mayhap we can cause a distraction, or earn trust and find a perfect time to slip into the woods, right, Naleem?"

But Naleem was already fast asleep. His steady breaths matched the rhythm of the boys', all three of them tucked where their worries could not touch them.

Hadwin sighed and burrowed under the blankets. "Goodnight, brother."

Chapter 15

Raegna

Summer light poured into the open dome of Judr's temple. The heat caused Raegna to break into a sweat. The thick maroon robe did not help despite the wide collar that exposed the base of her chest. Gaea's statue towered at the altar, staring down the aisle between the wooden pews. Raegna tried to take comfort in Her warm gaze. The temple provoked flashes of lifting Syden's people in her mind's eye, and Raegna fought a cringe.

Two priestesses in matching maroon dresses under their robes stood beneath the statue. One held incense over a small basin to collect the ash. The other clenched a torch that flickered with an orange flame. Judr's eldest priestess planted herself before Raegna, her neck hunched like a crowing rooster. Her white hair was bound in a single braid that matched the other priestesses, though a few strands hung to frame her withered, dark-beige face.

Raegna let her eyes drop to the floor. Dust lingered above the empty pews and between the tapestry-adorned walls. At the front sat Iida and her husband, Asmund. All of this was Iida's idea. Though Raegna knew she would be due for true initiation into priestesshood, there had been more pressing matters to resolve than her legitimacy. Her ritual in Syden was between her and Gaea alone.

"It is time to finish your rites, Raegna," the eld-priestess said with a rough edge to her voice. "You've inflicted your own scar, and lifted a village, or so you say. But you've yet to be accepted into a sisterhood devoted to our All-Mother. We have yet to find out if Gaea has accepted you as well."

The way the flames of her fire in Syden flashed had told Raegna otherwise. She set her shoulders back. "I'm ready, eld-priestess."

The old woman sniffed and nodded to Raegna's wrapped hand. "Undo it."

Raegna obeyed, untying the bandage, and exposing her cut palm. Old blood caked the gash, rimmed with raised, red flesh. The eld-priestess sneered at the wound and stepped to the side, giving Raegna a path to Gaea's statue.

"You will give Her your blood before us."

Raegna drew a breath and strode to the altar. A stone pillar inscribed with runes sat before Gaea, stained red with the blood of priestesses throughout Judr's history. With a wince, Raegna pressed her palm to the stone and smeared her gash across the runes hard enough to open it again. Traces of her own blood spread and settled between the etchings.

When she finished, Raegna stepped back, folding her fingers over her cut that stung with the grit.

The eld-priestess took the torch from her sister and held it over the blood. She traced the flames along Raegna's mark. The fire swept over the runes. Raegna looked on as she chewed the inside of her cheek, her stomach floating.

A snort blew from the eld-priestess' nose, and she shoved the torch back into her sister's hand. Digging into a pouch that hung from her waistbelt, she retrieved tiny bones. Experienced priestesses often carried doe bones. Gaea's daughter, Sachi, transformed into a doe when she visited Jorde. If a doe fell, priestesses preserved her remains to aid in divine guidance when needed.

The eld-priestess shook the bones in her hand. "All-Mother, would You have this woman serve Your children on Your behalf? We pray You to speak to us through Sachi's being."

With that, she tossed them over the stone. The white pieces clattered and became still while the eld-priestess and her two sisters leaned over them. Raegna tilted her head but waited.

The eld-priestess straightened and pivoted to face her. Ancient, bag-encircled eyes picked Raegna apart before the eld-priestess said, "They read an approval."

Raegna fought to repress a sigh of relief. Instead, she pinned herself upright and cast her gaze sideways. The pews creaked as Iida bounced in place behind her.

"Come, then." The eld-priestess stepped to Raegna's level, the two other priestesses on either side of them. "Let's speak the rites."

The eld-priestess turned to the other with the incense and dipped her fingers into the ash basin. Gray powder coated her worn fingertips as she scooped it up.

"All-Mother," she spoke as she stared at Raegna, "may this woman do good in Your name."

The eld-priestess ran the ash from the top of her forehead to her brow. "Give her the wisdom to receive Your teachings and guidance."

She dragged the stuff from Raegna's chest, down to her heart between her breasts. "Give her strength to gift compassion and smite darkness."

Finally, the eld-priestess swept ash over Raegna's lips. "May she speak with all these gifts You bestow. Praise Gaea, Mother of All."

"Praise Gaea, Mother of All," everyone in attendance repeated.

"Give thanks to the All-Mother," a voice sounded from the temple entrance. "Her power blooms everlasting."

Everyone faced the double doors that shut behind Matriarch Viona and her sister, Femke. Viona clasped her hands together with a wry smile and started down the aisle. Her layered, gold-stitched skirts flowed about her legs. "Forgive me, eld-priestess, but I thought preparations would be set for tonight's ritual."

The eld-priestess nodded to her Matriarch. "They are underway, Matriarch. Your sister insisted this woman be ordained as a true priestess. Preparations had to be put on hold."

Before Raegna could wonder what kind of ritual, Matriarch Viona whirled on Iida sitting in the pew, raising a thin eyebrow at her. "Sister? You believe this to be a priority?"

Iida did not look at her sister but kept her chin high, her oval face serene. "I wish for Priestess Raegna to be ordained when she is by my side during the rest of my pregnancy."

"Ordained or not," Femke spoke up as she approached behind Viona, "priestesses belong in the temple. Why would you have her attend you as a servant would?"

"I want our child to be surrounded by Gaea's good nature," Iida answered with her mouth tight.

"The child is yours, little sister," Viona corrected and stepped in front of Iida. "No one else's."

Iida fidgeted, picking at her nails. "I did not create this child alone."

Beside her, Asmund lowered his head and shrank away from the Matriarch's presence. His blue eyes flitted beneath his soft brow, stealing glances at Iida. It had to be the most daring thing he had ever done.

Men did not speak unless spoken to. Seen and not heard. That was Viona and Femke's way, Iida had told Raegna before their day together started. She warned her of many harsh things her sisters practiced but assured her they meant no harm. Asmund's behavior was a product of keeping his sisters-in-law happy. Iida promised he was naturally shy.

Raegna reminded herself of Banu's explanation of Viona and Femke's childhood horrors and their father and could hardly blame them for their dealings with the men. Even she would have had Bai silenced, but that became more difficult with every passing day.

Viona straightened at Iida's remark and peered down her long nose at her. "You bear the child alone."

Iida stiffened. She met Viona's gaze and sighed, closing her own. In a swift movement, Iida took Asmund's hand in her own and laid it over her belly. Poor Asmund nearly jumped off the pew. When Iida brushed the little locks of his mousy hair, his shoulders relaxed, and he leaned close to her.

"I do not bear this child alone," Iida said, caressing his knuckles. "Asmund is always beside me."

Raegna gulped, frozen alongside the other priestesses. Viona straightened and held her deathly stare over the couple before whirling away.

"You curse your child," she spat.

A heavy blanket of silence suffocated the room. It wasn't Raegna's place to interfere with family conflict. She couldn't think of anything to change the conversation, anyway. Especially not with the Matriarch's vexation.

"No matter," Femke dismissed with a wave, tearing through the quiet. "We came here to see to the ritual preparations. With the crescent moon, we can cleanse our meddling sister and the village of Fan's wickedness, right, eld-priestess?"

The old woman blinked as she snapped to attention. "Er, of course, my lady. It will certainly deter the evil one's schemes amongst us. Rest assured, Matriarch, everything will be ready for tonight."

Viona rubbed her temple. "I suppose, at least you have one more priestess to help you until then."

"I would rather have Raegna with me today," Iida argued and recoiled with a hand over her belly. "There are enough priestesses for your... ritual."

"If I may ask," Raegna spoke up, drawing her robe over her chest, "what sort of ritual is being performed?"

Femke smoothed out her skirt as she circled Raegna. "Every crescent moon, Fan shows his grin in the sky. There isn't enough light to protect us from his imps. He is most powerful during this time, besides the harvest season and the night of Fan's Eye. Thus, we perform a cleansing ritual to clear our hearts, streets, and homes of his evil."

Raegna side-stepped from her. "Forgive me ...but doesn't the Arch Priestess in Stadt travel to Mork Skov to cleanse all of Galaenia and ward the demon off? Her efforts provide the power to guard the realms for another year."

"Unfortunately, it has become clear that the Arch Priestess' efforts are not enough," Viona said, her chest rising. "Our women have given birth to more sons than daughters. Some of our young men are difficult to break. There are reports in Vesten of men using their bodies to seduce perfectly good women into their beds. Our own Queen keeps her husband, though their marriage has produced no heir, and even allows him to speak on matters of the crown. Fan's grip on us is far greater than it has ever been."

"Not to mention we've let a gold-eyed man into our midst," Femke added with a twisted sneer.

Raegna lifted her gaze to Femke's as soon as the words left her lips. Why did she feed into the conflict this woman laid out? It couldn't be to defend Bai's honor, though the relentless degrading of his looks chipped at her patience.

"Nevertheless," Viona spoke up, unmoved. "Extra effort is never a harm. All of us must do what we can to protect ourselves."

"My babe is well protected, sister," Iida protested. "We all are. Gaea will protect us. That is why Raegna is here, to guide me through the birth."

Viona let out a strangled sigh, pinching the bridge of her nose. "As you wish, little sister. I'm too busy to aid you in this pregnancy."

The eld-priestess cleared her throat. "Matriarch, shall we discuss the ritual?"

"Yes," Viona sighed. "We shall."

An opportunity presented itself with Viona's presence, and if she left now, Raegna might not have another chance to speak up. "Matriarch, if I may take just one more moment."

Matriarch Viona paused before turning to follow the eld-priestess outside the temple. "You may."

Raegna's chest tightened, and she took a breath to loosen it. "Syden has suffered, and I have lost dear friends to the hands of Fan's men. Could this ritual be the beginning of an investigation for the attackers?"

The Matriarch's long eyelashes barely touched when they came to-gether. Then she turned away, flipping a braid. "The ritual is to protect my people. I have yet to decide if you are deceiving me in this matter of your village. For now, I will not waste any warriors on a journey that could be meaningless. Is that understood?"

"Matriarch, I swear to you it is not a lie—"

"That is not what I asked, priestess." Viona faced her again, her shoulders back and her brow arched. "Am I understood?"

Raegna almost wished she had a tongue such as Bai's, brave and cunning. But this Matriarch had a familiar coldness Raegna learned to fear since childhood. Instead, she lowered her head. "Yes, Matriarch."

"And do attend this ritual." Viona continued behind the eld-priestess. "This way, you can gain knowledge on how to deal with the evil one. Perhaps even cleanse your husband as well."

Raegna suppressed a grimace. "Of course, Matriarch."

"Very good."

Iida stood and took Raegna's arm. "Come, Raegna. I would like to rest at home. We can let my sisters take over from here."

Judr's people bustled about their business under the rich blue sky. Raegna walked alongside Iida and Asmund to the Matriarch's house, listening to whatever questions the expectant mother had on her mind. Fidgeting with the sleeves of her new priestess dress, Raegna answered and assuaged Iida's concerns.

"How long did you carry your daughter, Raegna?" Iida raised her voice when an old woman pushed a herd of goats past the three of them. The bell on the ram rang with a sharp toll.

"Eight moons," Raegna said. "She came earlier than expected."

"Did she kick so much?"

"Plenty." Raegna smirked at the faded memories spent alone in her room. "At one time, she terrified me, but I eventually grew used to it. Her movements reassured me everything was well."

"Why were you terrified?" Iida asked.

The goat herd clamored in the distance as Raegna faltered in her steps. Terrified because of the sudden realization there was truly a babe inside her. Yes, the village healer said pregnancy was the reason for her illnesses and the missed cycle, but the concept did not reach her until Adabelle rubbed against her womb. Her child and Bai's.

"Oh, um, just typical fear and nervousness," Raegna lied. "I didn't know what to expect."

"Neither do I," Iida confessed. "But I have you to help me."

Raegna forced a grin. "Yes. You do."

In the house, Raegna admired the main room with plush furniture standing over a fur rug. Matriarch Viona kept a desk against the far wall. A large fireplace of stone sat within the adjacent wall, waiting to be lit come fall and winter. Doors to other rooms remained closed.

As Iida approached the staircase, Asmund kept close behind her. His voice came in a deep whisper as he raised his arms to catch her. "Careful."

Iida rolled her eyes. "A round belly doesn't mean I can't climb stairs, love. I'm capable."

Raegna pressed her lips together to hide an amused smile. In the bedroom, Iida rested on the edge of the bed with Asmund at her side, her hand in his. He never spoke again, letting his eyes drift over the floor or lift to look between the women as they talked more of newborns and pregnancy, listening intently.

Raegna answered the new mother's various questions to the best of her ability, though some she saved for Banu to answer later. As the inexperienced Iida persisted with concerns about the babe's movement, well-being, and birth, memories of Raegna's own past fears surfaced. Because of the trust lost between her and her mother, Raegna went to Pinar for her troubles. Thus, she recounted everything her dear friend told her so long ago.

Iida cocked her head at Raegna's saddened expression. "What is it?"

"Hm?" Raegna lifted her gaze to the couple across the room from the chair she sat in, her hands placed in her lap. "Oh, our discussion reminds me of a good friend. See, she had two babes before I had my first, so I confided in her. I've known her since childhood ... She would know what to tell you."

Iida copied her bittersweet smile. "She lived in your village?"

"Yes."

Iida looked to her feet and up again. "What was her name?"

"...Pinar."

"A good name. May Gaea bless her and give her peace."

The edges of Raegna's heart crumbled, but she chewed on her trembling lip. "Thank you."

"And do not pay mind to my sister's words," Iida continued, the corners of her mouth curled. "We will avenge our sister village; you can be sure of it."

Raegna pursed her lips with a quick nod of gratitude. She counted herself lucky to find a friend and ally in the sweetest woman in Judr.

By evening, Raegna headed to the healing house and came to a halt halfway down the road. Before the porch, Turid stood with Bai and Adabelle, the sunset silhouetting their forms. Even from this distance, Turid's warm smile plumped her cheeks that burned as bright as her red hair.

"Good evening, priestess." Jora walked up behind her, buckles and hilts clinking with her stride. "Just in time for supper."

The warrior stopped beside her and Raegna gave her a sideways glance. Jora narrowed her eyes on Turid and Bai. "Ah. I forgot she took him on."

Raegna drew a breath to swallow a groan. "Is it strange that I allow it?"

"Allow what?" Jora asked with her head cocked.

The words wouldn't come then. Allow her husband to tend to another woman's household is what she wanted to say, but that wasn't quite it. Raegna's face scrunched as she contemplated how to explain it. Then Turid traced Bai's arm and let her touch linger.

Jora scoffed. "I see. I understand you wouldn't want to cause trouble, especially with your arrival. Your husband doesn't strike me as the unfaithful kind. But I would keep my eye on her."

Raegna's cheeks flushed. As Jora ushered her forward, Raegna clamped her mouth shut from saying, *It's not that*. She hastened her pace with heat firing through her.

"Mama!" Adabelle exclaimed when Raegna reached them. The little girl wrapped her arms around Raegna's legs.

"Good evening, priestess," Turid greeted. "Warrior Jora. How are you?"

Jora shrugged with dull eyes. Raegna brought Adabelle close, but could not hold back her frown. "Well. Everything is in order?"

"Oh, yes." Turid beamed at Bai, whose chest puffed. "He's been an incredible help. Thank you again for lending him."

Casting her eyes down, Raegna nodded and took Adabelle's hand in hers. "Let's get inside, now. I'm sure Banu is making dinner."

Bai's crooked grin never left. "Yes, wife."

"Goodnight, all," Turid called after them. "I'll see you in the morning, Bai."

"Goodnight, m' lady," Bai said. Raegna swallowed a snarl.

Adabelle skipped into the healer's house with the adults trailing behind her. A warm, seasoned scent of meat filled the room.

Banu set dinner on the table and grinned at their entrance. "Hello, everyone. I hope you all had a lovely day."

Jora set her sword against the wall and met Banu at the table with a kiss. "Lovelier to be back at home with good food."

"Mama, at Lady Turid's house, I made friends with Oda," Adabelle rambled as they took their seats. "Papa made us lunch. We made bracelets and played outside with Oda's brother and picked flowers. She even showed me how to make a crown with them. But mine wasn't very good."

"What a fine day you had," Raegna said. Her sight traveled to Bai. "You did well then?"

"Yes," Bai replied, digging into the rabbit stew Banu prepared. "While the children played, I cleaned. Turid was very impressed with my work and has more tasks for me tomorrow."

"That's good to hear," Raegna praised. Holding his gaze for a moment longer, she intended a silent *thank you for taking care of Adabelle.* His expression uncertain, a corner of Bai's lip twitched before he took another slurp.

"Oh, there's a crescent moon tonight," Raegna announced as she stirred her bowl. "Matriarch Viona has invited us to a Fan ritual."

"A what?" Bai asked.

Banu's ladle dropped into the cauldron with a splash. Jora's head jerked up with her lips parted and brow furrowed. The family looked between them.

"A crescent moon...?" Banu murmured and retrieved her ladle. "Already?"

"Yes." Raegna blew on her spoon. "Something about this being the night Fan is at his most powerful and having to do a cleansing ritual. We never did such a thing in Syden, so Viona wants us to attend and lend me more experience as a priestess."

She made sure not to mention the cleansing of Bai's presence.

"You mustn't take the child," Jora blurted.

"Why not?" both Raegna and Bai inquired, then exchanged a glance.

"There will be children at this ritual," Banu informed them, approaching the table. "But these things are not for a young one's eyes." She gestured to Adabelle. "This one has suffered enough."

At the woman's lowered tone, Adabelle shrank in her seat.

"What exactly do they do at these rituals?" Bai asked.

"It is not for young ears either," Jora warned. "I refuse to even let Banu attend. As a warrior, I must go to help keep the peace and serve our Matriarch."

Banu squeezed her wife's shoulders. "She always comes back in worse spirits."

Jora put a hand over Banu's. "But the Matriarch has invited you, thus you have no choice. If you do not go, she'll question your loyalty to her."

A nervous bug crawled in Raegna's stomach, and the stew did not appeal to her taste. "Banu... Is it all right if Adabelle stays with you for the evening?"

"Of course, girl."

"We're actually going?" Bai said.

"Trust me," Raegna mumbled bitterly. "We cannot refuse this Matriarch."

"I'm not afraid of her," he protested with a huff.

Raegna's eyes flashed. "Neither am I. But if we are to keep ourselves away from her wrath and earn her confidence to avenge Syden, we will go to this forsaken ritual. For our sake and the sake of our daughter."

Adabelle squeaked from her chair. "…Mama?"

She sensed the fear and revolt in all of them. Raegna's closed fists released and she let out a breath. "Everything is all right, my babe. Your father and I will just have to leave for the evening."

Defeated, Bai looked at the little girl. "You can stay here and help Banu around the house, can't you?"

Adabelle gave them both a determined nod. "I can."

At least she would be safe with Banu. The healer and her wife's warnings tied Raegna's stomach into knots. Was this ritual truly worth the Matriarch's goodwill? If Jora wouldn't let Banu take part in it, what on Jorde could become of Judr on the night of a crescent moon?

What's more, this outing would be Raegna's first alone with Bai since Adabelle was born. Not that she concerned herself with what he might do to her. He clearly had meant what he told her in the barn. He would never harm her again. But the very thought of being alone by his side made the ritual even more uncertain.

Chapter 16

Naleem

Naleem awoke to the shuffling of sheets. Hadwin crept across the floor and slipped out the door to work in the kitchen. Even in the dim light fed through the crack below the door, Naleem could not fall asleep again and waited for the sun to rise. When it did, he carried a dreaming Cadoc to the nursery with Dakarai dragging his feet behind them.

The sunlight streaked the rows of small beds where the young boys either slept or stretched awake. Yet again, there were no other caregivers to give him aid. He was all alone.

Naleem braced himself and set Cadoc down to turn his attention to the infants in their cradles. Three of them snoozed despite the sunshine about their heads. One was in his second year and the other two were about to see their first winter. Naleem went to the two-year-old, who had been fussy yesterday when he stayed in his tiny cradle too long.

He let the toddler sit and play as he tended to the others. Cadoc watched from the edge of another boy's bed all the while. More and more of them woke, climbing from their beds.

"Find clothes, all of you," Naleem instructed dryly. "We'll have breakfast soon."

Some would listen, some to an extent, and some not at all. There were eighteen of them, none of them older than nine years. Each had his own personality and temper; Naleem just had to learn them to understand and discipline them.

A few of the boys gathered clothing and considered dressing until they created a game. Leading the game was the oldest and most difficult: Ugo, a rough, red-headed boy with amber irises and a flushed, pink face that resembled the beast councilman Reynold. Ugo had been noteworthy for not caring about Naleem's authority over the boys. Naleem was a new caregiver; thus, Ugo could test his limits.

"Enough." Naleem scolded them as they shrieked and chased each other around the room. "I said find clothes. Now get dressed."

Ugo stuck his tongue out in reply.

Caught up in the excitement, Dakarai joined them, jumping onto beds and ducking underneath them. Cadoc observed the game from the edge of a bed, tracking the rush around him.

Naleem groaned and let them play. He had to feed the babes first.

A curt knock thudded against the door before it opened. At first, Naleem thought it was a caregiver who would come to look in and leave again. Instead, Thenalious appeared at the doorway, peering inside with a faint smile, dressed rather informally in a loose shirt and pants. He had trimmed his black beard shorter, and the mustache stretched with his grin. Naleem scowled.

"How are things?" Thenalious asked. His hazel eyes roamed over the nursery, merely glancing at the boys. "Have you straightened them out?"

The children or the caregivers? Naleem glowered at him as he bounced a babe in his arms. Thenalious cocked his head, made another scan of the room, and frowned. "Where are the other nannies?"

Naleem rolled his eyes. "One came yesterday. He left as soon as he saw me here. I watched over all of them alone."

"Alone," Thenalious repeated.

"Yes." Naleem allowed his frustration to drip from his voice. He fought to bounce the babe gently as his gaze narrowed on Thenalious. "So, you told the truth when you said they neglected them. You know I cannot continue like this when they outnumber me."

"No," Thenalious muttered, then blinked. "I mean, yes. Trust me, I am as disappointed as you are... I'll get to the bottom of it and send some help to you."

The opportunity unfolded before him, and Naleem snatched it up as quickly as a starved dog. "My brother works in the kitchen. He's very good with children as well. I would appreciate his help."

Thenalious stared at the floor, his hands on his hips, not looking at Naleem. "Of course. I'll send someone to summon him here immediately." He raised his head. "Is there anything else I can do to make this easier for you?"

A knife in your gut. "No. That is all."

"Well then, my apologies for the incompetence of my men," Thenalious offered before leaving, shutting the door behind him.

At least Hadwin would be there soon. Being favored by Thenalious had its perks. As far as being placed in Reynold's seat—his *lover's* seat—Naleem was uncertain how he would deal with that. For now, he had the councilman's attention and, so it seemed, his utter determination to please. With that in mind, Thenalious and his desires could be used to Naleem's advantage.

When Naleem finished feeding the two babes, Hadwin arrived with his shoulders straight and his eyes alight.

"I cannot tell you how happy I am to be rid of that place," he exclaimed with his arms out.

"I'm sure you were just making their breakfast," Naleem speculated, washing the babes' faces with a cloth.

"Cleaning up after the councilmen is more like it." Hadwin turned to the boys, who raced around the room. His sight landed on Cadoc, a familiar face. "Good morning, nephew."

Cadoc smiled at his uncle.

"Uncle Hadwin!" Dakarai cried out and ran into him, throwing his arms around his legs. "Will you come play with us?"

"Good morning to you too, Dak." Hadwin chuckled, ruffling the boy's hair. "I am not sure. Apparently, you all have breakfast downstairs waiting for you."

"Yes, and you should all be dressed," Naleem grumbled.

Not pleased with this answer, Dakarai's mouth twisted, and he dashed back to run with the others. Hadwin and Naleem looked on for a moment, silently concocting a plan to bring control into their own hands. Hadwin stepped forward, the fifteen young boys jumping about in front of him.

"I have a proposition for all of you," he stated loud enough for them to hear over their fun.

A few stopped in their tracks, intrigued, while others glanced at him but kept their motion.

"If you are all good and prepare yourselves for breakfast," Hadwin told them, "we can play outside today. Maybe see the barn animals."

This caused an uproar of shouts and squeals.

"I want to go outside!"

"I want to see animals!"

"Only if you dress and line up at the door," Hadwin warned, waving a finger before them.

In a flash, they dressed and filed in. The youngest needed an extra push but were eventually made ready and ushered out by their new caregivers. Naleem carried a babe on one hip and held the toddler's hand on the other side of him, with Cadoc at his heels. Hadwin hefted the third babe while the boys crowded him, intrigued by the promise of adventure.

In the dining hall, they filled a table where porridge, nut bread, and honey awaited them. Every boy gobbled up their breakfast while kitchen servants poured milk into their cups. With his brother at the table, Naleem relished the freedom to eat and drink his fill without having to monitor the children.

When they finished, they leaped for the front door, eager to go outside, so Hadwin led the way. The boys stampeded forth through the door, starting a game of chase before the long porch. Giddy from their contagious energy, Hadwin joined them while Naleem sat on the porch steps with the babes. Cadoc settled beside his father.

"You don't want to play, son?" Naleem asked him.

Cadoc shook his head.

Naleem brushed his son's hair with his fingers, scratching his scalp. "Will you help me watch them, then?"

Legs kicking out, Cadoc nodded. They oversaw the games the others played, the three babes crawling and exploring just behind them. The boys especially enjoyed Hadwin's participation in their roughhousing, chasing them, wrestling with them in the dirt, and tickling them into fits of laughter. For the first time since they arrived in Haven, Hadwin's youthful smile brightened his face in genuine happiness again.

The dread that had been sitting on top of Naleem's chest lifted a few inches, allowing him to breathe. Dakarai took hold of Hadwin's wrist to bring him down as he jogged, despite his small size. Hadwin shouted and scooped Dakarai into the air. Naleem held onto that image, a sight he thought might have been stolen away from him forever.

Heartache cut through him like a jagged blade. Naleem looked to Cadoc, who was watching with a grin. He must have felt his father's gaze before he turned back to him. Cadoc had his mother's eyes; such a light blue, they were more like cool gray. Pinar stared back at him through those eyes.

Swallowing a stone in his throat, Naleem scratched Cadoc's head again before planting a kiss on his forehead. "Sweet boy."

Hadwin panted on his way back to the steps. "Gaea, they have such energy. I wish I could keep up for so long."

"Better than scrubbing dishes?" Naleem asked.

"So much better," Hadwin agreed. "It almost reminds me of being home. Almost."

Almost.

The early afternoon became late as the sun reached its highest peak and dipped down into the west. They took the boys inside for their lunch, let them rest in their nursery, and emerge again for dinner. The sons of the councilmen ate before the men of Haven, for, the story went, they were its future. In truth, none of the men wanted to deal with the little ones pestering their tables during their great feast.

When all had eaten their fill, Hadwin and Naleem herded the boys upstairs. This night, having Hadwin made putting the lot to bed much easier. Each of them snuggled beneath blankets within an hour, half due to their exhaustion, the other half because they wished to please their new, fun-loving caregiver, Hadwin.

"Sweet dreams, everyone," he bid them all as soon as Naleem rocked the last babe to sleep. "Goodnight."

"Goodnight," a few murmured as the door closed with a soft creak.

Dakarai and Cadoc in hand, Naleem and Hadwin retreated to their room next door and breathed sighs of relief.

"All right," Naleem said. "Time for us to find sleep as well."

"Do we have to?" Dakarai whined as his father nudged him and his brother to the bed they shared. "Can we stay up a little longer?"

"You need your rest after a long day." Naleem picked them both up and placed them on the bed, then lifted the covers. "Go on."

Cadoc burrowed under, yawning. Dakarai did so reluctantly. Naleem tucked them in and gave each a kiss on the forehead. "Goodnight, my sons."

Though Cadoc had already drifted to sleep, Dakarai stubbornly kept his eyes open. They drooped as he declared, "I'm not tired, Papa."

"I'm sure you're not," Naleem uttered, smoothing the sheets. "Close your eyes."

They must have been too heavy, for Dakarai let his eyelids fall shut and within minutes, little snores began. Both Naleem and Hadwin chuckled and climbed into their beds, Naleem being careful not to disturb his sons.

"Goodnight, brother," Hadwin whispered across the room. "Tomorrow we'll see if there is a weak spot in this place."

"Hm. Sounds like a plan."

Hadwin lay his head on his pillow. "We'll take the little ones for a walk around the camp."

"One step at a time," Naleem suggested.

A deep yawn drifted his brother into sleep. As soon as Naleem found his own pillow, his vision went dark.

A sharp hiss woke him, followed by a harsh *crr-ack*. Naleem's eyes snapped open. He propped himself on an elbow, searching for any danger to his family.

Shadows hung over the furniture, but there was no one in sight. Hadwin slumbered in a ball on his bed, his tawny hair a tousled mess. Dakarai and Cadoc dozed on their sides, facing each other in their sleep. The serenity of the scene made Naleem believe he had only been hearing things.

Another hiss sounded, another *crr-ack,* and the pained cry of a man.

Heart pounding, Naleem sat up. There was no immediate threat in the room, but what of the outside? Well, perhaps so long as it remained outside, it didn't matter. Why would he care if any of Haven's men suffered from whatever was going on out there?

Through the stillness of the night, the sounds trailed each other in a disjointed rhythm, the next man's cry more strangled this time.

Fear for the children next door filled Naleem to the brim. They were the councilmen's sons, yes, but they were innocent in this. They were his responsibility now and if anything happened to them...

Naleem slipped out of bed. He let his bedroom door creak open and shut, then crept to the nursery, the hallway dimly lit by the torchlight that flickered from the walls. Inside, the air shifted with steady breaths and murmurs of the young boys who slept there. He studied each bed and cradle before allowing himself the comfort that they were safe.

The sounds came again. Naleem pulled the door closed to muffle them from the boys. He peered through the torches' glow, where the cries of pain echoed. Down the hall, all doors were shut but a yellow line shone through the gap below one. Black shadows broke up the light within, gliding back and forth.

Every fiber within Naleem refused to investigate further, especially once another hiss, crack, and scream erupted. Curiosity won over. If he were to escape this place, he must know everything about it. Even frightening night noises.

Naleem tiptoed over the floorboards, practicing a silence he had not had to replicate since he was a child, sneaking a treat in the middle of the night. The lit doorway was just a few paces down the hall. He halted before it.

A hiss, crack, and scream.

Wincing at the severity of it, at his own stupidity, Naleem reached and turned the doorknob. The hinges remained silent as he pushed them ajar just enough to peek through. One eye inspected the inside and grew wide.

Wyn stood with an elongated whip with barbs at its end in one hand. He wiped the sweat from his brow with the other, the few wisps of brown hair plastered to his head. Four men knelt in a line before him with their backs to him. Bright red blood streaked from the tops of their shoulders and down. They trembled and whimpered as Wynn raised the whip and brought it down again.

Hiss, crr-ack, and a scream. The third man arched backward as the barbs sliced him. To Naleem's disbelief, he recognized him as the care-giver who had abandoned him and the nursery on his first day.

On the opposite wall, Thenalious leaned, relaxed, as he supervised the scene with cool eyes. His bored gaze floated from the men to the door. He jolted when he noticed the slit in the doorway.

With a gasp, Naleem jumped, shutting the door louder than he wanted to. Before he could race back down the hall, Thenalious strode to reach the door and threw it open.

Naleem's back slammed against the wall behind him. The scraping of the wood stung the skin under his shirt. His mind mistook it for the gashes the other men now carried.

"I'm, I'm sorry," he blurted without meaning to. "I was just—I heard—The children, I was worried—"

"It's all right, son of Sigmund," Thenalious soothed and closed the door. He drew close to Naleem, too close. Their chests brushed and Naleem could go no farther. "You've done nothing wrong. I won't hurt you."

"But they—"

"They have disobeyed their duty to me," Thenalious finished for him. He moved to place a hand on Naleem's arm but when Naleem flinched away, he rested his palm next to him. "And their duty to Haven. This is a justice I am serving for you. Don't be afraid."

Lungs burning for air, Naleem said no more. He stared back at Thenalious, with flashes of bloodied backs behind his eyes.

"Don't be afraid, son of Sigmund." Thenalious leaned in. The warmth of his breath grazed Naleem's cheek, and he shuddered. "I will protect you. I will rid the world of those who cause you harm. All right?"

Nothing would pass over his lips, so Naleem simply nodded, his nails raking the wall. Thenalious remained close, beholding his face for a moment longer that lasted an eternity before he pulled away.

"Go now." His hand fell from the wall. "Get some rest. Tomorrow is bound to be as long as today."

Naleem nodded again. He ducked down the hallway, back to his family, leaving Thenalious standing before the sounds of the whip and the shouts of pain.

Safe inside his room, Naleem stood against the door, shaking, catching his breath. Any advantage with Thenalious' desire may prove itself useful, but Naleem would never be immune to his power. Thenalious was still the snake that ruled the beasts of Haven. He was still responsible for the blood of Syden. There was too much at stake to outplay his game.

Hadwin and the boys dozed, oblivious to the terror outside. Naleem choked on a sob at the sight of them. A hand over his mouth, he sank to the floor.

Gaea, why have you done this to us?

CHAPTER 17

RAEGNA

THE SHARP CRESCENT MOON curved in the deep night sky; stars dotted all around it. Galaenian legend described a full, yellow moon as Fan's eye peering into Jorde and the lives of Gaea's children. The people observed Fan's Eye as a holiday to deceive Fan by disguising themselves as his many imps and minions.

A crescent moon was his white-fanged grin and a reminder of his curse on Sachi and Sigmund's descendants. These were mere legends to Raegna. Nothing more than tales to frighten children and another excuse for a feast.

Banu retrieved cloaks to keep them warm, despite the season. She insisted she did not want to remedy fevers when her wife and guests returned. Adabelle watched from the kitchen table as her parents readied themselves for the outing, her blonde hair flowing with the tilt of her head.

Raegna knelt before her with a sad smile. "I'll see you in the morning. Banu will put you to bed tonight, so you will be good. All right?"

Adabelle nodded. Raegna gave her a kiss on her brow and a tight hug. "I love you, my babe."

"I love you, Mama," Adabelle replied.

Bai circled Raegna as she rose, placing his hand on Adabelle's cheek, which took up the whole side of her face. His thumb ran along her fair skin as he said, "Listen to your mother."

"Yes, Papa," Adabelle told him. He kissed her forehead.

They thanked Banu for watching over her and stepped out from the healer's house, and down the dirt path toward the main road. Their boots crunched on the gravel, cloaks floating above their heels. The air had cooled for the evening, but the temperature did not require such a heavy cloak.

Raegna kept a short distance from Bai, though it was customary for a woman to escort her husband by taking his arm. He did not seem very keen on physical touch either, as his arms remained at his sides, his wiry shoulders stiff while they walked. Blond strands fell above his brow, and the night softened the harsh angles of his face.

"How was working for the Matriarch's sister?" he asked, keeping pace alongside her.

It would have been too merciful of Gaea to keep him quiet.

Raegna focused on the path ahead. "Iida is very kind. More than I can say about her sisters."

"As pleasant as I'd expect them to be?" Bai guessed with a sideways glance at her.

Despite herself, Raegna smirked. "Yes, as you'd expect them to be. ... I tried to see if Viona would send warriors to Syden to confirm everything that's happened, but she is not moved. She still believes we are lying."

Bai rolled his eyes, which had turned a gloomy hue of gold. "She hates men so much; one would think she would leap at the opportunity to get rid of a coup they started."

"She doesn't trust us." Raegna lowered her chin. "I suppose I don't blame her. Our arrival is rather strange. And though I experienced the attack myself, I wouldn't believe us either. But I wish there were a way I could convince her."

He tilted his head back with a lift of his shoulder. "Perhaps we both could?"

A soft snort came from her nose. "She would not even consider listening to you. Attending this ritual will assure her of our trustworthiness."

"We both know we are worthy," he said. "I wonder, is she worthy to us? We can seek help elsewhere."

"Where else then?" she challenged, a brow raised at him.

Bai did not miss a beat. "Stadt. I've heard the Queen is kind. As kind as Iida. She would know what to do. She has the warriors and Maidens at her disposal."

"Even the Queen can't just send warriors to the other end of Galaenia at her own whim," Raegna countered. "The High Council would have to approve of the matter. The Maidens may belong to Galaenia itself, but there wouldn't be enough of them for the number of men that pillaged Syden. If we even receive an audience with her majesty."

"I still believe she would be more helpful than this Matriarch."

Raegna hushed him when the great house loomed ahead of them.

As Jora told them, a crowd gathered before the porch steps, circling a blooming fire. The orange flames flashed between the silhouettes and licked high above their heads, the smoke clouding the speckled stars in the sky.

"We will do what we can tonight," Raegna muttered to him instead. She took the crook of his arm, surprising him and herself, and escorted him toward the commotion.

Heat baked her skin as they approached the fire. The dense mob curtained the flames that were strong enough for a lifting, eating up large pieces of driftwood and logs, but not shaped for a human body. Sweat rose and dampened her dress. Raegna shuffled from Bai, conscious of his own warmth beside her.

The anticipation of Judr's people was as prevalent as the scorching blaze. They brushed and bumped into each other in a frenzy, trying for a better view. Raegna drew close to Bai once more. If she jumped away, she would only ram into someone else's shoulder and ricochet to him. Their muscles tightened against each other, but they tolerated the touch as they maneuvered through.

"Must be some important ritual," Bai speculated over the chatter of the surrounding people.

"Hush," Raegna hissed.

A hand clasped her bicep. Thinking it was Bai, Raegna whirled to snap at him but came face to face with Femke. Her large, deep-set eyes bore Raegna's above a wide, toothy grin. The flames flickered in her sage irises.

"Femke," Raegna gasped.

"Good evening, priestess," Femke greeted. She used a polite demeanor, one different from what Raegna was used to from her. "You've brought your husband, I see."

"Er, yes, I—"

"Come." Taking her wrist, Femke guided Raegna through the congregation. "You are a guest here. You will witness this cleansing up close."

Bai kept at her heels, twisting to avoid running into others. Raegna could hardly check to be sure he followed. Femke dragged her so quickly. What was the meaning of her cheerfulness when such flames danced over them?

Femke reached the inner circle, stopping Raegna beside her. Bai stumbled in tow.

"The perfect place for you to be," Femke announced. "Your husband will surely be cleansed this way."

"Cleansed?" Bai repeated. But Femke ignored him.

"Enjoy the ritual," she told them, a rasping edge to her voice. Then she trailed the rim of the crowd, taking a position before the fire, a step ahead of her people.

"What does she mean by cleansed?" Bai's voice rumbled through the background clamor of crackling flame and human tongue.

Raegna scoffed. "They believe you to be of Fan. Just like everyone else."

His brow furrowed, and a crease deepened in the crook of his nose. "Is that why we're here? To treat and cleanse me?"

"No, I told you the Matriarch invited me since I am a priestess." Raegna tapped her fingertips on her chest. "It's just another foolish idea they created to give them an excuse to distrust us."

Bai did not have an argument against her. He looked away, brooding, his eyes glimmering in the firelight. Shadows covered his face like the candlelight at Adabelle's birth. Raegna should not have felt a twinge of sympathy for him, for his hurt dignity, but her heart sank. She opened her mouth to reassure him with more comforting words—the first she would ever give him—but a drumbeat made them both jump.

Their gazes jerked to the middle of the circle, where people parted and made a path. A line of solemn priestesses shuffled through, their maroon robes dragging along the dry gravel and their heads bowed. Even so, Raegna recognized the hunched neck of the eld-priestess. Each of them walked with a hand extended from their sleeves, palms facing outward, and each bearing a long, pale scar.

The priestesses' line wrapped around the fire, ahead of the villagers. Behind them came Matriarch Viona wearing a crimson dress, dark brown furs, and a black cloak draping from her shoulders. Her unbound hair rushed in light sandy waves down her back, topped with a silver band like a crown. Most notable was the charcoal paint smeared over her green eyes.

War paint had its significance in great battles, and only the Maidens bore it across their eyes. In texts and stories of Galaenian history, all women painted their faces before a battle or during celebrations and rituals. This one resembled those of the old days. Perhaps Viona wished to recall them this way? It was anyone's guess.

The fact that they would perform such a ritual now was unusual. Since the end of Galaenia's shrouded past, only the Arch Priestess could execute sacred rituals. Yet the Matriarch stood before the flames, arms extended, palms up to the stars as women did in historical carvings.

The drumbeats slowed and Judr's voices dwindled.

"Judr," Viona greeted, her voice carrying over the popping fire. "Fan sneers at our world, mindless enough to believe he can slink about to project his wrath."

The people responded with disdainful grunts and murmurs.

"But Gaea is with us," their Matriarch continued. "Tonight, we stomp out Fan, his imps, and his tricks against us. Though potential vessels for his legion walk our streets, we are clever to snuff them out."

Shouts of agreement rang out.

Bai shifted his weight, shaking his head. "I'm not sure about this..."

His agitation echoed Raegna's. As she stood in place, an icicle settled in her belly and urged her to shrink back, but if she did, she would run into Bai. Instead, she focused on the heat to melt that aching fear, bracing herself between her husband and the Matriarch.

Viona raised her chin. "Bring the vessels!"

The crowd roared with approval. Drumbeats picked up and ravaged the air. The circle parted again as warriors marched through in their plated armor. The first warrior escorted an old man by his arm. He tripped as he tried to match her gait, his clothes waving and loose over his frail limbs. More warriors pushed three young men into the circle, no older than twenty. They hung their heads in defeat, except for one whose feet skidded over the gravel as he fought to be released. Two warriors held him and jostled with his frantic attempts to escape but refused to let go.

The last warriors carried two infants into the circle. Their image tore at Raegna's core. One screamed at the heat while the other was too sickly to lift his head. Each prisoner was handed off to a priestess, though the fighting boy remained in the warriors' custody. He grunted and growled as he struggled.

A sharp breath escaped Bai's lips. "Raegna."

"Nuisances, bachelors, and unwanted sons all." Matriarch Viona's gaze roamed over each priestess who gripped the men and children like vices. "Tonight, we rid our lives of them and place ourselves at ease knowing these creatures of Fan will be sent back to where they were spawned. Down in the flaming pits of Helved!"

She lifted her hands into the air as one might praise Gaea. All at once, the priestesses slipped daggers from their sleeves, brought the blades to the prisoners' throats, and cut deep. Blood spurted from exposed necks and poured over gaping mouths, thick and bright red. The old man gagged and choked before dropping alongside the young men. The fighting boy gave a yell before gargling on his own blood. The screaming babe was silenced.

"All-Mother Gaea, trap these wretches in damnation as You condemned Fan himself!" Viona declared, her eyes alight with fire. "Free us of this evil and give us the power to cast it out!"

As the people rejoiced, Raegna stumbled back, her entire body trembling. She landed in Bai's arms, strong and firm around her. Her fingers clutched them to anchor her to the world and her surroundings, terrifying as they were. Crimson puddles pooled over the gravel and inched their way to the circle's rim. The sight blurred as Raegna's mind swirled like the black smoke that rose to the crescent moon. Visions of Pinar and her daughters' blood drifted with the clouds. Ice burrowed under Raegna's skin.

"Raegna, I want to leave," Bai muttered into her ear, his voice as shaken as she felt.

All she could do was nod. Her eyes widened as the warriors tossed the bodies into the flames, blood sizzling. Their smoking figures lay among the logs and wood. Raegna could take no more of it. She whirled and clung to Bai as he drove through the gathering.

Raegna expected him to stop just outside the circle, but Bai continued all the way down the street back to the healer's house, where the frightening cheers grew faint. She let him. Pained faces contorted in her memory, drenched in blood. They unearthed the memories of corpses that had littered Syden. Neighbors who had fallen lifeless and gore-ridden on the ground. Pinar's body once rested beside both her daughters with the silent, twisted cradle flipped over in the room's corner. Gaea, the babe's scream snatched from his tiny throat. His empty eyes.

A sob broke from her, and Raegna's hand fled to her mouth. The other bunched Bai's shirt in a fist as they hurried back. He carried her up the porch steps to burst into the kitchen, lit only by candlelight.

Banu pored over a book at the table before she took in the sight of the terrified couple. They both panted at the door as it shut behind them.

"You've seen it then," she mumbled with a sorrowful face.

"They're sick!" Bai's voice boomed, startling Raegna in his arms. "How could they do this? To protect their village? They only fill it with more hate!"

"I know but be quiet." Banu turned in her chair to the healing room of cots. "She's asleep."

Raegna and Bai followed her gaze to find Adabelle folded on her side on top of a bed visible from their angle. Her pale blonde hair stretched across the pillow, and her tiny lips parted above her round chin. The serenity of the scene left Raegna speechless. The fire and shouts vanished in the distance. Another sob closed her throat.

Bai dipped his chin, his breath on her hairline. "Raegna, we cannot stay here any longer. This isn't right, isn't safe. We can't—"

But Raegna bolted from his arms. Her daughter was all she could see. She rushed to the healing room and knelt at her bedside. Raegna laid her head beside her, stroking her hair.

Her mother's breaths rattled, and tears streamed down her cheeks, but Adabelle did not wake. Her face carried on the sweet innocence and blissful obliviousness, which made her mother weep harder.

"I'll find some blankets for you all," Banu whispered in the kitchen.

Both she and Bai tiptoed through the house to make the healing beds more comfortable for the family. No one would sleep in the barn tonight. Raegna drew herself closer to the bed to let them pass over her.

Finally, Banu bid them goodnight and drearily retired to her bed. Raegna's sobs quieted by then, but her lip continued to tremble, and her vision fogged with tears. Her fingers combed through Adabelle's hair and lingered over each lock.

Precious Adabelle could not live here, not after the terror they'd witnessed. Babes and innocent men murdered and discarded into flames had no place in a sweet girl's childhood. Many of the things her family had witnessed had no place there.

Pinar's image rippled in Raegna's memory, growing fainter by the day. The rich life and pink hues were replaced by caked blood and charred remains. Raegna bit her lip hard with her shoulders shaking.

Bai crouched by her side, hesitant at first, but willing. He reached and let his palm rest between her shoulder blades with little weight to it, just enough for her to receive a delicate touch. Unused to a voluntary gesture from him, Raegna met his gaze.

Gold irises gleamed in the dark. The prominent brow pinched and bent upward. A sharp tongue hidden behind a sealed, frowning mouth. The face she feared for so long was a comfort, a site of solace. The hand she had vowed would never have her again now pressed against her back with reassurance. He would not hurt her or allow anyone else to.

Raegna relaxed and she tucked her wet eyes into her arm extended over their daughter. Bai wrapped one around her shoulders, the other around Adabelle's body, and pulled them both close.

CHAPTER 18

NALEEM

THE MORNING COLD CRAWLED beneath the sheets, though Naleem had them pulled up to his chin. He shivered and groaned awake as it dug under his skin. Grasping his bearings, he found Dakarai and Cadoc snuggled against him for warmth. Perhaps they drained the heat from him.

The sun had yet to appear, warm the air, and brighten the world. Despite this, Naleem could make out the breathing lump of blankets that was his brother on the bed opposite his, curled in a ball as he always slept. The image evoked childhood memories, waking early alongside a much younger Hadwin.

"Such a terrible habit," their mother complained all those years ago. "He'll become crippled sleeping like a cat, and no woman will want him."

Instead, Hadwin grew with a straight back, strong and capable. No woman wanted him because their mother hid him in Naleem's shadow. She favored her eldest. A sour taste bubbled into his mouth. Their mother's treatment of Hadwin never sat right with him, but Naleem never knew how to confront her without provoking her irritation. At least Pinar had taken Hadwin in. But now...

A fist pounded upon the door. Naleem jumped halfway off the bed, disturbing his sons' slumber. Hadwin sprang up, his tawny hair sticking up and his eyes wide. He and Naleem exchanged a look while the knocking persisted.

With a gulp and a deep breath, Naleem slipped out of the covers and padded across the wood floor. The door creaked open to Thenalious, winded with his face flushed red. His usually slicked black hair fell in unkempt strands over his temples.

"You have to come quickly," he gasped out. "Reynold's babe is to be born. A caregiver must be present to witness the birth. I'd rather it be you."

"What?" Naleem gaped, gripping the door panel. "But how could—"

"There's no time," Thenalious urged him. He took Naleem by the arm and hauled him past the threshold. "We have to go now!"

"But—Stop! Let go of me!" Naleem growled as he stumbled free. He glimpsed Hadwin inside, who had already placed himself in front of Dakarai and Cadoc. The boys stirred at the noise, raising their heads.

Thenalious' fingers squeezed around Naleem's arm before he released him. "You have to come. It could happen any minute."

Naleem turned to Hadwin. Drawing his shoulders forward, Hadwin removed his glower from Thenalious to give Naleem a somber gaze. A silent promise passed between them. He would stay and protect the boys, for it seemed Naleem had no choice but to follow the snake.

"Fine," Naleem grumbled and allowed Thenalious to lead him downstairs and out of the great house.

In a mad dash, Thenalious sprinted across Haven, through the maze of tents filled with sleeping men. Naleem struggled to keep up with him, though he was not built for running at such a speed. Even the sense of urgency was not enough for him to pump his legs faster, but he kept a pace just a short distance behind Thenalious. Cold air rushed over his skin, rang through his ears, and burned his eyes.

Haven began to wake with a few men emerging from tents, sleepy-eyed and stretching. A few looked on as Thenalious rounded a sharp corner with Naleem skidding in pursuit.

"How is Reynold's child being born?" Naleem panted as they ran. "You know we can't make children on our own."

"You're right," Thenalious said without a glance over his shoulder. "But you'll see."

The two of them plodded over a hill and a small, broken horse barn came into view, slanting sideways under crooked pine trees. A woman's scream burst from the weak wood walls. The shrill sound brimming with pain startled Naleem to a halt. Dirt clouded around his ankles.

He swayed before the old shack as another cry erupted. Thenalious turned back when he reached the shack door and waved for Naleem to follow. "Hurry!"

Naleem's muscles seized and refused to budge. He hadn't heard a woman's voice in what seemed like decades, and the sounds of her pained struggle unnerved him. Steeling himself, Naleem exhaled with his head bowed and followed Thenalious.

More faint female voices, both soothing and strangled, echoed from the door, which barely clung to its hinges. Whether from curiosity or a strange sense of terror, Naleem stepped inside on the balls of his feet. His vision adjusted to the world within.

The early morning darkness left the shack dim, cold, and damp. Hunched figures of women huddled against the cracking walls. A dozen of them cowered in the four corners of the barn, sitting on nothing but gritty mud and moldy hay. Their hair hung from their heads in terrible tangles, their eyes hollowed over sharp cheekbones and encircled with gray. Every one of them watched Naleem enter before turning their attention to the middle of the floor. Naleem tracked their gaze.

A woman with skin like frost and a swollen belly crouched and leaned against a woman who supported her weight. She held both of the new mother's hands that clawed hers through her agony, their touch like snow capping rich, black mountains. Sweat plastered the mother's honey hair to her forehead, neck, and shoulders as she fought with clenched teeth. A third woman knelt in front of her, observing between her spread legs.

"Almost there," she encouraged the mother, placing a gentle hand on her knee.

Reynold loomed over them, a hulking bull among meek sheep. Rust hair billowed over his back with a few thick braids entwined. The rough points of his brow and chin scrunched. He regarded Thenalious and his sharp amber eyes softened. That was until Naleem showed himself and the softness vanished, replaced by narrowed malice. His shoulders squared.

Seemingly oblivious to this, Thenalious went to his side. "Is everything all right?"

"Well," Reynold grumbled. "Fan willing."

Naleem hobbled over the hay and looked on from behind a wood beam, steadying himself against it. All of Haven's true nature hit him like a boulder rolling down a cliff. These had to be women they took captive from the raids. Women the men wanted to keep, breed, and use for pleasure.

The once beautiful women were nothing but bones, their tattered, frayed dresses hanging from their bodies. The mother would be as malnourished as the others, despite her round belly. Her drained, white skin pulled taut over her bow-like cheekbones and glistened with her sweat and tears. She might not survive this exertion.

"Never underestimate a woman, Naleem." His mother's words echoed in his mind. "She is stronger than you know. You may push the plow, lift a stone, and toil over fields. But only *she* can do all that and endure the pain of birth."

He never truly believed her until he married Pinar, and she gave birth to Dakarai. But Pinar was fit, well-fed, and guided by a proper midwife and healer. This poor woman had only her will and her companions.

"Nearly there," the third woman assured. She clasped the mother's leg, squeezing to embolden her.

The mother stifled a scream through her clenched teeth.

"It will be a son." Thenalious' hushed voice carried across the room. He rested his chin on Reynold's shoulder, clutching the crook of his arm. "It has to be."

Reynold remained still.

Finally, the woman playing midwife enfolded the babe and wrapped it in a threadbare cloth. The mother fell back against the woman who held her, her strength spent.

Reynold pulled out of Thenalious' grasp and towered above her. His lip curled over his teeth. "Well."

The mother couldn't lift her head, her eyelids drooping, her sight darting over the midwife with the babe. The woman behind her rubbed her arm, her cheek pressed to the mother's temple as they awaited an answer.

Back bent, the midwife cradled the babe, hiding it from the men against her torso. "It's... a girl."

A pitiful sob escaped the mother's throat, and Reynold's nostrils flared. He scruffed the woman's hair and snatched the babe from her. The newborn screamed as he yanked her aloft, dangling by an ankle and glistening in blood and fluid.

The mother wailed. The rest of the women whimpered and shied away. Naleem lunged forward, his feet taking him from his position in the shadows without his will and caught the babe's head in his hands.

"Stop!" he shouted, though the words burst from his mouth as if someone else were speaking. "Stop it!"

Reynold raised a fist at him. "I'll kill you too, worthless bitch!"

"She's just a babe," Naleem protested, holding his ground. "Leave her be!"

The beast's fist would have collided with Naleem's face if Thenalious did not speak first. "Rey."

He spun to him. Thenalious stayed a distance from the conflict, standing unnaturally still as weeping echoed around him. The sunlight sifted through the wood cracks and a ray brushed across his face, gleaming against the autumn undertone of his skin, brightening his hazel eyes.

"He doesn't understand" was all he said.

Reynold snarled, a rough and low sound from deep in his chest. His fingers constricted the babe's ankle, and she cried harder.

Thenalious' eyes flicked to Naleem. "Why do you wish to save this thing?"

Naleem should have surrendered and been grateful Thenalious spared him. But he had made it this far and spoke even as his throat closed. "Sh-she's only a babe. She's innocent... And, and I'll not let you kill anyone else."

"She is weak," Thenalious argued. "Meaningless to us. Even if we let her live, the men out there will not. She's doomed here."

"I'll protect her," Naleem blurted, and his gut wrenched. "I'll teach her to know who we are. Just please, leave her be."

"How could you—"

"I'll protect her and care for her myself," Naleem insisted. His arm ached from balancing her head. "I'll teach her she is below us and she can learn about Sigmund. Let her live."

Reynold jerked the babe from Naleem's touch and raised her higher. "No. It shall be gotten rid of."

"Give the child to him," Thenalious ordered.

The beast glared at him over his shoulder. "What?"

"You heard me."

"And you would allow this bitch to interfere whenever he likes?" Reynold growled, his face reddening. "To corrupt and destroy everything we worked for?"

"He is practically Sigmund himself," Thenalious stated with a shrug. "He sees the good in all and protects such an innocent babe... Give it to him."

Reynold seemed ready to unleash Helved, his muscles bulging. Instead, he held Thenalious' gaze for a moment longer, testing him, before dropping the babe.

Naleem snatched her in the air with a gasp and brought her close as she shrieked in his ears. Slick, small, and new. He wrapped her in her cloth again so she might at least be warmer.

"She is your responsibility and will not be protected by the council like the other children," Thenalious told him. "Is that clear?"

Naleem nodded while his mind spiraled. His words and actions came from him so fast that he couldn't comprehend what he had done. His heart slammed into his ribs against the newborn's body.

Thenalious walked past them and out the door, saying, "Besides, Reynold, we might as well put your nights fucking here to good use."

With hot fury, Reynold yelled back. "They won't last a week!" Then he stomped out of the old barn, slamming the rickety door shut behind him.

Naleem trembled once the two men were gone. The babe continued to scream as he held her, his fingers quaking beneath her.

The women stared at him, their eyes wide and mouths gaping. Naleem stared back, just catching his breath. Taking a step forward, he slumped to his knees beside the mother, offering the babe to her. She did not have the strength to lift her arms, so her friend took the child and laid her against the mother's chest. Finally, the babe's cries quieted. More tears spilled over her mother's eyes as she bent to kiss her forehead.

Naleem sat and let himself sigh, his bones rattling under weak muscles.

"Thank you," the mother managed through her sobs.

Naleem opened his mouth, but when nothing came out, he blinked and inclined his head.

CHAPTER 19

BAI

THE BRISTLED HAIRS OF the broom scratched the wood floorboards in a mismatched rhythm as Bai swept. His pile of dirt reached the edge of the porch to be pushed over the side and into the street. The mindless work Turid gave him was just what he needed after last night's events.

A squeal sounded at the steps, compelling Bai's attention upward. Adabelle and Turid's daughter, Oda, hopped from one step to the next as fast as they could. Oda had the same red locks as her mother, but with a pinker, freckled complexion. She had come up with this race as a new game for them to play. But Adabelle almost missed the last step to fall flat on the road, though she caught herself and regained her balance.

Oda laughed. "Hurry, Adabelle! Hurry!"

Adabelle twirled and hopped faster this time to keep up with the older girl.

"Be careful, Ada," Bai warned when she set foot on the top.

"Yes, Papa!" she said without looking his way, focused on the steps below. Her short arms hovered above her sides.

With a sigh, Bai shook his head. He envied them as they romped above the same street so recently pooled with blood. Bai clutched the broomstick and turned from them as if he could get rid of the thought.

Before the legs of a porch chair, Turid's son, Quinlan, flew a wooden horse through the air while mumbling neighs and hoofbeats in his throat. The boy had black hair and light brown skin that must have belonged to his father. The girls always left the poor boy out of their games. His sister denied him any part of them. Thus, Quinlan played alone, though he did not show any sign of disappointment as he giggled to himself.

Bai placed the broom beside the front door, close to the boy. "A fine horseman we have here."

Quinlan beamed and continued galloping the toy through invisible fields and forests. "He's my horse. I'll have one someday!"

He wouldn't, of course. Men did not own livestock or anything. Bai silently prayed he would find a good horsewoman for a wife, and she would give him one. That was, if such a woman existed in this forsaken village.

Last night's events resurfaced in his memory. The victims' throats slashed open, and villagers' faces filled with bloodlust. Raegna had been so horrified, she fell into his arms, the weight of her so heavy Bai thought she had fainted. He had never seen his wife so frightened since her mother forced them. A debilitating pang of guilt coupled with immense anger for the Matriarch writhed in Bai's chest. With the added concern for Raegna, it all became too much.

Bai retrieved the broom by the door to put it away. When he had woken to Raegna at his side this morning, her ivory face had been serene in sleep. The way her right eyebrow arched slightly higher than the other, full lashes brushing her cheekbones...

"Bai."

He turned as Turid made her way up the porch steps, lifting her skirt with one hand. Red hair falling loose, she gave a friendly smile that showed her teeth with the gap in the front, as she always did when she greeted him. He offered a weak grin.

"M' lady."

"Now, I've told you, you may call me by my name," she corrected when she reached the top of the steps. Her eyes caught the broom. "You were sweeping?"

"Yes, m' la—Turid," Bai stammered. He spun the broomstick in place. "The children needed fresh air as well."

Turid's smile crinkled the lines around her eyes as she clasped her hands together. "Very good. Ah, I do not know what I would do without you."

With her heart so kind and her manner so bright, Turid made it incredibly hard to believe she worked for that cruel Matriarch day after day. She continued to be cheerful and lovely despite all the surrounding hate. Bai admired that.

"Oh!" she exclaimed with eyebrows raised. "I have something for you, a sort of thank you." She gestured to the door. "Let the children play. Come inside."

"Of course." He followed, only turning back to say, "Be good, Adabelle. All of you."

"Yes, Papa!" Adabelle nodded, stooped on the ground with Oda as they devised a new game.

Turid shut the door behind them and straightened her collar over the base of her chest. "Children are always bored with adult conversation. Your Adabelle is such a darling."

Bai bounced on the balls of his feet. Not only did she praise Adabelle, but also acknowledged she was his as much as Raegna's. "Thank you."

"Here, let me get us drinks." Turid went to a pitcher on the kitchen table, cups already placed there from the children's breakfast. "I'm terribly parched from walking from the great house, but you must need this more than me, since you were working all morning."

"It is a warm summer," Bai agreed with a shrug.

She produced a little pouch from her sleeve and untied it. Dipping her fingers in, she pinched a bit of sparkling powder and let it shimmer into their cups. "I snatched a bit of ground lemon from the market. We receive little from Stadt but when we do, I must get my hands on it. It gives our water a better taste."

Turid handed him his cup. Thirst had dried the back of his throat, so Bai took it and drank deep. "Thank you."

"My pleasure." She sipped and swallowed with a satisfied sigh. "Much better. Now, Bai, I have compensation for all your hard work."

Her shoes thudded across the wood floor as she headed for the cupboard in the kitchen. Bai shook his head. "You don't need to give me anything. Raegna and I are grateful you have taken me on at all."

"Oh, don't be modest." Turid chuckled and returned with a small purse that jingled with coins. "Here you are. Payment for your trouble."

"Payment?" Men did not work for pay, they worked for their mandatory contribution to the village and all their credit went to their wives. Bai had never touched a coin in his life, let alone been offered an entire purse.

"Yes," Turid chirped and placed it on the table before him. The coins rang against each other. "Good enough for the next week. I thought of giving it to you early. You've done so well for us."

Bai rubbed his neck. "I... Turid, I cannot accept this. Wouldn't your Matriarch be furious?"

"My coin is mine to deal with." Turid leaned over the table with a palm on the surface, raising her chin and brow. "I want you to have it."

"Truly, I appreciate it." His mouth went dry. "But I can't. It isn't done."

Her bright brown eyes lowered, but the grin remained. "What if I required more of you? Made you more deserving of this payment?"

Bai's mind buzzed like a distant horde of bees. "What do you mean?"

Before he could blink, Turid drew so close to him that her breath blew hot on his neck. "You have other uses. Services to provide."

She reached between his legs and cupped him. Bai stumbled back and lost his footing. His vision blurred as he landed in the chair behind him. It would have tipped backward if Turid had not intervened, grasping the chair's backrest.

Bai shook his head and pressed it to stop the whirling. "What are you—"

"It's all right," Turid soothed and bent over him. She caressed his cheek, then combed his hair back with her fingers. "I haven't had the touch of a man since my husband fell ill. There is no brothel here to salve my aches."

Turid took his hand in hers and guided it up to her thighs under her skirt. Bai yanked away and his head swam, his heart convulsing. "I... I'm, I'm married. Raegna—"

"Your wife needn't know," Turid assured him. Her fingertips traced his shoulder and bicep. "You are here every day with me. It can be our secret. Besides, I sense little feeling between you two. She's cold and indifferent to you, isn't she? Sending you out to work when you're wounded, you poor thing."

All the while, her hand, slipped beneath the waist of his pants, stroked him, and he was hard despite the ice that flooded his veins.

Bai shrank in the chair, shutting his eyes tight to ward off the storm in his mind. "What... what have you... did you do?"

"I didn't mean for you to drink all of that so quickly, sweet one," she admitted as her face shimmered like rippling water. "Just something for pleasure."

"No." Bai moved to push her off. Not only was she heavy, but his arms were too. He merely held her back with his forearm pressed to her chest.

Turid resisted, pulling away and clutching his shoulder. "You would be the first to object. The first to refuse."

Swinging a leg over his lap, she straddled him and fiddled with the laces of his pants. A thick fog clouded Bai's mind, but he seized her wrists and hauled them up. "Stop."

With a halfhearted laugh, Turid slid out of his grasp. "You are ungrateful."

Instead of delicately loosening the laces, she ripped them open and dragged them down, exposing him. Muscles made of lead, Bai grabbed her and twisted to throw her off. Turid gasped and toppled sideways onto the floor with a hard thud. Bai's world spun with the sudden movement. He pulled his pants back up. What had she done to him? What was in that powder?

Turid rose with her teeth gritted. All memories of her smiles and cheerful faces dissolved as she glared at him. Her red face contorted with a hideous snarl, the whites of her eyes flashing.

"You stupid tramp," she growled when she got to her feet. Her hand raised and swiped across Bai's face. The tips of her nails clawed his skin. His head swung to the side. The force and motion of her strike swirled the room in loops.

"You have no right to harm me!" She struck him again. His cheek stung as it used to when he was young, when his mother struck him the same. The same as when Raegna slapped him in the woods.

The next blow was a punch. "You should consider yourself lucky that a woman such as myself would desire you! Offer herself to you!"

Another. "You must be daft and brainless. Or do you fancy men, you wretched bitch?"

This time Turid meant to scratch him. Bai cried out as she barely missed his eye. Blood oozed over the fresh cuts. One blow after another, she continued to lash at him. His lip split and his nose bled. Despite the blur and drowning of his mind, he threw a blind punch with his remaining strength.

Turid shrieked and teetered. Catching her footing, her hand fled to her cheekbone, where Bai's fist landed. Even he could see the bruise forming in a pale purple under her eye.

"You bitch!" she screeched. "The Matriarch will hear of what you've done!"

With that, Turid dashed outside, leaving the door open behind her. Her cries faded farther and farther away as she ran.

Struggling to comprehend what had just happened, Bai urged himself to stand, to reach the door. He grunted with the effort it took to move, and his arms trembled as he pushed himself up. His feet tripped over each other, and he dropped to the floor. A wave of pain plunged through his head when it hit the floorboard. He groaned as his skull seemed to crumble like an ocean cliffside.

Why could he not move? What was she going to do? His heart pounded faster than he could track it. His muscles spasmed under his skin.

Raegna. He had to get to Raegna.

Footsteps padded into the house. "Papa?"

No. Bai lifted his head. He could have wept at the sight of Adabelle looking over him. Her image crisscrossed in doubles. Her eyes went wide with her little brow knitted.

"Ada," he choked out, hefting himself on a forearm. "Go to—go to Banu."

"I'll get Mama," Adabelle decided.

"No, Banu," he told her, forcing himself to rise. He dropped and caught himself, both arms planted on the floorboards. "Go to Banu. Or Jora. They'll keep you safe."

Adabelle tilted her head. "... Because you're hurt. I'll get Banu."

Her little feet scraped across the floor, and she was gone too. She knew the way back to the healer's house. At least she would be far away from here and safe from whatever was to happen now.

What would happen now?

Turid would tell the Matriarch some horrific story and they would all believe her. He would have no chance. Raegna could not vouch for him, even if she wanted to. And why would she want to?

That moment with Adabelle would be the last Bai would ever have with her. This miserable state would be the last she would see of him. She would lose him. At the thought, his body collapsed, and his stomach heaved. Without warning, a sob broke free from his throat while he awaited his fate.

Chapter 20

Hadwin

After Naleem left with Thenalious at the crack of dawn, Hadwin could not find sleep again. He fidgeted and smoothed out his nephews' bed sheets while he waited and worried.

How long would this whole ordeal take? Would Naleem be back at all? Why did Thenalious want him especially? Besides the obvious favor he had shown, why Naleem when it was Reynold's child being born? Wouldn't that anger the beast?

When Dakarai and Cadoc woke, Hadwin gathered them up and prayed his brother would be all right before the three of them shuffled to the nursery.

Doing his best to care for the little ones, Hadwin kept a watchful eye on the older boys, who had risen to begin their morning antics. They could play all they wanted. He didn't mind for now. His thoughts were far too preoccupied. Only the creak of the door broke his attention from the babes.

Naleem stood at the threshold, his brown hair tousled, and his broad face paled with drooping eyes. A bundle of blankets rested in his arms.

"Naleem!" Hadwin leaped to his feet. In his excitement, a few of the children paused to see the reason. "Gaea, had they kept you any longer—well, I don't know what I would do."

Naleem let the door shut behind him and shifted the bundle. "It wasn't Thenalious who kept me, truly."

He pulled the blanket away, and Hadwin peered into the bundle. A newborn's fleshy, red face scrunched in a yawn before returning to peace again. Hadwin frowned. "Funny how something so small could be the product of that monster."

"There is more to this one than the others," Naleem said. "It is a girl."

A small burst of warmth filled Hadwin to the brim and diminished as the realization hit him. "Oh, no."

"She is our responsibility now." Naleem took the babe to the cradles. He chose one for her and placed her there. "Reynold was going to kill her right in front of her mother. I couldn't let him. Thenalious allowed her life to be spared."

Too many questions crowded Hadwin's mind at once. He could not ask even one before Naleem spoke again.

"I'm sorry I've done this to us, Hadwin." He stood over the cradle, watching over the babe. "There is no way to escape with one so young. She would give us away and we can't take her from her mother. And we can't leave her here."

Hadwin had not thought about that. He shook his head. "No, I would have done the same. I know why. They would kill her if we left her here."

Naleem nodded, stone-faced. "It's still early. Only Thenalious and Reynold know of her." He paced toward Hadwin, lowering his voice. "I intend to keep her safe with discretion for now. I don't know what Reynold might do to her, or to us... but the rest of the men can't know about her."

"I agree," Hadwin said at once. "She still needs her mother. Why did you bring her here?"

"For safety," Naleem told him. "Her mother insisted on it. Councilmen go to that old barn almost daily and she did not want the babe to be discovered. I thought we might take turns bringing her there to eat."

Hadwin blinked. "Oh, right. How often must we do that?"

"Often." Naleem nudged his shoulder with an amused huff. "Let's get these little beasts fed."

The morning routine ensued without a hitch. Hadwin preferred to keep Naleem in sight, but they could both leave the house to take the girl to her mother like clockwork. Hadwin couldn't recall how often Pinar nursed her newborns, but they seemed to always be suckling. Would it be easier to settle the mother in the nursery instead? The councilmen wouldn't approve of that idea, but Naleem might convince Thenalious of its wisdom.

After breakfast, they marched the boys upstairs, though they all begged to go outside. One pair of eyes on the outdoor games wouldn't be enough when Naleem took the first trip to the women's barn. Hadwin remained with the boys while Naleem gathered the newborn in his arms and left for the barn.

"Where's Papa going?" Dakarai asked Hadwin after pulling away from the fun of jumping on beds. He tilted his head as he peered up at his uncle.

"Don't worry, Dak," Hadwin assured. "Your Papa will be back. He's only taking the new babe to… to get something to eat."

"Papa doesn't play with us anymore," Dakarai whimpered, his lip pouting. "Doesn't he love us?"

Hadwin's heart caved in on itself. "Oh, Dak. Of course, he does. He's your Papa. I know it's difficult to understand after all that's happened…

But trust me, he loves you and cares for you just as he always has. All right?"

Dakarai frowned but tugged his uncle's hand. "Will you play with us, Uncle Hadwin?"

Hadwin pinched his shoulder. "I suppose I can find the time to."

Bounding after them, Hadwin scooped up his little victims before spinning until they were both too dizzy to run anymore. A heavy weight lifted from his shoulders as he played with them, a weight that had trapped him in Haven and disabled him from remembering his own childhood.

The boys slept wherever they dropped for their afternoon nap. It was the best Hadwin could do. Naleem returned from the barn without incident. The newborn girl dozed in her cradle like the other babes while Hadwin watched over them. Naleem sat on the edge of a bed where his sons fell asleep alongside two other boys, all of them lying horizontally across the vertical bed to fit. His eyelids dipped and he covered his mouth with a yawn.

Hadwin leaned against the wall. "Why don't you rest too, Naleem? You've had quite the day."

With a hesitant sigh, he inclined. "Just for a while."

"I'll keep watch," Hadwin told him. Naleem lay back across the bed as the boys had. A mere minute passed before his breath slowed to a slumbering pace.

Hadwin put his attention on the cradles when a babe cooed in their sleep. The newborn truly eliminated their chances of escape. The councilmen would protect the boys if Naleem and Hadwin fled. But they would not tolerate *her*. The strangulation of his youngest niece entered his mind in a horrific flash. Her struggling screams clamored between the walls. He shut his eyes tight to shake them away.

Yes, that is what they would do to her. No wonder Naleem could not stand to see another little girl suffer at the hands of these monsters. They could not abandon her here. But what were they supposed to do now?

First to wake was the girl, who gurgled a warning before erupting into an outcry. Hadwin pushed off the wall to take her just as Naleem jolted upright.

"Everything's fine." Hadwin raised his palms and stooped over the cradle.

The boys stirred at the sound. Naleem rubbed his eyes. "I can take her again."

She was already in Hadwin's arms, and he spoke as he went to the door. "No, you stay behind. It's my turn. Besides, you can afford to spend time with your sons. Dakarai misses you."

"Dakarai?" Naleem glimpsed at his son. He slept with his brother resting on his belly, with little room between them and another boy.

"Yes, maybe you can let him help you while I'm gone," Hadwin said and opened the door. "I'll be back."

"...All right," Naleem breathed, too dazed with exhaustion to give much input or argument.

Despite the peace within the nursery, Haven continued to work tirelessly. Servant boys scrambled upstairs while Hadwin stepped down. A few kitchen boys looked in his direction to identify where the infant cries came from, formed their own conclusion, and returned to their tasks.

Outside, Hadwin noted how few councilmen remained in the great house during the day. Perhaps they made rounds through Haven and evaluated all operations. Even as he paced past the tents, he caught no sign of a councilman. That was until Wyn's high-pitched barking echoed across the camp. Hadwin could not spot him but rolled his eyes at his orders.

Hadwin thought he knew where the old horse barn was based on what he had heard and followed the path. Like the servants, the men in the camp glanced up at the cries of a babe and went back to work. Unlike the servants, some sneered or kicked dirt at him. Hadwin raised his chin and ignored them.

Over a slight hill, tucked between the trees at the edge of the forest, the horse barn leaned against a tree. The brittle wood walls braced the rickety roof, barely supporting it to the sky. Inside, captives who were mere objects and breeding stock to the men of Haven lived like animals. Hadwin took a breath and proceeded as the babe's crying grew more fervent.

When he approached, scuffling resonated between the cracks in the wall and Hadwin paused. Deep, quiet grunts of a man echoed alongside the struggling gasps of a woman's voice. Hadwin frowned. Part of him wanted to interrupt and bring what went on behind the door to an end. But part of him feared Reynold may be on the other side. What would he do if Hadwin intervened?

Just as he devised a plan or distraction, the grunts and struggle ceased. Hadwin tightened his hold around the babe, pulling her closer to muffle her cries. Should Reynold emerge from the shack, he would have to hide. His heart leaped as footsteps came to the door.

Hadwin flinched when it opened, but Reynold did not exit. Instead, the man from the council meeting, Oberon, stood before him. Hoisting his belt farther up his waist, he cocked his head when he spotted Hadwin. "What— Oh, you're the new caregiver."

Blinking, Hadwin cleared his throat. "Um, yes."

"Hm." Oberon's long mouth broke into a grin. He nodded to the newborn in Hadwin's arms. "Do you enjoy this better than kitchen work?"

How could he be so casual after what he had done in there?

"I have to get inside." Hadwin walked past him, glad Oberon did nothing to stop him.

He had to adjust from bright summer sunlight to obscure darkness when he entered the barn. Hadwin gazed at the shadows of the women. Most of them curled against the walls, while a few tended to one in the middle: A woman with smooth ebony skin and hair billowing over her thin, hunched shoulders pulled away when her fellow women tried to comfort her. As Hadwin stepped inside, all eyes turned to him, either wide in fear or narrowed in calculation.

All of them were skin and bone. Large eyes peered from sunken sockets, and cheekbones protruded high above thin lips and chins. What once might have been beautiful, full locks hung loose and lank about their shoulders. Old, tattered dresses covered their bodies, which were bruised from abuse. They waited for what Hadwin might do. Some glared as if daring him to come close.

Then the newborn gave another cry. Their gazes shifted to the bundle in his arms.

"I, um, I'm Naleem's brother," Hadwin explained, standing stock-still. "He's the one who saved this babe. She's just hungry... Which of you is her—"

"Here." A warm voice called out from the back wall. She sat with her long legs stretched before her, her back and head propped up against the wall. Honey hair tangled around her pale white face, which was slack with exhaustion but held a gold tinge. Her clouded blue eyes bore into him. "I am her mother."

Hadwin nodded and went to her. Kneeling, he offered the baby to her, and she took her, preparing to nurse. The woman beside her leaned in to help her as she needed. Hadwin backed away, far enough to give her and the others space. He had no right to be among them. His presence intruded into their few moments of peace, and it made his heart ache.

"Why does Naleem send you here?" The question interrupted the quiet. It came from the reluctant woman in the middle of the barn, sitting with her legs folded beneath her on top of a hay pile. Her stark brow tightened with a glare, her rich onyx eyes staring daggers into Hadwin.

He gulped. "Well, we decided we would take turns bringing her here. I thought he would need the rest for a little while. So, I came instead."

The woman studied him with her lip curled.

"Farah," the woman beside the mother snapped, "so long as he brought the babe to us, it hardly matters who brings her."

"Forgive me, Sevda, for being apprehensive about this strange boy," Farah snapped back, the bridge of her nose crinkled. "But it is not your job to be my chiding mother."

"There's nothing you need to be afraid of." Hadwin stepped back. "If you like, I'll step out and wait."

"It's all right," the mother blurted, raising her head over her babe. "We've just grown fond of Naleem. I'm sure you're just as good as him but... Farah, do you wish for him to leave?"

Her words were gentle, genuinely asking for her request. Farah did not look at her, did not even glimpse. She fixed her jaded sight on the hay and gave a slight nod.

Hadwin obliged. Without another word, he left them alone and waited outside the door. The barn was hidden from the camp itself, so at least Hadwin did not have to look out over the Haven men and loathe them. The crest of the hill concealed the camp up to the tips of tents, but it could not drown out the voices and shouts of work.

After several minutes, Hadwin was called back into the shack. All the women drew themselves in a circle toward the center of the floor. They leaned close to each other in an urgent discussion. At his entrance, they turned to him, and each had a unique expression, eyebrows raised curiously or expectantly, or eyes cast down nervously. Farah regarded him with a scrutinizing gaze.

The mother finished nursing and cradled her babe in her lap. Her eyes locked onto Hadwin's. "You will protect her."

Her tone did not indicate a question, but it was not a demand. The words hung in the air as a statement, a fact.

Hadwin gulped and nodded. "Yes. We all will. We can protect each other."

She ushered him closer, though he hesitated, glancing at Farah's hostile expression. Hadwin knelt before the mother, careful not to inch too close.

She snatched his wrist and her nails sank into his skin, leaving red marks. Hadwin flinched, but she held him in place.

"You will not deceive us even if you try," she hissed under her breath. "You can trust none of these men. Every one of you is Thenalious' pawn to use to his own end. You will not jeopardize this girl because you think you can trick him. You cannot trick Fan himself; do you understand?"

Hadwin's throat closed. "I... but if we—"

"You will not risk her life." She forced every syllable through her teeth. "You will play the game. If you do not... they do unspeakable things to you."

Pinar had sacrificed herself at their command, yet those she wanted to protect were spared. Seagr wept for his lost wife in the aftermath of Syden's attack and defended her, only to be cut down by their steel. Obrecht, the old man of Gaea, defied their belief and fell, never to be lifted.

All this time, Naleem had played along, though reluctantly, by accepting Thenalious' offers to the nursery, to his table. However Thenalious intended to use him, whether to induce envy from Reynold or truly benefit Haven or both, Naleem and his family stood subject to his whims. The lives of these women and the girl in her mother's arms lay in Thenalious' hands.

"We cannot suffer here forever," Hadwin protested.

The mother released him and pulled the swaddle closer around her babe. "It is our fate. We can only survive and live another day."

Hadwin could not argue anymore. He cast his eyes down, but refused to let her words waver his resolve. There would be ways to escape this place. Haven was not Helved, despite its similarities. Thenalious was not Fan.

The mother bid her babe goodbye with a kiss before giving her to Hadwin. Guilt-ridden for taking her daughter from her, Hadwin stood and went toward the door. Farah's eyes followed him.

"Wait." The mother's voice reached out to him as his hand touched the doorknob. Hadwin turned to her, the babe gurgling in his arms.

"You'll name her Else," the mother told him. "My sister's name in her memory."

He nodded. "Else."

The men of Haven wrapped up their work for the end of the day while Hadwin walked past them and their tents. None kicked dirt at him or taunted him, all of them too enthused by the prospect of supper to worry about his presence. Hadwin relished the respite and stole a glance at the babe's face.

Just the size of a loaf of bread, she curled underneath her blanket and snuggled into his chest. She reminded him of peaceful times in his old home, the memory of his new nieces and nephews, for he had never seen newborns like them before. A sweetness crinkled in her pink, fleshy cheeks as she sighed and then yawned.

Hadwin smiled. "Else."

He found the porch steps and went for the door. It opened before he could move for the knob. Reynold appeared on the other side, a head-and-a-half taller than him. Rust braids fell over his bulky shoulders and his brow set in a permanent furrow. Hadwin's heart slammed against his chest. He stared wide-eyed at the beast.

Reynold recognized him and his amber eyes sharpened as Hadwin pulled Else closer to conceal her. He stalked forward like a bear through the woods and slowed at the steps beside Hadwin.

His voice rumbled so low it reverberated up Hadwin's spine. "Tell your brother Fan will have him."

His boots thudded on the wood steps and continued to the gravel dirt behind Hadwin. Breath finally returned after a few moments. Hadwin forced himself to straighten and dashed into the great house.

Chapter 21

Raegna

Summer beat down on Judr, baking the streets by afternoon. Sweat beaded Raegna's back between skin and dress as she sat with Iida, reading Gaea's scripture from leather-bound pages. Iida wove a blanket together with wool, tightening the strands to make it snug and durable. She insisted that come winter, her babe would need something thick to keep warm.

Winter seemed so far off with fall in between, but it would pass like a breeze. Would Raegna stay so long in this horrendous village?

The ritual had been all too much. The memory of blood and dead babes streaked through Raegna's mind, no matter how many times she shoved it away.

"Is something troubling you, Raegna?" Iida's clear voice cut through her thoughts. Her brown eyes studied Raegna's, her hands paused over her belly.

Raegna blinked and lifted her head from her book. "Oh. No, I'm all right. Truly."

The expectant mother's mouth twisted to the side, unconvinced. She fiddled with her weaving without another word. Raegna let her eyes fall upon the page again, the words and lines blurring in her shrouded vision. Her daughter had witnessed enough blood...

When she couldn't adjust her focus on the text, Raegna set the book down and scanned the room to get her bearings.

Femke lounged on a couch across from her, her legs propped over an armrest. Her sharp features flexed in concentration as she inspected her fingernails. Matriarch Viona's daughters sat on the furred rug before their aunt, engaged in a game of dice and cards. Such lighthearted girls to come from a mother like theirs.

The men remained against the opposite wall where they could be seen but out of the way. Viona's husband, a thin, tall man with a broad, square face, kept his eyes down beside Asmund. Raegna caught Asmund glancing up at Iida past his soft brow before looking away again. She hated seeing him pressed into the shadows. Of all the men Raegna had ever met—though there weren't many she grew close to in the slightest—Asmund presented the sweetest temper. No one would believe her if she told them he had a deep voice and spoke only to Iida in her sisters' absence.

Matriarch Viona stood in an adjacent room, speaking with Nairi, the stocky Lady of Labor. Before them was Ase, the commander of Judr's warriors, who had opened the gates for Raegna and her family. She donned thick leather armor, her black hair in a tight braid down the back of her neck. Raegna studied the length of the sword in its scabbard at her belt. A longing sparked within her.

If she were a warrior, perhaps Raegna would not be here. She would have more authority to bring news of the attack to sister villages and Matriarchs would trust her. If she were a warrior, her village and the lives of her friends, Pinar, and her children would already be avenged. Her daughter would be safe from all harm, and she would not have feared Bai.

Though when she thought of Bai these days, fear was no longer instilled in her.

Nothing was going to be done if Raegna scanned scripture and played priestess-in-waiting to an evil Matriarch's sister. Syden lay in ashes and Viona would do nothing, no matter how many times a meek priestess urged her otherwise. Raegna's nails glided over the cover of her book.

"We can seek help elsewhere," Bai had said the night before. "... the Queen is kind. As kind as Iida. She would know what to do. She has the warriors and Maidens at her disposal."

Raegna's eyes darted over the page of scripture as if it were a map, each line a forest road and each word a mile. They led to Galaenia's capital city, Stadt, where the Queen lived in her palace, Vakkar Hold. But how could a Queen listen to a lowly priestess and her common family?

"Matriarch!" a familiar voice wailed from outside.

Even the men looked up as the front door burst open with a crash. The Matriarch and her women peered from their room to investigate the commotion.

Turid teetered at the threshold, her cherry-wood hair sticking up in wild strands and her face drained of its rose color. Her eyes were crazed, the whites wide and unyielding. A purple bruise hung over her cheek and her dress creased with wrinkles. Every brow furrowed at her.

She panted as if she sprinted half the village. "Matriarch, you must help me! I— He— he's ruined me!"

Matriarch Viona stepped around the corner. "Who? What's happened?"

Turid yelped like a wounded dog and braced herself against the doorframe. "That tramp, that spawn of Fan... the priestess' husband, Bai. He... he raped me!"

She lost herself in a fit of sobs and fell to her knees. Her hands covered her face.

The world spun. Raegna was on her feet, her book tumbling from her grasp to the furred floor. "Bai...?"

"Where is he now?" Viona demanded.

"I..." Turid stammered over her words. "I fled. He had me pinned, but I fought and fled. From... my home." Her face stretched in slack terror. "My children. Oh, Gaea above, my children! He is there with them!"

"Ase," Viona snapped at the commander. "Have warriors at the gate, surround the village, and come seize this wretch. We will not let him escape or go unpunished."

"No!" Raegna shouted across the room.

Their heads spun to her, stealing the breath from her lungs. Raegna held her fists at her sides, and she forced her voice. "He wouldn't do that. He wouldn't hurt anyone!"

Viona peered down her nose, an eyebrow arched. "Naïve of you to think so, priestess. This is the way of men, so obsessed with a craving for intercourse, any of them will do what they can to take it. Your man is no different."

"No, not him," Raegna barked despite the bile that rose in her throat. Her gaze shifted to Turid, who knelt on the floor, watching the argument between the Matriarch and priestess with a twinge of calculation in glistening eyes.

Raegna ground her teeth. "She's lying."

Turid wrapped her arms around herself. "You insult me!"

"How dare you, priestess?" Viona spat.

"She's lying!" Raegna pointed her finger at the weeping woman like a spearhead. "He would not harm anyone!"

Viona threw her hands in the air. "Enough of this!" She gestured to her commander. "Ase, for Gaea's sake, find that man! We will punish him before this very house!" She turned on Raegna. "As for you, priestess, you will stay put here and watch the wretched pig die!"

"No, I will not!"

Raegna dashed out of the great house, screams following her through the door. She paid them no heed and tore across the gravel street. Her footsteps pounded with her heartbeat. Shapes and figures flew past her, and the wind tuned out shouts for her.

Not Bai. Her heart ached as it hammered against her ribcage. The darkness of her old room surrounded her. Her mother trapped her there, unlocking the door, only to drag Bai in.

Sweat rolled under her dress in the summer sun. Her hair would stick to her neck if it didn't whip behind her.

Not Bai. Jaleesa brought him to a halt before the bed, her nails sinking into his wrist. He winced, and she leaned into him and murmured in his ear.

Swords unsheathed from their scabbards as Raegna raced past a group of warriors. Jora's familiar voice called out, but Raegna didn't see her.

Not Bai. He shook his head and jerked away. Jaleesa held a knife to his throat. The edge pressed into his jugular. His eyes fell on Raegna, the richest gold brimming with fear. Her heart drummed as it did now, and her body trembled.

"He pinned me!" Turid's laughable words filled her ears.

With the knife between his shoulders, Bai came over to her and pinned her when she punched and kicked. It only slowed him and only angered her mother further.

Not Bai. Jaleesa kept the knife pointed at him as she struck Raegna with the back of her hand. Her knuckles bit Raegna's cheekbone. The hard smack echoed across the walls.

It was not Bai. Clamping her fingers under Raegna's chin, Jaleesa drove it up for her daughter to behold her seething face. Raegna's entire body seized, receiving the order without hearing a thing.

Bai's lip quivered over his clenched teeth. Tears fogged his gold irises. The first words he ever spoke to her shook with his voice. "I'm sorry."

With a painful lump in her throat, Raegna shut her eyes tight. Her own tears seeped through them and down her cheeks. She jerked her head from him. "Just get it over with."

When it was over, Bai let her go and wrenched away without another touch for years.

Turid's house came into view with the door open. The daughter, whatever her name was, who Adabelle loved, sat on the porch with her brother and leaped to her feet when Raegna appeared.

"Where is my mother?" the girl demanded with her hands on her hips. Raegna rushed past them, stopping just inside the house.

The air drifted thick and hot from wall to wall. The kitchen table in one corner held tipped cups that spilled their contents. Bai bent in a chair, his legs spread and his elbows resting on his knees. His head hung with his face covered behind his fists.

"Bai." Raegna took a knee in front of him. She brushed his leg with a tender hand and brought her voice to a faint whisper. "Bai, what's happened?"

He withdrew, curling in on himself.

"Please, Bai." She clutched the fabric of his pants. "You must tell me before…" No, she could not frighten him more. "I know you did nothing wrong. Tell me you did nothing wrong."

He stayed silent.

Then Turid's wailing sounded from the porch. "Oh, my babes! Thank Gaea you're safe! Thank Gaea!"

Old tears cracked over Raegna's eyelids as new hot ones surfaced. "Bai… you have to tell them the truth. I know you did not do this. Please, tell them."

"They won't listen." His voice sloshed.

A hard stone welled in her throat. "Please, Bai."

Footsteps started up and into the house. Bai raised his face from his fists and in a fleeting moment, Raegna caught sight of him. His lip split open and gushed blood, bruises stamped across his cheeks, claw marks slashed over his brow, crimson covering his nose. Tears added salt to mix with bloodied wounds.

Raegna stumbled but held onto his pants leg. Two pairs of hands hauled her up. Her world tilted on its axis. Bai shrank away as warriors came for him next, four of them grabbing him by his arms, shoulders, and neck. As they forced him up, one slammed the hilt of her sword into his gut and he collapsed in their grasp.

"No!" Raegna lurched forward. "Stop! Leave him alone!"

"Your love blinds your judgment, priestess." Matriarch Viona stepped through the threshold, as cool as a cat ready for an evening rest.

"Release him!" Raegna begged, hanging by her elbows in the warriors' grasps. "Can't you see he's hurt? He did nothing wrong and Turid is the one to blame! She's lying!"

"You will cease your insults to a suffering sister," Viona snarled.

"She insults *us*, Matriarch." Raegna pulled against her captors. "You and I have suffered this, and she believes it to be a tool and a game!"

Viona gaped and her cheeks and temples turned pink. She took a step back.

"Look at the man's face!" Raegna nodded to Bai. "He has suffered too!"

The Matriarch shut her eyes and growled. "I will not hear another word from you, priestess! Take them to the great house. Nairi will rip the hide from him!"

"Viona, listen to me!" Raegna yelled as the warriors obeyed. "Viona!"

Bai pushed against them when another hilt rammed into his chest. He doubled over, heaving for air. "Raegna!"

"Don't hurt him!" she cried.

The warriors hauled them from the house, feet dragging in the dirt. Many collected outside buildings and merchant tents to view the disturbance. Voices chattered over Raegna's desperate shouts and a crowd formed around the two prisoners and the warriors who held them. Their Matriarch led the way, striding back to her house.

Femke and Nairi waited there, Femke with her arms crossed below her breast and Nairi swinging the whip beside her leg. Its tails dangled with the rhythm. Iida stood at the front door, concealing her nieces behind her. Her mouth opened as if to say something, but no words came.

Matriarch Viona joined her sister and Nairi and gestured to the porch. The four warriors brought Bai to the rails and kicked the backs of his legs. He crumpled to the ground. Jerking his wrists in place, they tied him to the railing. They secured the rope and gave him a blow to the head. Bai's body went limp, his back facing the gathered crowd.

Raegna's captors kept her at a distance while she threw her weight to knock them off-balance.

Viona looked over her people. "This man has shamed and humiliated one of our sisters. Only Fan could conceive of something so horrid and cowardly. For this, he will die."

"No!" Raegna screamed over the calls for action.

The Matriarch waved Nairi on and she stepped in just behind Bai, wagging her whip. She launched it up and hurled it down with a crack that slashed Bai's back. The tails ripped through his shirt and skin. His head lurched back and his throat opened in a scream.

The crowd cheered.

Raegna lunged, but the warriors held her firm. "Please, let him go! Don't hurt him!"

Crack!

Bai yelled through gritted teeth. Droplets of blood splattered the ground and red soaked his torn shirt.

"No, let him go!"

Viona watched with dark shadows over her features. Femke smiled, tickled at the sight of a tortured man. At the front door of the great house, Asmund shielded Iida and the girls. All the while, the crowd roared for more. Nairi brought the whip to Bai's back over and over again. Blood spilled across her boots. Bai sobbed.

In a blur, Raegna twisted. Her arm tore loose from imprisonment. She drove her opposite forearm into the other warrior's chest. Raegna snagged the sword at her belt and peeled away, taking it with her.

"Stop!" was all the first warrior could manage, but Raegna rushed forward.

Nairi raised her whip once more. Raegna skidded between her and Bai, hoisting the blade above her. The whip came down on the steel and scraped it with a high-pitched *chink*. Raegna's maroon priestess skirts flowed out from her mad dash and the tails shredded them. A harsh sting snaked down her leg.

The crowd went silent. Nairi stumbled back in disbelief. All mouths gaped at the priestess as she held her sword aloft. Raegna glared with her chin down, her eyes flashing beneath her knitted brow.

"If another hand harms this man," she snarled at them, "I will drench this sword with your blood!"

Nairi flushed red as she prepared the whip. "I'll take care of you too, lunatic priestess!"

"Wait." Matriarch Viona raised a palm. She regarded Raegna, her face constricted with her affliction. "You have no right to interfere."

"I've the right to believe he has done nothing wrong." Raegna jutted her head toward Bai, holding the sword ready. "He is covered in wounds and *she* bears only a single mark."

"She fought well!" Femke spoke up.

"She lies and deceives us," Raegna countered. One scan of the gathering and she found Turid in front of them, clasping her children in her arms with an ashen expression. "She is the one who shamed my husband. He did nothing wrong!"

The crowd erupted in objection. Nairi and Femke waited on Viona, on her next command. Meanwhile, the Matriarch examined the ground as if the rocks and pebbles were puzzle pieces. She turned to Turid among her people, singling her out. Raegna followed her gaze.

Turid gulped and loosened her hold on her children. Her slack stare darted around the priestess and the blade that defended Bai. When her eyes met her Matriarch's, Turid froze in place, mouth bobbing as she tried to form words. Viona beheld the woman a moment longer before turning back to Raegna.

"You are lucky I do not behead him, priestess," she snapped. "Someone get her out of my sight!" Then she waved Nairi on. "Make him wish he were dead."

Warriors came forward and disarmed Raegna. One caught the hilt of the sword when she swung it. The other drove a knee into her belly. Raegna gasped as they pulled her away and Nairi resumed her position, lifting the whip above her shoulder.

Crack!

Bai yelped, and the crowd became a mix of protests and cheers. Raegna yanked at the warriors' arms as she choked out, "No, please."

She struggled for breath and forced her head up.

In the distance, over the crowds, Raegna spotted Banu walking with Adabelle clutching her hand and pulling her down the road. The healer paused at the gathered crowd.

Then Jora jogged toward them out of the mass. She hastily guided them in the opposite direction of the bloodthirsty shouts of insults, and back to the healing house. Both of them sheltered Adabelle from the sight.

Gloom and relief both ravaged Raegna's heart. The warriors twisted her back around to face Bai and Nairi. She looked on while blood spattered the ground and her daughter's beloved father cried out in agony.

Chapter 22
Naleem

SUPPER SPLAYED ACROSS ONE of the great hall's tables with bowls of soup and a small platter of fish. Naleem peered at the food while the boys took their seats. Digging the tiny bones out of the meat would be awful, but he couldn't risk the little ones choking. Hopefully, Hadwin would be back soon to help with the task. He ought to be.

As the boys chattered in their seats, two older voices carried over the hall, reaching Naleem's ears.

"A strike to the walls would do us good. According to the scouts, those broads only placed defenses at the front gate."

Naleem raised his attention from the boys. Before the double doors, Reynold and councilman Oberon murmured to one another.

Reynold's back faced the long table as he spoke, his large shoulders squared. "Ready everyone then. Thenalious will be quick to organize a raid. We need to get what we can to survive winter."

Oberon nodded, stole a glance at the boys, and took his leave toward the back hall. Reynold turned, meeting Naleem's eyes.

What Naleem should have done was look down, give the indication of submission or at least fearful respect. Yet after witnessing the brute attempt to kill a newborn in front of her mother as Naleem's own daughters were killed before him, he kept his gaze on the beast. Reynold would know he lost this time and he would lose again.

Reynold's nose wrinkled and he whirled to the doors.

With a shaking breath, Naleem settled in his seat with the boys.

The doors opened again, and Hadwin entered with the babe in his arms. He hurried to the staircase without a sideways glance at the table.

"Hadwin!" Naleem called.

Hadwin came to a halt at the second step and blinked at him. Naleem tilted his head but ushered his brother to join them. Hadwin paced over and rested on the bench in front of him with his nose down. Strands of his tawny hair fell in his eyes and he brushed them away. A few of the boys greeted him as they slurped their soup. He returned their greetings but wouldn't look their way. Naleem's stomach twisted.

"Hadwin, what is it?" he muttered so the boys would not hear over their own chatter.

"I..." Hadwin hesitated, refusing to meet Naleem's stare. He leaned over the tabletop instead, the newborn cradled close to his chest. "Reynold gave an exchange of words that frightened me, was all."

Naleem frowned. "What did he say?"

"I don't want to scare the boys," Hadwin admitted and drew back.

The thought of Reynold trying to threaten his brother sent heat through Naleem's veins. His jaw tightened as he forced himself to take a breath. "Ignore him for now. He's angry about being ordered around."

Hadwin nodded. "The women are very frightened as well."

His friendly nature had gotten the better of him, and the poor women were not ready for it. Naleem offered a weak grin. "They've been through much, Had. I don't blame them."

"We should still befriend them and let them trust us," Hadwin suggested. "We have an advantage in numbers." The babe gurgled as he rocked her. "Her name is Else. Her mother named her."

"Else," Naleem repeated. He folded his arms and rested them on the table. "Poor, pretty Else."

When they finished their meal, Naleem and Hadwin took the children upstairs for the rest of the evening. Naleem noted how Dakarai and Cadoc clung to him as they had on the journey to Haven.

A sad smile tugged at the corners of his mouth, and Naleem reached down to ruffle their hair. They giggled and swiped his hands away.

"Was your dinner good, boys?" he asked, lingering behind the group so the three of them might have a few moments alone.

"Yes, Papa." Dakarai skipped ahead and walked backwards. "But I don't like fish."

Naleem's smile grew and he rolled his eyes. "You've always liked fish, Dak."

"I like fish," Cadoc said.

Dakarai spun to walk forward and wagged his finger. "I like it when Mama cooks fish. Mama cooked it really good. With butter bread!"

At least she would remain in their memory, a place where they would never lose her. "Yes. She loved cooking for all of us."

Joining the others in the nursery, they prepared for bed. The clamor of the feast began with dish scrapes and the men's voices. The noise didn't ruin their slumber as they cuddled under the covers and received goodnights from their caregivers.

Hadwin and Naleem put the babes to sleep first, thus the older boys were told to keep silent. Most of them obeyed rather well, too tired to make trouble by this time of night.

A knock came at the door, and all of them jumped. Naleem and Hadwin exchanged a look. No one visited at this hour, for most everyone attended supper downstairs. As Naleem padded to answer, the knob turned with a click and the visitor pushed in. Naleem stopped.

Thenalious stood at the doorway, wearing a leisurely, long white shirt and black pants overlapped with leather boots. Despite Naleem and Hadwin's calculating looks, he offered a friendly smile.

"Good evening, caregivers," he greeted. "Children."

The boys recognized him and some gave him polite nods, but nothing more. Cadoc hid behind Naleem's legs.

"What is it you need?" Naleem asked him, in no mood for games.

"Nothing drastic." Thenalious folded his hands behind his back. "I thought I might discuss some concerns for the nursery while the men eat. This way, we have no distractions. Come with me to my chamber?"

"We can't speak here?" Naleem asked, his voice drawling.

Thenalious laughed. "There's no reason to be nervous. Just a private matter. I had servants bring food and wine there. I will be speaking with you, but I am still famished."

Naleem resisted the urge to look back at Hadwin again, but his brother's tension made itself obvious enough as he placed himself between the door and the children.

Naleem studied Thenalious' movements and listened to his tone for any hint of a lie or play. Thenalious shifted his weight, placing his hands on his hips. If he meant to hide something, he gave no sign of it.

"Very well," Naleem grunted, then turned to Hadwin. "You can hold the fort while I'm away."

Hadwin nodded, eyes dragging from Thenalious to his brother. With that, Naleem ruffled Cadoc's hair and gave Dakarai a nudge on the shoulder before following Thenalious out of the nursery.

The councilman glided down the hallway with a lethal grace that made Naleem's stomach churn. "Truly, it is better to go to my chamber for secrets. It is a head councilman's chamber. No one enters without my invitation."

"What secrets would we be discussing?" Naleem questioned as he kept pace with him.

"The newborn you saved." Thenalious cocked his head over his shoulder. "That is a matter meant for closed doors."

Naleem opened his mouth to speak but Thenalious stopped at two wood doors at the end of the hallway. Iron braced the edges and doorknobs shaped in the likeness of beasts—lions or wolves, or maybe a hybrid of both, Naleem could not tell—snarled at those who may enter.

Thenalious twisted the knob. The heavy door groaned inward, and he gestured Naleem inside.

Within and to the left glowed a fireplace of gray stone, a small kindling of flame burning blackened logs. Above it hung deer antlers, curving over the wide stones, touching the ceiling. Before him, a large window poured moonlight into the room and illuminated a giant bed dressed in wool blankets and furs. Foxtails dangled from each corner of the frame. A grizzly bear's skin stretched over the blankets. Its head hung over the foot of the bed.

The hollow floor echoed Naleem's footsteps as he walked in and scanned the room for any exit besides the door. The only plausible one would be the window, though that had to include a long drop. He prayed this was just one of Thenalious' strange generosities, like when he invited Naleem to eat with him in his tent.

When Naleem turned to Thenalious at the closed door, his veins flowed with ice. Reynold leaned against the frame next to Thenalious, his face blank like the stones set in the fireplace. His arms were folded over his chest with his hulking shoulders pitched forward.

Thenalious noticed Naleem's reaction and chuckled. "Don't worry. Reynold has a right to listen to us. It is *his* child, after all."

Reynold shot him a swift glare but returned to the expressionless mask. Naleem kept him in his peripheral vision.

"The men will not be happy about this." Thenalious slunk toward the fireplace and rested a palm on the stones. The orange light flickered across his face. "If any find out what it is, they will want it killed."

"My brother and I have agreed to let the matter remain secret," Naleem told him without missing a beat. "I only wish for her safety."

Reynold grumbled like an old bear.

"I am glad you seek the good in everything, son of Sigmund," Thenalious said without looking away from the fireplace. "I wish to take you on as one of us. But I must be able to trust you."

Naleem tensed, though his voice broke through his tightening throat. "What exactly does it take to earn your trust?"

"An oath." Thenalious pushed off the stones. "A pledge and submission that you belong to us. We have a way of doing things here in Haven."

Reynold's eyes watched Naleem with a gleam.

His heart drummed against his ribs, but Naleem stood firm. "And what does pledging to you do to me?"

"It gives you my favor and a safe place in Haven," Thenalious explained. "It shows the others that you agree you belong to me and act alongside me, under my rule."

Naleem's mouth twisted. "That doesn't sound appealing."

Thenalious laughed, the breath of it low and deep in his throat. "That is why I must do this and find out if you are fit for us. You've proven yourself unruly and quick to betray. I cannot allow that to go on for very long."

"You merely appointed me as a caregiver to your children," Naleem said. "How can I betray you?"

"I am not daft, caregiver." Thenalious' voice rose. "There have been plenty of weak-hearted men before you who befriended the women and tried to escape with them. Your actions this morning may prove useful to me, but they can also ignite hope in them. That is the last thing I need.

"I have to know you will not do the same again. You will bring none of them to hope or conspire against us. You will raise the little brat to submit to our rule and if I sense the slightest glimmer of revolt, you will suffer the consequences. So I may know you understand this, you will pledge to me."

Naleem's eyes narrowed. "I see. You are frightened of us. Of me."

Reynold straightened.

Thenalious tilted his head in Naleem's direction, hazel irises catching the firelight as he leered into his soul. "I have ways of eradicating your bravery. Will you swear an oath and be mine?"

Pinar's broken eyes took in the image of her husband a final time in Naleem's memory before the blade slashed her open. His daughters' blood pooled on the floor in the bedroom they were born, the place that was safest for them. All of it was torn away by this man, his men, and the injustice they reaped.

But with all the things Thenalious offered, there was a game to be played. A choice he allowed Naleem to make. The outcome of each choice benefited Thenalious only.

Be mine.

I will never be yours. Perhaps one day, Naleem could twist the game and tilt the odds in his favor. For now, within himself, the determination and willpower would remain. The words he spoke were simply that: words.

Naleem thumbed the raven pendant around his neck. "I'll swear your oath if it means that much to you. In return, the girl and my family will be kept safe."

"Of course." Thenalious pivoted to face him. "That goes both ways. If you break this oath, all protection and status will be revoked."

"Very well." Naleem folded his arms over his chest. "What will you have me say?"

Thenalious chuckled and drew closer to him. "It's not exactly what you say." He stopped inches away from him, their chests nearly touching, and tucked a lock of Naleem's hair behind his ear. "It's what we'll do."

Naleem pulled away and swiped Thenalious' arm. "I'll say your words and that's it."

"Oh, you'll say them." Thenalious followed him. "You'll be screaming them out for Haven to hear. Come now, it won't take long."

Reynold moved to the middle of the room, too close for comfort. Naleem's pulse throbbed in his ears. "This can't be a requirement. I'll swear whatever loyalty or allegiance to you. You can trust me after that."

Thenalious cornered him until his back hit the wall. "Not like I trust the others. Do this for me, son of Sigmund, and everything I promise to you will be yours."

Just as he had in the hallway when Naleem found the former caregivers under the lash of a whip, Thenalious pressed a hand against the wall above Naleem's shoulder. He clasped the other over Naleem's hip and tugged him in. Naleem squirmed with a shudder, and he gritted his teeth.

"No," he growled and shoved Thenalious back.

Reynold skulked forward, his broad shoulders preparing for a lunge. Thenalious regained his balance and raised a hand to stop him. "You'd be making a grave mistake, son of Sigmund."

"I said I will take your oath, and that is it," Naleem snarled. "Tell me what you want to hear and I'll say it. That's as far as it will go."

Thenalious chuckled. "You reveal your scheme like a frightened child. I'll tell you what I want to hear, then you'll turn your back on me. I must know that I have you, so I can keep you close."

"The answer to that is no," Naleem said.

"Then you do this to yourself." Thenalious' voice came like the tuning of a harp. "We will have to break you."

He moved aside and Reynold stepped in. Before Naleem could think to defend himself, Reynold's massive fist collided with his ear, then his gut. As he doubled over, the beast took his head and hurled his knee right into Naleem's face. The room went black before he woke in a heap on the floor.

Blood seeped over Naleem's lips. The metallic taste of it filled his mouth at the back of his throat. A tooth wiggled in his gums. He wiped the blood from his nose.

Reynold grabbed a fistful of Naleem's hair and hauled him to his feet. Naleem grunted and swung a fist at him. Catching his wrist, Reynold twisted his arm behind his back. Naleem cried out and kicked. But the beast threw him belly-first onto the bed.

Naleem's skull pounded with pain. The entire room tilted and swam in his vision. Reynold had him pinned with his arm wrenched behind him, agony striking through his shoulder down to the bone.

He kicked his legs out from beneath him, arching his back to throw the beast off. Reynold remained unmoved. A soreness pulsed through Naleem's shoulder and down his spine. When Reynold grew tired of it, he threw another fist against Naleem's head so hard he yelped. Then again, and again.

"That's enough, love," Thenalious said as he would have whispered into Reynold's ear.

One more punch and Reynold ceased, keeping a hand around Naleem's wrist at his back. Naleem sank to his knees. He rested his pounding head on the edge of the bed and stifled a groan. Thenalious loomed over him.

"It's only fitting, son of Sigmund, that you would refuse, I suppose," Thenalious hummed. His voice echoed as if it were distant. "That was the story your sniveling brother told in the tent, wasn't it? How Sigmund refused Fan's advances, and for what? The honor of a woman."

Naleem urged himself to get to his feet, but a mighty wave of agony crashed over him. Reynold held his wrist between his shoulder blades. The slightest pressure kept him down.

"We have our own way of appealing to Fan and gaining his power and favor, as you would have gained mine." Thenalious stopped behind him. The clinking of metal against metal sounded; a belt buckle loosening.

"It has been so difficult not bringing you into my bed sooner."

Panic flooded Naleem's nerves, and he shot up, catching Reynold by surprise. He pitched all his weight against the beast, but even that was not enough to knock him off-balance. Reynold took him by the nape and slammed him against the bedframe, the plush foxtails unable to soften the blow.

Then the beast tossed him onto the bed, blood smeared over the bear fur. Naleem's face swelled and blood oozed from the new wounds across his brow and cheek. He fought for consciousness, but the pain flourished through his skull. The darkness swallowed him again.

He woke to a new pain that he had never felt before. Naleem gasped and threw his head back. Reynold had him again and shoved him down. Thenalious grunted behind him with a hand at the base of his neck, the other at his waist. In the haze of consciousness, Naleem's throbbing mind assessed his surroundings and what was happening to him.

Reynold's palm held his head down and Thenalious pinned him, his hips thrusting behind him, within him.

Naleem cried out, arching and kicking, but Thenalious' strength rose against him. Naleem sobbed. He reached and clawed at Reynold. His nails sank into flesh and Reynold snarled. He swiped and clamped Naleem's wrist against the bed, shoving his face deeper into the furs, suffocating him.

Thenalious' fingers glided from Naleem's neck and between his shoulders before grunting with pleasure. Another sob erupted from Naleem's throat. Thenalious pulled away, leaving his body ravaged and trembling.

"Now you're mine," Thenalious panted. The hissing of a snake. His fingertips traced the back of Naleem's thigh. "Now you are mine."

Then Reynold hauled him farther onto the bed and took him. Naleem forced himself elsewhere, his entire being going numb. Tears soaked the fur around his eyes and he bit the bear's skin, muffling cries and sobs. He imagined Pinar's sweet face, her tender voice comforting him. He focused on the memory of her touch, light and warm.

Reynold finished and lifted from him. Naleem's muscles shook, cold despite the balmy summer night and the heat of the fire. The bear's fur scratched at his skin.

"Do you understand now, son of Sigmund?" Thenalious asked across the room. "You will heed my instruction, or you will suffer. In time, so will your brother and your sons."

Naleem whimpered and curled in on himself. He wept at the thought of Hadwin and wept harder at the thought of Dakarai and Cadoc. They were all so far away, in another world.

"What do you want to be done with him now?" Reynold asked, his voice moving to the fireplace.

Thenalious breathed a tired sigh. "I haven't decided. Let's eat first. I'm starving."

Every bit of Naleem's being wished to stay pressed into the furs, to drown in them. He dug up the courage to peek with one eye at the others. The two men feasted on fowl legs from a platter that rested above the mantel, their faces light in good spirits. Thenalious sat with a leg over an armrest. Reynold selected his next bite.

Naleem clenched his jaw. He propped himself on one elbow, then the other. The raven pendant swayed from his neck and he clutched it in his fist. His muscles spasmed as he sobbed.

Thenalious perked and gave Naleem a playful smirk, his eyes gleaming. "What is it, son of Sigmund? Did you not like it?"

With a hard swallow, Naleem bowed his head as his chest tightened. "May I go…"

"You'll have to speak up."

Naleem lifted his chin. "May. I. Go."

Thenalious froze mid-bite and frowned. "Careful of that defiant voice and remember where you stand. You and I still have matters to discuss. Rey and I still need you for tonight."

Every fiber in Naleem begged him to shrink back. To crawl into a dark hole, never to be seen again. But he sat firm, one arm trembling under his weight, the other holding the pendant. "What matters to discuss?"

"It's not your place to ask." Thenalious tore meat from a leg and chewed with more grace than Reynold, who ripped through the fowl like a ravenous dog. "We'll get to it. Supper is first. Why don't you come and eat?"

"I'm not hungry."

"I didn't ask if you were." Thenalious waved him over and offered a hand. "Come eat."

Naleem would have rather peeled his own skin before he stood next to them, but he would have to. His head swam when he rose and his feet crossed over each other as he braced against the bedframe. With a wincing breath, he limped to stand before them. His fingers pressed to the pendant, the one comfort in this form of Helved.

Thenalious looked him over, his gaze roaming from head to toe. "Don't be so glum, son of Sigmund. I offer you the greatest protection, respect, and status in Haven. All you need to do is spread your legs for it. Now you understand what happens when you keep up that cold attitude I hate so much."

While his stomach retched, Naleem fixed his sight on the floor. His body swayed and he fought to stay on his feet. Thenalious ripped a piece of meat off the bone and raised it to Naleem. "Here. You'll need your strength."

Bile rose to his throat, but Naleem reached for it. Thenalious yanked the meat away and lifted it again, peering at Naleem with scolding eyes. Naleem fought a curled lip and leaned down to bite it from his hand.

Thenalious brushed the backs of his fingers across Naleem's cheek. "Good. See, love? I told you it wouldn't take much."

"He still gives ugly faces," Reynold growled with a full mouth. "Good for a rough fuck, but not to keep for a caregiver."

Naleem grimaced as he chewed and swallowed, the meat slithering down his throat. He breathed deep to keep it down.

Thenalious watched him as he ate, head tilted and shoulders relaxed. "He makes a fine caregiver. Saving a babe's life would make Sigmund proud. But under Fan's rule, there is a give-and-take. Where there is life, there is death. And we can only feed so many mouths."

Play the game. Naleem looked him in the eye, brow knitted. "What can we do then?"

Setting a bare bone onto the platter, Thenalious grinned. He plucked a cloth from the side table and wiped his hands. "We will raid in the morning. Take down Judr like we did Syden. They have walls, but it's nothing a strong, cut trunk can't bring down. We'll take what we need to last through winter. Without either village, the game in the woods is ours for the taking through fall."

Screams from Syden flooded Naleem's memory. He shook off a wince, but the heat of the fires baked his skin as if he were still there. "I see."

"One more thing." Thenalious stood from his chair and wrapped an arm around Reynold's waist. "Your plea for the babe's life must come at a cost. If the men are to eventually know about her, I must make an example of you. And we must hold to Fan's ways."

Naleem's stomach twisted, and his portion of supper nearly came up. "What kind of example?"

"Where there is life," Thenalious started as he pulled away from Reynold, "there is death."

He went to the closet and found a sword, unsheathing it. The blade sang as it emerged. Naleem's heart dropped into his stomach.

"Let us see what our other caregiver is up to, shall we?" Thenalious went for the door.

"No," Naleem started, but Reynold pushed him forward.

The chatter and feasting downstairs still echoed from the great hall. Had an eternity in Helved truly been mere minutes?

At the end of the hallway, in time to bring the boys to bed, Hadwin was leaving the nursery with Dakarai and Cadoc at his sides. He shut the door and turned for the bedroom, but caught sight of Thenalious and Reynold marching toward him with Naleem in tow.

"Naleem?" Hadwin blurted. The look of horror said it all. Naleem must have appeared as torn as he felt. What pained him more were his sons' frightened faces, eyes wide as they shrank behind their uncle.

More footsteps came up the stairs and around the corner. The councilman Oberon stumbled upon the scene and halted in place. "Thenalious. What is this?"

His sudden presence did not thwart Thenalious' plan. He raised the blade to Naleem's throat, its edge grazing his skin. "This one has been conspiring against us. Soon he'll get his rightful punishment. Call your sons here."

The air fled Naleem's lungs. "Please—"

"Do it now." His voice rumbled like thunder.

"You won't have them!" Hadwin pulled the boys close, glaring with his chin high. "Let my brother go!"

Thenalious rolled his eyes. "Oberon, seize the caregiver."

Oberon obeyed, though apprehensively, and clasped Hadwin's arms.

"Call your sons here," Thenalious repeated to Naleem.

A stone raked Naleem's throat. "Thenalious, please."

The blade pierced his skin, and blood dripped from his neck. Thenalious faced the boys. "You brats will come forward now or your father dies."

Cadoc cried, but Dakarai bit his lip and took his brother's hand. Tears streaming down his reddening cheeks, he stepped into the space between all of them. His large, dark-brown eyes glimmered on his father, shredding Naleem's heart.

Hadwin wrestled in Oberon's grip. "Leave them alone!"

Naleem could only wriggle under Reynold's hold. "Please, Thenalious, do what you will with me, but don't hurt them. I'll do whatever you want."

Thenalious snorted. "I wish I could believe that." He looked upon the boys, taking the sword from Naleem. "It says in scripture that when Fan committed the first kill, 'Sigmund crumbled in a fit of sorrow.'"

The blade drew closer to the boys, and Naleem jerked on his captor. "Please."

Thenalious raised the sword above them and slashed. In that split second, Dakarai pushed his little brother down. The sword sliced his belly and the boy screamed. Blood flew and splattered across the floor and wall as Hadwin cried out.

"*Dak*!" Naleem wailed.

Dakarai dropped. His blood seeped over the floorboards. Naleem tore free from Reynold and fell past Thenalious, landing on his knees beside his son. He covered the gaping wound in Dakarai's belly with one hand and cradled the boy's head with the other.

"Dakarai, my babe," he wept. Cadoc sobbed before them.

"You wretched bastard!" Hadwin managed a hand free of Oberon. His fist swung in Thenalious' direction, but Oberon regained his hold. "You craven, vile snake! You'll rot in Helved!"

Dakarai's gasps filled Naleem's ears as he hung onto every one of them. Hot blood covered his hand in the deep gash in Dakarai's belly. More blood rose in his mouth and spilled over his chin. "P-Papa..."

"I'm here," Naleem whispered close to him. "You'll be all right, I'm here."

But Reynold grabbed him by the hair and hoisted him up, pushing him towards the bedchamber. Naleem went ballistic and whirled, dodging a punch only to be snatched again. His feet scraped against the wood floor. "No!"

Dakarai gasped on his back, Cadoc crying beside him. He had to reach them. He had to get to them. With the strength left within him, Naleem battled and writhed, kicking and throwing his weight. His sight fixed on Dakarai and watched from afar as his son, his firstborn, drew a final breath. His little chest wavered and lowered a last time.

All light turned to black smoke. Naleem's heart transformed into lead and his legs gave out from under him. A scream raked his throat raw. His head spun and his veins surged with heat. He shook Reynold away, but the beast caught him and slammed him into the wall.

"Lock up the caregiver and the other brat before I make them bleed too," Thenalious ordered Oberon. He started down the hallway. "We'll keep this one in our chamber while we prepare to raid."

"Tonight?" Oberon asked.

"Fan is satisfied tonight," Thenalious told him. "Before dawn, we'll reach Judr. Do as I say."

Though Hadwin fought, Oberon dragged him in the other direction. He, too, was no match for the councilman. "Naleem!"

A crater formed in Naleem's chest and Reynold followed Thenalious back to the bedchamber. Thenalious confronted him and took his chin in his hand. "You will never take matters into your own hands again. I am your lord here."

Naleem snapped and his teeth sank into Thenalious' palm. He cried out. A hard slap connected to Naleem's cheek just as Reynold pushed him into the wall again.

Thenalious' fingers clawed Naleem's hair and wrenched him to meet his eyes, blurred with tears. "When we're done, every man in Haven will have his way with you. That's a promise."

Chapter 23

Raegna

THE CHAOS DWINDLED AFTER Nairi struck Bai for the last time, and the crowd dissipated. The Matriarch and her village left him there to suffer for the night. Had Raegna not cared, had she gone with them, he might have died.

Instead, she hefted him with an arm over her shoulder and braced his weight to carry him to the healer's house. Though she kept a deliberate pace, Bai flinched and grunted with each step. The sun set and evening cooled the air while they inched down the dirt path.

Raegna tenderly touched his back, his shirt blood-soaked and brittle, when they neared the house and then the porch steps. Jora emerged and hurried to support Bai's other side. Bai gritted his teeth as they ascended. Banu held the door as Raegna and Jora guided him to the healing room. They lay him down on one of the sickbeds. He groaned and shut his eyes tight as he settled on his stomach.

Banu rolled up her sleeves and collected her supplies in the kitchen and cupboards. She instructed Jora as they both hovered over him. Raegna watched Bai on the sickbed, unsure of what more she could do. Part of her urged her to hold his hand, give him a comforting touch, something. Another part kept her still, watching the man she had despised and feared for so long coil in pain.

"Mama." The small voice tore her from her thoughts.

Adabelle stood at the open door. Her cherub cheeks paled and matched her blonde hair that tangled over her little shoulders. Stubby fingers fidgeted with her sleeve as she beheld the familiar shape of her father upon the sickbed with round eyes. Banu began her work, lifting the bloodied shirt from Bai's back, making him wince.

Raegna knelt before her daughter and rubbed her arms, brushing her hair away. She ran the backs of her fingers along her temple. "It's all right, sweet babe."

"What's wrong with Papa?" Adabelle squeaked.

Raegna hesitated. What was she supposed to say? How could she help her understand? Tears brimmed Adabelle's eyelids, though she kept a stiff lip, trying to be brave. Then Banu cut the bloody shirt away and Bai inhaled through his teeth. Adabelle shrank back.

"He..." Raegna searched for words as she pulled the girl close, stroking her hair. "They, they hurt him because they believed he hurt Turid."

The room grew dark, turning Bai and his healers into shadows of agony. Raegna looked over her shoulder and glimpsed Bai's torn back. No skin could be seen, only blood, wound, and muscle. Crimson streams dripped from his back and onto the white bedsheets, but Banu cleaned it up. Bai growled with fists clenched at every touch.

"He didn't hurt Miss Turid," Adabelle protested rather loudly. The tears rolled down her face. "Papa doesn't hurt anyone. He's like Sigmund, like the story, Mama. Remember?"

A hard stone formed in Raegna's throat. She wiped Adabelle's tears with her thumbs. "I know..."

The girl sniffled and huddled into her mother, resting her head under Raegna's chin. Raegna embraced her, rubbed her back, and listened to

Bai's grunts and growls. The lump in her throat throbbed when she forced a swallow. Adabelle trembled with each pained noise her father made.

"Come, sweetling," Raegna whispered and hefted Adabelle into her arms. "Let's get you to bed."

"But Papa..."

"Banu is taking care of him," Raegna assured her as she carried her out. "He'll be all right."

Banu spoke as she worked. "You may use our room, girl. It'll be peaceful for her to sleep there."

Raegna nodded her thanks and found the bedroom on the other side of the house. Inside stood a simple bed and dresser, everything the old healer and warrior would need for their rest. Raegna placed Adabelle on the mattress and lifted the blankets for her to snuggle under. Adabelle plopped on the pillow.

"Tomorrow things will be better," Raegna promised as she tucked her in. "For now, we must get some rest."

Adabelle ran her hand under her nose. "Will you stay here, Mama? I can't sleep."

"Of course, my heart." She sat on the edge of the bed and smoothed the blankets out. Taking a long breath, she said, "Your... your Papa will be all right. You'll see."

"Truly?" Adabelle whimpered.

"Truly." The words quaked over Raegna's lips. "He is... he is strong, you know that."

"He's a good papa," Adabelle declared. Her eyelids drooped and her breathing steadied. "He wouldn't hurt anyone..."

Raegna chewed the inside of her cheek. "I know."

Within a few minutes, the girl fell fast asleep, her face flushed and puffy from crying. Raegna leaned in and kissed her forehead, once and then twice. "Goodnight, sweetheart."

Everything will be all right, she assured herself and prayed somehow Adabelle would grasp this, too. After her daughter remained asleep, Raegna left her and let the door fall open just a crack behind her.

In the healing room, Jora looked on while Banu soaked a cloth with an ointment and placed it on Bai's wounds. He tensed but lay quiet, spent from his exertion. Raegna waited at the door and looked on without a word. Her lips pressed into a thin line as she clutched the doorframe, watching blood trail over his sides along with the substance Banu had added.

"You're doing fine," Banu praised him in a gentle whisper. "You're all right now. You're doing fine."

Jora nodded with her arm propped on the wall. "A fine warrior, you are."

Bai said nothing.

When she finished her work, the healer gathered her things and returned to her patient with a green biscuit. Raegna's nose crinkled at the sight of it.

"Eat this," Banu instructed as she put the biscuit to his lips. "It's stale, but it will help you sleep."

Bai took it and ground it between his teeth. He chewed for a long time, unable to get it down. A curt grunt escaped him when he finally did. Whatever Banu made the biscuit from took effect in less than a minute. Bai snored, on his stomach with his head resting on his pillow over folded arms.

"With proper care," Banu spoke up, breaking the silence, "those will turn into scars. I cannot heal scars. There are more than just the physical ones."

Raegna tensed and released her hold on the doorframe. "How long do you think it will take?"

"A few days before he will want to stand," Banu told her. "Maybe more. But months before they heal completely."

"When will he be fit for travel?"

Banu blinked, but didn't look at her. "That depends on him. He won't be able to sit on horseback for a few weeks, perhaps."

"And if I got a wagon?" Raegna asked urgently. "He could rest as we go."

"A rocking wagon would make him ache." Banu laced her hands over her belly as she leaned back in her chair. "And unfortunately, we do not have a wagon to spare."

"I believe I know someone who does." Iida could do this one favor for her. She would understand.

Banu straightened and set her hands on her lap. Jora stood behind her, resting weathered hands on her wife's shoulders. The dusk through the windows cast thin shadows on every wrinkled feature, but the hint of pity swam in the warrior's imploring eyes. "Where will you go, priestess?"

Raegna drew a breath. "Somewhere else. Somewhere better, and perhaps somewhere people will listen to us... The next village is Surleid in Ostern."

Jora tilted her head. "That is a long journey. Those villages are close to being cities. They are very wealthy. You cannot reach Matriarchs so easily there."

"Then Vesten." Raegna ran her fingers over her scalp. "Or Norden or even Stadt, like he told me. I hardly care! I should have listened to him!"

Tears stung her eyes and her palm went to her mouth, either to stop the words from spilling or to hide the quivering of her lip. She gave in and choked on a sob. "I should have listened to him..."

The warrior strode across the room and placed a hand on her shoulder. "Girl, do not blame yourself. None of this is your fault, do you understand?"

Her chest heaved and Raegna nodded, though the tears persisted. Then Jora raised her hand to her face, and Raegna flinched. The old warrior retracted her touch and rested it on Raegna's arm instead.

"You're a strong young woman, Raegna," Jora said. "When I met you, I saw you had the soul of a warrior. Like most of us, you blame yourself for things out of your control. Things you can't physically fight. Know that you have done all you can and more for your family and your village. I saw you defend this man today. He knows it. You did everything you could."

Raegna lifted her gaze to Bai as he slept on the sickbed. Blood seeped through the bandages Banu wrapped over his back, but he was not bothered by that now. An unbelievable ache pulsed in Raegna's heart with every beat. Unbelievable because it was an ache for him.

Just as she should have heeded him before the wolves in the forest attacked them, she should have before the wolves of Judr grew bloodthirsty. She tried to accept Jora's words of reassurance, but her heart blocked them like a shield against arrows. Still, Raegna gave a nod of understanding. Banu found a blanket and draped it over Raegna's shoulders, guiding her to a bed beside Bai.

Raegna shook her head. "I'll watch over him. I would rather give you rest so you can treat him tomorrow."

"If you wish, priestess," Banu agreed, and pulled up the chair for her.

Raegna sat and hovered over Bai's side as he slept. Banu and Jora slumbered on the bed across from them. Despite his injuries, Bai's face showed no sign of suffering. Every sharp angle seemed almost angelic, even his long, crooked nose and the curve of his jawline. No pain lived there, not even in the flickering of his eyelids. Though she had hated and feared him all these years, he was good and kind, especially to their daughter. And he had never touched her again...

All night, Raegna prayed Gaea would protect him and heal him. For Adabelle's sake. For her own sake, for if it weren't for Bai, she would not be there sitting with him.

Before she knew it, dawn appeared through the windows. Raegna woke with her head resting on her folded arms beside Bai. Whatever Banu gave him had a powerful potency, for he still slept like a babe. The familiar soft snores emitted from his parted lips. The corner of her mouth quirked, and she fought the urge to brush the fallen strands of his blond hair into place.

Dishes clanked in the kitchen, muffled by the closed door. Raegna stretched and yawned. Then she gave Bai one last look over before wobbling to her feet and leaving him in the healing room.

Jora fitted her armor around her torso before the table. Banu handed clean dishes to Adabelle to dry with a cloth. The girl wiped them down and carefully placed them on a rack near the front window. When Raegna emerged, she turned and beamed at her.

"Good morning, Mama!"

"Good morning, sweetling," Raegna greeted, offering a grin as she leaned against a chair. "How very helpful you are."

"Banu said to let you and Papa sleep," Adabelle told her.

Raegna's face fell. "Well, he... Your father is still sleeping..."

"Don't worry, girl," Banu assured her as she picked up another plate to wash. "He'll open his eyes soon. That sunlight will hit him and he'll know what to do, and we'll be there when he wakes."

Yes, Raegna thought. Regaining consciousness to the mutilation of his back and remembering the events last night would terrify him.

A swift knock at the door made Raegna nearly jump out of her skin. Jora straightened to attention. Banu dried her hands with a furrowed brow and went to answer. Had Viona sent warriors to take Bai and get rid of him for good? Perhaps he wasn't supposed to be dragged from the fate of dying before the Matriarch's house. Raegna put herself between the doorway and Adabelle as Banu opened it to reveal the visitor.

Iida's husband, Asmund, stood before them, his head tilted down and his shoulders pitched forward. His mouse-brown hair fell above his brow. Raegna blinked at him, squirming under Banu's stare.

"What is it, boy?" the healer questioned.

"My wife," he stammered, glancing up. "She wanted me to, she wanted me to summon the priestess. Her sisters are away."

Raegna stepped in to see him better. "Away? Where?"

Surprised by her sudden appearance, Asmund shrank back. "To, um, to your village. To Syden. Viona went with Femke and a few warriors."

Her gut froze over. What exactly had driven Viona to inspect Syden? Even Banu exchanged a look with her, the wrinkles in her forehead deepening.

"We are without a Matriarch for a few days then," Banu noted.

"But Iida is in pain," Asmund spoke a little louder. "She has been having pains since last night. She sent me to find both of you. She's frightened..."

All suspicion vanished, and the priestess and the healer snapped to attention. Iida could finally be in labor.

Banu tapped Raegna's arm. "You go with him, girl. I'll gather my things and meet you at the great house."

"What of Bai?" Raegna asked. "Surely Jora has to be on her way. We cannot leave him alone."

"I can stay with Papa," Adabelle volunteered with her hand raised.

Raegna turned to her with her eyebrows drawn together. "Are you sure, sweetheart? He might wake up... afraid."

"I can also stay as long as needed, priestess," Jora piped in.

"And I may still be here when he wakes," Banu said as she found a bag and began stuffing it with blankets and cloth. "You must go on ahead and comfort the new mother and not leave her by herself."

"Of course." Raegna bent over Adabelle and gave her a quick peck on the forehead. "Take good care of him, all right? I'll be back soon."

Adabelle rocked on her toes with her hands behind her back. "I will, Mama."

With that, Raegna followed Asmund out of the healer's house and down the dirt road. They hastened their pace, not meeting the gaze of any who watched them pass. Asmund trekked the path rather quickly for how still Raegna had usually seen him. He flew over the porch steps when they reached the Matriarch's house and shoved the front door open.

He let Raegna in first. "She's upstairs in our room. She's been in bed all night."

"It's all right," Raegna told him, though she moved on light feet. "She'll be fine, Asmund."

Tucked away in their bedroom, Iida lay on top of the sheets. A single braid held her hair that curled beside her neck. Her swollen belly bulged under her simple blue dress. She arched her legs and her oval face pinched in pain, then released. Taking a breath, she looked to the doorway where her friend and husband stood.

"Oh," she sighed, settling upright against the pillows. "You're both here."

Asmund perched on the edge of the bed and took her hand in his. Iida let her head rest on his shoulder.

Raegna clasped the foot of the frame. "How do you feel, Iida?"

"Almost ready." Iida's tired eyes flicked to Raegna's. "The pains are not so close to each other. There's time. I just thought now that it is morning, you and Banu would be awake."

"Oh, Iida, you could have woken us."

She shook her head. "Not after yesterday. Your husband needed you more... And my sisters bickered in the main room until dawn."

Raegna raised her chin. "Asmund said they left for Syden. Why?"

Iida straightened, but kept a hold of Asmund's hand. "My sisters can be... challenging, but only because they have been through much. Some I have not been told before." She paused. "I believe Viona may have been moved by your actions. As soon as she returned home, she ordered a party to prepare for the journey to our sister village.

"Femke argued you were lying and a traitor for defending a criminal. That both of you should have been killed... But Viona ignored her. Turid had always been a conniving and promiscuous one, she said. She should have listened to both sides, but her pride had gotten the best of her."

Raegna could conjure no words for a proper response. Her knuckles turned white as she gripped the bedframe tighter. "I... I will have to thank her."

A soft smile showed on Iida's front teeth. "I'm sure she will apologize to you directly when she returns and together you can send word to her majesty."

Her heart lifted to the ceiling. Justice could be served and the deaths of Pinar, her daughters, and all who perished in Syden would be avenged. The Queen and the Maidens could ride in and destroy the brutes who wreaked havoc and ripped lives and families apart. Raegna could not wait to tell Bai. Some good news might subdue his pain.

"I'm glad" was all she could offer. "For now, we will deliver this babe."

"There is a condition, a favor to ask of you if I can, my friend," Iida spoke up.

Raegna hesitated. "What is it?"

"Viona may have a change of heart, and she may very well still when she returns." She swallowed. "Femke, I am not so sure... Either way, deep within me, I feel my child might be a boy. I would love a son, but I do not think he is safe here."

Fan's ritual blazed in Raegna's memory. *Viona's first husband gave her only sons, and she killed him for it.* "They wouldn't take your babe."

"They might just," Iida admitted with her eyes down. She dragged them up to meet Raegna's gaze. "I cannot risk it. So I pray you keep its gender a secret from the village. If it is a boy."

"I will, my friend," Raegna agreed with a nod. "But you can't keep that secret forever."

"That is why we are leaving," Iida said. "We wanted to leave for Stadt."

Raegna blinked. "Stadt?"

Iida stroked Asmund's thumb with her own. "It's a grand place. I've been there before with my mother during Harvest Union when the Matriarchs visit the Queen and High Council. We can afford a small house there and live simply. And our child would be safe."

"Stadt is—well, it's very far away."

"We can bring the Queen your message of Syden," Iida explained. "Viona won't like it, but I know she will let me go after all of this. I believe she wants to make things right with you. I am a sister of a Matriarch. Her majesty and the Council will listen to me."

"Yes…" Raegna drummed her nails on the footboard, her vision unfocused in thought. She could not stay either. This was not the place for Bai, nor the place she wanted to raise Adabelle. "Perhaps then I could go with you? I don't wish to stay long. And you are my only friends here, both of you."

Asmund stared at her, blue eyes wide and fluttering. Raegna could not help but feel for him. She, too, would not have believed she would find even the smallest friendship with a man. Yet she was growing attached to Iida's shy husband and maybe… even her own.

Iida beamed. "We would love to have you!"

Her face tightened as she pitched forward, drawing her knees up. She could do nothing but allow the pain to come and go. Raegna remembered that from her labor. She moved to take Iida's hand, resting a comforting palm on her arm to guide her through it.

Then a faint scream sounded from outside, causing the three of them to jump. Iida grunted as her pain dwindled. "What was that?"

"Asmund, stay with her," Raegna ordered and left the room.

She jogged downstairs, her feet drumming against the steps. In the main room, Viona's two daughters appeared from the kitchen after breakfast. Both of them craned their necks and peered at the front windows.

"Priestess," the eldest said as soon as she recognized Raegna, "what is wrong?"

Screams multiplied, shrieking through the streets across Judr and approaching the great house. Horses thundered after them as if being chased by the outcries. Memories of her terrifying escape from Syden surfaced in Raegna's mind, and her gut somersaulted, begging her to flee.

"Stay where you are," she told the girls and turned the doorknob with a shaking hand. The door shuddered open.

The hoofbeats ceased as two horses cantered up to the house. They heaved when they came to a halt. Their female riders fell lopsided, with torsos lying over the horses' withers. Raegna's heart seized.

Blood poured down the horses' hides from the gaping, beheaded necks of the riders. The crimson soaked their gowns and chests that dangled from the saddles. Tied to the saddle horns by their hair hung the heads of Femke and her sister, Matriarch Viona, their jaws slack, and their eyes rolled back.

A scream tore from Raegna's throat.

CHAPTER 24

HADWIN

OBERON PRACTICALLY CARRIED HADWIN downstairs, past the dining hall. A new corridor led to more stairs descending to a cellar. Barrels of ale lined on top of each other along the walls. They passed in a blur as Oberon hauled Hadwin to a small closet and shoved him inside.

The door slammed shut behind him. Hadwin threw himself against it as the lock clicked. Darkness swallowed him as he smashed his fists on the door. It would not give, but he hardly cared, raging and fighting his imprisonment until his skin broke along his knuckles and fingers.

Soon, Hadwin ran out of breath, and his lungs burned. Tears stung his eyes and his body quaked, the adrenaline fading and despair taking over.

Dakarai did not deserve that kind of end... He deserved to grow, experience life, and be lifted to Heimelle when his time came. Not wander through the world between Heimelle and Helved with his mother and sisters. Hadwin's knees buckled, and he collapsed, cut fists clenched in his lap.

Footsteps hurried on the other side of the door. It burst open before Hadwin could react. A pair of hands tossed Cadoc in and the door shut and locked once more. In a deep state of shock, the poor boy shed no more tears. He whimpered in the room's darkness, curling in on himself. Reaching out to him, Hadwin took his nephew into his arms and pulled him close. He had no words for him, just the comfort of an embrace. Cadoc buried his face in his uncle's chest.

In the pitch black, the cool night crept through the timber walls. The cellar did not need to be heated by fire and hearth, thus all Hadwin and Cadoc had for warmth was each other. The last of their once whole family.

Faint bumps rumbled above their heads. Otherwise, the closet shrouded them in silence and they listened to the thud of their heartbeats and their own shaking breaths. Cadoc shivered between Hadwin's arms and he held him tighter.

Hadwin forced all dark thoughts aside and focused on how he would escape, find Naleem, and leave this place for good. How would he be able to free his family and survive these terrifying minions of Fan? Where had they taken Naleem? Was he locked inside a similar cell, alone and full of grief? Or would they rid him of this world along with his son?

Hadwin's chest caved on itself. Better days came to his mind: chasing his brother's children in front of their home as they squealed and giggled, their parents looking on with bright smiles. Good meat sizzled for dinner and when the children went to sleep, Hadwin, Naleem, and Pinar enjoyed wine as they told stories in front of the fire.

He let tears swell and drop into Cadoc's hair.

Time must have passed, though Hadwin could not tell how much. Sunlight did not shine under the ground. Neither he nor Cadoc slept through the night.

An eternity later, the door opened and dim light entered. Hadwin peered up at the intruder.

Oberon towered over him, clad in a long shirt and pants overlapped by leather boots. The light silhouetted him and highlighted his deep brown skin and the strands in his coarse, black beard over a hard frown. His rounded brow tightened as he studied his prisoners. Hadwin braced for another rough journey to a new cell. But the councilman's voice reached him with a gentle tone. "They've gone to Judr. No one will hurt you."

Hadwin fixed his eyes on him, heavy and unrelenting.

Oberon's features shifted and fell. He drew a breath and squared his shoulders. "They took your brother with them... I don't know what they intend to do with him. I'm sorry."

A meaningless apology that drifted to the floor like a fall leaf, meant to disintegrate and shrivel in the cold. Why did he bring this news to Hadwin now? What was his game, pouring salt over the wound?

When Hadwin still did not speak, Oberon continued. "I've covered the boy's body in the hallway. I thought that while they were away, you could give him a proper lifting."

Hadwin did not budge.

"...I can take you to a pyre I've made in the woods—"

"Why?" His voice came in a dry croak.

Oberon put his weight on one foot and then the other. "Because the men here do not believe in Gaea and Heimelle but... A child so young does not need to suffer such—"

Hadwin spoke through his teeth, though his voice wavered. "Why are you doing this?"

The councilman's black eyes met Hadwin's and swayed at the force behind them. The quaint, frightened caregiver had all but vanished.

"Because... I have my reasons for being here, and Thenalious has his," Oberon explained. "May we leave it at that?"

Hadwin dropped his gaze. "Where is my nephew?"

"Come with me."

Oberon stepped aside. On wobbling legs, Hadwin stood and supported Cadoc on his hip. They left the cellar and ascended to the first floor. The sunrise shed into the dining hall, which was incredibly quiet without servant boys to prepare breakfast. No sounds of metalwork, commanding shouts, or livestock sounded outside. Only the morning songs of birds fluttered into the great house. Though Hadwin's world was broken and shredded, life carried on.

Upstairs, the air grew dense and too thick for Hadwin to breathe. Oberon walked through the hallway without effort, but Hadwin struggled to find his footing, to see clearly. Then they stopped before the body. He halted mid-step, ordering his taut muscles to shield Cadoc from the view.

Dakarai remained where he had fallen the night before, but he was now covered in a white wool blanket, a small red stain of blood settled in the middle. Sunlight spanned over him from the window across from them. Dust fluttered through the yellow rays.

Oberon gave Hadwin a wide berth, lingering at the end of the hallway. After a deep breath, Hadwin set Cadoc down and instructed him to look away. Cadoc sniffled and turned so his back faced his brother's body.

Hadwin approached the surreal sight of the body and knelt to pick Dakarai up. He cradled him as if he were a babe again. Blood stained the wood floor, more than should have spilled from such a young body.

When he was ready, Hadwin stood before Oberon and waited for him to lead on to this pyre in the woods. Without a word, Oberon nodded toward the stairs to begin their journey. Cadoc stumbled after his uncle.

Songbirds greeted them outside, and Haven lay barren. No men woke from their tents or bustled to start the day. Those who had stayed behind worked in the barn on the other side of camp. Oberon avoided that direction. Instead, he took to the surrounding tree line and guided Hadwin to a thin trail marked by a few tracks and footfalls.

The trees loomed over them, but the rising sun painted them with more light and color, so their branches did not claw at them and their trunks were not shadows. Redwoods rose proud and homely while pine trees flickered and bobbed as the birds played and sang within them.

Too fair for a child's corpse to pass through, but perhaps this was how Gaea meant for it to be. Her land burst with life, waiting on a young soul to rise to her. Hadwin tried to think of it that way.

Oberon paused and Hadwin looked up. In the middle of a clearing, a bed of branches, twigs, and fallen wood waited. A lifting bed.

Hadwin inhaled through constrained lungs and went to it, Dakarai's body growing heavier and Hadwin's own feet dragging across the dirt. Cadoc remained behind him, and Oberon gave them room to grieve, stepping beyond the forest growth.

At the bed, Hadwin halted and knelt to lay his nephew across the branches. He cupped the back of his head in one hand and slipped it away so he would rest on a pillow of pine needles. His heart thudded as he unveiled the boy's face from underneath the blanket. He expected the brown eyes to stare back at him, but they were closed as if in sleep. His lips parted just slightly and dried blood covered his ghost-white skin over his chin. Hot tears dripped from Hadwin's eyes.

"Sweet nephew." He brushed the black hair from Dakarai's face. "You'll be all right... You'll be with the All-Mother soon. Say hello to Her for me. Watch over your father... and your brother."

The density of his body gave under a slow shudder. A sob stopped short under his swollen throat. He leaned forward and kissed the boy's forehead one last time. "Rest now, little one."

Hadwin rose and backed away. Oberon approached him, offering something in his hand. Pieces of flint. Hadwin clutched them. Traditionally, it was a priestess' duty to lift the dead, but there were no priestesses in Haven. Better Hadwin than anyone else. He crouched before the lifting bed again and struck the flint over the twigs.

A spark caught and bloomed beneath Dakarai, spreading larger and larger. Hadwin retreated and stood with Cadoc clinging to his side. Tears rolled down his cheeks, an arm draped over Cadoc as they watched the orange flames consume the small body and turn flesh into ash.

Hadwin traced the smoke that climbed into the morning sky with his gaze. The sun's rays reflected through the pale wisps. Dakarai's soul lifted towards Heimelle.

Chapter 25

Bai

FIGURES SWIRLED BAI'S DREAMS. Hands clawed and shoved him. Jeering voices shook the ground. The first strike of the whip snaked and ripped his skin. The ceaseless pain forced him to the present, lying on his belly and unable to move.

Raegna slept over her folded arms on the edge of his bed. Her dark red-tinged hair waved over her shoulders. Faint gray circles curved under her long eyelashes, still damp from tears. Her cheeks had a flushed pink hue even in the dim light. She stayed with him.

A chink of a sword echoed in his memory. Raegna's voice demanded to be heard. She stopped the pain for as long as she could, and after everything—*everything*—she stayed by his side.

Her presence lulled him back to sleep, safe under her guard.

Then he woke, the morning sun warming the room. Bai peeked around the healing room as he pulled himself to consciousness. Vague memories surfaced of hobbling across Judr with Raegna beside him, allowing his body so close to hers to support his weight. He took a deep breath and winced.

A thin layer of dried blood cracked over Bai's back. A million cat scratches etched over his wounds and his fists bunched the sheets of the sickbed. He groaned with his teeth clenched. When he dared to open his eyes again, he found Adabelle at the doorway.

Tangles of blonde hair haloed her face. Her soft eyebrows raised as she sucked in a gasp. "Papa! You're awake."

Seeing her brought joy and sadness both. Joy that she stood there before him and she was safe, but sadness because she would see him in this state, torn and broken. He opened his mouth to reassure her he was fine, but his voice failed him. He gaped like a fish for a moment before Adabelle called over her shoulder, "Miss Banu, Papa's awake!"

"Already?" Banu hurried in with bandages and two jars in her hands. One jar contained greenish biscuits, the other filled with a pulpy, lighter green liquid.

Behind her, Jora stood at the threshold, fully armed with a smile on her face. "Good morning, warrior. Bright-eyed as ever."

Banu dragged a stool to Bai's bedside and set the jars and bandages on a side table. "How do you feel this morning, boy?"

Bai opened his mouth again, but in shifting to see her, another wave of claws raked his back and he flinched.

"As I thought." Banu plucked one of the green biscuits and broke off a corner. Then she held it to his lips. "Eat this. It should help with the pain."

Whatever it took. Bai ate the biscuit and swallowed. The bitter taste of it lingered with flaky crumbs on his tongue. As Banu treated him, Bai let his eyes follow Adabelle, who sat on the sickbed across from him. Her face served as a distraction while Banu dabbed a cloth over the gashes. Her feet kicked over the floor with her little hands folded in her lap. He forced a smile, just the corners of his mouth pulling back slightly. She copied him.

But a face was missing from the healing house.

"Where is your mother?" he grunted.

"Mama went to Lady Iida," Adabelle told him.

"The Matriarch's sister is in labor," Banu added as she worked. "And Matriarch Viona has gone to inspect Syden. Iida requested your wife to be at her side."

Bai's brow furrowed. Why would the Matriarch decide to scout Syden now? And after all that happened? Perhaps it was for the best Raegna could not attend to him. She must have wished for time away from him. His chest constricted like both sides of his rib cage were being pulled together in the middle. He winced at the ache of it and the raw throbbing of his back.

Banu reached for the jar of green liquid and opened it. She dipped cloth into the contents and smeared it over Bai's back. The substance spread more like jelly and cooled the striped gouges. Once it sank into them, stinging needle pricks dotted along his back. Bai took a sharp breath through his teeth.

"Relax," Banu soothed. "This will speed up the healing process and keep it from festering."

"It's all right, Papa." Adabelle bore into him with concerned eyes.

Bai forced another grin. "I know, sweetheart."

The girl slipped off the sickbed and went to take his hand in hers. Her small hands wrapped around his fingers as she clutched them. Despite the pain, as soon as he felt her touch, Bai's agony eased. But the tension still squeezed his muscles.

Banu nudged the girl with her elbow, smiling. "What a good little nurse. Do you feel better now, young man?"

Bai prepared himself to nod when screams pierced the peaceful morning outside. The others jumped and peered out the window.

"What in Gaea's name?" Jora breathed.

The screams persisted, growing in number and volume. The thundering of horses rumbled through the streets. Shouts cut off. Bai gripped Adabelle's hands tighter as he fought to lift his head. "No…"

The four of them froze in place for several moments, listening closely to the sounds through the windows. Adabelle quivered while Banu set her medicine down. Victimized cries transformed into rough commands from deep, masculine voices. "Search every house. Spare the males. You know what to do. Move!"

Bai's veins became winter streams.

Jora turned to the kitchen and Banu rose to her feet. Her wife held a palm to stop her and tiptoed toward the door. Banu fixed Adabelle beside Bai and followed out of the healing room. Bai pushed himself up to call to them, to stop them, but he struggled to swallow a yelp for his movements. His grasp closed around Adabelle's wrist.

Protect Ada. Bai rose, gritting his teeth, and pulled her close. Adabelle scooped herself into his lap and curled into his torso. She knew as well as he did what was happening, and she buried her face in his chest, too frightened to do anything else. He would shield her and they would survive as they did last time. Bai searched for an escape route.

Heavy boots marched and steel clanked against steel as the men began their search just outside the healing house. Jora unsheathed her sword with a quiet ring. Banu plucked a bread knife from the table. The porch boards creaked, and Jora held her ground. Bai watched from his sickbed, able to view a quarter of the table from his position.

The front door burst open and two men shoved in. Bai had no time to witness what happened or worry about his agony. He stood, leaving Adabelle behind, and took three strides to slam the door shut. He drove a chair beneath the knob.

Blades clashed and Jora yelled. A soft swipe cut, and Jora shouted. A great thud vibrated across the floor.

"Jora!" Banu's feet pounded the floor. Then the sound of a blow against flesh echoed and she cried out. Another thud hit the floor.

Bai scurried and collapsed on the sickbed, taking Adabelle into his arms. Each gash on his back throbbed with every beat of his racing heart. Bai gulped afflicted growls. He could not let them hear him. He had to protect Adabelle.

Dishes crashed in the kitchen. Wood splintered as the table flipped with the tumbling of books and papers. Vials and jars shattered.

Footsteps shuffled over the floorboards. "Stop breaking things. We could use that medicine."

"That door was open when we came in," another man noted.

Bai held his breath, pressing his mouth into Adabelle's hair.

Footsteps approached. The doorknob wriggled, then shook. The chair wedged under it shuddered, but remained in place. When the knob wouldn't budge, they bashed against the door. The door caved in but braced, though it would not for long.

Adabelle whimpered while Bai searched for an escape. The small windows hung high above the sickbeds, allowing light in but not accessible to climb through. He could push Adabelle out, but she may not make the fall on the other side and who knew how many more men raided nearby?

There were no other doors except the one the men fought to break. Bai glanced at the floor and tapped the boards with his toe. An echo drummed beneath them. There would be space underneath the house, but how much? Enough for at least Adabelle to be hidden?

Bai set his daughter aside and knelt to pry the boards. His back screamed as he bent, but he clenched his jaw and yanked at the floorboards, digging his fingers in the spaces between them. An ax blade cut through the door, wrenching a hole above the knob. The men could see into the healing room.

"There's a girl!"

"Open it then," a cool, malicious voice ordered.

Bai growled as he pulled at the board with all his strength, ignoring his shredded back. They had already seen them. What was the point? A sharp lump formed in his throat. His pulse quickened with a surge of blood. He had to protect her.

The door crashed open. The chair snapped and crumbled. Adabelle shrieked and Bai released the board. He whirled to face the intruders, but staggered and caught himself across the sickbed. His muscles spasmed under his skin but he sat up. If he could keep himself between the men and Adabelle...

The two men stood at the doorway, one covered in grime with blood splattered across his leather armor and pale pink face, staining the blade of his ax. Rust-colored locks tumbled in braids and a matching beard reached his brimming chest.

The other entered with unnatural grace, his short-cropped black hair and beard clean and kept despite being part of a village raid. Crimson flecks spotted his own armor. He wielded a sword that had barely tasted the blood of his victims. He studied Bai with sharp hazel eyes under a straight brow.

His gaze flickered from Bai to Adabelle and back again with a smirk. "Surrender, and I won't hurt you."

Bai glared at him, lower than him, yet daring him to come closer. There had to be weapons in the healing room, surgical tools, or something he could invent. He would have to find them.

The man raised a palm and the tip of his blade. "Step away from the girl, and we will spare you."

Bai spat, a spray of saliva landing on the man's boot. "Burn in Helved."

The man frowned and his long nose wrinkled. He lifted his sword higher. "Not the first time I would have been told that as of late."

Leaping to his feet, Bai countered the man's attack by throwing his weight against him. The sword edge brushed his right bicep and thigh. The man grabbed a fistful of Bai's hair and tore him upward. Bai sent kicks at the man's groin and belly, fighting for a good angle. With little effort, the man threw him to the ground, flat on his back.

Bai screamed as the splintery wood floor slammed and grated his open wounds. The second man stepped beside him and kicked into Bai's side, the force so great Bai twisted and gagged for air.

"Papa!" Adabelle screeched.

The man snatched her hair and the back of her neck, then held her in the air. Adabelle sobbed and kicked out her dangling legs. Bai snarled as he forced himself up. The pain hit him like a storm wave crashing against a cliff side. He faltered and tried again.

"Don't hurt her!" he shouted at them. "Please, Gaea, don't hurt her!"

"Even though they have harmed you, you still wish for her safety," the man mused, with a thick eyebrow arched. "You still pray to your All-Mother."

"Papa!" Adabelle wept and scratched the man's fingers at her nape. "Papa! Mama!"

"Let her go," Bai begged, as he struggled to prop his weight on an elbow. His voice quivered with his heaving shoulders. "Please, I'll do anything. Let her go."

The man watched him and brought his sword beneath Adabelle's chin. "Where is your All-Mother now?"

His blade sliced through her skin, and Adabelle screamed. Blood flooded over her chest in dark crimson. Bai let out a cry so pitiful and loud, Gaea above could hear it. It tore at his throat and left it raw. The man dropped Adabelle to the floor and stepped over her. Bai scrambled to reach her.

He turned her onto her back as she gagged and coughed up blood. He put a hand to her gaping throat to stop the bleeding, but it sank into her jugular, the blood rising over his knuckles.

"No, Adabelle," he sobbed. "My Adabelle."

"End him if you wish, love," the man told his rust-haired companion as he left the room. "I'm done here."

But the other man followed him. "Let's see if Gaea saves him."

Bai could not afford to pay any more attention to them. He enfolded Adabelle with one arm and pressed the wound with his other hand. Hot tears rolled down his cheeks.

"It's all right, Ada," he whispered, stroking her hair. "Everything's going to be all right. You're fine."

Blood bubbled over her teeth as she rasped. "P-Pa... Pa...pa."

"Shh, it's all right now." Bai held her gaze, holding on to those sweet eyes. "You're safe... just—just sleep. Sleep, my Adabelle. I love you."

Adabelle fought for another breath and exhaled. Her body fell limp in his grasp and the light dimmed from her eyes. He watched her go as she stared back at him, but there was nothing there. She was gone. His entire world was gone.

Bai took his hand from her throat and stroked her face and hair, smearing her blood over her skin, which was drained of color. His heart swelled as he leaned over her, so close his tears pricked her nose. A bellow of sorrow and rage released from deep within his chest. Then another and another. Her blood pooled around them, and the suffering that washed over him outdid the throbbing of his shredded back. He let loose another cry and wept over his daughter's body.

CHAPTER 26

RAEGNA

RAEGNA SLAMMED THE DOOR and locked the bolt. In a whirl, she faced Viona's daughters. Both of them stared at her with slack jaws, hands drawing to their chests.

"Priestess?" the eldest squeaked.

"We have to go," Raegna told them and hurried upstairs. "Don't move, I'm going to get Iida and Asmund."

She raced to their bedroom and threw the door open. Iida had risen to her feet with Asmund's help in the time Raegna had gone. He helped her balance beside him. Iida trembled and raised her head. "Raegna, what is happening?"

"Judr is under attack," Raegna blurted. "We need to get all of you out of here. The girls are downstairs. What would be the best escape route?"

"There's a back door that leads to an alley," Asmund said at once.

"We can use the alleys to reach the walls," Iida added, one hand clamped around her belly. "We would have to climb the wall and we could be seen."

"But it is a chance." Raegna offered her hand to Iida. "Let's go."

Asmund and Raegna guided Iida downstairs as quickly as possible. Viona's daughters waited at the bottom of the staircase, shaking with dread. Asmund led everyone to the back door he knew of. Raegna took up the rear.

This attack had to have been by the same invaders that struck Syden. Male voices shouted and growled in every direction when they slipped out the back of the great house. A pitiful shriek followed each murderous roar. How could they strike again, a mere few days later, and in daylight?

Syden lay in ashes miles away, and no one would notice the smoke of their fires. Though it was the typical pass from Sorelle into Ostern, the next village of Surleid rested far from Judr. Too far for battle fire and black smoke to be visible.

Judr was on its own.

The group wove through alleys with Asmund in the lead, his arm around Iida. Their nieces sniffled behind them while Raegna made sure they kept a swift pace from the back, chastising herself for leaving her sword at the healing house. Her attention jerked forward when a blade sang too close. Asmund came to a complete stop, and everyone froze.

Ahead of them, a village man fought an invader with a broken rake, to no avail. The invader twisted the rake out of his grasp with the sword. As the man shrank back, he slashed him down in a spray of blood. The invader squared his shoulders with a sniff and passed.

Asmund scanned the alley and continued his path.

Once or twice, Iida inhaled through her teeth, her body doubled over. She buried her face in Asmund's shoulder, fists bunching his shirt as she stifled a cry of pain. Raegna silently prayed Gaea would show her friend mercy. When the contraction let up and Iida raised her head, Asmund led the group on.

Raegna followed, her prayers persisting for her own family. A healing house was defenseless against a raid, full of crucial resources the men could take for themselves. They would not overlook it. Would Jora be able to defend her home with one sword? Could Bai and Adabelle hide until the invasion was over? If they did, wouldn't the men light the house and burn them alive or flush them out?

She shook the thoughts and pleaded to Gaea, Sachi, and Sigmund to protect them. Bai was strong despite his wounds and clever enough to find an escape. Perhaps even Banu and Jora knew a route to the wall as Asmund did. There was still hope.

At last, the wall came into view and Asmund halted before it. He tilted his head to take in the sheer height of the wood pillars. They towered over them like tree trunks, just smashed together to form the barrier. Raegna recalled her days playing Maiden in the woods.

"Asmund," she prompted him, "can you climb?"

He didn't remove his eyes from the wall. "Barely."

Raegna pursed her lips and started up a pillar, using all the strength in her arms and thighs to hoist herself upwards. She could make it with time and effort, though time was not something she could afford. The true miracle would be none of the invaders catching sight of a small woman shimmying up the wall like a bear cub.

The wood scratched through her skirt, and splinters drove into her fingers and palms. When she reached the top, Raegna straddled the wall with much discomfort and leaned over to not draw attention to herself. She offered a hand to her friends below.

"Iida, you're first," she said.

Iida stepped back. "No, the girls go first."

"Aunt Iida!" the eldest protested, turning on her.

"Hush, now," Iida hissed at them. "Take Raegna's hand."

Asmund knelt, laced his fingers as a step, and pushed them to reach Raegna and scramble over. Raegna instructed how they would swing one leg after the other over the top and drop as gracefully as they could. The eldest managed her escape with a hard crash through the foliage. Her young sister slipped on her way down and yelped at the bottom. There would be a sprained ankle by the end of this.

Her older sister took care of her at the bottom, so Raegna peered down at Iida. "Now you will come up."

Iida gulped and clenched her jaw. Like her nieces, she stepped into Asmund's hand, and he hefted her upward. Raegna's shoulders strained to help her friend. Iida gasped and struggled, clawing at the wood, but scaled the height. She prepared to swing herself over, but Raegna brushed her shoulder. They both leaned down as far as they could over the top of the wall.

"Asmund," Raegna called down. "You jump over first so you can catch her on the other side."

He clambered up as best he could and leaped over. The girls jumped away when he landed. Raegna aided Iida as she swung a leg over and Asmund raised his arms to break her fall. Iida slipped off. Asmund staggered when he caught her and pulled her close, her toes touching the ground.

Iida flattened her feet and spun. "Wait. Raegna! You must let Asmund catch you!"

Raegna shook her head. "No, I have to find my family. You all run into the woods and do not look back. No matter what. Do you understand?"

Iida faltered with her brow drawn tight but nodded. "We'll see you in Stadt, then?"

For just a moment, Raegna allowed herself one long gaze at her friend. Unlike Pinar, Iida and her family had been saved. All of them looked back at her, shaken but alive. She dismounted the wall like a horse's saddle and readied herself for the descent. "Of course, my friend. Until Stadt."

"Until Stadt," Iida agreed. She, Asmund, and the girls turned to disappear beyond the trees, quickly for a party with a woman in labor and a girl with a sprained ankle.

Gaea, protect them, Raegna prayed as she leveled down, dropping and landing in a crouch. Any frightened woman might have followed them for a chance at life. Raegna had to find Bai and Adabelle.

***

Raegna stuck to the alleys, practicing more caution than Asmund had since she did not know Judr as well. The ringing of steel against steel and yells of anguish and triumph burst around her, making a safe route difficult to navigate.

Ahead of her, Ase, the Matriarch's commanding warrior, raged against an invader twice her size. Raegna ducked behind a pile of wood crates and watched with the man's back to her. Ase made a blow for his chest; he parried and pushed her backward.

Raegna gritted her teeth and picked up a crate, raising it over her head. She steeled herself and approached the fight. "Behind you, you dumb cock!"

The invader turned away from Ase, living up to Raegna's insult. Raegna hurled the crate into his face. The rickety thing slammed into his temple and cut him up. Ase side-stepped and thrust her blade into his gut. The man cried out and fell, his hands on his belly to hold his pouring innards.

"Priestess." Ase looked her over as Raegna did the same. In the chaos, the only armor she had slipped into was a leather chest plate. Her ink-like braids spilled down her back, hanging past muscle-cut arms. Blood dotted her left cheek, but that was nothing compared to her crimson blade. "Thank you. You... You tried to tell us. I'm sorry."

Raegna shook her head. "There's no time for that now. Judr will fall if we don't stop them."

"We don't have enough women." Ase's sword lowered. "It would take the village to at least make them yield. Everyone saw Viona's horse... The despair might be too great."

"You're their commander," Raegna told her. "If you gathered warriors and women together, maybe we have a chance."

Ase studied her, her eyes darting around Raegna's face. Then she shoved her sword hilt into Raegna's hand. "Take this." She nodded to the man she had slain. "I'll take his. Follow me."

Raegna tested the weight in her hand, missing her own sword. She hoped either Bai or Banu would get their hands on it and not some foul invader. Ase plucked her opponent's sword from the dirt and led the way down the alley.

On the main road, Raegna's stomach dropped. Groups of armored men ransacked homes or battled warriors. Common women and men fell under an ax or sword. Children screamed across the road, but Raegna could not take in all the carnage as Ase dashed ahead.

Ase approached a warrior with long gray hair and wrinkles over her tanned gold skin battling an invader. She fought in a plain blue dress she must have thrown on when the invasion began. The man struck, and she blocked with her shield. Ase sliced the backs of his knees, and he tumbled with a yelp. The older warrior beheld her commander and the priestess.

"Moja." Ase nodded to her. "You have your horn?"

The old warrior, Moja, twisted her hip to reveal a black and white horn at her belt. "Yes, Commander."

"Make the call for attention to us," Ase instructed, jutting a thumb over her shoulder. "Not all can answer, but whoever can will hear what I have to say. Priestess, guard her with me."

Something fired within Raegna like flint to a flame. "Yes, Commander."

"To that merchant booth, there." Ase pointed with her new sword.

A few men swarmed them, raising swords and axes. Ase and Raegna countered their attacks. The strike between Raegna's blade and her opponent's reverberated through her arms and shoulders. His strength pushed through her and Raegna gave him more ground. Moja ducked from behind her and angled herself beneath the man's chest. There, she ran her sword through him.

Raegna's heart plummeted with him. She braced for a reprimand from the more experienced warrior, but Moja glanced at her over her shoulder as they trailed Ase.

"You're strong, Priestess," she said, "but you cannot use that alone. You are also small and cunning. Use that to your advantage."

Raegna drew a breath, expanding her lungs to their limit, and pumped her legs faster.

When they reached the booth, Moja brought her horn to her lips and blew a long note. The sound alerted several women and men of Judr, but it caught the invaders' attention. Ase climbed on top of the counter and lifted her voice over the chaos.

"Women of Judr! If we are to save our home, we must band together! Take up a weapon and get into formation on my order. We will slaughter these beasts and send them to Helved!"

Singular shouts echoed over the road. Raegna assumed a stance as a dozen invaders raced at them. Moja stepped forward.

"Men, guard our children!" Ase screamed as she held her sword aloft. "Gaea is with us! For our Matriarch! For Judr!"

Raegna, Moja, and others released a battle cry. Ase jumped down and ran toward the invaders, with Raegna and Moja at her sides. The fire lit within Raegna consumed her as she charged. Pinar's face smiled behind her eyes as she faced the men who took her. She bared her teeth and angled her sword down.

You are also small and cunning. Use that to your advantage.

The forces slammed against each other. Raegna dipped beneath the first man and snaked the edge of her blade through his side. He cried out and stumbled at her heels. She had no time to soak in the small victory and countered the next man's blow. This one threw his shield into her. Raegna dodged and slashed between his shoulder blades as he twisted.

More women appeared in their battle. All of them shrieked in victory or cried out with a suffered wound. Raegna confronted man after man until a shield half her size rammed into her. She yelped and rolled, keeping hold of her sword. When she raised her head, a man towered above her, pointing his blade over her ribs. Before he plunged it down, a woman screamed, leaped over Raegna, and cut him down with an ax.

Grunting, Raegna got to her feet. The number of women emerging from the alleys and crumbling homes matched that of the invaders. Soon, more armored men littered the ground than Judr's own people. In the shadows, Judr's men hid with children under their guard. Raegna wouldn't look over at them long and reveal them. Bai and Adabelle would be in the same position somewhere.

In the middle of the road, a wagon pulled by two horses came to a halt. The invaders that filled it jumped down and joined the battle. Raegna cursed under her breath.

Two men did not leave the wagon. One was a weasel of a man, with a few brown wisps atop his head. He sneered at the other, who folded and plastered himself to the wall.

The black hair that tumbled in short locks struck a chord. His thick brow above sorrowful eyes brought Raegna back to Syden the day before the village was lost.

"Naleem."

Raegna bolted for the wagon. Gaea help any man that stood in her way. She slashed with her eyes trained on her target until she crouched behind a wheel. Raegna crept around to take the weasel by surprise. Instead, his ax swiped down and grazed her shoulder.

A scream left her. Raegna snarled and hauled herself into the wagon. The weasel countered her initial attack. His lip curled, showing brown teeth. Raegna shouted and blocked his ax until she found an opening. She meant to drive her sword through his chest, but her angle missed and sliced his side. The weasel howled and toppled over the side with a thud.

Raegna lowered to hide in the wagon. She studied Naleem, who wouldn't look her way, and her breath caught. His legs drew to his chest with his arms wrapped around them. He leaned against the wagon wall, staring somewhere distant. Bruises covered his skin with cuts and scrapes among them. His brow, temple, and nose were swollen. Blood clustered at his nostrils and smeared at his lips and chin.

"Naleem?" Raegna inched closer to him. "Naleem. Can you look at me? Can you hear me?"

Naleem tilted his head, craning an ear in her direction. A woman's voice must have been new to him. Raegna tried again. "It's me, Naleem. You're all right."

"Pinar?" he whispered as he turned to her. Any hope in his eyes died when he took her in.

Raegna choked down a sob. "No... It's Raegna. You know me."

Naleem's swollen brow furrowed. "Raegna..."

She offered her hand. "Let's get you somewhere safe."

Naleem didn't budge. His gaze shifted past her, and he shrank back. "Raegna."

She whirled and gasped, face-to-face with a man with tousled black hair and a cropped beard that glistened with blood. A tight smirk morphed above his long, clenched jaw and a fire bloomed in his hazel irises that absorbed the morning's light.

"Have you found yourself a new woman, son of Sigmund?" the man growled like a wolf. "No matter. We'll kill this one too."

Raegna roared and surged forward. The man blocked her attack. His blade was swift, practicing more prowess than his comrades. The edge flitted close, but Raegna's sword met his attempts to cut her. She remained low, searching for a good angle. He obstructed her focus with every clang of his sword. When her concentration slipped, the point pierced under her collarbone.

Pain shot through her neck and arm, slithering down her spine. Raegna screamed. Her sword clattered over the wood. The man pulled the blade from her, and she sobbed, heat searing in her fresh wound. She clutched her shoulder and wept.

"So much for the strength of a woman." The man kicked her sword closer to him. "This is the natural order of things. A man above you, and you below. If you knew what was good for you, you would stand down now."

Dizziness swept over her like a blizzard wind. Raegna breathed through clenched teeth and released her arm, driving the pain down. She planted her feet as blood dripped from her fingers. "Like Helved I will."

Raegna pivoted as if she would make an escape over the wagon. The man poised his blade as she wanted him to. Raegna ducked beneath him and slid on her knees. Snatching her sword beside his boot, she sliced it into his thigh as she brought it up.

The man dropped to one knee. "You rotten cunt!"

"Naleem!" Raegna shouted as she jumped off the wagon.

A second of hesitation passed before Naleem perked up and got to his feet. He followed her to the ground on shaking legs. The man bellowed behind them as they scrambled away. Raegna rushed Naleem ahead of her as they fled the battle. Across the road, Moja's horn resounded, blowing three times.

A different man's voice carried with it. "Thenalious! There are too many!"

Raegna could not watch what happened next. She knew to put distance between herself and that man. Naleem ran, zigzagging and stumbling. Raegna's chest and neck throbbed as she pushed for speed to navigate him in a favored direction. Her exertion pumped more blood over her dress.

She nudged him with the fist that held her sword. "Come with me. "My family is in the healing house. We have to find them."

***

The calls between the men to retreat and the victorious cries of Judr's people diminished behind them as Raegna and Naleem jogged to the healer's house. Raegna skidded to a stop when they reached the porch. The front door slanted wide open. A hollow rattle clinked from the beads that hung with furs from the rafters. No sound came from within the house.

Raegna whimpered as she rushed up the stairs. Naleem followed.

The table flipped with Banu's books, papers, and medicines dispersed over the floor. Pieces of dishes were strewn about the kitchen, and among them lay Banu. Jora sat against a chair leg, holding a bloodied gash above her hip.

Raegna gasped and knelt beside her. "You're bleeding."

"Never mind me." The warrior's growl cracked with desperation. "Tend to my wife. She hasn't moved."

Raegna shuffled to Banu's side. Careful not to brush the old healer with the sword pommel in her hand, Raegna pushed her gray hair back. A gash bruised above Banu's forehead. It wasn't deep, but blood oozed from it and trickled down the side of her face. At Raegna's touch, Banu stirred and grumbled under her breath.

"She's alive!" Raegna exclaimed. "Naleem, see if you can wake her up. I'll find Bai and Adabelle."

She left them without another word, investigating the last half of the kitchen until she discovered the healing room's door hanging off one broken hinge. A heavy, soft weeping came from inside.

Raegna's gut knotted. "Bai?"

The room remained the same. Bai lay across the floor, balanced on an elbow. His mangled back faced her, streaming in red. His shoulders shook, and he hunched over what she could not see.

Where is Adabelle?

A puddle of blood seeped around him that stretched its perimeter as she crept closer. Her heart drummed so fast, it seemed to float in her chest. "Bai..."

First, Raegna caught the color of Adabelle's dress, the same as she wore this morning. Shaking, her eyes traced the girl's body beneath Bai's and found the source of the blood.

Raegna dropped her sword, lunged, and shoved Bai aside. He rolled just inches away and wept. Adabelle lay limp before her, blood pouring over her neck and into her hair to stain the wood boards. Her skin was pale with death and gray and purple rimmed her eyelids.

Raegna's throat was torn raw by a scream and shrieking sobs.

Epilogue

Raegna

I NCENSE KINDLED IN LANTERNS in every nook within Gaea's temple. The gray-blue morning sky peaked through the open dome where smoke could escape. Raegna stood alongside Bai just inside the double-door entry, a basket of wildflowers and petals hanging from her good arm. The other rested in a sling with stitches in her shoulder wound.

Bai cradled Adabelle, still and blanketed in linen from head to toe. Her temple rested on his shoulder, her hands were stacked under her chest, and her legs dangled over his forearm. Bai's jaw was set, and his eyes glazed over, but he tilted his chin toward Adabelle as if waiting for her to wake.

Raegna took a breath that stretched her stiff, aching ribs. Her heart throbbed with every pulse. She peered at her daughter, willing her to stir. To return to them so the nightmare would end.

At the head of the temple, a mother mourned her husband and child as they burned on their lifting beds. Two more children hugged her sides, shedding tears into her skirts. More families preceded her and more lined behind the doors to follow Raegna and Bai. Despite Judr's victory, the invaders had taken their toll on the village and its people.

When the mother and her remaining children shuffled from the altar, two priestesses cleansed the beds of ashes. A third ushered Raegna and Bai forward.

Tears sprang to Raegna's eyes, and she choked on the thorn in her throat. Adabelle wouldn't wake up before they would take her. Raegna took slow steps with Bai. His shoulders trembled as he moved. The pain in his shredded back had to be agonizing, though not quite like carrying their daughter to her lifting bed as he had carried her when she was born.

The bed of driftwood sat beneath the altar, the stone-carved statue of Gaea looking out over the temple congregation and pillars. Raegna trailed Bai up the steps, his gait wavering. The third priestess waited, holding a small torch that crackled and stung Raegna's heart with the sound.

Bai settled Adabelle down and gathered the blanket as he had so many times, tucking her in for bed.

Raegna arranged the wildflowers in her hair, and in between her hands. Daisies and violets were all she could find along the hills. Neither she nor Bai exchanged a glance, as the inevitable approached with every passing moment.

Bai went first, smoothing Adabelle's blonde locks as he bent and kissed her forehead twice. He swallowed tears while he pressed his brow to hers in a silent goodbye. Then he pulled away.

Raegna knelt at Adabelle's side. She, too, brushed strands of her daughter's hair behind her ears, and flattened the creases in her skirt. Then she kissed her cheek.

"Sweet girl," she whispered, her voice thick. "Gaea will truly protect you now, as I always said She would. I will have no fear for you anymore, darling daughter. But I will keep your beautiful light in my heart so long as I live... until I see you again."

Another kiss on the other cheek, lingering this time. "Farewell, my sweet babe."

A dull pain drummed through her head, but Raegna rose and stepped from the lifting bed. Adabelle lay alone, unmoving, and surrounded by wildflowers.

The priestess handed the torch to Raegna, and she took it. On one knee, she placed the fire among the pieces of driftwood.

Even the flames seemed reluctant to take on such a task, enveloping the edge of the bed before catching the blanket, then her dress. The fabric blackened and curled. Then they flickered over her skin. Raegna's knees trembled, threatening to collapse, and her stomach heaved. Warm tears streamed down her face as she remained firm. Bai stood rigid beside her.

Crackling upwards, the fire consumed her before her parents. White smoke plumed and lifted her soul to Heimelle, into the care of the All-Mother.

And it was over.

***

War raged within Raegna as she trudged back to the healing house, her arm slung beneath her breast. Her sword rocked from her belt beside her swishing skirts. Tendrils of sharp pain stretched from under her collarbone and outward, throbbing with every stride of her gait. The last four days of Judr's liftings tore at her. The flames of hundreds of beds flickered in her memory. Women, men, and children.

And then Adabelle.

A metallic taste eased over her tongue when Raegna bit her lip. She picked up her pace. Judr bustled around her as many helped to re-build homes and buildings. Two women carrying a long plank of timber passed, too engrossed in their conversation to notice her.

One hefted the plank for a better hold. "There has been no news of them. They may have escaped, but who knows where they went? Or if they survived. We have to hold a vote to decide on a Matriarch."

"But the title belongs to Lady Iida," the other protested. "She is the most eligible."

"She would be more eligible in the village. Not in the wilderness."

Raegna clutched the hilt of her sword tight, the tendons in her fingers screaming. She shut their voices out. They were all so stupid and selfish for not trying harder. They did not scour the woods hard enough for Iida and her family. The four of them were out there somewhere. But no, Judr must appoint a new Matriarch.

Clouds covered the sky with the promise of summer rain, casting shadows over the healer's house. The beads and bones hanging from the porch clicked. The wind brushed the furs on the wall as Raegna climbed the steps and entered.

Banu stood over a cauldron at her small fireplace, turning to give Raegna a nod in greeting. Regardless of all the injured for whom she cared, the healer stayed on her feet. Her tired gaze hovered over Raegna and her bound arm.

Jora sat at the table, her waist bound in bandages under a loose shirt. Black hair curled around her head, unbraided, and she flinched when she attempted to lean for a sip of soup. Naleem sat beside her, mindlessly stirring his bowl. His square chin rested on a fist and glazed eyes revealed nothing. Neither he nor Raegna looked at each other when she took the chair across from him, wincing at her wound.

"Would you like some too, girl?" Banu murmured.

Raegna shook her head. "Not hungry."

"Come now." Banu poured the soup, anyway. "You've done much for the village yet again today. You'll need your strength."

She placed a bowl in front of the priestess and nudged it toward her like an encouraging mother. Raegna leveled her gaze at the bowl and closed her eyes. "When is the next search party?"

Jora reclined in her chair. "There is word they will cease the search."

Raegna's free hand slammed against the tabletop, clattering the bowls. Naleem jolted, and his clouded stare became sharp.

"They refuse?" Raegna hissed.

The old warrior sighed and shook her head.

Banu raised her palms as she turned for the cauldron. "It's been weeks, girl. They have not been found. These people yearn for a leader who will guide them out of this turmoil. There is no telling what happened to them or where they have gone, and Judr can wait no longer."

"Stadt," Raegna blurted. "That is where they are. That is where they are headed." She held her chin higher than she had in days. "And I promised Iida I would follow."

Jora frowned. "All the way to Stadt?"

"Iida wanted to go there to keep her son safe from her sisters," Raegna explained, tapping the side of her hand on the table. "She said she would be happy to report Syden's attack to the Queen since she was the sister of a Matriarch. Before we parted, she told me she would go. I said I would be behind her. We have to tell the Queen before these monsters take any more lives."

Banu opened her mouth to say something, but Naleem was quicker.

"My brother and son are at their base." He left his spoon in his bowl, and he met Raegna's eyes. "I know where it is. In the hills."

Raegna gave no time to ask why and straightened in her chair. "Then it is settled. Naleem, if you will come with me, we can go to Stadt as soon as possible. We may find Iida and Asmund on the road."

Naleem nodded in agreement and picked up his spoon to consume the soup.

"I would rather see you both heal before any kind of journey." Banu added wood to the fire under the cauldron. "Perhaps I can manage a wagon in the meantime."

"We'll stay for those injured in their homes," Jora added. "I wish you the best of luck. How could the Queen ignore this?"

With her muscles taut and her shoulder aching, Raegna ate her soup with Naleem, both of them driven with more purpose than they had in days. When she finished, Raegna brought her bowl to Banu.

"How will you get a wagon?" she asked the healer. "Many of the village's resources have been destroyed."

"In a time of uncertainty, when there is a Matriarch to be replaced," Banu started, "some women can be sold on the promise of a vote. There is one I have in mind. Let me handle it, girl."

It seemed a cheap and deceptive way of getting what they wanted. Especially when word spread that a majority preferred Ase to be the succeeding Matriarch after her courage in protecting Judr. But Raegna wouldn't argue with it. So long as they reached Stadt in something.

"Will you tell him then?" Banu whispered, taking Raegna's bowl.

Fighting a twitch, Raegna glowered and averted her eyes.

Banu pursed her lips. "It might do you both good to speak to each other. Come from a place of mutual understanding."

You don't know us. Raegna held her breath and fled outside, clicking the door shut. The porch rail stopped her, her sword hilt banging against it. She gripped the cracking wood in her hand until it dug into her skin. Still, it could not overcome the pain in her chest.

Raegna's lip quivered. The empty road clouded with her tears. Distant thunder rolled over the hills. A gust of wind rattled the beads above her. Raegna dropped and stooped to balance her weight on the balls of her feet. Her scabbard scraped the floor. She hung by her good hand on the rail to keep herself upright. Then her shoulders shook with her stifled sobs, pinching nerves in her stitched wound.

Pressing her forehead to the harsh wood, Raegna cried as she had every day for the past week. Adabelle's smiling face appeared behind her eyelids. Raegna rocked on her heels, twisting into a fetal position against the railing. Her sword guard poked under her ribs. She buried her face into her folded arm over her knees and wept until the rain poured over Judr.

Half-drenched in water, Raegna returned inside. She kept her reddened eyes down and crossed the kitchen to the healing room, not daring to look up. Once she reached its threshold, Raegna beheld her husband.

Bai rested on his stomach on the sickbed. He turned his head toward the wall, away from her, as she entered. The red gashes striped his back, open and exposed to the humid air.

Nothing tied them together now. Not her mother and not Adabelle. She could leave him if she truly wanted to. Her anger urged her to, her heart twisted and torn at the fact that he was the one Adabelle had spent her last moments with...

Raegna pushed that agony aside, along with all the other emotions that plagued her. She went to her bed and sat on its edge. Her eyes traced the lines on the horrible floor, stained with blood.

"We leave for Stadt," she said at once. "You... You can come with. Or you can stay behind."

A woman could divorce or disown a husband however she saw fit. She had never wanted Bai to be under her. Hopefully, he would hear this from her, releasing him from her name. Perhaps he would want the same.

A minute passed, and he remained silent. Raegna did not care to wait any longer. Let him say nothing as they had for years. She lay on her back, turning to avoid his image.

His voice rumbled like the thunder outside: distant and forlorn. "I'll come with."

Raegna coiled at the sound and the acknowledgment, the willingness. Yet some small part of her, deep within her, bloomed with relief. Raegna grimaced at that release in her heart as she stared into the grooves in the wall.

"Very well."

GALAENIAN GLOSSARY

A-B

Adabelle – Raegna and Bai's daughter.

Alv (AHlv) – Matriarch of Syden.

Ase (AH-seh) – Commander of Judr.

Asmund – Iida's husband.

Bai (BYE) – Raegna's husband.

Banu (BAH-noo) – Healer of Judr.

Berthe (BEHr-theh) – Commander of Syden.

Bjarni (Byarn-ee) — Man of Syden

C-E

Cadoc – Pinar and Naleem's youngest son.

Dakarai (DAH-kah-rye) – Pinar and Naleem's oldest son.

Else (EHl-seh) – Talia's daughter.

Estrid (EH-stread) – Pinar and Naleem's oldest daughter.

F-G

Fan — The Evil One and overlord of Helved.

Farah – A Haven captive.

Femke (FEHm-keh) – Matriarch Viona's second sister.

Fritjof (Frit-yoff) — Farmer of Haven

Gaea (GAY-ah) – The high goddess or All-Mother, creator of Jorde.

Galaenia (GAH-lay-nee-ah) – The country of the four realms: Ostern, Sorelle, Vesten, and Norden.

H-I

Hadwin – Naleem's brother.

Heimelle (HIE-mehl) – The paradise afterlife, heaven.

Helved (HEHl-vehd) – The underworld.

Iida (EE-dah) – Matriarch Viona's youngest sister, Asmund's wife.

J

Jaleesa (YAH-lee-sah) – Raegna's mother.

Jora (YOH-rah) – Warrior of Judr.

Jorde (YOHr-deh) – The world, the planet.

Judr (YOO-der) – A village in Sorelle, east of Syden.

M-O

Moja (MOE-yah) – Warrior of Judr.

Nairi — Judr's Lady of Labor.

Nalani (NAH-lah-nea) – Pinar and Naleem's youngest daughter.

Naleem – Hadwin's brother. Pinar's husband.

Oberon (OH-behr-ohn) – Councilman of Haven.

Obrecht (OH-brehckt) – Elder of Syden.

Oda (OH-dah) – Turid's daughter.

P-R

Pinar (PEA-nahr) – Naleem's wife.

Quinlan – Turid's son.

Raegna (RAYg-nah) – Bai's wife.

Reynold – Councilman of Haven.

S

Sachi (SAH-ckea) – Daughter of Gaea, Mother and goddess of women.

Seagr (SEE-ger) – A friend of Hadwin.

Sigmund – A god, Sachi's husband.

Sorelle – The southern realm of Galaenia.

Stadt (Sh-tAH-dt) – The capital of Galaenia.

Surlied (SOOr-leed) – A village in Ostern, north-east of Judr.

Syden (SUU-dehn) – A village in Sorelle, west of Judr.

T-Z

Talia – A Haven captive.

Thenalious (THEH-nah-lee-us) – The Leader of Haven.

Turid (TOO-read) – Woman of Judr, works for Matriarch Viona.

Ugo (OO-goh) – Reynold's son.

Viona (VEA-oh-nah) – Matriarch of Judr.

Wyn (Win or WUUn) – Councilman of Haven.

Thank You, Reader.

Thank you for reading *The Maiden's Husband*.

Explore Galaenia, and sign up for my newsletter to receive updates, behind-the-scenes, and bonus content!

www.morganrchristensen.wixsite.com/author

You can also follow me on social media!

TikTok: @morganchristensen_author

Instagram: @morgan_christensen_author

Acknowledgments

Thank you to my family and friends who have been nothing but supportive through this publishing journey. The dedication says it all, but thank you again, Dad, for indirectly inspiring the story by introducing me to *Vikings*. Your support has been immensely encouraging and assured me I am on the right path.

Thank you to my brother, Joe, for tolerating my brainstorming. Thank you to my friend, Taylor, *The Matriarch Chronicles'* first reader, for your feedback. You both have made your mark on the series.

A special thank you to all my beta readers. You all impacted *The Maiden's Husband* and changed the book for the better.

Thank you to my editors for going above and beyond! This book wouldn't be half as good without you.

Finally, thank you to author Jenna Moreci for all your resources and tips. I only knew about self-publishing because of you, and I'm eternally grateful for everything you do to educate and uplift other authors, no matter their path.

CREDITS

The Matriarch Chronicles: The Maiden's Husband
was created and written by
Morgan Christensen

Beta Read by
Taylor Anderson
Aaron Daggit
C.M. Howe
Finnegan
R.E. Sanders, Author of *A Path of Blades*
Hannah Greer, Short Story Author

Development Edit and Sensitivity Read by
Samantha Kassè

Copy & Line Edit by
Jocelyn Holler Smith

Proofread by
Claire Cronshaw, Cherry Edits

Map of Galaenia by

Alyssa Hurlbert

Cover Art by

MiblArt

Morgan Christensen began writing *The Matriarch Chronicles* in high school, discovering a passion for gritty legends filled with rigid emotions and bloody swords.

In the heat of Arizona, she can be found bingeing shows like *The Last Kingdom* and *Vikings* while snuggling her cat, Freyja. By day, she works as an office admin to stock her bookshelves and plan her next visit to the Renaissance Fair.